ARMED 'N' READY

FEDERAL K-9 SERIES

ARMED 'N' READY

FEDERAL K-9 SERIES

TEE O'FALLON

Entangled Publishing, LLC
2614 South Timberline Road
Suite 105, PMB 159
Fort Collins, CO 80525
rights@entangledpublishing.com

Amara is an imprint of Entangled Publishing, LLC.

Edited by Candace Havens
Cover design by EDH Graphics
Cover photography from Getty Images, Shutterstock, and Deposit Photos

Manufactured in the United States of America

First Edition February 2019

To Yarmouth Police Department K-9 Sgt. Sean Gannon, shot and killed in the line of duty on April 12, 2018, while executing a warrant. Your courage and dedication to protecting others will never be forgotten, nor will your ultimate sacrifice. And to Nero, Sgt. Gannon's K-9 partner, who was also shot during this incident. May you live out the rest of your years in comfort, and surrounded by love.

To the Massachusetts State Police K-9 Unit—this book is for you!

Chapter One

"No!" Andi cried. *Too late.*

Stray shook, sending suds flying. A fluffy white dollop of doggie shampoo hit her smack in the middle of her forehead. Uttering an exasperated sigh, she swiped it away. "If you don't stop doing that, we'll be here all day."

Dark brown, soulful eyes stared up at her from a soggy face. Andi narrowed her eyes. "Don't think I don't see right through your tactics, young lady." She pointed an admonishing finger. "You know I can't stay mad at you, and you're using that against m—"

A muffled thump came from somewhere in the house. She straightened and twisted her neck to look through the glass shower door into the master bedroom. Condensation blocked her view, so she cracked open the door, being careful not to let Stray escape. She held her breath, listening, but the only sounds were from the shower spray and Stray's occasional disgruntled snort.

She gave a shake of her head. *I'm imagining things.*

After closing the door, she leaned over and squeezed

another bead of shampoo across the dog's spine. "Now, where were we?"

A shadow fell across the shower stall. Stray stiffened and growled.

Movement caught her eye, and she looked up just as the shower door flew open and whacked against the wall.

For less than a second, she froze. Then, she screamed.

She stumbled backward, flinging out her arms for balance. The bottle of dog shampoo fell from her hand, and her feet nearly skidded out from under her. Somehow, she remained upright and braced her back and palms against the cool tile wall. Beside her, Stray began barking at the top of her lungs.

Oh my God oh my God oh my God. This was like something out of a bad high school movie. A giant black dog with the biggest, longest teeth she'd ever seen, and a huge, hulking man were in her bathroom. And—holy shit—*he's pointing a gun at me.*

Her heart hammered so hard against her rib cage, she could actually hear it above the pounding spray and the ferocious barking from the dogs. She sucked in quick breaths.

The hulk said something to his dog. *In German?* It stopped barking but still looked like it wanted to eat her alive. Stray didn't understand German and kept barking and snarling.

The black shepherd's lips curled back, giving her another look at those frighteningly sharp incisors. The man spoke, but with all the noise she couldn't make out what he was saying. Her mind was too busy spinning with the implications of what was happening.

I'm trapped. He's going to rape me. Then kill me. Stray, too.

Do something, idiot. Don't go down without a fight.

She grabbed the bar of soap on the shower shelf.

"Pol—"

She hurled the soap at him. A large hand snapped it from midair and flung it behind him, where it made a *thunk* as it hit the wall.

Andi grabbed a bottle of shampoo and raised her arm to throw that at him, too.

"*Police*, dammit," he shouted in an incredibly smooth, sinfully rich baritone. "Don't even *think* of throwing that shampoo at me."

"*What?*" She widened her eyes, sucking in deeper breaths while her heart beat madly. For the first time, she took in his clothes. His *uniform*. Blue with triangular patches on his chest and shoulders. *Massachusetts State Police.*

Piercing, deep-set, gunmetal gray eyes stared coldly at her from a face so hard it had to have been chiseled from rock. Her gaze traveled the length of him from head to toe, noting he was tall and with shoulders so wide they completely filled the shower door opening. Only then did she notice that, somewhere in the middle of all this, he'd put away his gun, the butt of which now stuck out of the holster on his belt.

The giant black German shepherd glowered up at her with glowing, satanic eyes, still looking as if it wanted to tear every square inch of flesh from her bones.

"What are you doing here?" she breathed between gasps, crouching to wrap her arms around Stray's neck and chest. The last thing she wanted was a dog fight in her shower, one Stray would undoubtedly lose. "How did you get in? You have no right to be here."

"Serving a search warrant, through the front door, and yes, I *do* have a right to be here."

"Sarge, you okay?" another male voice said.

With his gaze locked on hers, he extended his arm, holding out his hand, palm facing whoever was about to enter the bathroom. "Stop."

She caught brief glimpses of two other officers just

.

outside the bathroom door, although she was somewhat protected from their view by the mist-covered shower glass and the hulking body standing directly in front of her. *The house has to be crawling with cops.*

"I'm good," the state trooper said, still watching her like a hawk. "Get Malloy up here. *Now.*"

"You got it." The other men disappeared.

The black dog growled deep in its throat, and she flinched, hauling Stray backward until they were pressed against the tile wall. Between Stray's incessant barking and the shock, she barely registered the thickly muscled arm that reached into the stall and shut off the water.

"Ma'am," she vaguely heard him say, although everything happening was so surreal she had a difficult time concentrating. "*Ma'am.*" The voice was infinitely more insistent now and laced with a hint of annoyance.

Stray let loose with a series of ear-splitting barks that echoed in the confines of the shower. "No bark," she said, resting her hand on the top of the dog's head.

"Take this."

"What?" She snapped her gaze back to the trooper, who was holding out a towel to her.

Oh, shit. I'm practically naked. In front of a cop. Double shit.

Stray's wet body still trembled beneath her arms, but the dog had calmed significantly and seemed content to stay within the safety of the shower stall.

She snatched the towel from his outstretched hand, quickly wrapping it around her bikini-clad body and twisting the top into a knot between her breasts. Until that moment, she'd been so completely and utterly freaked out by the intrusion of the man and his scary-as-hell dog, she hadn't given a thought to the fact that the only thing she had on was a very old, very skimpy string bikini that barely concealed her ass and breasts. The only reason she'd kept it was for washing dogs. In private, that was.

"Easy girl." She began stroking the dog's quivering body, flattening the hair on her spine where it stood straight up. "Easy now." Stray had stopped barking, settling for an occasional low growl in the back of her throat.

Andi stared up at the trooper. "What the hell is going on? Why do you have a search warrant for my house?" Technically it wasn't *her* house. She was only staying there for a couple of nights.

His piercing gaze remained securely focused on her face. "As for the *what*," that deep, clear voice resonated, "like I said, we're serving a warrant. As for the *why*, all in good time."

"What in the world are you serving a warrant for?" She dug her fingers into Stray's thick ruff, massaging the dog's neck to keep her calm. "This *has* to be a mistake. You can't just barge into someone's home."

"No mistake." He glanced at the dog that stood obediently at his side, glaring at her with the same intensity his handler did. The shepherd didn't pay any heed to Stray. "Are you the only one in the house?"

"Y-yes," she answered, her body beginning to chill.

"Are you Andromeda Hardt?"

She shivered. "Yes. I'm Andi. Andi Hardt. What's your name?" The name tag on his chest said Houston but didn't have his first name.

He ignored her question and clicked the mic on his lapel. "Tell Cox we have a guest up here. Andi Hardt, owner of the Dog Park Café."

How does he know who I am?

"Copy that," a voice came back.

Sgt. Houston refocused his attention on her. "Where's Joe Myer?" he demanded, more than asked.

"Out of town," she answered truthfully.

"Where?"

"I don't know." A giant knot of fear and worry began wedging its way solidly into her gut. Joe had been unusually cryptic about his most recent business trip. Now state troopers were serving a warrant at his house. *This is* so *not good*.

That knot gnawed more at her belly, burrowing deeper and writhing like a mass of snakes.

"I can call him. In fact, I should tell him what's going on here." She glanced down at Stray. "Sit," she said, and when the dog complied, added, "Stay." When she made a move to get out of the shower, she nearly slammed into Sgt. Houston's solid, unmoving chest. "Are you *kidding* me? I haven't done anything wrong. Am I under arrest?"

He stared down at her, his eyes narrowing to slits. "No," he said in a flat tone devoid of emotion. "You can call Myer later."

"Okay, then. Thank you." It was obvious she had no control over the situation, and that both frightened and bothered the crap out of her. She might not be under arrest, but she sure felt like a prisoner. "Could I at least have some privacy, so I can get dressed?" It might be eighty-plus outside, but with the air conditioning blasting on her wet hair and skin, her teeth were beginning to chatter.

"Sorry, ma'am, I can't let you do that just now."

"Then when *can* you do that?" she cried with more force than intended. Now that her initial shock was wearing off, reality was kicking in hard and fast, leaving her confused and scared. "And stop looking at me. What are you, one of those perverted voyeurs? A peeping Tom?"

God, what had made her say that? She was acting like a petulant child, which would only make things worse. And actually, she hadn't caught him checking her out once. Not that she'd seen, anyway.

"I'm sorry." She clamped a hand over her forehead. "I just don't understand why this is happening."

His square jaw clenched, then he took a deep breath that made his massive chest even wider. "You will, ma'am. For the record, my name is Sgt. Houston. I'm with the Massachusetts State Police."

She rolled her eyes but kept her big mouth shut this time. They were probably around the same age, and if he called her *ma'am* one more time, she'd be tempted to slug him. *Probably a bad idea.*

"Step out of the shower. Slowly." He backed away, as did his dog, although both kept their eyes glued to her, as if any quick movement on her part and she'd find herself in handcuffs, or the main course of that demonic dog's breakfast.

Only now did it register that the dog wore a protective vest over its torso, as did the cop, she assumed. Normally, she loved dogs and they loved her back. Her mother once told her it was a gift. Dogs inherently sensed when someone liked them, and they returned the sentiment a hundred times over. But this dog was a cop, and one of the largest shepherds she'd ever seen. It had to be over ninety pounds.

Hesitantly, she placed one foot on the bath mat outside the shower door, pausing to glance over her shoulder, gratified that Stray hadn't budged, although the dog's ears were laid back, her head lowered. When Andi turned, her gaze quickly took in the rest of the trooper. It was impossible not to. She was around five-seven, and he had to be close to six-three or four. He could easily crush her with one hand tied behind his back.

A muscle in one of his sunken cheeks flexed as he clicked the mic on his lapel. "Malloy, this is Sgt. Houston. I need you upstairs. What's the delay?"

"A little tied up, Sarge," a female voice responded, making her realize he was doing his best to get a female officer on scene.

Seriously chiseled jaws clenched again. "Get up here ASAP."

"Ten-four."

He made a quick motion with one arm, and his dog trotted out of the bathroom. Next, he surprised her by reaching for the other towel on the rack, extending it to her.

Not understanding, she gave him a questioning look.

He tipped his head to where Stray still sat obediently in the shower. "For the dog."

Well, huh. His unexpected thoughtfulness momentarily fried her brain synapses, and all she could do was stare at him in disbelief.

"You don't want her shaking all over this pricey marble tile." He arched a brow. "Do you?"

"Um, no. Thanks." She accepted the towel then made quick work of giving Stray a rubdown that made her reasonably dry. Oblivious to the seriousness of what was going on, Stray groaned with pleasure at the body massage, then shook. When Andi turned to hang the towel back on the rack, she glimpsed the smattering of water spots on the trooper's uniform shirt. His face remained impassive. Either he hadn't noticed, or he didn't care.

"After you." He indicated the bedroom, and when she started for the door, Stray began to follow. "Probably wise to keep her in here for now."

Andi turned and held up her hand. "No, girl. Stay."

Uttering a low whine, the dog stopped and looked at her with mournful, disappointed eyes.

"Have a seat on the bed," he said after closing the bathroom door behind them.

She stepped into the bedroom to find the black K-9 sitting in front of the door to the hall. *No escape.*

A chill crawled up her spine as the enormity and

seriousness of what was happening sunk in deeper.

Turning, she planted her hands on her hips but thought better of it when the towel began slipping. Grabbing the edges just in time, she held it tightly to her breasts. "Not before you tell me what's going on here. I have a right to know. And I'd *really* like to get dressed. If you don't mind, that is." Without waiting for a response, she turned and strode toward her unpacked suitcase resting on the luggage rack. She reached for the zipper, and the next instant found herself lifted into the air as if she were no heavier than a matchstick.

"*What* are you doing?" *This is unbelievable.*

Strong hands grasped her waist, and her legs dangled as Sgt. Houston walked her back to the bed and deposited her ass-first on the mattress.

"*Pass auf,*" he said to the dog, which came closer, ears pricked high, golden gaze fixated on her every move.

Sgt. Houston pointed at her with a long finger. "Stay."

"*Stay?*" She barked out a laugh. "I am *not* a dog, and I don't respond on command."

Chiseled jaws tightened. "Stay. On. The bed."

"Or you'll what?" She raised her chin in the hope it would stop her lower lip from trembling. Being so antagonistic to a cop might not be the smartest move, but this was all scary as hell, and it was the only way she knew to conceal her fear. What was supposed to be a relaxing couple of days at Joe's house while the plumbing at her place was being overhauled was turning into a nightmare.

"Or," he said, towering over her, "I'll have to handcuff you, and if I do, I seriously doubt that towel will stay put." His gaze dipped briefly to where the previously knotted towel now hung practically wide open.

Though she wore a bikini beneath the towel, it didn't conceal much. She snatched at the parted towel and yanked it together, re-knotting it as best she could.

"Ma'am." He took a deep breath then let it out. "A female officer is on her way up here to assist. In the meantime, I'd appreciate your cooperation. It would make this a lot easier. On both of us."

"Fine," she reluctantly agreed, knowing it was the right thing to do. "But you could have knocked before breaking in. I would have *let* you in."

"We *did* knock. You didn't answer."

"Well, duh. I was in the shower washing the dog and didn't hear you."

"Clearly, ma'am."

"Andi. Call me *Andi*. If you call me *ma'am* one more time, I'll—"

"You'll what?" he asked, throwing her own words back at her.

Oh hell. He's right. If he wanted to call her ma'am all day, there was nothing she could do to stop him. It was just so annoying.

He snorted. "That's what I thought. Look," he began in a tone that was only slightly less patronizing. "You can't touch anything until the room's been searched. Tell me what you need, and I'll get it for you." He went to the suitcase, pausing to look at her before unzipping it. "Got any weapons in here, anything sharp?"

"An eyebrow plucker? A curling iron?" She couldn't help grinning when his brows lowered in obvious irritation. "Oh wait, be careful. I have a box of tampons in there somewhere. Those little things can do some damage if you handle them incorrectly. If I were you, I'd treat them like unexploded ordinance." She smirked, but in reality, her snarky comebacks were a sad effort to mask her growing anxiety.

He gave her a fake smile that crinkled the skin at the corners of his eyes. If the smile hadn't been so facetious, and if he wasn't about to search her personal belongings, she would have said he was somewhat handsome. In a kick-ass, take-no-shit, I-eat-nails-for-breakfast kinda way.

"Cute." He arched a brow as if to say: *right back atcha, babe.* Then he began digging through the suitcase. "After you're dressed, I'll take you downstairs, and we'll explain more to you about what's going on."

"Aren't you afraid I might attack you from behind and club you over the head when you're not looking?"

"No." He didn't spare her so much as a glance.

"Why not?" Testing her theory, she pushed from the mattress, watching as he rifled through her suitcase, searching it for weapons, she supposed, and whatever evidence they'd come to Joe's place for. "See, I'm getting closer." She continued edging toward his broad back. "I could easily incapacitate you with my hair dryer."

Again, he didn't bother to look at her. "Turn around."

She did and froze. Her only movement was the instantaneous widening of her eyes.

The black shepherd stood closer now, only a few feet away, with its demonic eyes burning into her. "Oh. Right." This time it was her turn to sit obediently. And she did. Slowly. "If I attack you, your partner will tear me to shreds, won't he?"

He pulled a pair of khaki shorts and a light-blue tank from the suitcase and tossed them behind him onto the bed. "Pretty much, so I'd strongly advise against it."

"Ten-four, Sarge." She wanted to smack her forehead. Joe's house was being searched by an army of cops, she was being guarded by a cop-dog bigger than any wolf she'd seen in a zoo, and here she was cracking jokes. *Not smart.*

She gave him a mock salute behind his back. Unfortunately, he turned just in time to catch it and pursed his lips. Her gaze was drawn to his duty belt, and her eyes again went wide, this time for a completely different reason.

Her face heated as if someone was blasting a blowtorch at her head.

Looped over the handle of his gun was one of her prettiest pair of undies—pale pink satin with lacy scalloped trim. She clamped a hand over her eyes.

Could this get any more embarrassing?

Don't answer that.

"Uh, Sergeant?" *Might as well meet the situation head-on.* "Can you grab me the matching bra, too?"

Clearly not understanding to what she was referring, he frowned, and when she dipped her eyes in the direction of his gun, he figured it out. Again, that seriously chiseled jaw flexed as he reached for the lacy garment, hooking it with two fingers. With a flick of his hand, he tossed it on top of her shorts and shirt as if it was burning his flesh and he couldn't wait to get rid of it.

She wanted to laugh at the image of her panties dangling from a hand big enough to pound a six-inch spike through a board *without* a hammer. Maybe it was the stress, or the embarrassment, but she couldn't hold back a tiny snicker. And was he—

No way.

Blushing?

Beside her, the black shepherd huffed and took a step closer, cutting short the full-on laughter about to escape her throat. She scrambled to the center of the bed. Her heart began hammering, and she half expected the dog to leap onto the bed and clamp its jaws around her leg.

"*Platz*," Sgt. Houston ordered the dog, who lay down next to the bed, still eyeing her with an intensity that was unnerving.

"Easy, Saxon." He knelt by the dog, laying one of those massive hands on its neck. Almost instantly, the tension in the animal's body seemed to ease. "He won't hurt y—"

She followed Sgt. Houston's gaze and looked down to see that in her mad dash to the center of the bed, her towel had slipped again. Her nipples jutted against the thin blue bikini fabric, reminding her of two blueberries. She gasped and clutched the towel to her chest.

"*Malloy*," he shouted into his mic. "Where the *hell* are you?"

"Right here, Sarge." A female officer in uniform stood at the bedroom doorway. "Sorry, I got tied up with—"

"There's another dog in the bathroom, and she"—he nodded to Andi—"needs to get dressed," he growled. "Bring her downstairs ASAP. Aside from the suitcase, this room hasn't been searched." Without waiting for a response, he yanked a leash from his belt and clipped it to the dog's harness. "*Fuss*."

The dog—Saxon—trotted to his side, and both of them went out the door.

She stared at the open doorway, then looked at Officer Malloy, who was also staring after him, a curious expression on her face.

"What's *his* problem?" Andi grabbed her clothes from the bed and began to dress. "*I'm* the one whose privacy just got trashed." She yanked on her panties and shorts, then tossed the towel on the bed and began putting on her bra.

"I understand completely, ma'am." Malloy nodded.

She tugged the blue tank over her head. "*Please* don't you start in with the ma'am thing, too."

"No, *ma'am*." She grinned. "I'd better get you downstairs before Nick—Sgt. Houston—pops a blood vessel."

Andi fished a brush from her suitcase, then paused before running it through her damp hair. *Nick. Sgt. Nicholas Houston.* She didn't know why, but the name suited him. A manly name that implied he could conquer an entire city. Single-handed, since he was obviously accustomed to people jumping at his command. Then again, she supposed he was only doing his job.

The army of cops she could now hear rummaging around downstairs had complete control of the house, which just punched all her control-freak buttons—a throwback to her days as a financial planner. And after what had happened in her old job, calling the shots on everything in her life was more important now than ever.

She sat heavily on the bed, staring at the brush in her hand. Whatever was happening was serious but had nothing to do with her. This wasn't even her house. She happened to be in the wrong place at a really, *really* bad time.

The worry that had been brewing inside her now stung her gut like a swarm of bees. Clearly Joe—one of her best friends—was in deep, deep trouble. The only question was *how* deep.

• • •

While Nick waited for Ms. Andi Hardt and her dog to make guest appearances, he removed Saxon's body armor and stowed it by the front door. His dog's coat was matted down with sweat, and as he ruffled the damp fur, Saxon uttered an appreciative groan.

They went into the kitchen, the only room downstairs yet to be searched. He gave his dog ample leash to search the cupboards and storage bins for drugs, firearms, ammo, and any other black powder items.

Saxon's tail waved back and forth as he sniffed and processed scents on the floor, in the air, and near the cupboards, then circled twice to be sure he didn't miss anything. The place was as neat as a pin. Aside from a sparkling clean coffee maker, the gleaming black granite counters and island were bare.

When Saxon had completed his search, Nick began opening upper cabinet doors. Next to an expensive-looking cream-colored china bowl, he discovered a box of frosted strawberry Pop-Tarts. Sure enough, when he looked down, Saxon was eyeing the box intently. Nick gave a low chuckle. Two years ago, he'd caught his ten-year-old twin nephews feeding Saxon an entire box of that same flavor of Pop-Tart. Since then, his dog craved them.

The refrigerator contained only milk, condiments, and salad fixings. The last, he'd guess, had been put there by the woman upstairs. With such an athletic body, he figured her for one of those strict fruit, nut, and salad-eating women who stayed as far away from meat as she could possibly get. Yeah, he'd tried not to look, but when he'd whipped open the shower door, it had been impossible not to notice.

She had long, supple runner's legs up to her neck, and every inch of damp, toned skin he could see was sun-kissed in a light golden hue. But the most striking thing about her was her eyes—the prettiest cornflower-blue ones he'd ever seen. Looks aside, there was more to the woman than what that little bikini covered.

Despite being scared by what was happening, she'd exhibited spunk in spades, doing her best to hide her fear behind the verbal lashing she'd given him. Most women would have experienced a total meltdown at finding a cop and his K-9 in her bathroom. Her reaction had taken a one-eighty from that. After belting out a skull-splitting scream, she'd actually thrown stuff at him.

The memory had him chuckling, and it took a few seconds for him to realize Saxon was waiting for his next command, canting his head as if thinking: get *yours* out of your ass and back in the game.

"Sorry, buddy." He'd seen plenty of bikini-clad women before, and it pissed him off that this one was messing with his professionalism *and* his concentration.

Leaning over, he gave Saxon a few hearty pats on the back. "Good boy." Even though Saxon had come up empty, he'd done his job. Myer definitely wasn't housing any firearms and ammo in the house.

"Got anything?" Eric Miller, an ATF agent—and one of Nick's best friends—had stuck his head through the kitchen door leading to the backyard.

A brown snout appeared as Eric's Dutch shepherd, Tiger, pushed his muzzle through the partially open door. The dog's black nostrils flared as he scented Saxon close by. In response, Saxon gave a snort of acknowledgment.

"Negative." Nick shook his head. "Tiger find anything outside?"

"Nada. Place is as clean as a newly smelted baby Glock. I've gotta put Tiger up in the cruiser before he melts into a puddle of hair." He shut the door and led Tiger into the yard.

Nick and Saxon headed into the dining room that now served as a makeshift command center for the search warrant team. Along the way, he caught sight of two officers already searching a roll-top desk in the office, while the locksmith was busy cracking into a wall safe. Troopers and agents were searching the hallway closet and the many other pieces of furniture on the main floor. From what he could see in the practically empty cardboard evidence boxes, they weren't finding much to seize, except for the pink cell phone he'd taken from the master bedroom.

Normally he'd have left it for the evidence team to photograph in place, but cell phones were too important for establishing critical links between people, and he hadn't wanted to take a chance that the woman would squirrel it away before it could be seized and searched for recent phone calls, contacts, and text messages.

Sitting around the dining room table were FBI Special

Agent Randy Cox and several other feds clicking away at laptops.

"Stick around, would ya, Nick?" Cox paused in the middle of placing a call on his cell phone.

Cox placed the call on speakerphone and Nick immediately recognized the voice of AUSA Ted Bennett, lead federal prosecutor for the Western Massachusetts Federal Gang Task Force. Bennett wasn't happy about Myer being MIA and that the most critical piece of evidence was missing.

"No computers at all?" Bennett asked.

"Nothing." Cox shook his head. "Not even a single storage device. No CDs, DVDs, thumb drives, or external drives."

"What about Myer's office in town?" he asked, referring to the other search team.

"Two desktop computers and a few thumb drives." Cox was frowning. "Our guys took a quick look at the hard copy docs, and so far, they're all associated with what look like legitimate accounts. We found some old bills indicating there was a six-month stretch during which Myer couldn't make payments on his mortgage, his Mercedes, and two credit cards. Then he suddenly paid off all his outstanding debts. And before you ask, we called in Myer's secretary, who confirmed that he does have a laptop but takes it home every day."

Bennett swore. "Myer's smart enough to keep the tainted account files on his laptop so he can take them with him wherever he goes. Was anyone else at the house when you got there?"

"Andi Hardt," Cox said. "We're about to interview her."

"What's she doing there?" Bennett asked. "You guys said she and Myer didn't have a relationship."

Cox caught Nick's eye, indicating he should respond.

"None that we knew of." He moved closer to the cell phone in Cox's hand. "*Sitz. Blieb*," he said to Saxon. After Saxon sat, Nick dropped the leash on the carpet. "Apparently we were wrong. There's a framed photo of the two of them in Myer's bedroom." One in which they looked mighty cozy. He'd instantly recognized Andi Hardt from her driver license photo and from surveillance he'd done outside the Dog Park Café.

"Assuming they're involved," Bennett continued, "she'll be less likely to cooperate than we originally thought. Find out exactly what her personal connection is to Myer."

"Will do." Nick shot a look at the stairs. Ms. Hardt should have had more than enough time to dress and get downstairs by now.

Saxon leaned over to sniff the table, leaving a condensation mark on the edge of the gleaming surface. *Mahogany?* No, something even more exotic, he guessed. He'd once seen an imported rosewood table at some snooty-falooty furniture store, and the price tag had been in the thousands.

Looks like it cost more than two of my paychecks. As did everything else in the house. Money laundering for a gun dealer evidently paid well.

Saxon cracked his jaws, panting as his long pink tongue fell from the side of his mouth. He'd have to get his dog water soon. Even with the AC cranked on high and blasting through the two vents in the dining room, the house was getting stuffy.

Cox ended the call. "I rechecked, and the lady has no criminal history, not even a parking ticket. Been a long time since I ran someone with such a squeaky-clean record."

Nick nodded. Seemed like everyone had a history of doing something wrong. *Even me.* But that hadn't been illegal. Just something he wished for a do-over on every freaking day of his life.

"Where's her file?" he asked Cox, wanting to review her

background and the bank documents before they interviewed her.

"O'Reilly? Get Sgt. Houston the file." Cox tipped his head to a young FBI agent.

The baby-faced Feeb quickly produced a manila folder. "Yes, sir. Here you go, Sergeant. Let me know if you need anything else."

"Thanks, kid." He sat and flipped open the folder. "First task-force assignment?"

"Yes, sir." The kid nodded overemphatically.

He'd been a newbie once, too. Twice, actually. First in the Marines with Force Recon, later with the Mass State Police.

A soft huff had him glancing at Saxon, who still sat obediently a few feet away. The dog's haunches bunched as he resisted the urge to come closer to Nick.

Before he could finish saying, "*Hier,*" Saxon bolted closer to the table and lay down at Nick's feet.

"Good boy." He gave the dog a quick pat on the head and began reading.

The first document was a DMV printout and photo. A smiling Andi Hardt stared back at him. Thick blond hair framed her face, but again it was her eyes that drew his attention. Not even a lousy DMV photo could hide her spirit that practically jumped off the page.

The next document was a *Springfield Ledger* article. The *Ledger* had interviewed Ms. Hardt over a year ago when she'd first opened the Dog Park Café in Wilbraham. The article had said it was risky opening up a restaurant so far from any big city.

Other documents filled the folder, but the most important ones were her bank records. Those, he couldn't wait to grill her about.

His cell vibrated, and he pulled it from his shirt pocket. It was an incoming text message from Kade Sampson, a

Department of Homeland Security K-9 officer stationed at JFK Airport in New York, and another of his best friends. They'd gone through K-9 training school together in Texas, along with Eric and a few other stand-up guys. Since then, their small group had been as tight as blood brothers.

Nick read Kade's text and frowned.

"Bad news?" Cox asked.

"Myer hasn't crossed any borders. Wherever he is, he hasn't left the country. Legally that is." They all knew it was entirely possible that he'd escaped through an unmonitored section of the border.

"Speaking of missing persons"—Cox canted his head toward the staircase—"where is she?"

"Still getting dressed, I assume." *And taking her sweet time doing it.*

"We made entry nearly an hour ago." Cox tapped a pen on the table. "How long does it take to get dressed?"

"Good question." By his count, she should have been down already. Then again, he hadn't lived with a woman in years. Five to be exact. Since his wife put a bullet in her brain. A painful, brutal reminder of his biggest failure—letting down the person he'd loved most.

He swallowed and stared at the phone in his hand, no longer seeing what was on the screen. It had taken years for him to stop grieving every single damned day of the week. He'd finally managed, but no way could he go through that again. Giving his heart away only to have it shatter into a million fucking pieces... *Not gonna happen.*

"Was she awake when you found her?"

He looked at Cox. "What?"

"I asked if she was awake when you found her?"

The agent wore an expression that told Nick he needed to pull his shit together and pay attention.

"Yeah. In the shower. Washing her dog," he added as a

quasi-plausible explanation as to what could be taking her so long.

Several agents and other officers looked his way and snickered. Word traveled fast during a search warrant, so he assumed everyone else knew exactly where he'd located Ms. Hardt.

"I see." Cox grinned. "Not as much as you did, I'm guessing."

He glared at Cox, making no effort to disguise his irritation. "She was wearing a bathing suit." Granted, a little one.

For a Feeb, Cox was okay, but the implication that Nick really was a voyeur pissed him off. Not only had he done his best to minimize the woman's embarrassment by keeping the other uniforms from entering the bathroom, but he'd tried to get the only female officer on site upstairs ASAP to deal with the situation.

Ignoring the jibe, he returned his gaze to the Accurint report in the folder. "Andi Hardt received her master's from Columbia School of Business, then became a financial planner at an investment firm in New York City. After ten years with the firm, she picked up stakes, moved to Massachusetts, and opened the Dog Park Café." Attached to the Accurint report was a printout from the restaurant's website dated yesterday. He noted the ad in the upper right corner of the page. *Bartender Wanted. Call Andi.* A phone number was included, and he guessed it was either the number for the pink cell he'd grabbed upstairs, or another phone associated with the café.

"Interesting." Cox made a few notes on a pad. "She and Myer both graduated from the Columbia School of Business, and they're into financial planning. I'd say there's a history there. With what we got from her bank, it looks like she's buried at least up to her ass in Myer's mess."

"Looks like." Nick tapped the keyboard idly with his fingers. "Photo upstairs aside, we've been surveilling him for six months and until now, never caught her once at the house. The only people we saw coming and going besides him were the cash mules dropping off envelopes in the mailbox. Could be something changed between them."

Cox made another note. "Let's get a subpoena for his and Andi Hardt's cell phone records. Eventually we'll get the laptop, and maybe we'll see a pattern of calls between the two of them right before he makes a dirty financial transaction."

"Possibly." Nick closed the folder. "But the subpoena requested records going back five years, and there was only one transaction between Myer's tainted account and one of Andi's accounts. If she's his accomplice, I would have expected to see more than one."

"Agreed." Cox nodded. "We'll have to ask her about that. No matter her answer, she won't be happy when she finds out what we did to her account. The court order was served on her bank yesterday just before closing."

"That oughta get her attention." Of that, he had no doubt.

It sure looked like she was Myer's accomplice, but he'd learned long ago that not everything was what it seemed, and people weren't always who you thought they were. Some kept their personal torment carefully hidden beneath a veneer of happiness.

Until it's too late to help them. He knew that firsthand.

He tossed the folder on the table then stood, preparing to storm upstairs and throw Ms. Hardt over his shoulder, regardless of whether she was dressed or not.

Calm your ass down.

Just because she triggered all his switches was no reason to behave like a total dick and make a fool of himself. He clicked his mic. "Malloy. Where *is* she?"

Malloy came back instantly, only not over the radio.

"Right here, Sarge."

His—and every other man's—eyes were riveted to the stairs. The room went totally silent as Andi Hardt glided down the staircase with what Nick could only describe as a combination of athletic grace and royal bearing. On anyone else, the khaki shorts and blue tank he'd grabbed for her would have looked drab. On her it was alluring. With her blond hair braided and a few wispy strands escaping around her high cheekbones, Daisy Duke had nothing on her.

Again, get your head out of your ass.

She was a suspect and most likely a player in a major money laundering scheme. On top of that, she was sleeping in Myer's house and was probably his girlfriend, his accomplice, or both. Whichever one it was, he'd get the truth out of her, including finding out where Myer was holing up.

A few steps from the bottom, she paused. Cornflower-blue eyes looked straight at him. When she quickly averted her gaze, he detected a faint blush on her high cheekbones, and he understood why.

Unlike the other men in the room, *he* was the only one who'd seen her practically naked.

Chapter Two

At the bottom of the stairs, eight sets of male heads turned to Andi, although only two men stood when she entered the dining room—one wearing a dark blue shirt that said *Federal Agent* on the front, and Sgt. Nicholas Houston.

When she met his penetrating gray eyes, her face heated. Groaning inwardly, she wondered if he'd regaled the rest of the cops and agents in the house about discovering her in the shower. They probably assumed she'd been totally nude.

Reality check.

With that itty-bitty bikini, she might as well have *been* naked. Though she hated to admit it, he'd exhibited surprising chivalry by preventing his colleagues from storming into the bathroom before she could cover herself.

"Miss Hardt," the agent said as he indicated the chair Sgt. Houston had vacated. "I'm FBI Special Agent Randy Cox. Please, have a seat."

Crossing her arms, she gave his proposition some thought. "Am I under arrest?" Couldn't hurt to ask that question again.

"No," he said without hesitation, alleviating only a speck of her mounting unease. "You're free to leave at any time, but we'd appreciate your cooperation."

"What *kind* of cooperation?" She moved closer to the dining room table and found the other officers in the room watching her with obvious curiosity. "I'm not sure I want to answer any questions until you tell me exactly what's going on and why you have a search warrant for this house."

"Fair enough." Cox sat, then beckoned her again to do the same.

Reluctantly, she did. Next to the chair lay the giant black K-9, although the dog's head remained on the floor. The animal's only movement was a flick of his golden gaze in her direction.

He really is beautiful. Resisting the urge to run her fingers through the thick black coat, she refocused on her predicament.

These men were being extremely evasive, but she'd play their game. At least long enough to get some answers. Not that she would automatically believe anything that came from their mouths. She'd learned the hard way to exercise more caution before trusting people. The one time she hadn't, she'd nearly been burned to a crisp.

She noted Sgt. Houston remained standing behind her, and she felt his presence like the grim reaper waiting for her to drop dead so he could collect her soul. Something about him unnerved her, and it wasn't because of the awkward way they'd met. He was trying to intimidate her, and it was working.

No, it's more than that. It's *him.* He was way too masculine and unyielding.

Like a solid brick wall.

"This is a copy of the search warrant." Cox handed her a document consisting of several pages stapled together. "Take a few minutes to look it over."

She picked up the warrant and began reading. At the top of the first page in bold letters were the words *U.S. District Court*. She'd only dealt with the courts one other time in her life. *A time I'd rather forget.* The document was signed by a District Court judge and authorized federal agents to search Joe's house and his office in Springfield.

"Flip to Attachment A, the second page." Cox did the same with what looked like a duplicate of the warrant. "This is a list of the items we're authorized to seize."

She scanned the dozen or so numbered items on Attachment A. Articles of incorporation for Joe's business, business licenses, emails, computers, laptops, various storage devices such as thumb drives and DVDs, and cash. But it was the last item that took her completely by surprise.

"Guns?" She snapped her gaze to Cox then twisted her neck to look behind her at Houston. Sgt. Houston watched her impassively, without a flicker of emotion, although she noted a hardening of that rock-solid jawline. She began shaking her head. "You can't be serious. This has to be a mistake."

"Again, there's no mistake." Houston repositioned himself at the edge of the table. "You and your boyfriend are up to your eyeballs in money laundering for a gunrunner."

"Whoa. Wait a minute. *Me?*" She stared at Houston, her eyes as wide as they could possibly go. "You must have me confused with someone else. I don't have *anything* to do with money laundering *or* a gunrunner. And what do you mean, my *boyfriend*?" For a second, she didn't know what shocked her more, that she and Joe were being investigated by the FBI and the state police for money laundering and gunrunning, or that they all assumed she was his girlfriend. Then again, she'd been in his bathroom at six in the morning, so it shouldn't come as a shock that they'd jumped to that conclusion. "He's *not* my boyfriend," she insisted.

Houston's tone hardened. "Then why are you here?"

"My place has plumbing problems, and since Joe was going to be out of town for a while, he offered me his place to crash for a couple nights."

"Where is he now?" Cox asked.

"I already told Sgt. Houston I don't know, and Joe didn't say. Did you ask his parents, or his brother or sisters?"

"We did," Houston confirmed. "They have no idea where he is. When was the last time you talked to him?"

He looked at her so intently that she felt his gaze boring into her like twin lasers, and she had the distinct impression he was angry. *Well, I didn't do anything.*

"Yesterday," she answered. "Right before he left. He gave me keys to the house."

Cox jotted something on a pad. "Did he say when he'd be back?"

"No." She twisted the edges of the warrant in her hands. Again, it hit her that he'd always let her know when he'd be returning. This time he hadn't.

Cox tapped his pen on the pad. "You used to be a financial planner in New York City. You and Myer both went to Columbia for your business degrees. Did you ever work together?"

"No. After graduation, Joe moved to Massachusetts. I stayed in New York."

"Are you working together now?" Cox asked.

"No." The warrant audibly crinkled as she all but gouged her nails clean through the papers.

"There's a photo of you and Myer upstairs in his bedroom," Houston interjected. "The two of you look pretty cozy. If you're not his girlfriend, and you're not his accomplice, what's your connection to the guy?"

"We're friends." When Houston arched an eyebrow, it was obvious he wasn't buying her story, but it was true. *Now, anyway.* "Okay, we dated and lived together while we were at Columbia, then after we graduated, we decided our romance had died a quiet death and we were just good friends, so we broke it off." And in all the years since, she hadn't had a meaningful relationship with anyone. Except for Steve, and that had been a disaster that still haunted her.

Maybe it's my fault for being so gullible.

She swallowed the shame inside her. Given the dire predicament Joe was in at the moment, there were more important things at hand than whining about her personal crisis. And as for her gullibility, she lived with Joe for two years and knew every aspect of his personality. There was no way she could have missed such a huge part of who he was. It wasn't possible. *There has to be an explanation.*

"After we broke up," she continued, "Joe moved here to Springfield and opened his own company, but we remained friends and spoke regularly on the phone."

"About what?" Sgt. Houston asked.

"About everything. Business, his new clients, his new house, restaurants he'd been to lately." That was something they'd shared—a love of good food, wine, and beer. While they'd been together, they frequented so many restaurants and wine tastings she'd lost count.

Cox looked up from his notes. "What did you discuss about his business?"

"That it was going well, but not quite as well as he'd expected." She bit her lower lip. The first time she'd seen Joe's three-story McMansion and pricy new silver Mercedes, she *had* thought they were a bit extravagant considering the income he said he was pulling in. "But recently, he told me he got a new client and business was picking up."

Cox's brows drew together sharply. "What new client?"

"He didn't say." Her gut twisted with more worry. She hadn't thought much of it at the time, but she *had* asked who the new client was, and he'd smoothly avoided telling her.

"What's your connection with his business?" This from Sgt. Houston.

"There *is* no connection. I told you already, we never worked together." Their suspicion and mistrust were beginning to piss her off.

"Then what brought you from New York City to Springfield?" Cox asked.

Christ, these two are relentless. She'd been swinging her head back and forth, answering their questions as best she could, but it was getting annoying.

"Joe knew I was fed up with the grinding commute into Manhattan and that I was looking for a change. He said there was an old restaurant on a nice piece of property about to go up for sale, and he suggested it might be the perfect location for me to open my place." That was only part of the reason she'd moved. The real truth was that she'd needed to get as far away as possible from Steve and her former employers. But Cox and Houston didn't need to know that.

"I opened the Dog Park Café about a year ago." *The best decision of my life, and I'm damned proud of it.*

The only good thing to come from Steve's treachery was that it pushed—no, *forced*—her to discover her brass ovaries and then do whatever it took to realize her dream: opening a cozy, inviting café and dog park that catered to humans *and* canines. She'd never regret the monumental change, but at thirty-five she was starting a brand-new life for herself. *Alone.*

Cox threw down his pen. "You left what had to be a highly lucrative income in a big city to open a restaurant in the middle of the woods?"

She nodded. "Lots of people try new things when they get fed up with the rat race. New York is a place of incredible opportunity, but after a while it sucks the life out of you." And it had. "The commute alone is enough to drive a person crazy." That part was true. Even her language had deteriorated during the daily drive into lower Manhattan. She'd invented several new curse words that would make a truck driver applaud her ingenuity.

Sgt. Houston made a *hmph* sound. "Are you and Myer still intimate?"

She glared at him. "That's none of your business."

"It is if you're working with him," he shot back.

Gray eyes bored into her, and she really did feel as if she were under a spotlight. *His* spotlight. Not for the first time since she'd come down the stairs, her face heated until she squirmed uncomfortably in her chair. Looking away from those piercing, knowing eyes, she swallowed before answering.

"I am *not* sleeping with him. We haven't been together since grad school." When her response was met with silence, her face grew hotter, and she clenched her fists, glaring at Houston. "And for the last time, I'm *not* working with him."

"Did Joe invest in your restaurant?" Cox asked, rescuing her from more of Houston's humiliating interrogation.

"No, I bought it with my own money. I put everything I had into the place." Including cashing out most of her retirement nest egg. If her venture failed, she was toast.

She realized this was a tag-team thing, the two men intentionally peppering her with question after question in an attempt to catch her off guard, so she'd inadvertently spill some kind of secret or get caught in a lie. But she *had* no secrets. *Well, almost none.* And she definitely wasn't lying.

"What's really going on here?" Again, she swiveled her gaze from Cox to Houston and back again. They might not be lying outright, but they definitely weren't telling her everything. "Joe isn't the kind of person to have anything to do with guns. He doesn't even *like* guns."

"Maybe not." Cox leaned back in his chair. "But he has

no qualms about laundering money for those who do. The question is how much *you're* involved."

"I'm *not*. How many times do I have to tell you that?" Her stomach clenched with the shocked realization that despite what she kept telling them, they still thought she was Joe's accomplice.

She noticed for the first time that when she spoke, the baby-faced agent sitting at one of the laptops clicked away on the keyboard. Whenever she stopped talking, he stopped typing.

He's making a transcript of everything I say.

"I'm thinking I may need a lawyer."

Cox let out an audible breath, then crossed his arms, giving her the clear impression that he was annoyed with her threat to seek legal counsel. "That's your prerogative."

"Yes, it is." She mimicked him by crossing her arms. "I know my Constitutional rights."

"Before you decide to lawyer up"—Sgt. Houston leaned down until his face was inches from hers, giving her a massive dose of his manly fresh scent—"allow me to put this in perspective for you. Last week, I was first on scene at a shooting. A fourteen-year-old girl was caught in gang crossfire. She took a bullet to the head. Her brains were splattered all over the sidewalk. *Your* ex-boyfriend is a bookkeeper for the same dealer who put that gun—and hundreds, if not thousands of others just like it—on the street. Thanks to them, Springfield is now a mini war zone. So, if you're sincere about cooperating, then you'll answer the man's questions. *All* his questions. If Myer's innocent, then the facts will support it. If he's not, he'll have to answer for his crimes. Trust me, we wouldn't be here if he were innocent. *Your* innocence is also in question."

Contempt flared hotly in the man's eyes. *Finally, some emotion.* She'd thought he was angry, but in actuality, he was royally pissed. And he was right. The only thing she knew for certain was that she was innocent. If Joe hadn't violated the federal crimes outlined in the warrant , then nothing she said to these men could hurt either of them. If he really was guilty, something she still had difficulty wrapping her brain around, could her responses to their questions make things worse?

I don't know anything, so how can I hurt him?

Then again, talking about him to the police seemed like a betrayal. She needed to hear it directly from Joe. He wouldn't dare lie to her. *I'd know if he was lying. Wouldn't I?*

She didn't know anything, not for sure. They'd lied to her at her old job, and she hadn't known until it was almost too late. A sob rose in her throat. *Maybe Joe's been lying to me for years.*

Then something else occurred to her, and she narrowed her eyes on Sgt. Houston. "Aside from me being in his house, why do you seem so certain that I'm involved in whatever Joe is doing?"

Without hesitation, he grabbed a folder from the table and pulled out a sheet of paper and handed it to her. As he did, his eyes were as hard as shards of gray ice. She took the document and began reading. It was a wire transfer from her bank dated less than a month ago. Her name was listed as the account holder, but she couldn't recall making any wire transfer from that account. Ever. And was that… "*A hundred thousand dollars?*" She jerked her gaze first to Houston's then Cox's. "What is this? *I* didn't authorize this transfer. I couldn't have. I don't *have* a hundred thousand dollars."

Since the day she'd opened the DPC—the Dog Park Café—she'd been struggling to bring in new customers and stay in the black. The most she'd ever had in that account at any given time was about twenty grand, and that was used to pay all the restaurant's monthly bills, salaries, and the mortgage.

Houston stared her down. "If you didn't authorize that wire, then who did?"

"I don't know." She looked away, her mind reeling with how this could possibly have happened.

A memory popped into her head, one of Joe sitting in her office at the DPC while she'd been writing monthly checks. Could he have somehow taken note of her bank account information? But how could he have gone so far as to authorize the transfer of so much money without her knowing it? It had never shown up on any of her monthly statements.

Or had it?

"Something you want to tell us?" Cox looked at her with raised brows.

"Last month my bank statement didn't come in the mail." She liked paper, so had opted for hardcopy delivery. "I realize I could have checked my account online, but I was so busy with the restaurant, I didn't bother. I'm meticulous with my money, and I balance my checkbook to the penny, so I wasn't worried about missing a transaction." Clearly, she'd missed one. A very, very critical one.

Her heart began beating faster. Numbly, she handed the document back to Houston. "I swear I didn't authorize this. Someone had to have deposited a hundred grand into my account and wired it out right away because I didn't see it in this month's statement, and my account balance has always been correct."

Sgt. Houston pursed his lips. "The money was wired in, then wired out less than twenty-four hours later."

"Then there should be a record of where it came from and where it went, right?" She held out her hand in question.

Cox adjusted his chair to face her directly. "As for the source account, we don't have that information yet, but we will. The money was transferred to an offshore account in Belize."

"Look." She fisted her hands. "This is ridiculous. I have nothing to do with this, and I don't want to talk to you anymore."

Sgt. Houston sat on the edge of the table, too close to her for comfort. "We froze your bank account."

"What?" she whispered, praying she'd misheard him.

"Yesterday, we served your bank with a court order freezing all assets in that account." Sgt. Houston nodded to the document in his hand. "Because of this wire transfer, your entire account is now considered tainted. You can't touch anything in it until we say otherwise."

"You can't do that." She stared in disbelief at the crumpled paper. Panic spread through her like wildfire. "That account is all I have for the café. It's how I pay my bills. *All* my bills. We're hanging on by a thread as it is, and if I can't pay the bills, I may have to shut down."

To her dismay, neither Houston nor Cox showed anything resembling remorse or an iota of understanding.

This is not good. This is beyond *not good.* Someone—*Joe?*—had used her bank account without her knowledge, and right now she couldn't prove it. She covered her face with her hands and groaned.

"Talk to us," Sgt. Houston said. "Could Myer have initiated this wire?"

"I don't—I don't know."

"What are you thinking?" Houston asked, clearly picking up on her hesitancy.

In an effort to put more space between them, she leaned back in her chair and let her hands drop to her lap. "He helped me set up that account when I moved here. He introduced me to one of the managers, a personal friend of his." Could he have used that connection to access her account?

"I want to call Joe." She pressed her lips together, growing angrier by the second. "I need to talk to him. If he really did this—and I'm not saying he did—then he'll clear my name. I'm sure of it. My phone is upstairs. If you let me get it, I'll call and ask him directly."

The two men exchanged looks.

"Nick? What do you think?"

"Can't hurt," he said to Cox. To her, he added, "As long as you put the call on speakerphone, so we can hear what he says and record the conversation. Will you consent to that?"

"Don't you need a wiretap or something?" Even she knew the police couldn't just listen in and record phone conversations anytime they wanted.

"Not a wiretap," Cox said. "We have blanket authorization from the U.S. Attorney's Office to monitor and record any conversations for this investigation. All we need from you is your consent to utilize *your* phone to do it."

Sgt. Houston pulled her phone from his thigh pocket but didn't hand it to her. Until that moment she hadn't known he'd taken it from the bedroom.

"Fine. I consent." She held out her hand, but Houston ignored her.

"What's the passcode?" One of his fingers hovered over the phone.

She narrowed her eyes. "What if I don't want to give it to you?"

Houston pursed his lips, emphasizing the concavity of his lean cheeks. "If you cooperate and give us the code, you stand a significantly greater chance of getting it back sooner, rather than later. *Much* later."

Reluctantly, she rattled off the code and watched him enter it before handing the phone to her. The pink case was still warm from being against his leg. "Can I tell him about the search warrant?" she asked.

"Yes." Houston nodded. "If he answers, ask him where he is, then try to convince him to come home. If he doesn't answer, leave a message that it's urgent he calls you back."

After pulling up Joe's cell number from her contacts, she was about to make the call but hesitated when Cox clicked a button on a small digital recorder and set it on the table in front of her. A tiny red light glowed steadily on the top of the device. "Are you going to arrest him?"

Houston didn't hesitate. "Eventually, yes."

She held his gaze for a moment. The thought of Joe— her former lover and friend—in handcuffs was positively frightening. *Please let this be the right thing to do.*

Taking a deep breath, she touched the call button, then the phone's speaker button. It went directly to voicemail, and she found herself somewhat relieved. She let the message play out, then left word about the search warrant and that he should call her urgently. She ended the call, but before she could pocket the phone, Sgt. Houston smoothly took it away.

"Hey, give that back!" She jumped up and made a grab for it, plowing into his chest—a chest so hard she bounced off him and practically fell right back into the chair she'd been sitting on.

"No can do." He extended his long arm and handed the phone across the table to the baby-faced agent, who slipped it into a clear plastic bag. "This phone is now evidence."

"I don't understand." She shook her head. "That phone is mine, not Joe's, and it has nothing to do with his business dealings."

"The phone was located on the premises during service of a federal search warrant." Cox pointed to the warrant. "You'll get the phone back, but it will probably be months before we can return it to you. Right now, it's seizable pursuant to Attachment A, paragraph eight, describing cell phones and computers."

"Speaking of which," Houston interjected, again towering over her, "does Myer have a laptop?"

"Yes." She frowned. In addition to his expensive house and car, he'd been inordinately proud of his brand-new, lightweight Mac Air.

"We didn't find it here or at his office. Did he hide it somewhere on the premises?"

"No. I don't know. At least, I don't think so." Again, she twisted her hands together. "He never used to hide his computer." *Or anything else, for that matter.*

"Do you and he send emails to each other?" When she nodded, Cox slid his pad to her, handing her a pen. "Write down your full email address and his."

She did, knowing they could pull that information off her phone, anyway. If she gave it to them outright, maybe she'd get the phone back sooner.

"Found something." Officer Malloy handed Cox a stack of envelopes, cash, and several sheets of paper stapled together. "We found cash in the safe, and these envelopes in the locked mailbox. The envelopes are loaded with more cash."

"Did you count it yet?" Houston asked.

Malloy pulled a piece of paper from her vest pocket. "Thirty grand, total."

What is Joe doing with that much cash? They both knew that any cash not in a bank was lazy money because it wasn't earning interest.

Cox handed the bills to the baby-faced agent, then began flipping through the other documents. The only words Andi had been able to make out were in a large font on the first page: *Last Will and Testament.*

He looked up from reading. "Is your real name really Andromeda Hardt?"

She nodded, a little embarrassed by the celestial name her astronomy-loving parents had seen fit to bestow upon her at birth. "Too many syllables. Everyone calls me Andi."

"Understandable." Sgt. Houston smiled, making him appear only slightly less serious. As a distraction, she tried visualizing what a genuine smile would do to his chiseled-from-rock face.

Probably nothing. And probably wouldn't change his similarly humorless personality, either.

"Did you know you're the sole beneficiary of Joe Myer's estate?" Cox raised both brows.

"*What?*" Her mouth fell open.

He handed her the document, and she quickly read the section to which he referred. *I, Joseph A. Myer, bequeath 100% of my estate to Andromeda Hardt.* The will was dated only a month ago.

"I don't understand any of this," she whispered, more to herself than to the men seated around her. For Joe to do this without telling her...something was very, *very* wrong.

They were friends now, but nothing more. *Why would he give me everything if he died?* He had family—a mother, father, two sisters and a brother. What was going on with him that he'd drawn up a will only a month ago? The presence of state troopers and federal agents in his house did, in fact, give her a major clue.

She shut her eyes as reality slammed her in the face all over again. Whatever was going on, Joe was in deep, deep trouble, and he'd dragged her into his mess.

An ominous silence pervaded the room, and she opened her eyes to find everyone staring at her, waiting for her to say something. "I wasn't aware he'd designated me his beneficiary. I swear I had no knowledge of this." Why she felt she had to swear to it, she didn't know. Then again, she could understand their perspective.

A person didn't normally make someone his sole beneficiary unless there was a close personal relationship. If nothing else, Joe's will made her look guilty of lying. Again, begging the question as to whether or not she should seek legal representation before answering more questions.

"Do *you* know where Joe is?" she asked Cox, thinking they might be lying to her for some reason. It wouldn't be the first time a man had lied to her. The FBI agent seemed to be in charge, but the way Cox repeatedly deferred to Houston left her with the certainty that the state trooper was a major player in this investigation.

Cox shook his head. "We don't, and we're concerned for his safety. He booked a flight from Logan to Vegas but never boarded the plane. That's pretty odd behavior, don't you think?"

With everyone eyeing her suspiciously, she suddenly made the connection between Joe being missing and his will. "You think I knew about the will and killed him to inherit his estate? You've *got* to be kidding me." She stood, clenching her hands.

A growl came from beneath the table, and the black shepherd leaped to its feet. She uttered a shriek and stepped back, nearly tripping over the chair. Sgt. Houston grabbed her upper arms, tugging her against his chest until she'd regained her balance. She automatically reached for him, her fingers closing over the hardest, thickest biceps she'd ever felt.

"*Platz*," he said, and the dog immediately backed off and lay down.

Her heart beat faster, partly because the K-9 was so intimidating and partly from the shock of being pressed up against Sgt. Houston so intimately from her head to her toes.

"You all right?" he asked. "Saxon won't hurt you."

The dog still lay on the floor, his head tilted so that he could watch Houston. The intensity of those gold canine eyes was alarming, although she understood dogs well enough to know this one was only trying to protect what it perceived as an imminent threat to its master.

"I'm fine." She lifted her gaze to find Houston watching her with undisguised suspicion. "Except for the fact that you actually think I could have murdered Joe. I love him as a friend. I don't ever want to see him hurt."

He released her abruptly. The tightness of his mouth and the frigid animosity in his eyes obliterated any images she'd been trying to conjure up of how a smile might transform all those hard planes and angles. She'd been wrong. No way would this man ever smile, let alone exhibit even the tiniest morsel of warmth toward another human being.

"I didn't say that," he answered in a flat tone.

She rested her fists at her hips, still glaring at him. "Then why are you concerned for his safety?"

"Because"—he crossed his arms—"there's a bounty on his head, and no one knows where he is. When someone in the illegal gun business disappears, they tend to show up only when someone finds their body."

• • •

For some reason Nick couldn't pinpoint, the image of Andi stuck behind bars didn't sit well with him.

Not your problem.

Fear and worry spread across her features as she absorbed his words, and he was hit with the irrational urge to comfort her—a suspect.

What the hell?

Needing space, he reached for Saxon's leash. His dog leaped to his feet, ready to go to work again. "Back in five," he said to Cox, then headed for the kitchen, taking his first breath in the last ten minutes that wasn't mingled with the distracting scent of Andi's shampoo or whatever was making her smell like that flower in the boutonniere he'd worn at his sister's wedding.

He began opening cupboards, searching for a plastic bowl for Saxon, when a female voice came from behind him.

"Looking for a water bowl?"

He turned to find Andi had followed him into the kitchen. As she passed Saxon, she paused, hesitantly laying a hand on his dog's back and running it along his spine. Saxon turned his head, his nostrils flaring as he gave the back of her hand a sniff.

"You're gorgeous." She continued stroking, and since Saxon didn't seem to mind, Nick didn't stop her.

As her fingers sifted through the thick, shiny coat, he stared at her blunt, neatly manicured nails. Saxon had scared her at least twice, but she'd barely hesitated to pet him, and it was done in such a natural way.

No shit, Sherlock. She owns the Dog Park Café. Shouldn't come as a shock that she likes dogs. Speaking of which… "Where's your dog?"

"Locked in the bedroom." She jerked her head up, worry filling her eyes. "Why?"

"Will she be okay up there?" Not that he gave a shit if the dog crapped all over Myer's pristine bedroom carpeting or tore everything in the master bedroom to shreds, but he didn't want the animal stressed more than she must be already by being locked up.

"We were up early and went for a long walk. She'll be fine." Her gaze narrowed on him.

"What?" For some reason, his inquiry about the dog's welfare seemed to make her think he had some kind of ulterior motive.

"Nothing. I was just…" She shook her head as if to clear it. "Trying to figure you out."

Don't, he wanted to say. The last thing he needed was a woman rummaging around in his messed-up head. "Cox give up questioning you?" he asked, sorely needing to shortcut her train of thought.

"One can only hope." She scrunched her lips in a way that made her look cute. "He's filling out paperwork for me to sign, so we're taking a break." She opened another cupboard door and reached for the china bowl next to the box of Pop-Tarts. As she did, the box fell on the floor, and Saxon lunged for it.

Nick got there first, snatching it away and setting it on the counter. "Not a chance, buddy."

A high-pitched whimper sounded from the back of Saxon's throat, and he lowered his head as if he were pouting.

Andi laughed and began filling the bowl with water. "Loves sweet treats, does he?"

Nick nodded. "Too much." Renewed suspicion rankled his gut. "For someone who doesn't live here, you seem to know your way around this kitchen."

She groaned. "Don't start that again. I told you the truth about my relationship with Joe. On the few occasions I've been in this house, he and I spent most of the time in the kitchen. Before the restaurant's kitchen was renovated, I'd come here to try out recipes on him. Poor guy. I think he got sick of my cooking." She set the bowl on the floor, giving Saxon's ears a quick massage as he bent his head to begin lapping at the water.

He watched in surprise when Saxon turned to give her hand a quick lick, as if to say thanks. His dog was trained not to attack someone just because they touched him, but bestowing an affectionate lick on a total stranger was definitely not in his repertoire.

He'd occasionally seen that kind of instant rapport between humans and canines, and Andi Hardt seemed to have it. He also trusted Saxon's instincts the way he trusted only a few people in his life—friends like Eric and the other guys he'd gone through K-9 school with. Saxon was a good judge of character, and it wasn't lost on him that the dog's immediate acceptance of Andi didn't jibe with her being a criminal.

It would take time to prove her innocence *or* complicity. His dirtbag radar was pretty damned infallible, but he wasn't sure about anything. Still, he could count on one hand the number of times he'd been surprised by someone.

Loud slurping had them watching Saxon as he made quick work of drinking every drop in the bowl. When he was done, he continued licking until the bowl began inching across the hardwood floor. Then Saxon sat in front of Andi, panting with a gratified look on his face. His long tongue slipped from the side of his muzzle. Droplets fell onto her sandals, calling attention to the pale-pink nail polish on her toes. Even his dog was drooling over her.

She picked up the bowl and filled it again. After Andi reset it on the floor, Saxon got to work lapping up more water. "He looks purebred. Is he?" Nick nodded. "I've heard black shepherds are rare. Either the sire, the dam, or both have to have the recessive black shepherd gene."

He leaned his hip against the black granite counter, also watching Saxon as he took great, sloppy gulps of water. "You know your shepherds."

"I love dogs." She shrugged then quickly looked away.

A moment of awkward silence passed between them. As if there could be any other kind, under the circumstances.

"I'm sorry about the girl," she said quietly. He must have had a puzzled expression on his face because a moment later, she added, "The teenager caught in the crossfire last week. It must have been horrible finding her that way. I can't imagine what goes through your mind at a moment like that." Her eyes clouded with genuine sorrow.

"You get used to it," he lied. He'd *never* gotten used to it.

"Really?" The clear skin on her forehead wrinkled.

"How?"

"By keeping it impersonal so I can do my job." The acid boiling in his gut made him feel sick. Five years after the fact, and the grisly images of his dead wife remained imprinted in his memory as if they'd been stamped there yesterday. There'd been no need for an autopsy. Even if she hadn't left a suicide note, the unregistered firearm in her lifeless hand and the bullet wound to her head told the story.

Except for where she got the gun. A gun with its serial number filed off—the same as the guns sold by this dealer.

"If I let it get to me every time I see a gunshot victim, I'd be worthless."

Every cop knew that, although why he was confiding in her, he had no clue.

Someone cleared his throat, and Nick found Cox standing in the doorway. "We're just about done here." He gestured for Andi to return to the other room. "I need you to sign a property receipt for the few items we're seizing."

Ignoring Nick, she patted Saxon one last time. "Goodbye, Saxon."

He stopped slurping and fixed his gaze on her, watching with obvious longing as she went out the kitchen door.

If Nick didn't know better, he'd say his dog was in love.

"What's up?" Cox glanced briefly in the direction Andi had gone.

"Nothing." He shook his head, annoyed with his thoughts. There was just something about her that stayed with him, and it had nothing to do with the case. "What d'ya need?"

"Your opinion." He leaned his forearms on the granite island. "Think she's bullshitting us?"

"Maybe, but it's too soon to tell. I'd like to see her full background check first, especially the rest of her financials." He looked around Cox's shoulder, noting the way Andi's khaki shorts tightened across her backside as she leaned over the dining room table to sign the property receipt. "Whether she's innocent or not, my guess is Myer will try to contact her. Despite what she says, he obviously still has feelings for her. She's his sole beneficiary. A man doesn't do that without a darned good reason."

Cox turned to follow Nick's gaze. "Should we work her?"

"Yeah." He nodded, then quickly outlined a plan for doing just that. "Given what we're holding over her head, I'd be surprised if she doesn't go for it." Didn't matter whether she was innocent or not. If she could be exploited for the good of the investigation, they should do it. She was the best lead they had to find Myer before he got his money-laundering ass killed and they lost their best witness.

"Something wrong?" Cox asked. They'd been working together long enough that the man had picked up on Nick's reluctance. "You having second thoughts about using her?"

"No," he lied. "She's a means to an end. Nothing more."

"I'll pitch it to Bennett. See what he thinks."

As Cox placed a call to the AUSA, Nick snagged Saxon's body armor at the door, then led his dog outside to the Explorer. He didn't care how they got to Myer, as long they did.

He popped open the side door for Saxon, who leaped up and settled on the kennel bench. When he shut the door, Andi's white pickup parked in the driveway caught his eye.

She'd definitely tell him to go to hell, but the best person to work Ms. Andromeda Hardt...

Is me.

He wanted to wipe this gun dealer off the planet, and he wouldn't let anyone stand in his way. If they did, he'd steamroll over their ass without hesitation. If necessary, he'd back up and grind them into the pavement.

Because for him, this was personal.

Chapter Three

By the time Andi pulled into the lot at the DPC, it was after ten a.m., still an hour and a half before lunch service kicked off. There were only a handful of other vehicles, some of which belonged to her staff, some to patrons running their dogs in the hundred-by-two-hundred-foot dog run.

She parked and let out a heavy sigh. Behind her on the truck's bench seat, Stray responded with a whine that had Andi glancing in the rearview mirror. The lingering smells of slightly damp dog mixed with baby shampoo filled the cab. Seemed like Stray had recovered from her surprise encounter with that giant K-9.

Better than I have. Holy cow, what a way to start the week.

In the end, all Cox had said was that he'd be in touch. "In touch." She laughed bitterly. Yeah, she knew what they'd be in touch about. Her cooperation, which she undoubtedly had to keep giving if there was any hope of getting her bank account unfrozen.

Opening a restaurant was risky business in any town, let alone in a suburb without a big city to provide patronage.

In order to add the dog park aspect to the place, she'd had to buy land outside Springfield. The location had been less expensive, but the necessary renovations had sucked her account close to dry. She'd done the research, though, and discovered there wasn't another dog park within a hundred miles, let alone one with a restaurant. She was counting on that unique combination to draw in customers who loved good food and spending time outdoors with their furry friends. The DPC was everything she could have hoped for, and she'd finally found a reason to be optimistic about the future.

Until now.

Using her bank account was a betrayal of everything she and Joe had once shared. *And it hurts, dammit.* She tightened her fingers around the steering wheel. Not for the first time that morning she began questioning her judgment where men were concerned.

It had been nearly two years since she'd seen Steve. His duplicity had been the nail in her dating coffin, and since then, she'd sworn off men altogether. That conniving bastard had slept with her, pretending to want a real relationship, when in fact, he'd only been trying to get close to her to further his career. He'd said he wanted to help with her clients' portfolios, and in the end, he tried bilking them out of their annuities to bring in more money for the firm. All to pad his accomplishments and grab the next VP promotion. One that should have been hers.

After wising up, she'd confronted her bosses about Steve's illegal activities, and the sons of bitches actually backed him up. Then they tried to buy her silence. She'd quit on the spot, then walked out the door and turned over evidence to the Attorney General's Office.

She let out a disgusted huff.

It's in the past. Forget it and move on.

There were plenty of problems to deal with in the here and now.

Shaking her head, she gazed out the windshield at the dog run, watching a medium-size Schnauzer cavorting with a large gray Bouvier. *Stray's friends.*

She'd temporarily named the dog Stray after the animal had wandered into the DPC about a month ago. The café was turning out to be a magnet for wayward dogs, and thus far she'd been 100 percent successful in finding good homes for all of them. Since Stray was a beautiful female with a sunny temperament, she figured the dog would be adopted any day now, and she was already sad at the prospect of not having her around.

Unable to drag her butt inside, she sat in the truck with the engine running. She frowned, wishing she could call Joe, but that wasn't possible. Federal agents had seized her personal phone.

Who writes phone numbers down anymore?

The cell at work didn't have any of her personal contacts, but at least she could borrow it for a bit.

Even sitting in the truck with the AC on, she began to sweat into her blue tank and khaki shorts—the clothes Sgt. Houston had selected for her. Funny how he was so completely not the kind of man she'd be interested in, yet something about him stuck in her mind. Like a burr. *No, make that one big-ass burr.*

The man was as big and strong as an oak tree. Even his dog was enormous, looking as if it should be housed in a barn, not a kennel. The two of them were made for each other. Although the dog—Saxon—was significantly friendlier than the man. No, she much preferred a warm, affable man who actually knew how to smile. Definitely not one who obviously spent every spare moment pumping iron in a gym.

Ironically, he seemed to have a soft spot for dogs. His

concern for Stray's wellbeing had taken her totally by surprise.

No sooner had she stepped out of the truck than the midmorning heat and oppressive humidity slammed into her. She opened the rear door, and Stray leaped out, charging to the dog run's fence. Her golden-brown body wriggled as she stood on her hind legs and rested her front paws on the top rail.

Andi readjusted her leather shoulder bag then joined Stray at the fence. She ruffled the hair on the dog's head and massaged her soft ears. Stray groaned in obvious pleasure, leaning into her hand. She didn't know who got more out of these moments, her or the dog. There was something so soothing about petting a dog.

Stray barked and pushed her wet nose against Andi's hand.

"Okay, okay, girl." She laughed. "Go play with your friends."

The second she'd opened the inner gate to the run, Stray took off like a shot and bolted after the other dogs.

Back outside the gates, Andi joined two of her customers, Frank Feldman and Meera Devine. Frank owned Penny, the Schnauzer, while Scottie, the Bouvier, belonged to Meera.

Frank was a nice-looking man, around forty-five and with only a touch of gray in his hair. He was absolutely crazy about dogs *and* the DPC's broccoli rabe and pulled pork panini with a side of mac 'n' cheese. Meera was around the same age as Frank and worked part-time as a secretary. Despite the woman being ten years her senior, Andi enjoyed the many chats they'd had since the restaurant opened.

"Morning, Frank. Morning, Meera."

"Morning, Andi," they replied in unison.

"Stray is certainly full of energy today." Meera nodded to where Stray ran circles around the other dogs.

"That she is." Whereas Andi felt positively drained.

When she glanced at the other woman, she couldn't miss how close Frank stood to Meera or how their shoulders remained in constant contact.

Hmm, sweet. The possibility that the DPC had brought two of her favorite customers together added a touch of much-needed brightness to what had begun as a depressingly awful morning.

She smiled inwardly. Frank and Meera were perfect for each other. "I'd better get inside before the lunch rush kicks in." More importantly, she suspected they were still in the "puppy love" stage and would prefer being alone.

After exchanging goodbyes, she headed to the cafe's rear entrance and pulled open the door that led directly into the kitchen to find Marty Machatto, her head chef, leaning over to inspect something in the panini press.

"'Bout time you showed up." He lifted the lid of the panini press and slid out an expertly toasted sandwich, complete with perfect golden-brown grill lines. He placed it on a cutting board and made quick work of cutting it into four squares. "It's my new invention."

"Ingredients?" She didn't know which happened first, her mouth watering or her stomach growling.

He grabbed a napkin, then handed her a piece of the sandwich. "Smoked turkey, avocado, homemade mozzarella with a pine-nut pesto spread, on potato-dill bread."

"Sounds delicious." She bit into the crusty sandwich, then chewed slowly. The garlicky pesto hit her taste buds first, followed by the mozzarella and all the other fresh ingredients that blended harmoniously on her tongue. Closing her eyes, she swallowed, then sighed her approval. "Chef, you've outdone yourself. It's orgasmic. Start it out as a special, and we'll see if everyone else loves it as much as I do."

"Hoped you'd say that." He was about to bite into one of the other pieces of sandwich when Tess McTavish, the

DPC's manager, flew into the kitchen, her long, curly red hair bouncing. "Here." He handed her a wedge. "Try this and tell me if you don't think it's the best panini you ever had. This one's vegetarian. Just for you."

"Hey, Andi." Tess's green eyes sparkled as she smiled in a bubbly way that lit up any room. With her dangly crystal earrings, multicolored tie-dyed tank tucked into cut-off jeans, and Birkenstocks, she was a throwback to hippie-Woodstock days. The woman was only five foot two, but no one would ever overlook her.

"Thanks, Marty." She accepted the sandwich and was about to take a bite when she gave Andi another look and frowned. "You okay?"

"Rough morning." *And then some.* "Fill you in later. Cappuccino first."

Along with being the manager, Tess had also become Andi's best friend, and every morning before the lunch rush they gabbed over coffee, and no topic was off-limits. Movies, makeup…and men, of course.

Andi stowed her bag in a locker against the wall then began scooping espresso into the stainless-steel Gaggia.

"Wow," Tess mumbled between chews then pointed to the plate with the remaining two pieces of panini. "Can I take these out to Kara and Zoe?"

"Sure." Marty handed her the plate, and she disappeared out the door to share the panini with the senior waitresses. As if twenty-five could be considered *senior.*

The espresso machine began dripping into two ceramic cups, and Andi started foaming milk. Minutes later, she was sitting at the gleaming, square wooden bar next to Tess, watching Kara wipe down the dozen or so beer taps until they gleamed. Zoe busied herself setting one of the twenty rustic wood tables situated around the dining area.

Andi pivoted on her stool, taking in the earthy decor.

Between the tables and bar seating, the café's legal seating capacity maxed out at about a hundred, less since she'd removed several tables to accommodate a small black piano. To bring in more business, she'd booked a musician for two weeks from this Saturday.

Funny how Joe had shared her love of music and food, but not dogs. He'd hidden that fact at first. That should have been her first clue that not only wasn't he the right man for her, but he was capable of concealing things from her. *Important* things.

Next, she gazed fondly at her favorite part of the DPC. The Wall of Dog.

On the south side of the dining room, covering nearly every inch of wall space, were framed photos of dogs, some posing with their owners, some without. It was a decor idea she'd come up with, and her customers loved it. After spending a hundred dollars at the DPC, a customer could hang one framed photo of their pooch. The only exceptions were photos of the stray dogs she'd found homes for and a copy of the photo on the bureau in Joe's bedroom. The same one Sgt. Houston had said she and Joe looked "pretty cozy" in.

She couldn't stop her lips from lifting. Since Joe didn't like dogs, he hadn't appreciated being tacked to the center of a wall surrounded by canines. She'd hung it there as a joke, intending to take it down right after he'd seen it. Then it had grown on her, and she'd left it there for posterity.

After what he'd done with her bank account... *Serves the bastard right.*

"Earth to Andi." Her friend eyed her with concern. "What's going on?"

She lowered her voice so Kara and Zoe wouldn't hear. Ten minutes later, she'd related everything about the search warrant.

"Holy crap." Tess's green eyes went wide as she set down her cup.

Andi put her finger to her lips, glancing at the two waitresses to see if they'd heard anything. Luckily, they'd moved on to the deck to set the exterior tables. "Trust me, there's nothing holy about it. If it's true, then these are bad people Joe's gotten involved with. You have to promise me that you'll keep this quiet."

"Cross my heart." She dragged her finger down her chest, then from side to side in the shape of a cross. "And the police actually broke into the house while you were still in bed?"

"Not exactly." She took a sip of cappuccino, and her face flamed, although she couldn't be certain if it was from the hot coffee or from Sgt. Houston catching her clad only in her oldest, saggiest bathing suit. "I was washing Stray in the shower."

"Did you hear them come in?" Tess leaned forward on the stool. "I mean, did they at least knock?"

"He *said* they knocked. Unfortunately, I didn't hear it, so they had to break in."

"*He* said they knocked? He who?" After saying "who," Tess's lips remained puckered as if she were whistling.

"Sgt. Nicholas Houston of the Massachusetts State Police, that's who." Again, her cheeks heated. "And his K-9 sidekick."

Tess straightened on the stool. "Are you telling me a state trooper and his dog found you naked in the shower?" She struggled to keep from grinning.

"Of course not." She rolled her eyes. "I was wearing a bathing suit. I don't normally wash dogs in the buff. The important thing is that he was pointing a gun at me, and I thought his dog—which turned out to be a very *nice* dog—was going to tear me to shreds."

"Was it that old blue string bikini? That thing doesn't

cover much." Tess laughed. "Was he hot?"

Andi let out an exasperated breath. "No." *Yes.* In a rugged, tough-guy way, though admitting it—even to herself—really chapped her ass. "Anyway, since they took my phone, I have no way of contacting Joe. I'll keep the DPC's business cell phone with me at all times, so if he calls on the landline, come get me right away. Can you do that, please?"

Tess hunched her shoulders, holding up both hands in a defensive posture. "Okay, okay. I'm sorry. And I'm sorry for laughing." Worry lines creased her brow. "In all seriousness, you need to be careful of police, and especially federal agents."

Andi paused with the cup midway to her mouth. *Where did* that *come from?* While she didn't want to pry, it sounded disturbingly like Tess had experience in these matters, and that couldn't be good.

"I'll let you know if Joe calls. I promise." Tess squeezed Andi's shoulder, then her face suddenly brightened. "Your plumber called and said the work on your house is done and you can move back in."

"Thank God." That meant she could move out of Joe's after work.

Since police and federal agents had been crawling through the house *and* her personal things, she hadn't relished the idea of sleeping there again. *Maybe because Sgt. Houston touched everything in my suitcase.* Including the lacy bra and panties she currently wore.

The memory of her panties clinging irreverently to his gun, and his long fingers tossing them onto the bed while a distinct blush crept up his neck and chiseled jaw, nearly had her laughing.

Forget it. Forget him.

She and Tess finished their cappuccinos, then got down to reviewing the weekly specials Marty had left on the bar.

But her mind still wasn't totally focused on business. The tally of evidence against Joe had become too high to ignore. Her heart might be in denial, but her gut knew the truth.

Joe really is laundering money for a gunrunner.

At four thirty that afternoon, Andi took a break before the dinner rush and headed back to Joe's place to collect her things. As she drove up the driveway, she was reminded of how, not six hours ago, it had been jammed with police vehicles.

She got out of the truck and was headed for the front door when something on the front step caught her eye. *A cigarette butt.* She hadn't noticed it earlier. She wrinkled her nose. Using the tip of her sandal, she kicked it into the adjacent flower bed, being careful not touch it with her bare toes. "Disgusting habit." Odd, but she hadn't smelled smoke while everyone had been there. Then again, she'd been so freaked out she could easily have missed it.

She pulled Joe's house key from her shorts pocket and was about to insert it into the lock when she froze. The paint on the doorjamb next to the lock was scratched and scuffed. She distinctly remembered putting the key into the lock that morning to turn the deadbolt, and those marks hadn't been there.

So who did this? And when?

The back of her neck prickled. She whipped around, expecting to get hit over the head, but no one was there. Her heart rate kicked up, and she tiptoed off the front porch, peeking around the corner to look into the backyard.

Nothing. Empty. Aside from grass.

Her pulse slowed, and she began making her way back to the front door, checking over her shoulder several times along the way. She took a deep breath. The plan was to take a quick look, and if anything was out of place, she'd get the hell out of there.

Her hand trembled as she inserted the key into the lock and turned it. Slowly, she pushed open the door and peeked inside. For a moment she stood there, unable to move as she took it all in.

Oh my God.

She yanked the door shut with enough force that she stumbled backward, nearly falling off the front step. With her heart hammering, she bolted to her truck.

Chapter Four

Nick wiped the sweat from his brow then reached into the refrigerator and pulled out a beer and one of the dinosaur-size, double-cut rib eyes he'd bought yesterday.

The first things he normally did when he got home were to let Saxon have some dog time in his fenced-in backyard, then peel off his uniform before uncapping a beer. Today he was so hot, tired, and thirsty that the beer took priority. He twisted off the cap and took a long slug. In the corner of the kitchen, Saxon slurped noisily at the fresh water Nick had set out for him.

After leaving Myer's house, he and Cox had gone back to the FBI office and tried calling Myer on Andi's cell phone again, but he never answered. Then Nick and Saxon hit the streets, talking to every informant he could find, trying to dig up information on where Myer was hiding out, or whether the guy was already dead. But he'd come up empty. Either everyone was lying their asses off, or nobody knew where he was.

Nick was certain the guy would reach out to Andi. The

only question was when. And he worried that if he returned the phone to her, she couldn't be trusted to notify them when Myer called—unless he was around when it happened. If AUSA Bennett approved of Nick's plan, he'd start first thing in the morning.

Knowing his grill's ignition switch was on the fritz, he dug into a kitchen drawer and found a butane lighter on top of a strip of photos he'd tossed in there a few years ago. He stared at the photos without picking them up. Tanya had convinced him to snuggle up in one of those curtained photo booths in the middle of a shopping mall.

Better times. Before three miscarriages killed Tanya's soul.

No matter how much he'd tried to help her, nothing did. Each miscarriage chipped away at her self-worth until there was nothing left of the woman he'd fallen in love with.

By the time Tanya had died, their marriage was long over, and both of them knew it. It had taken years for him to admit that without feeling any guilt or pain, but the healing process had taken its toll. Since then, he'd frozen himself off from attachments that could make him experience any real feelings. It was easier that way. Easier than going through the pain again of losing someone he loved.

Saxon's presence kept him grounded. His dog's claws clicked on the tile as he came to stand in front of Nick, looking up at him with an intensity that told him his dog knew he was upset. That was the thing about dogs—they picked up on human behavior and emotion, and K-9s were probably even more attuned to their partners. Emotions traveled up *and* down the leash, so when Nick was bothered, so was his dog and vice versa.

He set the beer on the counter and patted his chest. "Up." Slowly, Saxon rose on his hind legs and planted his front paws on Nick's chest, allowing him to bear-hug the dog and bury his face in Saxon's soft ruff. "Thanks, buddy," he said after a minute, looking down into his dog's sympathetic golden eyes. "I needed that. Now let's get outside and grill us a big-ass steak."

Snorting in agreement, Saxon dropped his front paws and followed Nick out the back door onto the deck. He watched the dog bound down the stairs and leap from the third step onto the yard before charging across the freshly cut grass. The yard was entirely enclosed by four-foot high picket fencing, although Saxon could easily jump the fence anytime he chose.

As he lit the grill, Andi Hardt's lightly tanned, peaches 'n' cream complexion came to mind. Between his time in the military, then ten years with the state police, three of which had been with SWAT, he'd had a lot of things thrown at him... sticks, rocks, bullets, even grenades...but never a bar of soap or a bottle of shampoo.

Taking the beer with him, he sat in one of his Adirondack chairs, positioning himself to watch Saxon walk up one side of the teeter-totter he'd bought to hone the dog's balance. Like people, some K-9s' sense of balance was better than others, and Nick had noticed his dog occasionally hesitated on nonstationary surfaces. The teeter-totter was the perfect training mechanism.

Saxon tensed as the back end of the teeter-totter he'd walked up lifted until both ends of the narrow board were in the air. For a moment his dog froze, waiting for the board to level off before walking slowly down the other side.

Nick grinned as Saxon pirouetted on the grass. He was improving every day, but he wanted his dog in peak condition and ready for anything.

He leaned back to watch Saxon take off like a gazelle and race along the fence line.

The phone in his shirt pocket vibrated. He pulled it out and looked at the display. *Cox.*

"Sorry to intrude on your evening," Cox said when Nick answered. "Thought you'd want to know ASAP. Bennett approved your plan. You've been green-lighted to do whatever it takes to bring Myer in. Eric will be your backup."

Nick did a quick fist pump. "I'll hit her up tomorrow morning."

"You think she'll really go for it?" Cox asked.

"She will if she wants to clear her name and get her money back."

"Good points." Cox chuckled. "We've been monitoring her cell phone continuously. Myer called once, and we had a female agent answer. He must have recognized that it wasn't Andi, because he hung up. We tried calling him back, but it went right to voicemail."

"No surprise. He wants to talk only to her." Making the success of his op all the more critical.

Saxon trotted up the stairs and sat directly in front of Nick. The dog's ears twitched, and he cocked his head. Anytime Nick got on his cell phone there was the likelihood they'd be doing his dog's favorite thing: working.

He pointed to the floor of the deck, and Saxon lay down, resting his massive head between his paws, but his eyes remained focused on Nick.

Through the phone, he heard Cox yawning. "I ordered a more complete background check on Andi Hardt and an updated set of financials, but it could be a week or more before we get everything back, and the AUSA doesn't want to wait. If Myer winds up dead before we get to him, our case goes out the window."

The phone clicked. "Stand by," Cox said, telling Nick the agent had gotten another call. "That was Andi Hardt," Cox said when he came back on a minute later. "Someone broke into Myer's house and trashed it."

Nick suppressed a groan. His evening of relaxation had just gone to shit.

Chapter Five

Andi sat in her truck in front of the house, rocking back and forth as she waited impatiently for Agent Cox to arrive. Her stomach twisted into knots, and she rocked faster, biting her lower lip. Cox didn't have to tell her to wait outside, because she had less than zero intention of going in there alone. Based upon what little she'd seen, whoever had done this was angry. *Really* angry.

Sofa and chair cushions slashed open and thrown to the floor, white springy stuffing everywhere. Furniture broken as if someone had taken an ax to things. She could only imagine the damage inflicted on the rest of the house.

Groaning, she replayed her conversation with Special Agent Cox. She'd railed at the poor man, mistakenly assuming he and his band of merry agents and state troopers had returned to search the house again after she'd left for the DPC. "What a jackass I am."

There'd been no need for them to come back and trash the place. Logic aside, there was something so violent about the way the house had been ransacked, as if whoever had done this wanted to send a message. A thoroughly *mean* message.

She let out an unsteady breath, thankful she hadn't been there when they'd broken in. Who knew what they would have done to her?

Engines purred as two vehicles came down the road then slowed before pulling into the driveway. The first was a black Charger, and the second was a state police Explorer. *Nick Houston?* Perhaps, although just because it was a state police vehicle didn't mean it was *him* behind the wheel. The state police must have hundreds of officers. But when the Explorer came to a stop, she noticed the K-9 emblem on the side door panel, and her heart beat a little faster. After the embarrassing shower debacle, she'd prefer to never lay eyes on him again.

She left her truck parked on the street and headed up the driveway. Cox got out of the Charger. A moment later, Nick Houston rounded the hood of the Explorer, pausing to look at the house across the street, then to the properties on either side of Joe's.

Nervous energy invaded her body. Something about seeing Nick again made her feel... *What?* She struggled to find the correct word to describe her prickly, charged response to the man's presence. *Annoyed?* No, that didn't explain her nervousness. *Edgy?* Yes, definitely that, but why? *Because he has a badge and a gun?* No. Cox was a gun-toting, badge-carrying federal agent, but he didn't elicit any of those feelings in her, not even close. *Make that not at all.*

Unlike Cox's, Nick's sharp gaze didn't immediately settle on her the second he got out of his vehicle. As she joined them in front of the house, he continued surveying his surroundings, searching for threats with subtle yet calculated glances. The man had a soldier-like air of invincibility about him, as if no one could get past his deadly defenses.

"Ms. Hardt," he said, coming to stand beside her, and

when he canted his head, she noted the color of his hair reminded her of sandy New England beaches and caramel. *Rich sandy-brown.*

"Call me Andi." She cleared her throat, focusing on his eyes, which were softer than gunmetal gray, her original assessment. *More like sterling silver with a touch of blue. Blue steel.* "After all, since I'm still a suspect there may be silver bracelets in my future, and I like to be on a first-name basis with any man who gives me jewelry."

His lips twitched. Full, sensual lips. And was that a glimmer of humor twinkling in his eyes?

Couldn't be. She must have imagined it.

"Andi, then," he said unexpectedly. She'd have bet twenty cappuccinos that he wouldn't have embraced such informality. Not a take-no-prisoners kind of cop like him.

A warm breeze whispered through the trees, bringing with it his clean, citrusy aftershave mixed with the smell of freshly oiled leather. An entire day in this heat and humidity and the man still smelled great and looked all clean and pressed. The only evidence of the long day he'd had was the faint growth of beard on his jaw.

No fair. With her shorts and shirt sticking to her, she must look worse than something the cat dragged in.

"Agent Cox," she said, quickly holding out her hand to Mr. FBI, which he shook. "I need to apologize for my rude behavior over the phone. I realize now that you had nothing to do with this."

"No need for apologies." He held up his other hand, stopping her from continuing with more contrite explanations. "You've had a rough day."

Ya think? "I definitely have. When this is all over and you unfreeze my account and stop believing that I'm part of a criminal organization, I'd like to extend an invitation to both of you to stop by the DPC for lunch. On me, of course."

Cox smiled, then shot Nick a conspiratorial look. She narrowed her eyes. *What's up with that?* "Thank you for the invitation," the agent said, his smile gone now. "Someday, perhaps. Now let's go inside and have a look."

She led the way to the front door and pointed out the scratch marks near the lock. When they entered the house, it was worse than the brief glimpse she'd gotten earlier.

There wasn't one piece of furniture in the living room that remained unscathed. Splintered wood lay everywhere. Cushion filling hung from the hallway chandelier. As they walked into the dining room, she sucked in a breath. Joe's beautiful wood dining table had deep cut marks over most of the surface.

"I'll call it in." Nick clicked the microphone on his shoulder and reported the break-in to the Ludlow police department.

"You won't be the investigating officers?" She looked from Nick to Cox. Not that she totally trusted them, but she had to admit that, under the circumstances, they'd been fair and courteous in their dealings with her.

"At this point, we can't be sure this has anything to do with our investigation," Nick said. "Even if it does, burglary isn't a federal crime. Local police will retain jurisdiction on this."

Cox took a few photos with his cell phone. "Don't worry. We'll maintain contact with the locals. They're already aware that we served a search warrant here today. In fact, two of their officers were here with us this morning."

She hadn't known that, although when she thought about it there *had* been several different uniforms present during the warrant.

"Let's check out the second floor." Nick led the way as she and Cox followed him up the staircase and into the master bedroom.

"Oh no." She covered her mouth with her hand. The sheets and duvet had been torn apart, the mattress upended, padding and springs spilling out from a deep gash in the center. The box spring had been destroyed, its fabric cover ripped off. Every drawer in the bureau and bedside tables had been pulled out, their contents scattered. Even her small suitcase had been dumped on the floor, her clothes thrown everywhere.

Nick turned slowly in a three-sixty, his eyes constantly moving as he took in the damage. "They were looking for something."

Cox took more photos on his phone. "The only question is whether they found it."

"Found what?" she asked. "You guys served a search warrant less than twelve hours ago. Didn't you find everything there was to find?"

Nick turned on her. "We didn't find your boyfriend's laptop."

"For the last time"—she clenched her hands—"he's *not* my boyfriend. And don't you think this is too big a coincidence? A search warrant *and* a break-in all in the same day?"

"Yeah," he said flatly. "I do."

Cox put his cell phone to his ear and headed for the door, turning at the last second. "I have to make some calls."

Nick slipped a small pad from his breast pocket. "What time did you get here?"

"Around five o'clock."

He scribbled on the pad. "Was the front door locked?"

"Yes, but I noticed those scratch marks on the door and a cigarette butt on the front stoop that wasn't here when I left this morning."

"You'll have to point out the butt to the evidence collection team. We might be able to get a DNA hit." He paused from making notes on the pad. "There's an alarm system installed in the house. It wasn't on when we served the warrant this morning. Did you activate it when you left today?"

"No," she admitted, realizing if she'd been in the habit of setting it, she would have known the second Nick and the other officers had gotten in that morning.

He raised his brows. "Why not?"

"Well, it seems stupid now." She let out a sarcastic laugh. "I was afraid I'd screw up the code and the police would come running and arrest me for breaking in to a house that's not mine."

Again, Nick's eyes twinkled with humor. The corners of his mouth lifted, stopping just short of a full smile. Not for the first time, she wondered how an honest-to-God smile would transform the hardness of his features.

"Can you tell if anything's missing?"

"Not really." She went to her upended suitcase and kneeled beside it on the floor. "I've hardly been anywhere in the house except the kitchen, so aside from my own things, no."

Andi turned to find him arching a brow. Disbelief screamed from every nuance of the subtle gesture.

She got to her feet and came to stand in front of him, parking her fists on her hips. "*What* is your problem? I've told you more than once that Joe and I haven't had any real relationship for years. We're friends. *Just* friends. And I am *not* part of his criminal network."

For several seconds, he stared down at her silently, as if gauging her truthfulness. "So you keep telling me."

The air conditioning took that moment to kick on, blowing a whiff of his scent her way, and it was distracting as hell.

Needing space, she took a step back. "You don't believe a word I've said to you. You're so suspicious and untrusting you lack the ability to perceive truth when it smacks you in the face. You see criminals everywhere, don't you?"

"It's my job." He took a step closer, so that he once again loomed over her, but at this point she was getting used to that tactic and stood her ground, craning her neck to meet his steely gaze. "In fact," he continued in a smooth, deep voice, "a lot of taxpayer money is spent training me to do just that."

"Do they also train you to identify that rare"—she hooked her fingers into quotation marks—"*honest* taxpayer?"

"I'm trained to gather the facts, *ma'am*," he added, and she understood he'd used that word to intentionally be annoying, since she'd specifically told him to quit using it on her. "Contrary to what you obviously think, I don't pass judgment. A judge or a jury decide if the facts warrant a conviction."

"You really don't care if someone is innocent or guilty." She pointed a finger at his chest without touching him. "You're a just-the-facts-ma'am kind of guy?"

His eyes flashed with subdued anger, and she found it gratifying to have finally penetrated his emotional armor. "I don't deal bullshit, and I don't tolerate it, if that's what you're implying."

"Then what do I have to do to prove I'm innocent and not bullshitting you?"

"Cooperate. *Fully.*"

"I *have* been cooperating. *Fully*," she said, throwing his word back at him.

"Just how far are you willing to go to prove your cooperation?"

She crossed her arms. "As far as it takes."

He shocked her with a full-fledged smile, and she had the answer to her question. When Sgt. Nicholas Houston smiled, he was devastatingly handsome.

Big whoop. So he's good looking.

Oh hell. There was no sense deluding herself anymore.

I'm attracted to him. Physically, anyway.

"I'll hold you to that," he said calmly, although there was an undecipherable look in his eyes that gave her the disquieting feeling she'd been expertly herded into a trap.

"What about the photo?" He tipped his head to Joe's high-top bureau. More specifically, to the exact location where the framed photo of her and Joe had been—and wasn't now. "The one of you and your *not*-boyfriend. Did you move it?"

Ignoring his jibe, she walked to the bureau. Until he'd pointed it out, she hadn't realized the photo was no longer there. "I didn't touch it." Turning, she found him standing directly behind her. She hadn't heard him move and wondered how such a big man could get around so soundlessly. The skin over the bridge of his nose was creased, leaving her puzzled about the implications of the missing photo. "Why would they take it?"

"I don't know." He tucked the small pad back into his breast pocket. "We don't even know who 'they' is. If we assume whoever broke in is connected to this investigation, then chances are they already know what Joe looks like." His frown deepened. "But they may not have known what *you* look like."

"I have nothing to do with whatever Joe's involved in, so why would they want a picture of me? I don't have his laptop, and I can't give them any useful information. I can't even give *you* anything useful."

"We'll figure this out." His eyes took on a look of determination. "I promise."

Despite their constant sparring, something about the sincerity in his eyes made her believe him.

"Do you have another place to stay tonight?" he asked.

"Yes." She walked back to where her suitcase lay on the floor. "The plumbing work on my house is done, so I can move back in. The only reason I came here was to collect my things." She knelt and reached out to right the suitcase and start dumping her clothes back into it when strong fingers clamped gently over her hand.

Nick knelt beside her, so close that their thighs touched, and she could feel the muscular strength of his. "Don't touch anything. The evidence team has to photograph everything and dust for prints. They'll need a set of your fingerprints to compare to any others left behind."

Warmth emanating from his large body washed over her in gentle waves, and every place his long, strong fingers touched hers tingled with awareness. Of what, she didn't know.

Their gazes locked, and his hand still covered hers, curling her fingers beneath his own. As she stared into his eyes, her heart slammed against her ribs. While she understood Nick's touch was purely for professional reasons—to preserve evidence—it was disconcerting.

Footsteps sounded outside the bedroom, and she yanked her hand from beneath his as they both rose to their feet. Cox and two uniformed officers entered the room.

"You good, Nick?" Cox stood in the open doorway, a quizzical expression on his face that made her realize he must have misinterpreted what he'd seen as her and Nick holding hands.

As. If.

"We are, but there's something you should know." He succinctly explained to Cox and the uniforms about the missing framed photograph.

Cox nodded. "All the more reason to move forward with things as planned."

"What things?" She crossed her arms as a now-familiar sense of foreboding spread through her.

One of the local officers interrupted. "Ma'am, I'd like to

ask you some questions."

Rolling her eyes, she groaned. "What is this, a cop thing? My name is Andi. Andi Hardt, *not* ma'am."

"Sorry, ma'am." The cop winced. "Ms. Hardt."

Beside her, Nick chuckled.

It was nearly midnight when Andi fell into bed. Her entire body was exhausted, yet her mind couldn't stop buzzing. Just when she'd thought the day couldn't get any worse, it had, culminating with getting fingerprinted for elimination purposes. She'd completely missed the evening shift at the DPC, but Tuesdays were slow, and Tess had closed up early. She really was counting on that musician to beef up business. If that didn't bring in more customers, her dream café might die a horrible death.

Nails clicked on the bedroom's hardwood floors as Stray walked in. The dog nuzzled her arm before lying down beside the bed with a contented *huff.* Normally, Stray overnighted in the garage, happy to sleep in the comfy doghouse Andi had purchased for the occasional wayward dog. Tonight, she'd needed canine companionship.

Cox had followed her home, insisting on checking out every room in her house before allowing her to enter. He'd explained that until they deduced why the photo of her and Joe had been taken by the burglars, she should exercise additional caution.

Flipping onto her belly, she snuggled against the fluffy down pillow and reached out to run her fingers over Stray's soft coat. In response, the dog touched her wet nose to Andi's hand, as if giving her a good night kiss.

In the darkness, she smiled, but it was fleeting. The only reason she'd worked in the financial world was because she'd seen her parents struggling for money and wanted to help them. They'd been scientists, living from grant to grant, and when one grant after the next dried up, things were rough. But they'd loved doing what they did, so when she quit her job in New York, she decided to emulate them and follow her dream.

At least her parents had each other. She, on the other hand, was destined to wind up alone. Dogs were the most wonderful creatures on the planet, but they could never be a substitute for a family of her own.

Time to face facts.

Life had thrown her a cruel curve ball. For her, a family wasn't in the cards.

With quick, angry motions she swiped at her tears, wishing she could wipe away her pain and worries that easily.

She'd been relieved that it had been Cox inside her home, rather than Nick. Around him, she felt compelled to stay extra sharp, and it was exhausting. Sparring with him left her body and mind totally energized, but afterward, it was as if all remaining life had been sucked from her.

Before she nodded off, his melodic voice sounded in her head as surely as if he were standing in her bedroom. *Just how far are you willing to go to prove your cooperation?*

Her eyelids closed, and she began falling into an uneasy sleep, unable to shake the worry that she really was being herded into a trap. *What* trap remained to be seen.

Chapter Six

The only times Nick had been inside what was now the Dog Park Café were when it had been a shabby, rundown bar in serious need of renovation. Located thirty minutes outside Springfield in Wilbraham, the place was a little remote, and he'd only been there to break up a few drunken brawls and haul some of the locals to jail. Ironically, this was one of the city's few suburbs that miraculously hadn't been touched by the rash of shootings plaguing the city.

As he parked his Tahoe in the lot facing the fenced-in dog run, he noted Andi's white pickup. *You gotta love a woman who drives a truck.*

Shit. Bad choice of words. He'd let her get to him, and he seriously needed to slam the brakes on that before it happened again. When she'd given him a verbal smackdown about his job, he'd goaded her right back about the boyfriend thing. It had been unprofessional, and he prided himself on his professionalism. He had to be more careful. Especially given what he was about to dump on her head.

He looked at the outside of the café and was impressed

with the changes. Once-moldy gray stain had been replaced by fresh yellow paint and white trim around the windows and doors. A hand-painted sign in flowing black script hung over the entrance. About a hundred yards north of the restaurant was a small Colonial in the same colors that he assumed was Andi's house.

Several dogs were in the run, including an Australian sheepdog, a mixed breed that looked like the one at Myer's house yesterday, and a big Bouvier des Flandres. At nearly ninety pounds and with a long gray coat, thick beard, mustache, and eyebrows, the Bouvier was a dog no one would forget. Leaning against the railing were a woman about Andi's height but with dark brown hair, and a man a few inches taller. The two had their heads together as they watched the dogs.

Another man leashed up the Aussie and led the dog outside the run to a dark green Porsche on the far side of the lot. Nick immediately recognized him. Paul Nelson—chief of the Springfield PD. As the Porsche drove off, he tapped his fingers on the wheel. *What's the chief of police doing here on a Wednesday morning?*

Most department chiefs worked a day shift, Monday through Friday. He could have taken a day off, but that wasn't what Nick found most odd. He happened to know that Chief Nelson lived an hour from Wilbraham, making this one heck of a long drive just to run his dog. Then again…*maybe not so long with all those expensive horses under the hood.*

Saxon craned his head over the console, uttering a series of whines as he caught sight of the other dogs through the windshield.

Nick shifted on the seat, laughing at the excitement brimming in Saxon's eyes. Playing with other dogs was a rare treat for a K-9. "Ready to go undercover, buddy?" *Woof.* "Make nice with the other dogs while I go to work. At least *they* don't know you're a cop." But Andi would know.

Before responding to the break-in yesterday, he and Cox had decided not to overwhelm her with Nick's operational plan. Even though they held all the cards, the woman had been through enough for one day. If they pushed too hard and too fast, they risked her refusing to cooperate. Still, he'd bet a week patrolling on foot that she'd hit the roof when he told her how this would go down.

Saxon gave a high-pitched bark, prancing in place, a sign of impatience Nick understood all too well.

"We got this, pal." *Whether Andi likes it or not.*

He shut off the engine, then got out and opened up the door behind him. Saxon obediently waited for him to hook the six-foot leather leash onto the dog's civilian collar. A second later Saxon leaped from the truck.

"*Fuss*," he commanded, and Saxon glued himself to Nick's left side, glancing up at him occasionally as they made their way down the slight incline to the dog run. Given how well-trained Saxon was, the leash hadn't really been necessary. He only used it to make others feel comfortable with his dog's size and presence.

As they got closer, the other dogs ran over to greet the newcomer, tails in the air, ears alert. Like people, dogs sized up their kind to determine who would be the dominant one.

From his position at the gate, he had a better view of the raised wood deck that ran end-to-end along the backside of the restaurant. Though it was only ten a.m., several tables were already occupied by customers.

A bead of sweat trickled between his shoulder blades. The sweltering temps didn't seem to bother the dogs, although with Saxon's pure black coat, he'd have to keep his dog hydrated more than usual. Funny how he would always think of Saxon as "his dog" when in fiscal reality, he was the property of the Commonwealth of Massachusetts and worth nearly twenty grand.

After letting Saxon into the run, he secured the inner and outer gates, then leaned his forearms on the top rail, watching to make sure everyone got along.

Saxon bounded into the circle of dogs, then stood at full attention, looking like the king of his domain, barely moving except for a stiff tail wag. The other dogs circled and sniffed. His K-9 was unusual in that he was definitely an alpha but able to get along with other dogs without asserting aggressive dominance. Like any human confident in who and what he was, Saxon didn't feel the need to throw his weight around. Unless he was working. Then, he was positively fearsome and would make even the biggest, meanest badass think twice before getting anywhere near those snapping jaws.

He watched a few minutes longer, then made his way up the stairs to the deck and sat at a shade-covered table that gave him a good view not only of the dog run but also the small lake off to the side of the property.

Several laminated menus were propped in a wire holder in the center of the table. He grabbed one and began checking out the sandwiches. Within a minute, his stomach was growling from the mouth-watering list of paninis on freshly baked ciabatta and loaded with locally cured meats and cheeses.

A sharp bark had him scanning the dog run to find the pretty mixed breed flirting with Saxon, pirouetting and getting in an occasional nip on his flanks. Looked like she didn't hold a grudge against his dog after having her bath interrupted yesterday.

Saxon raised his head high and strutted slowly, deliberately around the female in a show-dog pose meant to advertise his assets. When the two dogs went nose-to-nose, Nick laughed. Even in the dog world, the signals between opposite sexes were the same as for humans. Unlike the dogs, he didn't think Andi would be so quick to forget *their* encounter.

This was a quasi-undercover plan he'd concocted. Technically, Eric was better suited for the job, having worked a lot of UC gigs for the ATF down south before transferring to the northeast. His friend had gone to a lengthy undercover school at the Federal Law Enforcement Training Center, whereas Nick had no such training—unless he counted high school plays and college musicals. But he wanted this gig and wanted it badly. He had a score to settle with this gun dealer, and no way would he pass this job off to anyone else.

He adjusted his chair and found Saxon and the golden-brown female lying a few feet from each other beneath one of several large shade trees, panting but seemingly content. Nick glimpsed Andi coming through the screen door carrying a tray loaded with silverware.

Her blond hair was loose, hanging halfway down her back. Some of the golden strands curled softly at her temples. She headed to the opposite side of the deck from where he was sitting, greeting most customers by name. *Smart.* No better way to get repeat customers than to make them feel welcome. He watched the easy way she interacted with patrons and staff, pausing to chat briefly at each table.

When she got to a table where a young couple was attending to a baby perched in a high chair, she set down the tray, and a beautiful smile lit her face. She stroked the back of the baby's head with such gentle tenderness Nick couldn't take his eyes off her.

She went on to finish setting a table at the far end of the deck, then paused to look into the dog run. Her profile was to him, and he could see a smile forming on her lips, but it was short-lived. Slowly, she turned, searching the tables she hadn't gotten to yet, and he understood what she was looking for. *Him.* Dogs like Saxon were distinctive in size and color.

There was only one of him within at least a several-hundred-mile radius, and wherever Saxon was, Nick was.

When she finally found him, her eyes narrowed to slits and her lips compressed into a thin line. With the tray still in her hand, she took a deep breath and headed straight to his table with long, determined strides.

So much for their little truce yesterday afternoon. She had to know something was up.

"Good morning," he said when she came to stand beside his outstretched legs. From the irritated gleam in her eyes, he thought she might dump the tray over his head.

She set it down, instead, and crossed her arms. "What are you doing here?"

A light breeze brought with it her scent, all flowery and pretty. No matter how much he wished otherwise, he couldn't deny it. Something about her torqued every one of his senses.

"Can't a guy get some relaxation while he's watching his dog play?" He locked his hands behind his head and looked up at her.

"I have no doubt this is *not* a social call. For you *or* your partner." She jerked her head to the dog run.

"And you accused *me* of being overly suspicious?" He clucked his tongue. He was beginning to enjoy this. "*Now* who's being suspicious?"

Her lips compressed into an even thinner line. "I'm not stupid, Sgt. Houston." She yanked out the chair next to his, then sat and leaned into his personal space. With her blue eyes and sun-kissed complexion, she was just as lovely as he remembered. "I know you want something. You said you don't deal in bullshit, so how about doing me the courtesy of getting to the *real* reason you're here."

"Fine." He unlocked his hands from behind his head and leaned in until their faces were only inches apart. *Bad idea.* This close and his senses were more than going into overdrive—they were sparking with ignition.

Her sweet scent was in his nose and lungs. Her warm breath fanned his face like a gentle caress.

The job, he reminded himself.

He hadn't acted since college, but he could do it, and he wouldn't fail.

Showtime. Act I, scene I, starring Nick Houston.

"Until Joe Myer shows up, I'm your new bartender."

• • •

Andi must have misheard him. "You're *what*?"

"Your new bartender," Nick repeated with a deadpan expression. "I've seen your want ad, and I'm your guy."

"You can't be serious." But the look on his face said otherwise, and in her gut, she knew he was. "No, no, *no*." She shook her head slowly, deliberately, and repeatedly to ram home the point that there wasn't a chance in Hades that she'd entertain such a bizarre proposition. "I have interviews this morning for a new bartender. I don't need you."

"Cancel them," he said in a harsh tone.

"No." She straightened then glanced at the nearest table, making sure no one could overhear their conversation. The one thing she had that was all hers was the café, and he was trying to force his way into it. *Not. A. Chance.* "You must be out of your mind if you think I'm going to allow you to work here. Besides, you already have a job."

"You said you'd do anything to show the extent of your cooperation. Don't make a liar out of yourself," he added.

Damn the man for knowing just which of her buttons to push. Before she could respond, he reached behind him, the movement tightening the dove-gray T-shirt over his body, giving her an up close and personal view of just how well defined his chest and shoulder muscles were. Until now she'd only seen him in his stiff, starched uniform, protective vest, and so much equipment on his belt that she hadn't realized how narrow his waist was.

When he leaned slightly to the side, her eyes dipped to where the T-shirt was tucked into a pair of seriously faded jeans. A worn brown leather belt with a rectangular brass buckle snugged tight emphasized the fact that there wasn't a single roll of fat on the man. "Here."

Huh? She tore her gaze from his perfect torso, embarrassed at the smile tugging at his lips. *Crap.* She'd *so* been caught ogling him, and he was eating it up.

"Want your phone back?" He grinned openly now, those sensual lips a stark contrast to all the chiseled planes and angles of his normally serious, now incredibly handsome face.

He was holding something out to her. Her pink cell phone. She automatically reached for it, but stopped, jerking her hand back. Suspicion prickled sharply in her brain. This was way too soon. Only yesterday Cox had informed her in no uncertain terms that it could be months before the phone was returned to her.

She glared at him. "What's the catch?"

He set the phone on the table. "While your phone was in our custody, Joe called, but he wouldn't talk to us. We had a female officer answer, but he knew it wasn't you."

Now she understood why she was getting her phone back. "You want me to call him. I already tried that yesterday, and he wouldn't answer. What makes you think he'll answer if I call him now?"

"He probably won't. I think he's savvy enough to power off the phone when he's not using it, so he can't be traced or tracked by the phone's signal. But you two are obviously... close." She could swear his jaw clenched. "He's been trying to reach you, and I think he'll do it again," he continued. "You and this phone are our only link to him. Try calling him once. Assuming he doesn't answer, leave another message reiterating the sense of urgency that he calls you back."

There didn't seem to be any harm in that. "What if he *does* answer?"

"Try to talk him in."

"Why?" She let out a sarcastic laugh. "You'll arrest him if he turns himself in."

"That's true." He leaned in closer and lowered his voice. "I *will* arrest him, but I can't do that if he's dead, and dead is exactly what he'll be if we don't get to him first. Whoever Joe's laundering money for put a hit out on him so he can't be a witness against them."

Despite the rising heat, a chill went through her. She covered her face with her hands, struggling to process what Nick had just told her. Large, warm fingers closed around her forearms, tugging her hands from her face. She looked into his eyes, frightened by their glittering intensity.

"You said you didn't authorize that wire transfer. If that's true, then by talking him in, he can clear you *and* you'll be saving his life. He can't hide forever, from us *or* the gun dealer who wants to kill him. The difference between us and them is that when *we* get to him, we won't put a bullet in his head. If he cooperates, there will probably still be prison time, but at least he'll be alive to serve it."

Her stomach clenched as the heavy weight of his words sank in. Sure, she wanted her bank account released, but Joe really was in mortal danger, and she had no choice. Talking him in was the best thing she could do for both of them.

"Okay," she whispered, staring at her phone on the table.

"You can do this. I know you can." He released her wrists. "Here's how this will go down. You'll keep that phone with you at all times. I'll be here with you most of the day and into the night, bartending inside. If he shows up, I'll be here. He'll probably call, rather than take the chance of showing his face with things being so hot. The minute he calls, you let me know, and you keep him on the phone. I'll tell you what to say."

Nick Houston dictating what she said irked her on so many levels she couldn't tally them fast enough. "What if he calls at night after we've closed down and you're not here? You can't be with me twenty-four seven."

"We checked your phone out. You have conference call capability. If I'm not here when he calls, you conference me in. I already programmed my number into your phone."

She picked up the phone and scrolled through her contacts until she found his entry. *Nick*. There was something so disturbingly personal about seeing his name in her phone contacts.

"Call him now. When voicemail kicks in, leave the message we discussed. Don't say anything else."

Swallowing her pride, she took a deep breath, then cued up Joe's number. As Nick had predicted, it went straight to voicemail, and she left another urgent message to call her back. She ended the call and set the phone back on the table, noting that her fingers were trembling. *I'm so not cut out for this stuff.*

"Good job." He covered her hand with his, squeezing it.

She knew the contact was merely a show of support, an *atta girl* for not screwing up her first assignment. But when his fingers closed around hers, the heat from his hand spread outward and upward, making her feel as if his entire body was wrapped around hers like a warm glove.

He removed his hand. "Now let's discuss the terms of my employment."

"Employment?" Her fingers still tingled from his touch, something that was short-circuiting her other senses. *Oh, right.* Bartending.

She hated how she'd been forced into this deal. Worse,

she despised how he could light up her body like a Roman candle. As if losing control of her restaurant to him wasn't bad enough, now she'd lost command of her own body's responses. Like it or not, she was stuck with him for a while.

"Fine." She sat back and crossed her arms. "I'll let you work here, but these are *my* ground rules." He arched a brow and smirked, which only needled her more. "You can keep your tips, but I won't pay you a dime. Not only are you salaried by the state police, but with my bank account on ice I don't know if I can pay my *real* employees. And"—she leaned forward—"you'll have to sit through an interview just like everyone else. I need to know what your experience is. Have you ever bartended before?"

"In college," he answered.

"College?" She barked out a laugh. "That's a long time ago. You sure you remember how to do it?"

"I'm not *that* old." He cracked a lopsided smile that she found unexpectedly and irritatingly charming. "I think I remember how to pour a beer and mix a gin and tonic."

No, he wasn't that old. Mid-thirties, she'd guess. "Perhaps, but there's more to bartending than pouring a draft and mixing a drink. Social rapport is the most essential element of the job. A good bartender can bring in more customers. Conversely, a bad one can drive them right out the door and leave the DPC with a bad reputation, something I can't afford, particularly since you've frozen my bank account."

He began rubbing his chin. "You don't think I can do the job?"

"It isn't that." *Well, not exactly.* She grimaced.

"Then what is it?"

"I'm afraid you'll scare away all the customers."

He frowned. "How do you figure that?"

"Well, you're so...so..." She twisted her lips, struggling to find the right word. *Annoying? Obnoxious? Controlling?*

As much as she wanted to say all those things, she couldn't without worsening the situation.

"I'm so *what*?"

"Big," she blurted out, settling on something not quite so insulting. "And intimidating. You've got cop written all over you, and frankly, I don't think you know how to be social without sizing someone up for an orange jumpsuit and a prison cell."

He smiled, revealing a set of even, white teeth, then he pulled his chair closer to hers, the legs scraping on the deck. He rested a muscular forearm on the table, and she was hyperaware of his nearness. She held her breath, and when she finally inhaled, his citrusy scent invaded her lungs. He smelled too damned good.

"You'd be surprised at the skills I possess."

While she processed his words, his gaze held hers captive with a potency that made her heartbeat thrum in her ears. She couldn't tell if he was sending her a warning, boasting, or whether there was a double entendre tangled up there somewhere. In any case, there was definitely a challenging gleam in his eyes.

"We'll see about that." She pushed back her chair and grabbed the tray as she stood. "We're open for lunch and dinner. Lunch starts at eleven thirty. Don't be late."

It took all her willpower not to glance over her shoulder as she walked away and pulled open the screen door. Once inside, she deposited the tray onto the bar and went directly to her office. She shut the door and fell into her desk chair. The stack of unpaid bills on her desk was getting higher.

Irritation had her grinding her teeth. She'd been manipulated into making a deal with the devil. Unfortunately, Satan came in the form of one very hunky, incredibly sexy state trooper.

Chapter Seven

Nick grabbed two beer glasses from beneath the bar and flipped down the tap's handle. He'd been working at the cafe for three days now, and things had been quiet. Other than Andi, only Tess knew who he really was and why he was there. Tess was due in shortly, and Andi was busy helping Kara and Zoe with the dining room.

He glanced at the photo across the room on the Wall of Dog. It was a copy of the one that had been stolen from Myer's house during the break-in. It shouldn't, but for some reason the idea of Andi and Myer together annoyed him. More importantly, instinct and experience told him there was a bad reason why the photo was snatched. If unexpected shit went down, he'd be there front and center to stop it.

And Myer still hadn't called her.

Unless she hasn't told me.

He served up drafts to the two men in business suits at the end of the bar. Michael Sullivan and Stan Barrow were tax attorneys in Springfield. Despite the twenty-minute drive, they stopped in every day for lunch at the same time and both ordered the green chili burger with cheddar and two beers.

"Your burgers will be out in a few minutes," he said as he cleared away dirty plates left by two female customers who'd just walked out the door.

"Thanks, Nick." Michael lifted his glass in mock salute. "Nothing better than a DPC burger. Just don't tell the wife. She says if I don't get my cholesterol under one-eighty, she'll divorce me."

"Wouldn't dream of it." He held back a laugh. Michael's cholesterol might be high, but he was about five-ten and couldn't have weighed more than one-forty.

"Care for a beer?" Stan asked before taking a sip. "It's on us."

"Thanks, guys." He began wiping down the bar with a dry cloth. "No can do. The boss would fire me for drinking on the job."

"Nah." Stan waved a dismissive hand. "Andi's a good woman. All her employees love her. *Everyone* loves her."

"I can see that." And he had.

Since the lunch crowd had begun trickling in an hour and a half ago, no fewer than half a dozen men had made a point of personally greeting her. From the way their hands had lingered at her waist as they hugged her or kissed her on the cheek, they all wanted to get into her pants. *Don't have to be a cop to see that.*

At first it was entertaining, watching her deftly maneuver and evade those who pushed too far. But seeing it day after day was beginning to irritate him. *That* pissed him off even more, and he didn't understand why. Although, he had to admire the easygoing way she had with her customers, and her ability to make nice with those she clearly couldn't stand.

He'd already identified the regulars Andi actually liked versus the ones whose pawing and slobbering she tolerated solely to be a courteous hostess. Frank Feldman and Meera

Devine were on her A-list.

Frank had been hunkered down at the far end of the bar with Meera for the last twenty minutes. It was clear from the way he constantly leaned in that he was sweet on her.

Meera had already confided that she worked as a secretary, but Frank hadn't been so open about his occupation. He'd come around, they always did. Eventually, everyone bared their souls to a bartender.

"Two more gimlets." Frank raised his and Meera's empty glasses.

"You got it." He quickly mixed together the gin and Rose's lime syrup, then set the drinks on the bar in front of Meera and Frank.

"You're a welcome addition to the DPC," Meera said, lifting her glass in a toast. "Thank you."

"Anytime." He made his way to the other side of the bar to finish cleaning up after the two young women who'd just left, but Andi had already cleared things away.

She held out a napkin with writing on it. "I believe this is for you."

He took the napkin and read the words neatly scrawled in flowing script. *Nick, call me. Gigi.* Instead of dots, Gigi had topped her i's with little flowers and written down her phone number. When he looked back at Andi, she was smirking, which only served to draw his attention to her mouth, and the rosy pink lip gloss she wore. Not that he was thinking of kissing her or anything

She dipped her head to the napkin. "That must happen to you a lot."

"It's irrelevant." He tossed the napkin in the trash bin beneath the bar. Since he'd started working at the café, women gave him their numbers all the time, but he'd never felt the remotest desire to hook up with any of them. Funny how he never paid attention to whether *those* women wore rosy pink lip gloss. *Shit.*

"That's the fifth napkin in three days, and those are just the ones we know about. The staff has been collecting them. We call them the Napkin Girls." She narrowed her eyes. "Remember, you're here to work. Not to get laid."

"Wouldn't dream of it." He grinned, but she didn't grin back at him. It was obvious she didn't like having him in her place. Control was her thing, and allowing him in her restaurant was tantamount to submission. But he sensed there was more to it. She didn't like *him.* Understandable, given the circumstances. *Probably for the best.*

As she turned and walked into the kitchen, he followed the motion of her gently swaying hips, then his eyes were drawn to the cell phone clipped to the waistband of her short khaki skirt. Most women didn't wear their cell phones, so he was gratified to see she was taking their deal seriously. If— no, *when*—Myer called, she'd be able to answer right away.

Andi emerged from the kitchen, expertly balancing four plates, which she brought to a table in the corner. He liked that she didn't hesitate to lend a hand to help out the waitresses, and that she took pride in her establishment. The place wouldn't have survived this long without hard work and perseverance, things she clearly wasn't afraid of.

After chatting for a minute with the party of four, she went to the coffee maker adjacent to the bar and began setting up a fresh pot to brew. Nick was heading her way when she picked up a cheeseburger from a plate Kara had set for her at the end of the bar, took two hefty bites then groaned in obvious pleasure. Standing over her shoulder now, he *hmphed.* "You're a carnivore. I had you pegged as a strict fruit, nut, and salad-eating woman."

Without turning, she set down the cheeseburger and dabbed at her mouth with a napkin. "Technically, I'm an omnivore. And why does it come as such a shock to you that

I eat meat? Are you profiling me?"

"No, I—"

Something shattered. Andi spun as they both jerked their heads to the source of the noise—plates crashing to the floor. Not realizing he was so close, she plowed headfirst into him. As he clasped her arms, her hands flew to his chest. As gentle and soft as her touch was, it burned straight through his shirt to his skin. *Holy hell.* He hadn't been this affected by a woman since he first met his wife. God help him if Andi ever touched him directly... The image of a fireball streaking across the sky came to mind.

"Sorry," she said. Their gazes locked, then she quickly averted hers.

"No problem." He released her arms but not before getting an eyeful of cleavage at the deep *V* of her pink blouse, and a disconcerting whiff of her flowery perfume that had him wondering if she'd dabbed some between her breasts. He cleared his throat. *Keep it professional.* "Can you cover the bar for a few minutes? I'll clean that up."

"Um, sure." She slipped past him to check on the few remaining people sitting at the end.

As he watched her go, he dragged a hand down his face. The air conditioning inside the restaurant was cranked high, but the place was hotter than a sauna. She might still be a suspect, but that didn't stop him from being attracted to her. That, he could live with. Attachment was where he'd drawn the line with any of the women who'd come and gone lately.

He grabbed a broom, waste pan, and an empty plastic dish bin from the kitchen then went out to the dining area where he found Zoe standing over the broken pile of plates. "I got this." He crouched and began collecting the larger pieces and putting them in the bin.

"Thanks, Nick." She smiled gratefully. "I'm a klutz, and you're a doll. A really *big* doll, but you're still a doll."

"Get out of here." He winked at her.

After he'd swept the area for smaller shards, he set the bin on a table and paused to look at one of the photos on the Wall of Dog. Andi's face was framed by a black hood as she knelt in the snow, flanked on one side by a black and white Alaskan malamute, and the other by a pure white Samoyed. All three were smiling.

He leaned in to read the handwritten notes on the matting. *Orion and Venus…gone from this earth, always in my heart. Love you always, Andi.*

Before she spoke, he knew she was standing behind him. Even if he hadn't heard her light footsteps, he recognized her flowery scent.

"They were my babies. My friends." Her voice didn't tremble, but there was deep emotion in her words.

"They were beautiful." He turned to see the sadness in her eyes, but there was also love, and he wondered how a woman like her was still single. She had a helluva lot going for her. Intelligence, beauty, guts. From what he'd seen, any man with half a brain would be stupid not to jump at the chance to have her on his arm.

Aside from the possible money laundering thing.

"They were." She nodded and swallowed. "Inside *and* out."

"How long has it been?" Judging by her reaction, he'd guess not long.

She reached across the table and straightened the photo. "Venus left me three years ago, and Orion's been gone almost five now."

Longer than he'd thought. She was a woman who loved and experienced loss deeply, canines being no exception. "What's with the celestial names?"

Aside from interacting with customers, he hadn't once caught her in a genuine moment of joy. Now she surprised him by giving a quick laugh. "Amateur astronomy runs in the family."

Interesting. "How long have you had Stray?"

She shook her head. "Stray's not mine. She wandered onto the deck about a month ago, looking for food. She was emaciated, poor thing. I'm only taking care of her until I can find someone to adopt her."

That explained why the dog wasn't named after a planet, or comet, or some other celestial body. "You should keep her. You two are good together."

Before lunch, they'd put Saxon and Stray up in Andi's garage kennel, and during the walk to the garage Stray had never left Andi's side. The dog was devoted to her.

She gave a wistful sigh, still staring at the photo. "I can't go through that again. It was too painful."

He understood that for some, the death of a dog could be as painful as the loss of a human family member. He resisted the urge to comfort her, to reach out and stroke her hair. "I'm sorry for your loss."

"Thank you. It isn't that I haven't thought about keeping Stray. After Orion and Venus died, the house was so empty without them. Empty and quiet. But this place"—she gestured to encompass the Wall of Dog and the dog run outside—"gives me my dog-fix every single day. This restaurant is my dream."

A gentle smile lit her face, one that tugged at his own deeply buried dreams. Dreams that included growing old with someone. Something that would never happen now. "After suffering a loss, it takes time. For some, longer than others. A dog's life is far too short, but our lives are far richer for it. When the time is right, you'll open your heart again."

For one infinitesimal second, he didn't know if he'd been referring to her heart, or his. Then a shot of cold, hard reality hit him over the head. *Not yours, that's for damned sure.* His heart had a big ol' "Closed for Business" sign hanging on it.

She turned from the photo. Cornflower-blue eyes pinned him, and he couldn't look away. He had the distinct impression that she knew he'd unintentionally revealed something about his personal life, and it left him feeling exposed and edgy.

Just as he cleared his throat, movement over her shoulder caught his eye. Eric stood just inside the front door, watching him. Nick subtly canted his head to the bar.

He returned his gaze to Andi's, wishing there was something he could say to make her feel better. There wasn't, and it was better that he maintained a professional distance, anyway. "I'd better get back to work. You never know when the boss is lurking around."

"Funny." She gave him a sarcastic look then eyed Eric. "He looks familiar."

"He should. He was at your boyfr—" He'd been about to say *boyfriend* but caught himself. "Correction. At your *ex*-boyfriend's house."

"You're learning." She feigned a glare of indignation.

By the time he made his way behind the bar, Eric had settled onto a stool at the corner near the outside deck. Without asking, Nick poured a Sam Adams on draft. He tossed a coaster on the bar, then set the glass on top.

"On the house."

"That's mighty generous of you." Eric lifted the glass and took a long swallow. "Nice place. How's the food?"

"Kick-ass. I was about to order lunch." He grabbed a menu and slapped it on the bar.

"No need," Eric said. "I'll have a turkey club."

Nick placed their orders then leaned closer so they wouldn't be overheard.

Eric took another swig. "You never said how Andi took it when you proposed working here?"

"Not well at first." He turned to watch the subject of their conversation cooing at yet another baby. When he looked back, his friend was grinning stupidly. "What?"

"Nothing." Eric held up his hands in surrender. "How'd you sweet talk her into it?"

"I appealed to her logical side. She wants to clear her name and get her money back." Nick picked up the soda dispenser and squirted club soda into a glass for himself. Again, he watched Andi as she lifted a hand and gently caressed the baby's cheek.

"She's hot," Eric said.

Nick set his glass onto the bar with more force than intended. Some of the contents sloshed over the rim.

Eric laughed. "Just checking."

"On what?"

"To see if you give a shit."

"I don't. She's a suspect, not a prospect."

"Right." He nodded, too emphatically for Nick's taste. "I only came by to give you an update."

"So start updating." He grabbed a cloth to clean up the mess he'd made. What Eric had said about Andi had royally pissed him off. More irritating was that he didn't understand why he cared.

"I called Kade again. Myer still hasn't crossed any borders. His trail is dead. So to speak. His family hasn't heard from him, and traces on his credit cards are still coming up empty."

"Then wherever he is, he's paying for everything in cash." He served Eric a bowl of pretzels. "Got any *good* news?"

"Not really." He grabbed a handful of pretzels. "Some of Andi's background check is in."

Nick froze. While he still had to treat her as a suspect, he hadn't really expected the feds to dig up more dirt on her.

"She paid for the Dog Park Café in cash." Eric stuffed a few pretzels into his mouth.

"How much?" He already had a bad feeling.

"One point five million," Eric said as he chewed. "For the restaurant, the house, and nearly ten acres. Based on county permit applications, she probably sank another half million into the renovation."

Not a good sign. Money launderers usually paid for big-ticket items with untraceable cash.

A flash of pink had him look over to see Andi rise and turn, a smile on her face. When she caught sight of him watching her, her smile disintegrated as she rightly interpreted his dark look to be bad news.

Marty took that moment to bring out their sandwiches. "Here ya go, guys."

"Thanks." Nick took the plates and set them on the bar.

"I know you want her to be innocent." Eric plucked a toothpick out of a wedge of club sandwich. "But maybe she's not."

"I don't *want* her to be innocent." He picked up his sandwich. "I don't *want* her to be *anything.* If she's got a role in Myer's money laundering scheme—let alone running guns—I'll arrest her myself." He grabbed his panini and bit into it. Based on the smell wafting into his nose, he was sure it was kick-ass. The possibility of arresting Andi made it taste like cardboard.

Eric picked up a fry and dipped it in ketchup. "Have you heard from Matt and the guys?"

"Yeah, they're—"

Nick spotted two burly guys in suits at a table near the front door, giving Kara a hard time. One of them had an arm around the waitress's waist, while the other was licking his lips in a sleazy, suggestive manner. Kara managed to extricate herself from the man's grasp, but the douchebag grabbed her arm. Other people in the restaurant were starting to stare.

"Ah, hell." Nick dropped his sandwich on the plate and

rounded the end of the bar. By the time he'd gotten to the table with the two assholes, A-hole #1 was on his feet, still trying to cop a feel.

"Got your back," Eric said from where he now stood behind Nick.

"Let her go. *Now.*" He towered over the jerk, who unwisely failed to follow his order. A-hole #2 wisely stayed in his chair.

Kara struggled to escape the guy's grip on her wrist, but he only tightened his hold, hooking his arm around her waist. From the corner of his eye, Nick caught Andi rushing over.

"Who the fuck are you?" A-hole #1 was about five ten, with beady, dark brown eyes and slicked back hair. *Great.* A friggin' mobster wannabe.

Nick leaned in, intentionally getting in the guy's face. He really wanted the little prick to take a swing at him so he could pound his face into the pavement. He had no tolerance for dumb shits who thought they could press themselves on women. "I'm the fucker who's about to throw you out on your ass."

"Nick." Andi touched his arm. "Don't."

"Oh, yeah?" A-hole released Kara and stupidly took a step closer to Nick.

Oh, yeah. Before the guy could react, Nick grabbed his wrist, spinning him, then wrenching his arm behind and high on his back. The guy struggled, but he was no match for him.

"You motherfu—"

Nick shoved the guy's arm higher, and he yelped. "Language." Then he propelled the A-hole straight out the front door. He released the guy's arm, and with more than a little shove, sent him stumbling into the parking lot.

Andi came up behind him, along with Eric, who'd escorted A-hole's buddy outside.

Nick clenched his fists. It was all he could do not to ram

his boot up the guy's ass or lock him up for assaulting Kara. "Show up here again, and I guarantee you won't leave looking so pretty." Not that the little fuck was pretty now.

"Sonofabitch," the guy muttered, massaging his shoulder as both men headed for a black BMW.

Eric chuckled. "You exercised great restraint. I'm proud of you. Personally, I would have mashed my fist in his face."

"Do me a favor, and follow them outta here."

"My pleasure." Eric headed out the door.

Andi rested her hand on Kara's shoulder. "Are you all right?"

The young waitress nodded. "I'm fine. Thanks."

"Are you sure?" Andi asked, concern evident in her eyes.

Kara nodded. "I did just what you trained us to do if male customers start harassing us or try to get physical. I kept calm and gave him the opportunity to back off."

"I know. You did great," Andi reassured her. "But remember, you don't ever have to accept a customer pawing you or making suggestive comments, and I'll back you up every time."

"Thanks. I was about to kick him in the nuts." Kara gave her a quick grin. "Like how you said we could."

Nick held back a snort. *Andi was telling her staff to kick sleazy customers in the nuts?* His admiration for her was growing every day. She had even more guts than he'd given her credit for.

After the waitress headed back into the dining room, Andi turned on Nick, giving him an undisguised look of irritation. "I appreciate you stepping in to help, but you didn't have to be so aggressive."

"Yeah. I did." He met her stare with a hard one of his own. Without waiting for a response, he turned and went back inside.

As soon as he crossed the threshold, customers began

clapping and cheering, including Zoe, Kara, and Marty. As he made his way behind the bar, the clapping died down. He picked up his sandwich, which had turned cold. *Figures. No good deed…*

Andi came behind the bar. "We need to talk. In my office. Now."

He took a deep breath and let it out. *Great.* He followed her into the little office off the kitchen.

"Close the door."

He did, and when he turned back, she got right in his face.

• • •

"I agree that guy deserved to get thrown out of here." Andi sat on a corner of her desk, then pointed a finger at herself. "But *I* would have taken care of it, and not so violently. Do you think this hasn't happened before? I've never had to resort to launching a customer out the door with enough force to land him in the next town." She jabbed a finger in his direction. "The way you handled him was unnecessary and bad for business."

"The asshole had it coming." Nick leaned back against the door, crossing his arms, drawing her attention to his thick biceps. "Trust me, once guys like him think they can get away with forcing themselves on a woman, they'll never stop."

She sighed. "I don't disagree with you on that, but we're not on the street, and you're not here to police the place. This is exactly what I was afraid of, that you'd scare customers away with your storm-trooper attitude."

"Do you have any idea how terrifying it is for a woman to be held against her will?" He pushed from the door and moved closer. "No, you don't. But Kara does, and so do the thousands of other women who get assaulted every year in this country by bullying trash like him."

She stared up at him as he loomed over her. "All I'm saying is that I can handle guys like him. I don't need you—"

His arm shot out, hauling her against his chest. His other arm angled across her back, holding her immobile. She tried pushing away, but he held her so firmly she couldn't wedge her hands between their chests.

Her breath came in quick gasps. She gripped his waist, feeling the solid muscles bunch beneath her fingers. Her heart pounded as his face inched closer to hers. Before he said the words, she understood what he was doing—teaching her a lesson.

"You want to be in control all the time, but you can't be." His nostrils flared as he stared down at her. "Doesn't feel so good, does it?" Warm breath washed over her face, and she breathed in his scent.

Actually, it does.

As it had behind the bar when she'd slammed into him, his touch made her skin tingle and her breath come in short, desperate gasps.

Don't let him get to you like this. He's only playing you.

Long, strong thighs pressed against her. His chest was rock hard. Steely, defined muscles flexed as she twisted his soft gray T-shirt in her hands.

"I know what you're doing." The huskiness in her voice surprised her.

"Do you?" He leaned in until his lips hovered over hers without touching them.

Their gazes locked, and she could swear he was about to kiss her. For an instant, she wondered what she would do if he did.

For a moment longer, he stared at her, then took a deep breath and raised his head, releasing her. "I have to get back to work." He spun and yanked open the door.

A startled sound came from the doorway. Tess stood on the threshold, her fist in the air, poised to knock. Nick glanced at her, then she stepped aside to let him past. Andi could no longer see him, but watched Tess as she stared after him.

Tess came into the office. "What was *that* about?"

Andi waited for her heart rate to slow. She didn't know what had just happened between them, but it had been intense. Rather than frightening her and driving home his point as he'd intended, he'd kick-started something else she hadn't experienced in a very long time. *Desire,* and with the very last man on the planet she should be thinking about that way.

Tess giggled. "You know, he really is a hunk. They make guys like him at Hunks-R-Us. Have you noticed the size of his biceps? The man's built like a tank. But remember..." Tess frowned. "Be careful with him. More importantly, *of* him."

"You don't have to tell me that." Although he *was* a hunk, she admitted silently, remembering how hard and solid he'd felt beneath her touch. She pressed her fingers to her lips, wondering what it would actually feel like to kiss him.

Stop it. Do not *go there.*

Least of all with a guy she knew up front was only there to "get his man."

"Boss?" Tess raised her brows. "Something I should know?"

"No." She shook her head. "Nothing. Hopefully all that hunkiness will bring in more business at the bar. We need it."

"Maybe we should make Thursdays Ladies Night." She grinned. "If there was ever a bartender who could reel in the ladies, it's him."

Andi began clearing away empties from the dining room

tables, casting occasional glances at Nick. Friday nights at the DPC still weren't as busy as she hoped. Most of the dining tables were empty, but Nick was managing to keep a full bar. Mostly women, she noted, and the Napkin Girls box was filling up quickly. Soon they'd need a bigger box, a spatial factoid that was beginning to annoy her.

"Just look at him work it." Tess eyed him appreciatively. "He might be a cop, but he's great eye candy. All that twisted steel and sex appeal." She let out a hearty sigh. "And he listens to people."

Andi grunted. It irked her how she'd unloaded on him earlier about missing her dogs so much, and she still didn't understand why she'd done it. One minute they'd been standing there, and the next she'd poured her heart out to him. Guess he really was a good listener.

Or a world class manipulator. Like Steve had been.

They watched as he poured Cosmos from a cocktail shaker for two women in their forties. With each shake, his biceps bunched, and she could make out the outline of carved abdominals beneath the T-shirt she knew firsthand was soft and worn. She couldn't hear the conversation, but one of the women spoke and he smiled, responding with something that made both women titter like a couple of teenage girls.

"Oh, for heaven's sake." All that flirtatious tittering made her want to puke.

After pouring three pints for a group of guys at the other end of the bar, he easily made conversation with the men as if he'd known them for years. She never would have guessed there was another side to the man—a social one. *But is that real, or an act?* She had to admit it seemed genuine, just part of who he was.

Tess eyed her speculatively. "You don't *have* to let him work here."

"I do if I want if I want my get-out-of-jail card and my

money back. Besides"—she bobbed her eyebrows—"he *is* great eye candy and good for business. The least he can do while he's here is make up for holding onto my money."

"True on both counts." Tess nodded. "Those women have been here for hours, and they ain't fixin' to leave anytime soon. Maybe it was fate that Nick showed up just when you needed a bartender."

"More like fate-ful." She wiped down another table. "You and Marty can take off. I already cut Kara and Zoe loose for the night. I can close up after last call."

"Thanks. I've got plans later." Tess waggled her eyebrows, leaving no mistake about what her *plans* were.

She admired Tess's free-spirited nature. It wasn't that her friend was easy or anything. Tess was very comfortable putting herself out there. Though, at times, she didn't think Tess was content working at the DPC. Her friend possessed keen business savvy and seemed destined for something greater. She hoped Tess made the right choices before too much more of her life passed her by.

Unlike me.

Again, she was hit by that all-too-familiar wave of regret about the decisions she'd made in her life. It had taken her too long to find what she loved most. Entertaining, meeting people, serving up great food at reasonable prices, and all in a dog-friendly atmosphere. Rather than seeming hectic, the restaurant gave her contentment and joy, and that's all she needed. Although, sometimes she wavered on that basic tenet.

On rare occasions, she found herself wishing there was someone to share her life with. Then the past—the part with Steve, in particular—smacked her in the face, and the stupid idea of sharing her life vanished with the bluntness of a wrecking ball. Now Joe had been added to her list of men who'd betrayed her.

Nick's deep, rumbling laughter came to her, and she paused at the screen door to find him watching her. That was nothing new. In the few days he'd been working at the DPC, she'd caught him tracking her on numerous occasions— to make sure she wasn't concealing a call from Joe, she assumed. But this time was different. It was subtle, but the way he watched her now wasn't his usual surveilling-a-suspect demeanor.

Gone was the suspicion and hardness she'd become accustomed to. In its place was an unexpected softness and something else she couldn't decipher. It was as if—

Don't be ridiculous. For one incredibly naive, incredibly stupid moment she could swear there'd been a tiny shadow of caring in his eyes.

Maybe she was simply getting to know him in a different light. *Yeah, that must be it.*

As annoying as it was to admit, he was turning out to be far different from the man she'd first met in the shower. Then, he'd been all hard-ass and taciturn. Now he was just a man she was beginning to like. *Another scary-as-hell thought.*

What other surprises is the man hiding?

She shook her head and went out the screen door to clear empties and make sure there were no other customers lingering on the deck. The air had cooled somewhat, but it was still a contrast from the air-conditioned interior of the restaurant.

As she reached for an empty glass, a flash of white at the base of a tree inside the dog run caught her attention. Was someone running a dog at this time of night?

She held her hand over her eyes to shield them from the glaring light from inside the cafe. Peering into the darkness, she still couldn't make out a dog or any definite shape. Whatever was there, though, wasn't moving. There'd been occasional sightings of an albino deer in the area, but it had yet to make an appearance at the DPC.

As she took a step closer to the railing, the white object took off, then vaulted over the dog fence and disappeared.

Andi's heart thumped faster. She backed up, nearly tripping over a chair. *That wasn't a dog* or *a deer.* It was a man, she was sure of it.

And he'd been watching her.

Why, she didn't know, but with everything going on, standing around waiting to find out... *Bad idea.*

She spun to haul ass back into the café, when something touched her waist. Flinching, she sucked in a quick breath, preparing to let loose with a scream loud enough to wake the dead. At the last second, she bit off the sound.

The cell phone clipped to her waist was vibrating.

A few steps from the door, she yanked the phone from its cradle and stared at the screen.

Joe.

Chapter Eight

Finally, the bar had slowed down, but Nick had been busting his ass mixing drinks and pouring drafts nonstop for the last hour. Good thing, because it kept him from reliving the near-kiss in Andi's office.

He'd only meant to make a point, but the instant he'd gotten close to her, he'd felt the sparks zapping between them. And when she'd grabbed his waist, he'd felt her touch in every cell of his body. He'd come less than a hair's breadth from kissing her, and he would have done it, too, if he hadn't had a moment of clarity about the supreme stupidity of pressing his lips to hers... of raking his fingers through all that thick, blond hair, and—

Across the dining room, Andi flung open the door to the deck. Even from this distance the panic was obvious in her wide eyes. She held up her hand. In it was her pink cell phone. Then she put the phone to her ear.

Myer.

He threw down the coaster he'd been holding, then hustled out from behind the bar. He wanted to run, but that would attract attention and cause others to think there was an emergency. Which there was, but he didn't want anyone else out there when he listened in on the call.

The screen door creaked as he pushed on it, then he urged Andi outside. Rather than let the door slam behind him, he quietly closed it. Luckily, the deck was empty of customers.

With the phone still pressed to her ear, she jerked her head left and right, looking over the railing toward the dog run, as if she were searching for something. Or some*one*. He made a mental note to ask her about that.

She glanced at him, and the phone shook in her hand. "Joe? Are you all right?"

He took the phone from her and put the call on speaker.

"I'm fine," a voice said in a hushed tone.

He made a circling gesture with his finger, indicating she should keep him talking.

She nodded. "Where are you?"

"It's better you don't know. You should stay out of this."

"*Stay out of this?*" She gave the phone a look of disbelief. "Thanks to you, I'm in this whether I like it or not. I already told you police and federal agents searched your house, and I had the extreme misfortune to be there when they broke in."

"Oh Jesus, baby." Nick clenched his jaw at Myer's term of affection. It shouldn't bother him, but it sure as shit did. "I'm so sorry. I didn't know that would happen. I never meant to involve you in this."

So is she? Involved? Christ, he hoped not. Fuck, Eric was right. Nick *did* want her to be innocent.

"I didn't know, I swear it," Myer continued, regret evident in his tone. "I never would have offered you my place if I had any idea that would happen. Are *you* okay? They didn't hurt you, did they?"

Nick suppressed a few choice expletives. The idea that he—or *any* of them—would have hurt Andi pissed him off.

"No, they just"—she flicked her gaze at him—"frightened

me."

An exhaled breath came through the phone. "Did they take anything?"

Nick nodded, indicating it was okay for her to tell him.

"Just a few papers and some cash. They left a property receipt. You didn't tell me I was your sole heir." Her forehead creased. "Why did you do that?"

"Because I care about you. That hasn't changed. I know I screwed us up a long time ago, but I never stopped loving you. If anything happens to me, I want…" His voice choked. "I want you to have my estate."

"No, Joe." She began shaking her head, and the angry look in her eyes softened. "Don't talk like that. Whatever you're involved in, I can help. But you should know they have a warrant for your arrest."

"I had a feeling that was coming, but I can't turn myself in."

She looked at him, the plea for help obvious on her face. He pressed his lips to her ear. "Tell him the gangs are looking for him and there's a bounty on his head. He can turn himself in and we'll protect him. He can't run forever."

"Joe, you have to turn yourself in. There are people trying to hurt you, but the police can help you."

"How, by throwing my ass in jail?"

"By protecting you." She grabbed Nick's wrist, tugging the phone closer. Despite the seriousness of the situation, he found it difficult to ignore how amazing her fingers felt on his skin. "You can't stay in hiding forever. Sooner or later, they'll find you."

"Who, the bad guys, or the police?"

The hold she had on his wrist tightened, and she leaned in closer. "You have to answer for what you've done, and you have to tell them I had nothing to do with it." The creases in her forehead deepened, and her voice began to shake. "But you can't do that if you're dead."

Several seconds of silence passed, and for a moment he

thought Myer had hung up. He strained his ears for sounds—something that would give him a clue as to where the guy was. A bell, a whistle, a foghorn, anything. But there was nothing.

"Come with me," Myer said, his voice tinged with desperation. "We can leave the country and start a new life somewhere else. I can make you happy, Andi. I know I can."

He scrutinized her reaction, irrationally gratified to see that she wasn't reacting the way a woman in love would. Or an accomplice.

She released his wrist, and her body stiffened. "You know I can't do that."

Another moment of silence passed, this one lengthier.

"I know. It was just a thought. A Hail Mary."

"Turn yourself in, dammit. I'll help you. I promise."

"I'll think about it. I have to go."

"No wait!" she cried, reaching for the phone. "Tell them I didn't wire any money for you."

But he was gone.

Nick set the phone onto a nearby table then turned back to Andi. "You did good." And she had. She'd held it together and said all the right things. Now it was up to Myer.

She took an unsteady breath. "I hope so. No matter what he's done, he doesn't deserve to die." Her words came tumbling out. "Deep down, he's a good man. I don't understand how he could have done all those things, especially to me." Despite the lingering warmth in the air, her body trembled.

"A lot of good people get into bad situations. Some think there's no other way out, except by doing something illegal." *Or by killing themselves.*

She blinked rapidly. "I don't understand how things could have spiraled so far out of control. I may lose a good friend *and* my business. This place is everything to me. It's all I have." Her slim body began shaking with sobs, and when she covered her face with her hands, something inside him, a barrier—professional *and* personal—cracked wide open.

Don't do it. You can't.

His brain didn't listen, and he took her in his arms. She shuddered as he tugged her against him. For an instant, she stood that way, with her arms locked around her waist. Then her hands crept up his back, allowing him to hold her closer.

"Shh," he whispered against her hair, rocking her gently. "It'll be all right." God, he hoped that wasn't a lie.

Sobbing openly now, she dug her fingers into his back, her breath warm against his chest. Her body was taut with tension, and he found himself rubbing his hands up and down her back, trying desperately to ease her pain. There was nothing else he could do.

Gradually her trembling eased. Her sobs lessened, and she relaxed against him, and damn if her body didn't feel good. Warm...yielding...and the way she smelled...

He took an unsteady breath, not understanding why he was thinking of her on any level other than a professional one. Getting involved with her was a thousand miles beyond out of the question. "He'll call again. I'm sure of it. When he does, you'll talk him in, and I'll be there to help you."

Lifting her head, she gazed up at him. The flow of tears had ceased, yet her eyes still shimmered, and grief showed in every nuance of her face. "Thank you. I know it's your job, and all, but—"

He pressed his lips to her forehead. He didn't know why, but it seemed the most natural thing for him to do. When he pulled back, their eyes met and held. Hers were filled with undisguised shock, no more than what he was certain was mirrored in his own.

That one little kiss on her forehead shouldn't have meant anything, but it had. He still needed her to get to Myer, but when he'd kissed her, he'd been scorched by an unexpected truth. In just a few days, he'd not only begun to care about her, but to seriously question his assumption of her guilt.

When she parted her lips, he involuntarily did the same. Startled awareness pounded in his brain. Professionally, this was wrong. Personally, this was a royally big mistake in judgment. He didn't *do* caring, not anymore.

That didn't stop him from slipping one hand to the small of her back, or from tugging her closer until her slim, curvy body pressed against his. When her fingers touched his waist, his resolve slipped more, leaving him dangling over the edge of a very dangerous wall. If he fell, he doubted he could climb back up.

"Hey, are you guys all ri—"

He released her, jerking his head to the screen door. Tess stood on the deck, her mouth agape. "Woops. Sorry. I seem to be making a habit of this." The screen door slammed as she spun and went back inside.

Andi eased away from him, her tongue swiping at her lower lip. She reached for her phone on the table and turned to the door, but he caught her arm. He dragged his other hand down his face. He must be out of his mind. No matter how strong the attraction was between them, this was a place he couldn't go. Neither of them could.

"We can't do this." As much as he wanted her, he knew it was the right thing to say and not just because she was a suspect. He'd frozen himself off from romantic entanglements the day his wife died. It was how he'd survived. It was the only way he knew how. They were flirting with disaster, and she would wind up seriously hurt. *We both might*, he had to admit.

The skin between her brows furrowed, and he couldn't decipher whether it was from anger, regret, or something else. "I know."

Then she was gone.

He turned and braced his hands on the railing, drawing in a ragged breath. With every passing day, whatever was sparking between them grew brighter and hotter.

Whatever that something was, it meant trouble. Big trouble.

Chapter Nine

Andi breathed harder, inhaling the scents of pine and moist earth as her feet pounded on the dirt trail. Sweat beaded on her forehead and upper lip, and she swiped it away. Despite the thick tree canopy shading her from the early morning sunlight, thick, dewy air pressed in on her from all sides. She didn't care and picked up her pace, but not before glancing over her shoulder for what had to be the hundredth time since she'd left the house.

It was Saturday, just over two weeks since Joe had called, and while there'd been no more sightings of the man who'd been watching her that night, the woods seemed to have eyes. With every bend in the path, she tensed, half anticipating someone would jump out from behind a tree and grab her. After telling Nick what she'd seen in the dog run, he'd warned her to notify him immediately if she saw him again, but there'd been no more sightings.

As if that wasn't enough to ruin the morning runs that were normally peaceful and mind-clearing, the memory of her second near-kiss with Nick had pretty much fried her brain cells for the duration of time.

Forget it. It hadn't meant a thing. To either of them. It was only the heat of the moment. Nothing more than that.

But she'd clung to him. *Actually, clung to him.* If Tess hadn't interrupted them, who knew what would have happened?

You know *what would have happened.* She would have given in to her crazed need to claw at his shirt to get to his bare skin and feel all those hard muscles beneath her fingertips. Joe had never come close to evoking that kind of no-holds-barred response from her. Yet another sign that they were better off as friends. "Friends" was something she and Nick could never be. Friends *or* lovers. It was just as well that his presence at the DPC was temporary.

The trail straightened, and she dug into her reserves, kicking up her pace until her muscles screamed.

A chipmunk dashed across the path in front of her, and she veered at the last second to keep from stepping on it.

Lately, she and Nick had avoided each other as much as humanly possible. When she needed to get something from behind the bar, she waited until he'd gone into the storeroom to restock supplies, or into the kitchen to grab another of Marty's experimental paninis.

Nick had afforded her the same treatment, although he always kept an eye on her, making sure she didn't receive another call from Joe without telling him. In fact, the only good things that had happened lately were that the bar was packed every night now and the musician she'd hired for this evening would bring in even more customers. *Maybe I'll get through this after all.*

With Tess covering for her, she had just enough time to get back and shower before the lunch crowd arrived. Good thing, because her shorts and tank top were thoroughly soaked with sweat and sticking to every inch of her skin.

The trail was silent, save for the sound of her breathing. *In. Out. In. Out.* A spooky sense crept up her spine and neck, spreading to her scalp. The sensation of being watched was overwhelming, and with every stride, her heart beat faster. *Maybe I should have told Nick where I was going, after all.*

Too late now, idiot. Besides, she refused to go all paranoid without any proof someone was actually stalking her.

Behind her, branches snapped. She clenched her fists and whipped around, planting her feet, readying for a fight. Her heart hammered, pounding in her ears.

A large deer broke through the brush and shot across the path. Andi let out a tiny shriek. Without breaking stride, the deer disappeared into the thicket. Her chest sawed in and out. "Holy shit." Gradually, she unclenched her fists. This whole thing with Joe and the mystery man outside was seriously spooking her, to the point where she'd begun to jump at every little noise.

Shaking her head, she took off again, this time at a slower pace. An uncomfortable foreboding still surrounded her, but she did her best to shrug it off and enjoy the rest of her run.

As she rounded the last bend that led to her property, whistles and barking came to her ears. After clearing the trees, the sight that greeted her made her mouth hang open, and not just because she was exhausted. *Hardly.*

She practically stumbled over a large rock, righting herself before face-planting in the grass. Slowing to a stop, she leaned over and rested her hands on her thighs. It was all she could do to catch her breath. Or stop staring.

Twenty feet away, Nick strode through the lake's shallows. Over one shoulder, he held a rope attached to the inflatable mattress she'd had leaning against the back of her house. Saxon stood atop the float, barking his head off and looking as if he were having the time of his life. Granted, watching the dog enjoy himself was entertaining, but that wasn't what had her blinking repeatedly to clear her vision.

No siree.

She swallowed. The only thing Nick had on was navy blue gym shorts and…nothing else.

Thick, incredibly defined muscles bulged and flexed all over his upper body. Pectorals. Biceps. Abs. All glistening with the sexiest sheen of lake water to ever grace a male body.

Andi wiped sweat from her forehead just before it dripped into her eyes. She'd known Nick had to be hiding a great body beneath his uniform, jeans, T-shirt, and everything else she'd seen him in, but this…Adonis…this Greek god… *Oh my.*

Apparently, her female customers agreed, because as he swung the float in a slow one-eighty and started back in the other direction toward the deck, he was greeted with applause and a bevy of whistles coming from the cluster of women leaning against the deck railing.

Through it all, Saxon barked happily, swaying as he continually adjusted his stance to keep from falling.

Sunlight glinted off Nick's broad back as he dragged the float another twenty feet before Saxon lost his balance and fell into the lake with a splash. He barked and swam circles around Nick as he dragged the float back to shore. The crowd along the railing now included Tess, Kara, Zoe, and Meera, all of whom cheered and hooted.

Nick dropped the rope, then grabbed a water bottle from the grass. He tipped it for a long swig, then dumped the rest of it over his head.

Saxon shook, sending droplets of water flying a good ten feet in all directions. The dog ran circles around Nick, as if he was trying to convince him to go another round.

Nick shook his head and said something to his dog. Andi couldn't make out what, but the animal calmed and pressed the side of his body against Nick's leg.

Andi straightened, and Saxon jerked his head in the air

as he caught sight of her. The dog bolted toward her, and she clapped her hands. When Saxon got closer, he slowed to a stop.

"Good morning, Saxon." She knelt to greet him.

Woof. The dog shoved his muzzle into her hand, and she scratched his long, damp black ears.

"I see you had fun out there." She ran her hands along his coat, which was quickly drying in the hot morning sun.

A pair of long, lightly haired legs appeared in her view, and her gaze slowly traveled up Nick's calves and powerful thighs, to the bulge beneath his wet trunks. She raised her eyes to his lower abs, where rivulets of water trickled down the many crevices before disappearing into the waistband of his shorts.

Stop. Staring.

It was hard not to.

Force yourself.

And speaking of hardness, all she wanted was to run her fingertips all over his glistening chest.

"What, exactly, were you doing?" She straightened and pointed to the float.

"Balance training." His gaze dipped to the sweat-soaked tank that sagged low on her breasts. "As K-9s go, Saxon is at the top of his game. But he needs more experience maintaining balance on uneven, unstable surfaces, and this is a good way to supplement his training."

Saxon's ears pricked as he listened avidly to their conversation.

"I see." *A whole lot of bare skin, to be precise.* She turned to leave, having taken her fill of glistening muscle for one morning.

"Wait." Nick stood motionless, his hands on his hips. Hips that were completely devoid of fat and without any evidence of impending love handles. "Where were you just now?"

"Running." Her attire should have made it obvious.

"I know that." He shot her an annoyed look. "I meant, *where*."

She tipped her head to the tree line. "The woods. It's got good shade cover."

When he turned to look at the trees, her gaze drank in the breadth of his muscled shoulders and back, his high, tight butt, and those long legs that looked strong enough to kick down a twelve-inch-thick wall of bricks.

"You shouldn't be out there alone." When he turned back to her, he was frowning. "Especially when some guy might be lurking around the café. Next time you go for a run, I'll go with you."

"You're exasperating." She threw her hands in the air. "I've been going for runs by myself in those woods for over a year. I promise you, there are no bad guys lurking behind the trees." Only a deer that had scared the shit out of her.

"Don't be so dismissive."

"Don't be so smothering." From the corner of her eye, she'd caught Saxon watching them, turning his head alternately from her to Nick as if he were a spectator at a ping-pong tournament.

"I'm not." Even though he'd begun to sweat, the look he sent her was as cool as ice. "What I am, is worried."

"About me? I'm not in any danger. Joe is."

"Humor me."

Knowing it probably wasn't worth arguing over, she sighed. "Fine." Then she turned and began walking to the house.

"Admit it," he called after her. "I'm growing on you."

"Not," she shouted over her shoulder.

Deep, rich laughter followed her as she walked briskly home and yanked open the screen door. Only when it slammed shut behind her, did she take an easy breath. She'd never admit it, but he was right. She *had* begun to like having him around.

Bar sales had gone up significantly since he'd started working at the café. That was the *only* reason his presence didn't annoy her quite as much as it had in the beginning. It definitely wasn't because she kinda liked him as a person, or that the man's body was more chiseled than Mount Rushmore. *Definitely not that.*

Continually reminding herself that he had a different set of priorities and couldn't be trusted was the best medicine for keeping her libido in check. That and the itsy-bitsy other thing about how he might throw her in jail for money laundering.

Without getting up from the ultra-cushy dog bed Andi had purchased at the local pet store, Stray raised her head, her dark eyes brimming with curiosity. A moment later, she rose from the bed and walked to where Andi stood by the door.

Since she'd started letting Stray stay in the house overnight, the dog had begun anticipating her moods even more. Stray sniffed her hand—the one she'd been petting Saxon with. Andi recognized the second Stray identified the smell of her new canine buddy. Her head lifted, and she let out a soft whimper, taking quick, mincing steps with her front paws and pushing at Andi's hand with her snout. The message was loud and clear: Stray was excited and wanted to play with Saxon.

As she stared at the dog, it struck her that Stray's reaction to Saxon was eerily similar to Andi's reaction to Nick. When the man was near, it was as if someone had flipped a toggle switch that sent electricity shooting through her body. This had to stop.

Cold. Shower.

She gave Stray a quick pat on the head, then grabbed a bottle of water and went upstairs. Before heading into the bathroom, she checked her phone on the nightstand. *No missed calls.*

After turning on the shower, she stripped off her damp clothes and stepped beneath the cool spray. When she began soaping up, far too realistic visions of what Nick's incredible physique would look like beneath the shower swam before her eyes. *Shame on me for having such thoughts.* Then again, he'd seen *her* practically naked in the shower, so she shouldn't have anything to be guilty about. *Fair's fair.*

That evening, Andi glanced around the DPC's dining room. The musician she'd hired was due in less than an hour for setup and sound check. Customers were starting to trickle in for dinner, but the real crowd wouldn't begin arriving for another hour to get seats for the show.

She set the last of the candles on one of the tables, then looked around the room with satisfaction. Everything was set for tonight. There wasn't anything left to do except wait for her musician.

Barry Schultz had been playing at a club in Boston when she'd first heard him. She'd been instantly drawn to his combination of contemporary, crowd-pleasing songs everyone was familiar with and his own original music. Barry was a one-man show, alternating between the piano and the guitar. She'd invested a fair amount in advertising, and it had paid off. The DPC had nearly sold out in advance. There was still a chance this live entertainment gig could carry her through until Joe showed up and exonerated her. Otherwise... *I can't fail. I won't.*

Across the room, Nick cleared away a few plates and glasses from a table, then carried them to a bin. She liked how he pitched in when things got busy. As she watched him head for the bar, she couldn't stop staring.

A black T-shirt stretched tightly across his back as he leaned over to deposit the dirty dishes in the bin. Faded jeans cupped his perfect ass and long legs.

Several women twisted their necks to check him out. One of them said something to him, and he walked over. She couldn't hear their conversation, but all the women were grinning like idiots. Even Nick was smiling as he carried on what she assumed was an inane, flirtatious conversation. One of the women handed him her business card. He accepted the card and slid it into the back pocket of his jeans. As he disappeared into the kitchen, the women leaned in to whisper amongst each other, giggling.

A spurt of unwanted jealousy shot up her spine. The Napkin Girls now had business cards. Groaning, she shook her head. She had no business tallying the number of times he'd been hit on.

Tucking the empty tray under her arm, she went to the bar and stowed it away. When she turned around, Nick was carrying a plate loaded with fries and a panini, something she'd learned was his favorite food.

With his free hand, he tugged the business card from his back pocket and surprised her by dropping it in the trash container under the bar. "Any calls?" He nodded at the phone clipped to her waist.

"No." She lifted her chin, incensed that he'd think she would keep something that important from him, and secretly pleased that he'd trashed the card.

When she began to walk away, he reached out to rest his hand on her bare shoulder.

"Hold on." The second his fingers contacted her skin, delicious tendrils of heat swirled up her neck, warming her face. "I didn't mean anything by that."

"Hey, Nick." Tess squeezed past them and grabbed the

soda dispenser, filling a glass with seltzer.

"Hey." He smiled, dropping his hand then heading to the other side of the bar. Along the way, he cast Andi a quizzical look over his shoulder.

Shit. I'm turning into a b-i-t-c-h.

Andi watched as he popped a fry in his mouth.

Tess leaned in. "I know you've sworn off men for all eternity, so what's going on between you two?"

"What do you mean?" She really didn't want to have this conversation.

"You know exactly what I mean." Tess urged her away from the bar and out of Nick's earshot. "Two weeks ago, I catch you guys in not one but two torrid embraces hot enough to fry an egg. Since then, you've been avoiding each other, but you both look like you're ready to rip each other's clothes off."

"That is *not* true." But it was, a little, and she was embarrassed that others had picked up on it. On *her* emotions, anyway. He probably hadn't given her another thought since the night he'd nearly kissed her. "If he wants to get laid while he's here, I'm sure he's got a long list of Napkin Girls waiting beside their phones for him to call."

"Puh-lease, girlfriend." Tess crossed her arms over her sequined tank top. "Marty, Kara, Zoe, and I have a betting pool as to when the two of you are gonna quit with the foreplay and just do it."

More heat crept up her neck to her face as she dragged Tess outside onto the deck. Luckily, it was still so hot only a few tables had customers. "Nothing is happening between us. *Nothing.*"

Tess laughed. "I know I warned you to be careful around him, but I really think the feeling is mutual on his part."

"What feeling? The only feeling he has for me is the hope that I cooperate with his investigation."

"Are you blind? He can't keep his eyes off you. As soon as your back is turned, he watches your every move."

"Yeah, but not for the reason you think. He's only keeping tabs on me so he doesn't miss me taking another call from Joe."

"Honey," she continued, "that's not the only reason he keeps tabs on you. Trust me. Hunky, gorgeous guys like him who actually have brains don't come along every day. For a cop, he might be all right after all."

"It doesn't matter." Andi shook her head. "He's off-limits to me, and I'm off-limits to him."

"And why is that?" Tess prodded.

"For starters, I'm still a suspect he thinks may be helping Joe. And my personal rule still stands. No. Men." At least until one she could trust again came along.

"If he really believed you were a suspect, I don't think he'd be making with the touchy-feely so much with you. What else you got?"

"He has zero sense of humor." Kind of, although she was beginning to think he really did have one.

"That's ridiculous." Tess leaned against the railing. "He laughs all the time, and the bar is packed every night because of him. The women love him, and the guys dig him, so how stiff can he be?" She giggled. "Okay, perhaps not the best choice of words, but you know what I mean."

Andi shook her head. "I can't trust him. He's twisting *my* life around to suit *his* needs." *Sound familiar?* she reminded herself. Just like Steve had done.

Tess turned to face her. "Has he lied to you?"

"Well, no. At least not that I know of." Andi watched a young woman in the dog run leash up her dog. "What's with the Team Nick thing? I seem to recall you warning me to be careful of cops, him in particular."

"*I* would never get involved with one." Tess pointed to

her chest then to Andi. "Doesn't mean *you* can't."

Again, she shook her head, although even she had to admit her resolve was slipping. "He's not my type. I need someone who likes music, and books, and who wouldn't feel like a sissy going to a musical with me."

"I give up." Tess flung her hands in the air and went back inside the restaurant.

Andi took a minute to scan the deck for empties. Satisfied the waitresses hadn't missed any, she joined Tess inside where she was standing at one end of the bar, grinning. Tess canted her head to where Nick was polishing off the last of his panini. On the bar next to his plate was an open book.

"Well, there ya go," she said. "Cops *can* read. Looks like you can put a check mark next to at least one of your criteria." She smiled smugly and walked into the kitchen.

He closed the book, tucking it under his arm, then picked up his plate and headed in her direction. "What?" His eyes narrowed suspiciously.

She pointed to the book—*The Count of Monte Cristo*—unable to hide the look of surprise on her face. "It's a book."

His mouth twisted, and not for the first time she noted the contrast between the hard, masculine features of his face and those soft lips that he'd pressed to her forehead. "I *can* read, you know."

"*The Count of Monte Cristo*?" She smiled. "I figured you'd read cop books, or books about federal agents and spies."

"I always wanted a sword," he said with a straight face.

She huffed. "You men and your phallic symbols."

He chuckled, a rich sound that sent tingles dancing up her spine.

Tess let out a low whistle from where she now stood at the kitchen doorway. "Who. Is. That?"

Eric stood just inside the front door. His gaze locked

with Nick's. If Eric's presence hadn't been enough to have her tensing with worry, the man standing next to him was. FBI Special Agent Cox.

Her heart sank. Something about the expression on Cox's face could only mean one thing... Bad news.

• • •

Feds working on a Saturday night?

Only if bad shit was going down that couldn't wait until Monday.

Nick set his book and empty plate on the ledge beneath the bar.

Andi grabbed his arm, her fingers cool against his skin. "Something's wrong, isn't it?" She glanced to where Eric and Cox were seating themselves at the other side of the bar.

He looked into her worried eyes. Lying to her was something he couldn't do. "Probably."

"Then I want to be part of this conversation." She started past him.

"Wait." He stretched out an arm, stopping her.

Anger flashed in her eyes. "Anything about this concerns me, too."

"Be patient. I need to speak with them first. Alone." Mainly because of the text message he'd received earlier in the day from Eric.

Cox had heard back from Andi's bank. The fact that the agent had shown up in person to deliver the results on a weekend didn't bode well.

"Okay." She held up her hands in defeat.

As she turned and walked to the front door, he glimpsed Meera and Frank waiting in line for a table. They both waved to him, smiling.

He flexed his fingers, still feeling the warmth from Andi's

slim body. Aside from putting his hand on her shoulder, that had been the first time he'd touched her in two weeks. *Two weeks of torture.*

Keeping physical distance from her was driving him out of his mind. But he couldn't go there. Not while she was still a suspect, and not while she was involved in this case.

Who am I kidding?

The real reason for keeping his distance was that his heart wasn't capable of deep attachment. Innocent or not, she would always be out of his reach. Although for the first time since his wife died, he felt the undeniable urge to bash through that self-imposed barrier and see where he landed.

He tipped his chin in the direction of the temporary bartender Andi had hired to back him up tonight. Mark, a thirty-something guy with dark hair and brown eyes, nodded back, acknowledging Nick's request that he cover him for a few minutes.

When he came around the outside of the bar to where Eric and Cox were seated, the first things he noted were the bags under Cox's eyes and the worry lines on the man's forehead.

"You look like shit. To what do I owe the honor of your presence on a Saturday night?" He looked from Eric to Cox, although his question was directed solely at the FBI agent.

Cox shot Nick a fuck-you look. "First off, there were no prints in Myer's house besides his, Andi's, and a housekeeper who cleans once a month."

"And the cigarette butt outside the front door?" Nick asked.

Cox shook his head. "No prints and not enough DNA to run through CODIS."

"You could have told me that Monday." Nick crossed his arms, knowing damn well there was another reason for Cox's visit.

"We still don't know about Andi."

His gut clenched. "Meaning?"

"Meaning," the agent continued, "the bank is dragging its ass getting back to us with more information on that wire transfer from her account. They said they'll call us on Monday." Cox's expression darkened. "Unfortunately, that's not all."

"What else?" Whatever the man was about to say was the real reason they'd shown up on a Saturday night.

"I'll take this one." Eric pulled a few papers from his back pocket. "Myer slipped across the Canadian border through Quebec two weeks ago, the day before the search warrant. We don't know how, but he did. Kade's been spot-checking for border crossings, and somehow it never made it into the system until last night."

"Two weeks ago?" He got in Cox's face. "How did that happen with a Red Notice in place?" In his years with the state police, he'd grabbed several foreign criminals on Interpol Red Notices.

Cox took a resigned breath. "Because there *was* no Red Notice."

"Come again?" Nick said in a pissed-off tone. "Because I must have misheard you."

"You didn't." The agent shook his head. "Apparently, the DOJ attorney implementing the Red Notice went home early that day. *Before* filing the notice with Interpol. Naturally, that was the same day Myer slipped across the border."

"Fuck." He took a calming breath, resisting the urge to heave a nearby glass at the wall.

"We're working with the Border Enforcement Security Task Force," Eric said, pausing to glance at Tess as she strode through the dining tables, balancing a tray laden with dinner plates. "Between DHS, the Bureau, and the Mounties, maybe we can track his ass down."

"Meanwhile," Cox said as he got off his stool, "the AUSA wants you to stay put here. He's convinced Myer will call Andi again."

So was Nick, and that couldn't happen soon enough. He'd concocted this plan for the sole purpose of getting to the gun dealer, but now what he needed more than anything was to get as far away from Andi as soon as possible. His personal feelings were more than beginning to cloud his professional judgment and mess with his impartiality. The only way to get reassigned was to see this case through to the end.

"Sorry, pal." Cox sent him an apologetic look. "Stay in touch."

"Right." *Hell.*

The minute Cox was out the door, Eric threw down a twenty. "Buy you a beer? You look like you need it."

He dragged a hand down his face. "You know it." He hadn't been drinking while on duty—bar duty, that was—but tonight, he could sure use a cold one.

As soon as Mark poured them both a Sam Adams, Nick held up his glass to Eric's. Eric, however, was staring across the dining room again.

"What's *her* story?" He nodded to the DPC's feisty manager. "She's cute."

Nick sent his friend a disapproving look. "Stay away from her. At least until this assignment's over. I don't want to complicate things more than they are already." Truthfully, in the past two weeks he'd come to like Tess, but Eric was commitment-phobic, and he didn't want to see Tess get hurt.

"You should talk, bro." Eric took a sip of his beer. "Every time I walk in here, you're eyeballing the lovely Ms. Andi Hardt."

He took a long drink of beer, not willing to admit anything. Not even to Eric, who was one of his best friends.

"You know," Eric continued, "I don't believe she's guilty

any more than you do. Once she's in the clear—"

"Not gonna happen." His gaze found the subject of their conversation chatting with Meera and Frank, who'd just sat down at a table near the piano. "There's too much riding on this case to fuck it up." Besides, he was no better than Eric at commitment, although their reasons for detachment were totally different.

Eric set down his glass, holding up a hand. "Just sayin'."

"Yeah, well, don't." He gripped his beer tighter.

Whether she was innocent or not, he'd be lying if he didn't admit that his motivations for bringing in Myer were becoming murky.

Since he'd found Tanya with the gun in her hand, he'd made it his life's mission to get illegal guns off the streets. It was his own personal brand of justice, and a way of saying his final goodbye. He still wanted to nail the gun dealer, but now his mission had a new component—proving Andi's innocence. To do that, he needed Myer.

"Something already happen between you two?"

He caught Eric watching him, concern in his eyes.

"No." *Liar.*

"Well?" his friend prodded.

"I almost kissed her." *Twice, but who the fuck's counting?*

"Ah." He smiled briefly, then nodded in understanding. "She *almost* kiss you back?"

Hell yeah.

Eric's face sobered. "Tanya's been gone a long time. She'd want you to be happy. We all do."

He knew that. Tanya *had* wanted him to be happy. She'd said so in the letter she'd written him the day she'd killed herself.

Someone touched him on the back. *Andi.* As always, her flowery scent preceded her.

She gazed up at him with a hopeful expression. "Do you

have any good news? Do you know where Joe is?"

"Hi, Andi." Eric smiled.

"Special Agent Miller," she said coolly.

"Call me Eric," he insisted.

"Eric, then." She smiled back, but her mouth was tight, and he knew her expressive face well enough to know it was forced.

"Joe crossed into Canada two weeks ago," Nick told her.

She let out a heavy breath. "Not exactly the sign of someone considering turning himself in, is it?"

He opened his mouth, about to agree with her assessment, when five men shouted in unison.

"Nick!"

Taking up every inch of the front doorway were his best friends. He'd all but forgotten they were coming into town to supplement security at the Northeast Expo.

"Sonofabitch," he muttered as the entire crew surged to the bar. He hoped Eric had filled them in that he was quasi-undercover. Customers—particularly women—were beginning to stare at the boisterous bunch.

"I take it these are friends of yours?" Andi watched as they clapped Eric on the back, then took up surrounding stools.

"Sadly, yes." In reality, he was always glad to see them.

She leaned in. "They're police, too?"

He nodded. "Police or federal agents."

"Wonderful." She pasted on a sarcastic smile. "A bar full of cops and feds. Did you call in backup to make sure I don't run off to meet Joe in Canada?"

He looked down and spoke the truth. "I never thought you'd do that. Despite what you think, I trust you to see this through."

For a moment she looked at him with disbelief, then her eyes softened. "Thank you."

Those two little words caused something inside him to shift, altering his perspective and forcing him to take a virtual step back. They'd come to a crossroads, where his personal and professional lanes intersected. Exercising caution was *the* paramount tenet of police training, so as he stood there, gazing down into her clear blue eyes, he was frozen in time and place, assessing and reassessing.

Questions and concerns jabbed at his brain and his memory, and when forced to make a choice, he honestly didn't know which way he'd turn. "You're welcome," he said finally, and was rewarded with the second genuine smile he'd ever seen on her face. One that had his gut twisting with the need to kiss her. For real, this time.

Matt was the first to extend his hand. "Good to see you, Nick."

He took Matt's hand, shaking it firmly. He'd walk through fire for any of his friends, but he and Matt knew each other's shit like nobody's business. "How's Trista?"

At the mention of his wife, Matt grinned like an idiot. "She's good."

A year ago, Matt had married a CIA analyst he'd fallen crazy-ass in love with. Nick had stood up for him at the wedding. Since then, he'd come to cherish his friendship with Matt's new wife almost as much as he valued Matt's. He still got a kick out of how a five-foot-one-inch sprite had tamed his best friend. Matt was over a foot taller than Trista, but he was a doting pile of mush where his wife was concerned.

"This is Matt Connors." He rested his hand at Andi's back, urging her closer to the bar. For a moment, she stiffened at his touch. Then, unless he was imagining it, she actually leaned back, increasing the contact. And damned if he didn't keep his hand right where it was.

"How do you do." She reached out to shake hands with Matt.

He went down the line, introducing Kade Sampson and Dayne Andrews next. Despite being the DHS's toughest K-9 cop, Kade's dimpled smile never failed to win over the ladies. Dayne's ruggedness and intense green eyes drew women like flies, but he remained his usual, reticent self.

As Andi shook hands with Markus York, Nick eyed the grisly scar over his friend's left eye. Markus had gotten into some kind of scuffle a few months back but wouldn't talk about it. Since he'd been wounded, his friend's obsidian eyes seemed darker than ever.

"And this," he said as he stopped in front of the man whose cocky grin and swagger were a source of never-ending amusement, "is Jaime Pataglia."

When Andi held out her hand, Jaime clasped it, then pressed his lips to her fingers. She grinned, and Nick ground his teeth, shooting Jaime a look that said it all. *Back the fuck off.* He knew his friend didn't mean anything by the overtly flirtatious display. Hardly. Jaime's excessively friendly manner was a time-perfected cover for some seriously heavy baggage the man had been carrying around for years.

"Romeo"—Eric dropped a hand on Jaime's shoulder and tugged him back onto the barstool—"I think the lady's had enough of your smoochy city ways." He shot the other man a warning look.

Somehow, Eric had known exactly what Nick had been thinking—that if Jaime didn't get his lips off Andi's fingers, he might have to take him out back and beat some sense into him.

Nick had no business going all Neanderthal-possessive on Andi. They'd *almost* kissed. Big deal. That didn't make her *his*. And Jaime was his friend, for fuck's sake.

But I want her.

That was the thought hammering in his brain as he watched her blush and take back her hand. The realization sent his possessive thoughts into overdrive, and he resisted his caveman need to brand her lips with his right then and there in front of his friends and everyone else in the restaurant.

"Gentlemen, it's been a pleasure." She glanced to the front door where Tess was playing hostess. The place was brimming with people trying to get in for the show. "I'd better get back to work."

He tracked her as she joined Tess at the front door. When he turned back to his friends, Matt chuckled. Eric and Jaime grinned. Dayne, Markus, and Kade rolled their eyes.

"Fuck all of you," Nick said as he went back behind the bar to pour his friends beers. Laughter followed him every step of the way.

He grabbed enough money from his tip jar to cover a round of beers, then stuffed the money into the register. When he turned around, Andi caught his attention. Her cell phone was glued to her ear.

Nick's heart rate kicked up.

She said something to Tess, then her eyes locked with his. She hastily made her way through the thickening crowd and came behind the bar. As she got closer, he glimpsed the sheer terror on her face.

This had to be the call they'd been waiting for.

Myer.

As she drew nearer, his pulse thrummed faster. Something was wrong. *Very* wrong.

Chapter Ten

Andi clenched the phone tighter. This was awful.

Her anxiety ratcheted up as she wended her way through the crowd. Odd how Nick was the first person she sought for help.

"What is it?" he asked when she reached him. Concern was evident in his eyes. The crowd was so loud he had to lean down to be heard. "Is it Myer?"

She shook her head, trying not to let panic consume her as she listened to the voice on the other end of the phone. "Okay," she said into her cell. "I understand completely. No worries. We'll be fine." *No, they wouldn't be.* There was no way out of this mess. She ended the call and reclipped the phone to her waist, looking around the room. Most of the dining tables were full. The front door was jammed with more people trying to get in. She wanted to scream.

Nick clasped her upper arms. "Andi. Talk to me. What's wrong, baby?"

Baby?

She didn't know why he'd called her that, but she liked

it, and his touch was a soothing balm to her frenzied nerves.

"I'm in trouble." *Six-foot-deep trouble.*

He cupped her chin. "Tell me what's wrong?"

"It's my musician," she cried. "His car broke down somewhere in Pennsylvania. He didn't have his phone with him, so he wasn't able to call sooner. He won't be coming tonight." She took an unsteady breath, her mind racing with entertainment alternatives, but there were none. None that could possibly justify the cover charge all these people had paid. "I've got a restaurant full of customers expecting entertainment, and he's *not coming.* This is the first live performance here. If word gets out that my singer didn't show, it could mean disaster for the DPC's reputation." Something she couldn't afford, especially now.

She looked around the dining room again, her panic growing. The crowd was getting antsy. Voices were getting louder. "I'm screwed." She looked first into Nick's eyes, then at Tess, who'd joined them. "What am I going to do?"

"Don't look at me." Tess held up her hands. "I can't play the piano, *or* the guitar, and I can't hold a tune to save my life."

"Nick?" Nick's friend, Matt, looked at him with raised brows, giving her the impression he was waiting for something.

"Nick," Eric repeated, banging his pint glass on the bar.

Each of Nick's other friends began banging their fists on the bar in unison, chanting, "Nick, Nick, Nick!"

Customers all around the bar started clapping and cheering, though they had no idea what they were cheering about. Heck, even *she* didn't know.

He narrowed his eyes, glaring at his friends. She didn't understand why, but he didn't seem happy.

"You can't leave a damsel in distress," Matt shouted over the chanting.

Nick took a deep breath, rolling his eyes to the ceiling as

if he were sending a prayer—or, a curse—to the heavens.

"Cover the bar with Mark," he said to Tess.

"Yes, sir." She gave him a jaunty salute as she took over at the beer taps.

His face softened, then he touched his fingers to Andi's cheek. "Give me a minute. I've got this." Then he slipped past her and disappeared into the kitchen.

Over the din, she barely heard the kitchen's side door bang shut. *Great. First my singer abandons me. Now, my bartender, too.* And what did "I've got this" mean?

Matt, Jaime, and Eric began clapping. Kade, Markus, and Dayne did a three-way fist bump. There was no time to dwell on what they were so happy about.

The din inside the DPC rose until she could barely hear herself think. Worry had her twisting a towel in her hands. She was a savvy businesswoman. Surely, she could come up with something.

A free round of drinks for everyone?

No, one drink could never make up for the cover charge, and she couldn't afford the loss in revenue.

A dance contest? Trivia?

All lousy ideas. She had to come up with something else, and fast.

She looked nervously over her shoulder. *Where is Nick?* The drink orders were backing up, and both Mark and Tess had their hands full. Looking back at Matt's friends, she caught Matt and Eric grinning expectantly.

"What did he mean by, 'I've got this'?" she shouted at them, looking from one man to the other.

"You'll see," Matt replied with a full-blown grin.

"See what?" When he didn't respond, she looked at Eric, but Eric now had his eyes glued to something behind her.

She followed his gaze to where Tess was shaking a martini. After she poured the drink and set it on the bar in front of a customer, Tess looked up and smiled shyly at Eric.

Oh, boy. Tess didn't know Eric was a cop—a federal agent. Not yet. But that was a conversation for another time. When she didn't have a restaurant full of people waiting for live entertainment that wasn't going to materialize.

The kitchen door banged shut, and a moment later, Nick strode in. Without stopping, he wound his way to the front of the room where she'd set up a stool and a microphone next to the piano.

She stared, not really comprehending the meaning of what she'd seen him carrying—a guitar case. She continued watching, dumbfounded, as he proceeded to unpack a gleaming wood guitar. After stowing the case behind him on the floor, he sat on the stool and began strumming the strings lightly, twisting the pegheads as he tuned the instrument. Then he turned on the microphone, and the crowd hushed.

"Good evening, ladies and gentlemen." His clear baritone was more pronounced with the mic. "Unfortunately, the person you came to hear tonight was unable to make it. So you'll have to settle for me. I'm Nick. Your bartender."

As a unit, his friends started whooping, hollering, and clapping, which got the entire crowd clapping and cheering with them.

"You go, Nicky-boy!" Matt shouted.

Eric, Jaime, and Kade whistled, as did many women. Even Markus, whom Andi had noticed didn't say much, wore a slight smile.

Nick began strumming the Troggs' "Wild Thing," and when he started to sing, her eyes went wide. Her jaw dropped. Nick's voice was…mesmerizing.

"Oh my God." Tess squeezed her shoulder. "Did you have any idea he could sing? Like *that*?"

Numbly, she shook her head. When they exchanged looks, she saw the same shocked expression on Tess's face that she knew was reflected on her own.

"Yeah," Andi mumbled. "Who knew?" That her state-trooper–bartender could not only play the guitar, but sing as well as anyone she'd heard on the radio. There really were two totally different people wrapped up in that gorgeous, hunky body.

As the song went on, people waved their arms in the air, swaying to the music and singing along. By the time Nick got to the last line—*"shake it, shake it, wild thing"*—most of the women were on their feet, shaking and gyrating their hips. Even Kara and Zoe had stopped serving and were dancing alongside everyone else.

When Nick finished, the crowd roared and clapped, and Andi found herself applauding right along with them.

"That man has hidden talents." Tess leaned closer. "Didn't you say he wasn't your type? That you need a man with common interests, like books and music? Can you say, 'check mark'?" She snickered before going back to mixing and pouring drinks.

"Hidden talents," Andi repeated. The man was amazing. His voice was incredible, and the way he got the crowd going within seconds was nothing short of a miracle. He'd saved her ass tonight.

And where did he learn to sing and play the guitar like that?

Next, he launched into a set that included, among others, "Brown-Eyed Girl," "Save a Horse Ride a Cowboy," culminating in Neil Diamond's "Sweet Caroline." She stayed behind the bar, helping Tess and Mark keep up with orders. Kara, Zoe, and the extra waitresses she'd hired for the night buzzed around the tables.

After thirty minutes, Nick took a break, and the applause was deafening. He laid down his guitar then headed to the bar where his friends were still clapping.

She grinned, still in disbelief as she moved closer to where Nick's friends were now clapping him on the back. Leaning over, she shouted, "Buy you a beer?"

"Maybe later." He winked. "For now, I'll take two glasses of water."

"Coming right up." She squeezed water from a nozzle into two glasses, unable to peel her eyes from him as he gave all his friends dirty looks. As she carried over his water glasses, it hit her. For some reason, he hadn't wanted to do this, and not just because it wasn't part of his job. His friends had heckled him into it. He'd done it for *her*.

That stony resolve she'd erected to stay away from men— Nick in particular—slipped a solid foot. As if he felt her eyes on him, he turned and met her gaze. Since he was too far away to hear, she mouthed the words *thank you*.

You're welcome, he mouthed back, then one corner of his mouth lifted into a lopsided grin.

Inexplicably, her heart began thumping harder. She set the water on the bar in front of him, and he guzzled the first glass without taking a breath. Her eyes went to his strong throat as he swallowed. *Wow.*

"Not bad, huh?"

She turned to find Matt watching her. The man really was handsome. All Nick's friends were, but Nick was the only one who got her blood pumping until she thought it would shoot out her ears.

"You're right. Not bad at all." And Tess was right, too. A man like Nick didn't come along every day.

Fifteen minutes later, he surprised her yet again by relocating the microphone to the top of the piano and sitting on the piano bench. Clapping greeted him, followed by whistling. The women in the crowd absolutely loved him.

"Thank you," Nick said. "I'd like to dedicate the next song to my best friends in the back of the bar."

This got his friends hooting even louder this time, lifting their beers to Nick as he launched into a raucous rendition of Garth Brooks's "Friends in Low Places."

For the next thirty minutes, the drinks flowed, and Marty sent out plate after plate of appetizers. Nick pounded the keys, engaging the crowd by taking requests and acknowledging two birthdays, one anniversary, and one couple who'd just gotten engaged. He finished up his last set with Jerry Lee Lewis's "Great Balls of Fire." She'd thought the applause had been deafening before, but that had been nothing compared to this. She resisted the impulse to cover her ears.

It was after one in the morning when she and Nick closed up the restaurant and let Saxon and Stray out of the kennel for a walk along the edge of the lake. The sky was clear, and the full moon reflected off the still water. With his dark coat, Saxon was barely visible, trotting ahead of them. Stray kept pace, her golden-brown coat shining in the moonlight, letting them know where the dogs were at all times.

For several minutes, they walked in comfortable silence broken only by the chirp of crickets and the hooting of an owl.

"Were you ever going to tell me you play the guitar and piano, and sing as well as anyone on the radio?"

"No," he said simply.

She laughed. "Why not?"

"Because it's not relevant."

"Not relevant?" She stopped walking and caught his arm. "But you're an amazing singer. The way you engaged the audience...you're a natural showman. How in the world did you wind up being a cop?"

"I used to love performing, but law enforcement was my

calling." He began walking again, giving her no choice but to fall in step.

"Where did you perform?"

"High school and college, mostly." He whistled softly, and both dogs came loping out of the darkness. "In school, I was torn between football and musicals, so I did both. I played football in the fall, and did musicals in the spring."

"Were you any good at football?" She couldn't imagine him not being as good at football as he was at performing, or at being a cop.

He laughed. "I could have gone pro, but I joined the marines right out of school."

"Why?"

"Helping others and protecting this country and what it stands for was a stronger calling. Running around a football field wouldn't have cut it."

"Were you one of those SEALs?"

He laughed. "No. I went with Force Recon."

"What's that?"

"Some consider it the marine equivalent of the SEALs."

"How come I've never heard of it?"

He gave a low chuckle. "Most people haven't. We like to joke that SEALs are a bunch of sissies compared to Force Recon. Everyone's heard of SEALS because there've been more books and movies about them than any other special ops team."

"How long were you in the marines?"

"Six years."

"After that?"

"I got hired by the state police."

"Is that why you stopped performing?"

It was a long moment before he responded. "I just didn't want to do it anymore."

The path veered sharply to the right, and their arms

brushed, giving her goose bumps. This was their first real conversation about something other than Joe, and she didn't want it to end.

"Why not?" Somehow, she sensed there was a specific reason he didn't perform anymore, and she found herself wanting to know more about him, and what made him tick.

"I was twenty-seven when I became a trooper. Shortly after that I got married and only played or sang occasionally for my wife."

Andi froze in mid-step. *He's married?* Her heart all but stopped beating. *This can't be happening.* God, she felt like a fool for starting to actually feel something for him.

"Andi?" He stood a few feet ahead of her. "You coming?"

"No." She called for Stray, then waited for the dog to sit at her side. "I'm tired. I need to go home." She turned to head back to the house, and he clasped her arm.

"Bull." With his thumb and forefinger, he gently forced her chin up. "My wife died five years ago. Since then, music stopped giving me any enjoyment. That's why the guitar was in my truck. I was going to donate it." In the moonlight, his gray eyes sparkled like polished silver. "I didn't mean for it to come out like that."

"I'm so sorry," she whispered, torn between relief that he wasn't married and sadness at his loss. He must have loved his wife very much. So much that her death had convinced him that he no longer deserved to experience the joy of his music.

"For what?" His brows furrowed as he dropped his hands first to her shoulders, then to her bare arms.

"Your wife." Curiosity had her wanting to ask how she died, but she didn't. "Is that why you didn't want to sing tonight?" *Because it was something special you did for her?*

Jealousy for a dead woman made her feel small and petty, but she couldn't help it. He'd loved someone enough to marry her. That's what *she* used to want—before she'd lost faith.

He ran his hands up and down her arms, sending delicious shivers shooting across her skin. "I wasn't prepared to sing tonight, but I wanted to help you."

"Thank you again for that. Truly. I'm sorry that it brought up bad memories for you."

"At first it did." His hands stilled. "Then it felt good. Cathartic."

"I'm glad." In the dim light, she detected a slight smile on his lips. "Music is a beautiful thing no one should have to live without."

Wordlessly, he cupped the back of her neck, his thumb grazing her cheek. His breath was warm on her face. "You smell like pretty flowers."

Involuntarily, her lips parted. "It's freesia," she whispered, and her heart began to race. He was going to kiss her. *And God help me, I want him to.*

"It's nice," he whispered back.

As he lowered his head, her gaze was drawn to his mouth. His lips were soft, feathering hers before adding light pressure, urging hers to part. The kiss was gentle, his touch exquisitely tender on her cheek.

His tongue sought hers, and she uttered a tiny gasp, moaning low in her throat, pressing her lips harder against his. Kissing him back might very well be a colossal mistake, but it was what she wanted more than anything, and when he began kissing her more deeply, something fierce and instinctive shot through her blood, a craving she could no longer deny. Every one of her nerve endings sparked for the first time in so many years she'd lost count.

She arched against him, sliding her hands around his waist and up his back. Beneath the soft T-shirt, solid muscle rippled at her touch. His heart hammered against her breasts, and his big body shuddered as if he were holding back.

Something wriggled between them. *Stray.* To her dismay, the dog forced them apart.

"Quite the protective little watchdog you've got." He uttered a low laugh then leaned down to give Stray a pat on the head.

Not to be outdone, Saxon pushed between their legs, panting and demanding attention. Andi rubbed the other dog's ears.

"C'mon." He laced his fingers with hers. "It's late. I'll walk you home."

With her pulse still fluttering, the walk back passed in silence, but inside she was smiling. She didn't understand how or why, but tonight there'd been a discernible shift in their relationship and her perception of him.

Her fingers were totally engulfed by his large, calloused hand, and as exhausted as she was, part of her wished the walk back to her house was longer than it was. The other part warned her she'd be a naive fool to forget that he held her future *and* the future of the DPC in his hands. Right now, she was incredibly vulnerable and still needed to tread carefully around him.

When they arrived at her back porch the motion sensor light kicked on.

Nick stopped short, pointing then insinuating his body between hers and the porch. "What *is* that?"

She looked around his shoulder in the direction of his outstretched arm, then giggled. "A telescope, silly. Don't worry. It won't attack you." Pushing past him, she headed up the stairs, as did the dogs, and walked onto the porch. "I told you amateur astronomy ran in my family. When my dad and uncle were kids, they made this telescope out of parts from the Williamsburg Bridge. My great-uncle was an engineer in the city and used to bring home spare pieces that were going to be thrown out as scrap. Those spare parts are now a telescope."

He followed her up the stairs, eyeing the telescope warily, as if he expected it to come to life and start shooting. With its spindly tripod legs and the long optical tube made from an old pipe, it did kind of look like a cross between a mounted machine gun and a rocket launcher.

"I'll see you tomorrow," he said, casting one more wary glance at the telescope before dropping a light kiss on her lips. "And don't forget to lock up behind you. This door *and* the front door."

"I won't." The door creaked as she pushed it open. Stray darted inside and trotted to her bowl, crunching on a few remaining kibble leftovers from that morning. When Andi stepped into the kitchen Nick and Saxon were still there, waiting, she knew, for her to close the door.

"Do you even have a deadbolt?"

"No."

He shook his head, frowning. "I'm calling a professional security company first thing in the morning."

"You will not." She parked her fists on her hips. "I lived in the city half my life. The last thing I want is to feel so paranoid that I need a security system."

"With everything going on, I don't want you taking any chances. Humor me."

"Again?" She'd come to realize he used those two words a lot. "You're incorrigible." Andi shook her head, although deep down, she was touched by his concern for her safety. "Good night." She grinned and shut the door.

Sighing, she leaned back against the doorframe. Part of her had wanted to invite him inside for a nightcap. *A nightcap. Right.* What she'd wanted was *him.* Kissing her more. Touching her. Undressing her with his big, strong hands. The enormity of the moment wasn't lost on her.

Despite who and what Nick was, let alone why he was

there, he was the first man since Steve that she'd thought about. *Really* thought about.

She unclipped her phone from her waist and set it on the counter. Except for the sound of Stray licking the inside of her kibble bowl, the house was quiet. *Eerily* quiet. Though she wasn't ready to admit it to Nick, maybe a security system wasn't such a bad idea. She flicked on the kitchen lights to see Stray pushing the dish along the floor until it hit the wall and could go no farther. She began noisily lapping water, but stopped abruptly.

Stray lifted her head, water dribbling back into the bowl. Her ears went back, and she let out a low growl. Hair on her spine stood straight up, then she bolted into the living room, her nails scrabbling on the kitchen tile.

Andi followed. "What's the matter, girl? Did another raccoon get inside?" That had happened only a month ago.

She'd taken one step into the darkened living room when a hand clamped around her mouth and an arm came around her waist, hauling her backward against something hard.

For a full second, shock overrode all rational thought, and she froze. *Oh my God. I'm going to die.*

Then fear and panic exploded in her mind, and her fighting instinct kicked in. Hard.

She began clawing frantically at her attacker's fingers, and when that didn't work, she swung her arms behind her, contacting her fist. Beneath the hand covering her mouth, she screamed, but the sound was muffled, and she doubted anyone outside the house would hear.

"Knock it off, bitch!" a male voice hissed.

Like hell I will.

With renewed vigor, she swung backward again with her fist and hit something soft.

"Fuck!"

Her heart raced painfully. The pulse at her throat roared

in her ears, and still she could only manage to move the smallest amount of air through her nostrils. *Not enough!*

The arm around her waist tightened, doubling the difficulty of breathing.

Escape! Don't give up without a fight! If she didn't get more air soon, she'd black out.

Do something!

Fingers tightened, jabbing into her cheek, forcing her to suck in loud, wheezing breaths through her nose. Her chest heaved from the effort. More panic escalated through her body, and with every inhalation came the nauseating smells of sweat and body odor.

Stray barked furiously, snapping at the attacker's legs. A shadow in the corner of the room moved. Another man emerged from the darkness, reared back his foot, and kicked Stray in the side. The dog yelped, but still had enough game in her to keep snapping. The booted foot lashed out again, this time kicking Stray so hard she hit the wall.

The dog whimpered and fell to the floor in a heap and didn't move again.

Bastards. Fueled by rage, Andi kicked backward and tried to bite the hand covering her mouth.

"I said knock it off, bitch, or I shoot the dog!" The second man in the room extended his arm toward Stray.

Andi froze. Light from the kitchen gleamed against something shiny in his hand—*a gun.*

No. It can't end this way.

There had to be something she could do. She racked her brain for an escape plan, for her *and* Stray. But as her gaze fixed on the gun, the futility of the situation became crystal clear. What little hope that ran through her mind trickled to a thin stream before ceasing entirely.

They were too strong for her to escape, and if she did…

…she'd be shot dead before ever making it to the door.

Chapter Eleven

Saxon trotted ahead, darting left and right as he followed one scent after another, seeing and smelling things Nick couldn't. By this time of night, his mind was usually crammed with thoughts about work. Tonight, his head was filled with thoughts of a woman.

Andi.

The kiss he'd given her hadn't scraped the surface of what he wanted: to carry her to her bedroom and make love to her all night. Whether he was prepared for it or not, she was getting to him.

Andi Hardt was everything a man could possibly want. Beauty and brains. Compassion and guts. Instinct shouted louder than ever that she was innocent, yet he was treading closer and closer to a line he should back the hell away from before he stepped right over it and plunged into quicksand. He couldn't—no, *shouldn't*—get involved or do any other stupid thing that might risk losing Andi's cooperation. Like kissing her again, or carrying her up to her bedroom and stripping them both down until they were totally naked. *Fuck, no.*

Andi was still a critical part of an active investigation that was nearing the boiling point, and sticking to the plan was the only thing that mattered. In the meantime, there'd be a lot of cold showers in his future.

As they neared the edge of the grass that abutted the DPC's parking lot, Saxon loped to Nick's side.

Until tonight, he wasn't sure he'd ever sing again, or pick up an instrument that he couldn't load with at least eleven rounds of ammo, but when he'd seen Andi so panicked about her MIA musician, he hadn't thought twice about helping her. For a few seconds he'd been pissed at his friends for goading him into it, then he realized it wasn't anger tearing him up inside. It was something else entirely.

Since Tanya died, he'd been getting up every morning and reporting for work, but he'd only been going through the motions. Until now, he'd been hiding under a blanket, scared shitless of exposing his heart for fear of having it ripped from his chest again. It had taken the right person to yank off that blanket and let sunlight into his world. Andi had done that.

Light from the adjacent streetlamps glinted off the bumper of his Tahoe in the parking lot. Saxon ran ahead, lowering his front legs to the grass then pushing off to leap easily over the four-foot fence skirting the lot. He cleared the top rail by well over a foot and with minimal effort.

Nick followed, vaulting over the fence. He was about to insert the key into the Tahoe's door, when Saxon alerted. The dog stood at full attention, staring at Andi's house. Nick did the same, straining to see or hear whatever it was Saxon had. At first, he sensed nothing out of place. Only the kitchen light glowed through one of the windows facing the lot. Then, a dog barked. *Stray.*

Saxon gave an angry snort. Nick knew his dog well enough to know something was off. Stray wasn't a barker.

Something moved outside Andi's front door. That's when

he noticed a dark van parked in the shadows in front of her house. Distant rumbling told him the engine was on, but the headlights were off.

When Stray barked again, fear coiled in his gut. Nick took off running. He didn't have to issue Saxon a command. His dog knew bad shit was going down.

He vaulted the fence on the other side of the parking lot at a dead run. Saxon leaped over the rail and charged ahead.

As they pounded across the grass, the kitchen light in Andi's house went out. Only the moon lit the front yard. His heart hammered so loudly he could hear it, feel it in his throat.

Shadowed figures came into view on the front lawn. Three people. Two larger, one smaller. *Andi*. Even in the semidarkness, he'd know her shape.

She struggled as two men dragged her across the lawn toward the van. The driver's door opened, and a third man stepped out.

Sonofabitch. They're kidnapping her.

Unbridled rage pushed him harder. He would *not* let this woman die. *This* time, he'd be there to stop it.

When he was still twenty feet away, Saxon launched himself at one of the men. The man screamed.

"Get it off, get it off!"

Nick tackled the other asshole, landing on top of him. He heard the breath *whoosh* from the guy's lungs as he hit the ground. Beside him, Andi fell and uttered a muffled scream.

"Andi!" he shouted, worried she'd been hurt. Her hands were tied behind her back and tape covered her mouth.

Saxon's jaws were clamped around the second asshole lying next to her. The man screamed as the dog tightened his hold on his arm.

Andi scrambled backward, trying to put distance between herself and the fight. The distraction was enough, and the guy beneath Nick landed a solid punch to his jaw. Pain exploded in the side of his face. He shook his head to clear it, then jumped to his feet in time to avoid a gut punch.

Breathing heavily, Nick dodged blow after blow, then landed a right cross and heard bone crunch. The man hit the ground and didn't get up again.

He spun, rearing back his arm, about to ram his fist into the other guy, when a gunshot blasted. Andi gave another muted cry. Nick's heart about stopped.

Is she hit?

The man whose upper arm Saxon had his jaws clamped around struggled to aim his weapon again. *At Saxon.*

Fuck, no.

His dog wasn't about to back down. Not even a gunshot would scare Saxon off.

Abandoning the driver, Nick leaped onto the man tangled up with Saxon and lunged for the gun. He got one hand on the guy's wrist, but not before he managed to crank off another round.

Andi's body jerked, chilling his soul, striking absolute terror in his heart.

"Police! Let go of the gun!"

Saxon growled, shaking his head back and forth, still gripping one of the guy's arms. The asshole grunted but still struggled to gain control of the firearm. Nick stuck his finger through the trigger guard, preventing the trigger from being pulled back, then he twisted the guy's wrist hard until he yelped and let go. With his free hand, he slammed his fist into the guy's jaw. The body beneath Nick went slack.

A door slammed, followed by tires screeching on pavement. The driver of the van was taking off.

Glancing behind him, Nick saw the first guy was still out cold, and he didn't have a single set of cuffs on him.

"*Aus.*"

Saxon released his hold and stood guard over the unconscious bodies, panting.

"Andi!" Nick jumped to his feet and went to her, dropping to her side. She lay curled into a ball on the grass, her body shaking. Carefully, he peeled the tape from her mouth. "Are you okay? Are you shot?"

When she didn't answer, his pulse rocketed into the stratosphere. There wasn't enough light to thoroughly inspect her for gunshot wounds, but he ran his hands down her arms, legs, belly, and back just the same. He didn't feel anything wet.

"Andi? Honey, talk to me."

She took a deep breath and let it out. The sound was music to his hears. He took her in his arms, cradling her against his chest. *Thank God.*

As she lay tucked against him, she gradually stopped shaking. Only then did his heart rate settle into normal range. Rocking her gently, he kept his eyes on the two motionless men, although Saxon wouldn't let either of them escape.

"I'm okay," she said finally. "I was just scared."

"I know." *So was I. Scared shitless that she'd been shot.*

For several gut-wrenching moments, he'd seen his past repeating. He'd seen Tanya, a small hole on one side of her head, the other side blown out, her brains splattered across the pristine white lace duvet.

Gulping in an unsteady breath, he pulled a pocketknife from his pants pocket and cut off the tape binding her wrists. "You're safe now." She stared at him, unmoving. In the dim light, her eyes were wide and glassy with shock. "Hey," he said softly. "Come back to me."

He stroked her cheek, her hair, then kissed her forehead, her lips, anything to bring her back.

Her fingers closed around his bicep. "I'm fine."

"Good." *That was an understatement.* But this wasn't

the time to analyze the life-altering relief he'd experienced at realizing she was alive and unhurt. He held up the tape he'd removed from her hands. "Do you have any tape like this in your house?"

She nodded. "I-I think so."

Sensing she was still a little out of it, he helped her to stand. "Can you find some and bring it to me? I need to tie these guys up." He knew she was still in shock from what had happened, but he couldn't risk the men escaping while he went into the house.

"Okay." She turned and went inside, although her movements were a bit wobbly.

Moving swiftly, he patted both men down for more weapons. Between the two of them, he found another .9mm and two switchblades. He also dug cell phones from their rear pockets.

While he waited for Andi to find tape, he set the weapons and phones on the front step next to the door, then pulled out his own phone. The first call he made was to his barracks, then he called Cox, Eric, and Matt. Despite him urging them not to, Eric and Matt insisted on rallying the rest of Nick's friends. Soon, the place would be crawling with police and feds.

The front lights flicked on, as did the lamppost near the curb. The screen door slammed as Andi came back outside, holding a roll of gray duct tape. He took it from her and made quick work of taping the men's hands behind their backs. They were both starting to regain consciousness, so he taped their ankles together, allowing only enough slack that they'd be able to shuffle to the patrol cars when they arrived.

Andi hadn't uttered a word since retrieving the tape. She stood on the front stoop, arms wrapped around herself, her hands tightly clasping her shoulders. When she lifted her gaze to his, he glimpsed the same shock and fear he'd seen in hundreds of victims' eyes. It was nearly enough to snap what little remained of his control.

Because he wanted to kill the men who'd touched her.

He climbed the few steps to where she stood. When he tugged her into his arms, she came willingly. Her body was soft, her breath warm against his chest.

Sirens wailed in the distance. An unexpected truth hit him like a brick. Andi was the only woman since Tanya who'd managed to get under his skin.

No murkiness about it now.

He'd still do everything in his power to nail the gun dealer, but his priorities had just shifted like tectonic plates in an earthquake. Now there was something far more important in his life—protecting the woman in his arms.

• • •

Red and blue lights flickered on the other side of the lake. Andi pressed her face to Nick's chest, burrowing closer. She breathed in his scent—his usual citrus, this time with a bit of freshly cut grass thrown in.

When she sighed, he kissed the top of her head. What she really wanted was for him to tip her chin up and kiss her deeply. Even with her face snugged against his chest, she could hear the emergency vehicles drawing nearer. She didn't want to leave his protective embrace, didn't want to think about what had just happened, or why. Those men tried to kidnap her. If it hadn't been for Nick and Saxon, she could be dead by now. Or worse.

What did they want?

The bastards had stuck a gun in her face and dragged her outside, but if they'd wanted to rob or rape her, they didn't have to kidnap her. They'd even hurt poor Stray. Luckily, her dog seemed to be okay. Andi had found Stray wandering around the house, frantically looking for her. Just the same, she'd bring her to the vet for x-rays as soon as the animal hospital opened.

Wait... Her dog?

Finding someone to adopt Stray had been the plan all along. That was why she'd never given her a proper name.

Keep telling yourself that.

She and Stray had bonded from the moment the beautiful golden-brown dog had wandered onto the DPC's deck. Now Stray had been injured trying to save her. She might not be a trained K-9, but she was just as fierce and protective in her own way. After taking her to the vet, Andi would stop at the grocery store for Stray's favorite food—ice cream.

Nick's arms around her tightened, then he released her. It was on the tip of her tongue to object, when he repositioned his arm, tucking her to his side. To increase the contact, she wrapped one of her arms around his waist, leaning into the warmth and security of his body.

Saxon stood proud and tall, tail erect as he guarded the two incapacitated men. Like Nick, the dog was all cop, and they'd both saved her life. She'd have to pick up some Pop-Tarts then sneak them to Saxon when Nick wasn't looking.

What seemed like ten police vehicles sped closer. The first two that pulled to a stop in front of the house were state police sedans, followed by local police cars, a few unmarked units, and several K-9 SUVs.

Radios squawked, and her front yard glowed with the ricochet of flashing red-and-blue strobes. The DPC and her house were situated on a quiet stretch of road, with no other houses for at least a quarter mile in either direction. Given the early hour, chances were her neighbors were asleep and wouldn't know anything about the incident unless it hit the newspapers.

At least a dozen officers packed her front yard, including

Special Agent Cox, Eric, and two of Nick's other friends—Matt and Kade.

Eric got to them first, resting a hand on Nick's shoulder. "You guys all right?" He looked from Nick to her, his eyes filled with concern.

"We're fine." Nick gave her waist a little squeeze, snugging her that much closer and making her feel totally protected.

She'd expected him to release her the minute the troops arrived, but he didn't, and she was grateful for the support. Mentally *and* physically. The adrenaline was beginning to wear off, and if his arm hadn't been around her, she might have slipped to the ground like a limp noodle.

Matt and Kade joined them.

Matt frowned. "You're bleeding."

"What?" She eased from Nick's embrace, placing one hand on his chest as she looked at his face.

A small cut beneath his right eye oozed blood, probably, judging by the split skin, from the fistfight he'd had with the three men. When she reached up to touch his face, he clasped her hand, pulling it away.

"It's nothing," he reassured her. "I'm fine."

He wasn't fine, and neither was she. Okay, so she hadn't been hurt, not physically, anyway, but she was so far from fine it wasn't funny. "Would someone tell me what just happened here?" Her voice had come out in a high-pitched squeak.

Cox joined them on the front step. "That's what I'd like to know."

"Three men tried to kidnap her." Nick's tone was hard as he released her and walked to where Saxon dutifully guarded the two prone figures.

She followed but stood off to the side as he succinctly described what had happened.

"These two assholes," he continued, "dragged her out of the house. Her hands were taped together. There was a third guy waiting in a van at the curb. He took off and left his buddies behind."

"I don't suppose you got the tag?" Cox asked.

Nick shook his head. "Too dark. Headlights never came on. Chevy, black or brown. Late-nineties model with a busted-up rear bumper. These guys"—he indicated the men on the ground, who were beginning to stir—"have gang tattoos."

How in the world did he take in that level of detail, let alone in the dark and while fighting off three armed men?

Because this was his world, a dangerous one, and she was so far out of her element it was pathetic.

He pointed to the front door. "Between them, they had two switchblades, two nine mils—Ruger and Glock—and two cell phones. The serial numbers on the guns were filed off. We can check all their recent texts and calls and see who they've been talking to lately. Based on their tats, these guys are low-level gang members, so you can bet they're taking orders from someone else."

Her heart squeezed as she listened to his voice—totally devoid of emotion. Tough as nails, cold as ice. As if someone had flipped a switch, he'd instantly morphed back into a hard-ass cop.

It wasn't that she'd forgotten who or what he was. It was the reaffirmation that there really were two distinct aspects of this man and his life. One, she now knew, was filled with warmth, passion, humor, and music. The other, shadowed by violence and ugliness, the depths of which she hadn't truly understood until now. This was the world he worked in, and it terrified her.

Turning, she went up the steps, pausing to glance at the guns and knives he'd taken off those men. It was hard to imagine how many lives could be snuffed out by those weapons. One bullet or knife strike was all it would take.

She shivered then put her hand on the screen doorknob,

clasping it tightly. She might not be a cop, but she didn't have to be one to understand with unerring certainty that this was all connected to whatever Joe was involved in. "I have to check on Stray," she said, looking at the men lying on the ground. "They kicked her."

Nick's expression softened, as did his tone when he spoke. "I'll be there in a minute."

Quietly, she turned the knob and went inside to the living room. Her stomach roiled with anger at the danger and chaos Joe had brought into her life. When he showed up, she fully intended to rip into him with every foul word in her verbal repertoire. Which wasn't much, really, but she'd concoct something special just for him.

In the corner of the living room, Stray lifted her head from the dog bed. "Oh, you poor thing," she crooned, sitting on the floor to stroke her soft, velvety ears. Her head filled with rage and her heart with sadness at what Stray had endured trying to protect her. "Thank you, girl." The dog nuzzled her hand then licked her arm. "I didn't mean for you to get hurt."

Uttering a long sigh, Stray lowered her head and rested her muzzle on the edge of the bed.

Men's voices drew her attention. Through the screen door, she watched Nick collect the guns, knives, and cell phones, dropping them into a plastic bag. Then the door opened, and Saxon entered first, followed by Nick, Matt, Eric, Kade, and Special Agent Cox.

Saxon went to Stray. The shepherd lowered his head to sniff the other dog, then gently licked her muzzle. The gesture was so tender and loving that Andi nearly laughed. Not at the sweet affection Nick's dog was showing to hers, but at yet another similarity between Saxon and his master.

Like Nick, Saxon was a cop who would take down an armed bad guy without hesitation, putting his life on the line for her and others. The dog's training and instincts to protect were just as fierce as Nick's, yet both could switch from badass to gentle and caring in a heartbeat.

Saxon lay on the floor on Stray's other side. It never ceased to amaze her how wonderful and loving dogs were. To humans and to each other.

Nick knelt before her and rested a hand on her arm. "We're transporting these guys to the barracks. We'll get them to talk." The look he gave her was tender and filled with concern.

"This is because of Joe, isn't it?"

"I'd say so." He nodded grimly, pausing to run his hand over the top of Stray's head. "We think they wanted to use you as bait. To lure him in."

Her eyes widened, and she grabbed his forearm. "But they'll kill him."

"And they'd have killed you, too." His jaw clenched, and a deadly gleam sparked in his eyes. "If they'd gotten you tonight, they'd have found a way to make sure he knew it. They'd have lied to him, told him that if he turned himself in, they'd let you go."

A chill crept up her spine. "But they wouldn't have. Would they?"

"No," he answered in a voice as hard as granite. "Where's your phone?"

"In the kitchen. Why?"

Releasing her arm, he stormed into the kitchen, returning a moment later with her phone. He punched in her code, then cued up a call and held the phone to his ear.

"Nick," Cox warned. "What are you doing?"

"Speeding things up."

"We don't want to scare the guy off," Cox countered, making a move to grab the phone.

Nick's tone was deadly. "I don't give a fuck what you want."

Saxon scrambled to his feet, planting himself in a protective stance between Nick and Cox.

As one, Eric, Matt, and Kade moved to Nick's side, as if in support.

"And I'm sure not gonna give these assholes another chance to grab her," he continued. "Myer needs to know his actions are putting Andi in harm's way, where she'll remain until he turns himself in. He may not answer the phone, but you can be sure he's checking his voicemail."

She knew the moment Joe's voicemail kicked on. Nick's eyes narrowed to slits. His lips compressed, and his nostrils flared. "Joe Myer," he said. "This is Sgt. Nick Houston with the Massachusetts State Police. Whoever you're laundering money for just tried to kidnap Andi and use her as bait to lure you in. She could have been killed, you sonofabitch. If you still love her like I think you do, you'll turn yourself in. To *me*." He recited his cell phone number then ended the call.

Andi hugged her knees to her chest, lowering her head to hide the tears trickling down her cheeks. *This wasn't supposed to happen. None of it.*

When she lifted her head, Nick was again kneeling in front of her.

"You can hate me for what I just did, but I'd do it again. Anything to keep you safe." The determination on his handsome face frightened her. "Nothing's going to happen to you. I won't let it." His face had softened again, and she believed him. "Matt and Kade will stay here while the rest of us go to the barracks to interrogate those men. I'll find out who's behind this."

"What will you do then?" she asked.

"You let me worry about that." He smiled, but there was no warmth. "A patrol car will stay out front overnight. You'll be safe. And did I mention that Kade is a veterinary technician? He'll give Stray a cursory exam and make sure she's okay. I'll be back later."

"When?" she asked, unable to contain the hopefulness in her voice.

"I don't know. I'll call." He handed her back her phone then dropped a quick kiss on her lips. "*Hier.*"

Saxon nuzzled Stray one last time then followed Nick out the door. Eric and Cox went with him. Even though Matt and Kade remained behind, the room suddenly felt empty. She didn't doubt Nick's words. She *would* be safe. Matt's friends and the officers stationed outside would protect her. But who would protect *them*? They were all highly trained, but they weren't bulletproof.

"Would you like me to look at Stray?" Kade gave her a warm smile that showed off his dimples. "Nick said she'd been hurt."

"Yes. Please." Numbly, she stroked Stray's ears while Kade carefully helped the dog to her feet. Then he ran his large hands methodically over both sides of Stray's rib cage.

"I don't think anything's broken. Bruised, probably, so she'll be walking unsteadily for a while."

"That's a relief." She looked gratefully at Kade and was rewarded with a full-fledged smile that not only emphasized his adorable dimples but how incredibly handsome the man was.

She yawned, wishing she could fall asleep and pretend this night had never happened. "We're going to bed. Help yourself to anything in the kitchen."

"Thanks," Matt said. "Let us know if you need anything."

She helped Stray climb the stairs then settle onto another dog bed in a corner of the bedroom. "Sleep well, girl." The dog lowered her head and uttered a throaty sigh.

Andi fell into bed fully clothed. Despite how tired she was, sleep didn't come easily.

Stuffing an extra pillow beneath her head, she gazed out

the window at the stars. It was nearly three in the morning. Venus stood guard over the peaceful, shimmering lake. While she was resting safely in her bed, Nick and other officers were tracking down the dangerous people who'd orchestrated her kidnapping. As much as she'd been worrying about Joe these last weeks, now she worried for Nick. Maybe more so.

She'd been given rare insight into what it must be like as a police officer's spouse or partner. You'd have to be willing to accept—and mentally capable of accepting—that person had the ability and authority to kill when necessary. And that they could be killed in the line of duty.

Do I have what it takes?

Lying there in the darkness, she didn't know quite what she felt for Nick. Somewhere along the line, annoyance had turned into respect, and she'd begun to like him. Then *like* had morphed into caring with something else thrown in— desire. God, how she wanted him to make love to her. But her feelings ran far deeper.

Fear curled in her belly. If anything happened to him…if he were killed…he would take a piece of her heart with him.

How much of her heart was too frightening to contemplate.

Chapter Twelve

Nick cuffed the gang member—Jose Matteo—to the metal chair in one of the barracks' interrogation rooms. Three doors down, Eric was busy with Matteo's partner-in-crime— Sonny Luther.

Matteo was a pathetic twenty-year-old, about five-foot-six, and a little chubby around the waistline. The entire right side of his face was turning purple from where Nick had smashed his fist into it. The sonofabitch had gotten off easy. If he hadn't knocked Matteo out cold, he would gladly have pummeled the rest of the guy's face to a bloody pulp for hurting Andi. He'd wanted to kill the guy ten times over then get to work on his buddy two doors down. But he needed them alive so they could talk, and talk fast.

Given that the third asshole had gotten away, it wouldn't be long before some shifty attorney showed up to represent the two men. After that, it would be too late, and the attorney would shut his clients down. Professionalism and the monitor in the corner of the ceiling held him in check. Everything that went down would be done right and recorded for posterity.

He sat on the edge of the table and crossed his arms, staring down at Matteo. Exercising sound tactics, he said nothing. Eventually, the little shit would start squirming.

Matteo leaned back, sending Nick his best defiant, punk-ass look. *Won't work.* He'd seen far too many young men *and* women absorbed by the gang system who'd been taught to act tough. The truth was that inside they were all scared, needing to take advantage of a gang's pack mentality in order to feel like they belonged.

At first, Matteo maintained eye contact. Then Nick glimpsed the telltale signs of weakening.

Sweat broke out on the kid's upper lip. He grabbed both sides of the seat and began to squirm. A few seconds later, Matteo broke eye contact and looked away. When he looked back, he lost it.

"Quit fucking staring at me."

"I'm making you nervous." He knew he was.

"Fuck no."

"Then it shouldn't matter if I stare at you."

He was careful not to ask questions. Matteo had been read his rights and claimed he wanted a lawyer. It was up to Nick to convince him otherwise. Without asking any questions.

"I ain't talkin', and you know it. So why am I here?"

Gotcha.

"Kidnapping. Assault. Unlawful possession of a switchblade. Unlawful possession of a firearm. Conspiracy. Resisting arrest. And my personal favorite—assault on a police officer."

Matteo leaned forward. "Didn't know you were a cop at first."

"Doesn't matter. You'll still be charged for that."

Matteo swore again. "That ain't fair."

"I couldn't care less." He paused, allowing the ramifications of all those charges to sink in. "This isn't your first arrest, which means you'll do hard time."

More sweat broke out on the kid's brow and neck. Damp patches darkened his armpits and the front of his shirt. Nick had already run Matteo's criminal history. For a gang member, it actually hadn't been that bad. Petty crimes mostly. These new charges would send him away for a long time.

He guessed the kidnapping was an initiation meant to launch Matteo and Sonny directly to full status, and he was betting this was a directive handed down from someone else.

"You're not a real gang member. You're a sad little wannabee who screwed up," Nick pressed. "Now you're going to prison for something someone else ordered you to do."

"I am, too, a gang member," Matteo shouted.

"Bullshit." He smacked his hand on the table, making the kid jerk back against the chair. "You're a sorry-ass nobody who's going to spend the next decade in prison."

"You motherfucker," Matteo hissed.

"That's *Sgt.* Motherfucker to you." He leaned in closer, waiting.

Less than a minute later, tears welled in Matteo's eyes, followed by sobs. Looked like this would be even easier than he'd anticipated. Probably meant there was still hope for the kid. After he did his time.

Now to nail him down with information he'd learned from a street informant during the drive from the DPC to the barracks.

Nick remained where he was, softening his voice. "You've got a girlfriend and a two-year-old son. I know you'd like to be out before your boy turns ten. You could do that. With good behavior and cooperation. The cooperation part starts now."

He straightened to give Matteo time to absorb and process the potential deal on the table. Not *too* much time.

Still defiant, Matteo stared at the ceiling.

Nick's patience was running thin. "Your buddy is in

another room down the hall. Whoever talks first gets the golden prize."

"Yeah?" The kid sneered. "What's that?"

"Reduced charges and a reduced sentence." It would take a prosecutor to make the specific offer, but in general that was the way the system worked.

Matteo continued to sneer, doing his best to intimidate Nick.

"If you don't start talking, you're looking at a full sentence with no chance at reduction. If that happens your kid won't remember you by the time you get out of prison. Chances are your girlfriend will have moved on by then and shacked up with someone else." He stood. "You've got exactly three seconds to start talking, or I walk out that door and the deal walks with me."

Another few seconds went by before Matteo sniffled and choked back a muffled sob. "What do you want to know?"

Nick whipped out a waiver of rights form from his back pocket, then grabbed another trooper from the hallway to sign as a witness and remain in the room during the interview.

"Who told you to kidnap the woman?"

"I don't know."

"How did you get the order?"

"By text. I got a photo and an address."

Photo? The one stolen from Myer's house, he assumed.

He tugged the evidence bag containing Matteo's phone from his back pocket and pulled out the phone. He pushed the *home* button, and the screen lit up. "What's your passcode?"

Matteo pressed his lips together, then squeezed his eyes shut for a moment. Now the kid was trying his patience. "Cooperation," he reminded him. "*Today.*"

The kid gave up his code, and Nick punched in the numbers. Figuring the order was recent, he tapped on the first text message. There was no sender name, only a phone number. A burner phone, most likely.

The first part of the text was Andi's home address. The second was another address in Holyoke, an area Nick knew had several abandoned buildings.

Before he tapped on the photo, he could already tell it was the same one that had been stolen from Myer's bedroom—the one with Andi in it.

"Were you supposed to take the woman to this other address?"

"Yeah." Matteo nodded.

"Then what?"

"Tie her to a chair, then wait for a guy to show."

"What guy?"

"I don't fuckin' know. We were just supposed to turn her over to whoever met us there. That's it. Not my business what happened after that."

He gripped the phone tighter, resisting the urge to bash it against Matteo's head. But time was ticking down fast. Sooner or later, it would go up the chain that they'd bungled the kidnapping. Nick was hoping for later.

Gears began spinning in his head. There was still a chance that whoever was on the receiving end of the delivery that wasn't going to happen was there now, waiting. They had a small window of opportunity before word got out, and that window was closing with every passing minute.

He grabbed the pen and a pad he'd set on the table and shoved them in front of Matteo. "Write it. *All* of it. Including the name of your cowardly buddy who drove off and left you to take the hit." He motioned to the other trooper to follow him out the door, leaving Matteo alone to pen his confession. Normally, he'd spend more time with an interrogation as important as this one. Time was not on his side.

Eric and Cox came out of another interrogation room. "He talk?" Eric asked.

"Yeah." He charged into his tour commander's office. Eric and Cox followed.

Five minutes later, they were speeding down the highway toward Holyoke with four marked state police vehicles in tow. Eric sat in the passenger seat of Nick's SUV.

"You okay?" Eric asked.

"Great." *Not even close.*

He'd called the number on Matteo's phone, but no one answered. That phone had probably been tossed down a sewer grate by now. He gunned the SUV faster down the highway, but his gut told him they were already too late to grab their quarry. At least the bastards hadn't gotten Andi.

He admired that she hadn't broken down and gone into hysterics. She might be soft and sleek on the outside, but there was a tough core at the center of that woman. Still, if he hadn't been there tonight, or if he'd been too late...

He clamped his fingers tighter around the wheel, his fury growing exponentially by the second. This time he *had* been there, but there'd been a time—five years ago—when he'd failed.

Tanya had needed protection. Protection he clearly hadn't been able to provide, something that would always tear into him. He should have been able to save her. He'd tried. God, how he'd tried. Maybe it was finally time to accept that. That and the fact he'd been alone long enough.

Never in his wildest imaginings did he expect to care so deeply for a woman again, or even let one get close enough to try.

He yanked the wheel to veer onto the exit ramp, barely slowing into the curve.

There was no telling what would or wouldn't happen next between him and Andi, but he was sure of one thing. What he'd said earlier about not letting anything happen to her had been a colossal understatement. If it came down to it...

...he'd die protecting her.

Chapter Thirteen

It was ten p.m. Sunday night, and Andi wiped down the gleaming bar for the tenth time in the last hour.

Nick was still out there searching for the people who'd tried to kidnap her. They were dangerous, and they were armed. She was thankful that Saxon was with him, but with every passing hour that he didn't show, her emotions coiled tighter and tighter until he was all she could think about.

Could she really open herself up and risk her heart again? In the depths of her soul, she knew the answer, and the thought was frightening.

I already have.

Ugly memories of Steve's lie and the damage he'd done to her career *and* her emotions edged its way front and center in her mind. She'd been royally burned before and had good reason to have sworn off men for all eternity.

Nick can't have been playing me. Not then, and not now. She'd know if he was.

She threw the damp cloth into the laundry bin then looked around the dining room. As soon as the dinner crowd had ended, she'd cut most of the staff loose, leaving only her and Tess to close up.

Tess wiped down the last of the tables. Matt and Kade sat in a corner, sipping coffee as they had during the entire time they'd been guarding her. Occasionally, one of them had gotten a phone call, and she'd pumped them for information on Nick. They wouldn't tell her a thing, and it was driving her crazy.

The only good part of the day had come at the vet clinic, when the doctor had confirmed that Stray's ribs weren't broken. She'd checked on her several times throughout the day, and each time Stray was resting comfortably in her bed.

"Ready to close?" Tess grabbed her purse from under the bar.

"Just about." She turned off the kitchen lights then tipped her head to Matt and Kade, who rose and waited for them by the front door.

Tess dug into her sparkly, multicolored leather bag for her keys. Even her key ring glittered with an assortment of dangling crystal charms. "Where's the Viking?"

"Who?" She tugged the deck door closed, locking it.

"The hunky guy with the spiky blond hair." Tess waggled her eyebrows. "The one I saw talking to Nick last night."

"Oh, him. Eric." She laughed, then pursed her lips. "Did I mention that he's a cop—a federal agent?"

The laughter in Tess's eyes died instantly. "Too bad."

Hmm. One day—after the dust settled on her own chaotic life—she'd have to put aside her determination not to pry and dig deeper into what *that* was about.

"Speaking of guys," Andi continued, changing course, "didn't you have a first date last night after work?"

"I did." She sighed. "My first *and* last with that jerk."

Andi flicked off the deck lights. "Where'd you meet this guy?"

"Here, a couple of weeks ago." She made a disgusted sound. "I should have known he'd be a jerk."

Andi raised her brows. "How could you have known?"

Tess stared at the keys in her hand. "Because he reminded me of my stepfather."

Now, Andi was certain there was a story there. Tess rarely spoke of her family. "You know you can talk to me. About anything."

"I know. Thanks." She gave Andi a wan, false smile and slung her bag over her shoulder. "My problems are nothing compared to yours. And likewise, I'm here for you, too."

Tess squeezed Andi's arm, then sauntered to the front door and began chatting with Matt and Kade.

"You coming?" Matt called out.

"Yeah." She nodded, then joined them at the door and waited for them to go outside so she could shut off the lights and set the alarm. Ironic how she'd alarmed the DPC but not her own home, yet it had been her house that was broken into by thugs who meant to do her harm. In hindsight...*dumb. Really dumb.*

With the alarm still beeping, she locked the door behind her. Kade walked Tess to her car while Matt stayed behind.

"Did you hear anything new?" she asked hopefully.

He shook his dark head. "The only thing I can tell you is that Nick and Eric interrogated the guys who tried to kidnap you. They've been following up on leads all day." He watched her closely for a moment. "He'll be okay. He's good at what he does."

"I know." They began walking to the house. "I didn't mean he wasn't, I'm just—" *Going absolutely nuts not hearing from him.*

"Worried, I get it," he said, filling in the blank. "My wife worries every time I walk out the door, but she accepts who I am and what I do. Even before we got married, it was hard on her. It took time for her to adjust and not let it get to her every second of the day."

"'Night, Andi," Tess called from the open window of her beat-up Camry as she drove past.

She waved back. "I don't have any right to feel this way," she mumbled, more to herself.

"Why not?" Matt chuckled. "From what I've seen, he feels the same way."

"*Who* feels the same way?" Kade asked as he caught up to them.

"Nick."

"Oh, that." Kade also chuckled, then walked ahead of them to the house.

"See?" Matt laughed again. "Everyone else does."

She glanced at him, unable to read his expression in the semi-darkness. "How can that be, when I'm still a suspect?"

"The house is clear." Kade leaned over the back porch railing. "Nick's on his way. ETA in ten."

"It just is," Matt responded matter-of-factly, and before she could ask what he meant by that, he added, "But that's for Nick to explain. For now, let's get you inside."

Twenty minutes later, she was pacing the living room. With every turn she made on the floor, Stray swung her head, watching her. Even with the patrol car outside, the two men remained alert, one at the front door, and one at the rear.

A knock sounded at the rear door. Matt and Kade drew their guns from beneath their shirts. She'd assumed they were armed, but hadn't detected their hidden weapons.

Matt nudged the kitchen door curtain aside, then nodded to Kade. They holstered, and Matt opened the door.

Saxon trotted in first and went straight for Stray's bed. The two dogs' noses touched. Saxon gave Stray a thorough sniffing, then lay down beside her, his muzzle touching the other dog's front paw.

When Nick walked in, Andi's breath caught. Their gazes met and held, his weary from lack of sleep. Her eyes roved his body, reassuring herself that he wasn't hurt. That was her greatest fear—that something would happen to him because of her.

He still wore the same jeans and black T-shirt he'd worked in the day before. The only additions were the badge and gun holstered on his belt. His jaw was covered with light stubble, but to her, he'd never looked better. *Or sexier.* She went to him and threw her arms around his neck, burying her face against his chest.

His arms came around her, and she sighed with relief, breathing him in and absorbing the heat from his body, letting it seep into her hers, melting away the tension. The worry-induced adrenaline that had kept her going all day vanished, and she was on the verge of falling asleep standing up.

"They talked," he began, gently easing her from his arms. "They were supposed to take you to Holyoke and hand you over to someone else."

Matt sat on the arm of the sofa. "Get a name?"

He shook his head. "They don't know who ordered the kidnapping or who they were going to meet. They were told to take her inside, tie her to a chair, then wait."

"You believe them?" Kade crossed his arms, the look on his face skeptical. "Generally, any time gang members' lips are moving, they're lying."

"I do believe them." He nodded. "So does Eric. He grilled the other guy and eventually got pretty much the same information out of him. We hauled ass to the location, but nobody was there. The whole street is abandoned, and I'm sure that was part of the plan. The guy who got away—the van driver—probably got the word out about the bungled kidnapping. We found the van in a strip mall, but the driver's in the wind. We'll get him. Eventually."

He tugged her closer to his side, and when she wrapped her arm around his waist, his muscles bunched beneath her fingers.

"No one on the street is talking," he continued. "And that's odd. There's always someone willing to dime out a brother for the right price. Not on this, though. The streets are eerily quiet, as if something heavy is about to hit the fan and everyone's scared shitless to talk about it."

Matt grunted, then massaged his chin. "The others have started their shifts at the Expo, but Kade and I don't go on for another forty-eight hours. We can follow up on any leads you've got."

"Right now, we've got nothing to go on," Nick said. "Eric went to the FBI lab to drop off the two cell phones we seized. They'll do a dump on the phones and analyze everything. Phone numbers, social media, photos. And speaking of photos, one of the guys we arrested had one on his phone of Andi and Myer—the same one stolen during a break-in at Myer's house two weeks ago. It was texted to him, so they'd know what she looked like."

She shuddered at how close she'd come to being tied to a chair, helpless. As if sensing her unease, Nick snugged her closer.

"Want us to stick around?" Matt asked.

"Nah, you guys can take off. The patrol car will stay out front all night. The restaurant's closed on Mondays. We can touch base in the morning."

"You sure? We can stay downstairs," Kade suggested.

Nick shook his head. "I got this. Saxon will watch our backs."

Hearing his name, Saxon came to sit at Nick's other side, leaning his head against Nick's thigh. Seeing that kind of complete adoration reaffirmed Andi's decision not to put Stray up for adoption. Somehow the dog had wiggled her way into her heart, and she couldn't bear the thought of her belonging to someone else.

"Call if you need us." Matt clapped a hand on Nick's shoulder. "'Night, Andi."

"Good night, Matt. Kade. And thank you."

"Our pleasure." Kade followed Matt out the front door.

No sooner had the door clicked shut than Nick's mouth crashed down on hers. His arms were iron bands around her back, holding her tightly against him.

She parted her lips, and he took full advantage until her head swam and her heart thudded crazily. When he finally pulled away, he was breathing hard. "Andi." His voice was ragged, gravelly. Steel-gray eyes looked down at her, fierce with emotion. Hunger and heat radiated off him in waves.

She half expected him to throw her over his shoulder and carry her upstairs like a conquering hero. But he didn't. Not that she would have minded if he had, because she wanted him. *God, how I want him.*

Gently, he trailed his fingers down her cheek, stroking across her lips, then along her jaw. Closing her eyes, she let her head fall back, giving him complete access to her neck.

His lips were warm as he kissed the sensitive spot near her ear. The stubble on his jaw grazed her flesh, sending tingles to her belly. To keep from slipping boneless to the floor, she fisted his T-shirt in her hands. Her nerve endings crackled, sensing every inch of his body pressed against hers. She opened her eyes, and what she saw took her by surprise. Flooring her, actually. Because in addition to the volcanic heat she'd glimpsed, something else simmered in the depths of his gaze, something that speared a hole straight through her heart.

Tenderness.

This man...this gorgeous protector who could undoubtedly have every woman whose name graced the napkins he'd thrown into the garbage, wanted *her.*

She didn't know what he felt for her, but she wasn't fool enough not to know her own feelings when they smacked her in the face. Despite her initial reservations, she was falling for him, and couldn't have prevented that fall if her life depended on it. It was that simple.

His lips closed again on hers, urging them apart as he slipped his tongue inside her mouth. He tugged her blouse from her skirt, skimming his hands along the sides of her rib cage then over her breasts.

Her nipples instantly puckered, and the muscles in her lower belly clenched. *I want this. I want* him.

It was a risk, perhaps the biggest of her life, but she was willing to take it. Wordlessly, she clasped his hand and led him to the base of the stairs.

"*Pass auf,*" he said to Saxon, whose head tilted in obvious curiosity at what they were doing.

In response, Saxon let out a guttural sound and sat straighter, as if coming to attention. She didn't know German but understood Nick had just commanded Saxon to guard the house.

As they climbed the stairs, her nerves ratcheted tighter. By the time they got to her bedroom, her heart was beating way too fast.

Light from the upstairs hallway spilled onto the bed. She turned on a lamp and found Nick surveying the room.

The bed was antique brass with a cream-colored cotton duvet, matching pillowcases, and a half dozen colorful fringed pillows in various sizes. A few equally colorful throw rugs dotted the wood floor. Since her bedroom windows faced the lake, she'd opted for no curtains, giving her an unobstructed view of the water.

"Pillows." A smile tugged at his lips. "I like it."

She swallowed, trying to slow her uneven breathing.

He looked so out of place in her bedroom. Not that she'd decorated with frilly, girly things, but he was so big and masculine he was a stark contrast to the neutral serenity she'd been going for.

Her hands shook. His presence in her bedroom pretty much blew any semblance of serenity out the window.

"You're nervous," he said, brushing the backs of his knuckles down her cheek. "You shouldn't be. I already know you're beautiful. Inside *and* out."

He smiled, and something in her heart went into overdrive, skipping every other beat yet hammering harder.

Getting a grip on her nervousness, she tugged his shirt from his waistband. He lifted his arms, so she could peel it up his chest and over his head. She sucked in a tight breath. His body was beyond beautiful. It was a work of art that she couldn't wait to explore. Dropping the shirt to the floor, she ran her hands down his bare chest, reveling in the warmth of his thick pectorals and undulating abdominal muscles.

When his body quivered at her touch, she froze. "You don't like that?"

He laughed, a deep, throaty sound that reminded her of what an amazing voice he had. "Are you kidding? I love it. Don't stop."

She didn't.

His skin beneath her fingers was warm and taut. His shoulders and arms were as thickly muscled as his chest. As she sifted her fingers through the thin coating of hair arrowing down his torso and disappearing beneath his beltline, her hands trembled again. This was all happening so fast. They hardly knew each other.

Then why does it feel so damned right? She didn't know, but could only hope Nick felt the same.

Wanting him this much was both exciting…and terrifying.

She unbuckled the belt, then unbuttoned his jeans before

tugging down the zipper. Snug, black undershorts covered the bulge of his massive erection, and she couldn't resist dragging her fingers over him.

A deep, guttural groan emanated from his throat, sending chills to her belly. "Do you like it when I touch you like that?" *She* did, and the only thing that could top it was to feel his hardened length without the encumbrance of his undershorts.

He laughed. "You can touch me anywhere you like."

"Promise?" When he nodded and gave her that lopsided grin, an excited shiver shot through her. She clasped the waistband of his jeans, intending to push them down his legs when her hand contacted his gun.

"I've got this." He pulled the holster and badge off the belt and set it on the bedside table. Next, he sat on the edge of the bed, untied his boots, and kicked them to the side before standing again. A grin quirked his lips. "Carry on."

"Yes, Sergeant." She gave him a coy smile, then slid her hands around his waist, shoving them beneath the waistbands of his jeans and undershorts to cup his bare muscled ass.

As she shoved his clothing farther down, her hands contacted more and more of his bare flesh, and he groaned again, louder this time. She loved having this effect on him.

His legs were long and strong, with a thin coating of dark hair. His eyes were closed, his jaw clenched. When she'd gotten his undershorts low enough, his erection sprang forth, and her eyes widened at how big he was. Could she really take him all in? For the past few years, her sex life had been all but nonexistent.

Unable to stop herself, she took him in her hands, gently stroking his hard length.

"Baby," he growled, removing her hand. "Keep that up, and we won't make it to the bed." The look he gave her was tight with tension.

For a man with such big hands and fingers, he deftly unbuttoned her blouse and slipped it from her shoulders, running his hands down her arms. Tingles raced up and down her body, hardening her nipples.

This is really happening. Part of her couldn't believe it, yet she'd sensed their relationship was coming to this. Despite her resistance, she'd known it deep in her heart.

He reached behind her and unzipped her skirt, letting it fall to the floor. Resting her hands on his shoulders, she stepped out of the skirt and kicked it aside. Her breaths came quicker, and her skin grew hot. With a flick of his thumb, he unhooked her bra, then tugged it off. His low rumble of appreciation made her hunger for him pulse hotter, faster, until she could barely breathe.

He cupped her breasts and rubbed her nipples with his thumbs until they were pert and erect. Watching his large, calloused hands caressing the smoothness of her bare breasts was the sexiest thing she'd ever seen. Shockwaves of heat, lust, and desire ignited in her core. Now it was her turn to groan, and she pushed her breasts into his hands, wanting to experience all that he could give her.

When she met his gaze again, his eyes smoldered like molten metal. His lips closed around one of the hardened peaks, and she moaned louder, arching into his mouth. Energy hummed in her veins, and the hot, burning craving between her legs intensified until she wanted to scream.

"More." She held his head tighter to her breast. "*More. Please.*"

He urged her backward to the bed, laying her down then slowly stripping off her panties. The tips of his fingers were rough against her skin, the motion gentle as he slid the silky material down her thighs. He was big and heavy as he lowered on top of her. "Am I crushing you?"

In answer, she wrapped her arms around his back,

tugging him tighter against her and digging her fingers into his corded flesh. "No." Then she pulled his head down for a kiss she hoped would drive him out of his mind because that was exactly what he was doing to her. The taste of him in her mouth, on her tongue, was nectar she could sip on for a long, long time.

While they kissed, his hand massaged her breast, his fingers fondling her nipple until she couldn't take it any longer and twisted in his grasp, urging him to take the hardened nub in his mouth again. The moment his lips closed around her nipple, a sharp bolt of lightning shot to her core, and she gasped.

He continued plucking and teasing her with his tongue and teeth, scalding her body from the outside in, and still, it wasn't enough. She moaned louder, cradling his head until he shifted position and teased her other nipple with the same enthusiasm.

Moments later, he kissed her again, deeper this time. So deeply it was as if he were touching her soul. She undulated her hips, rubbing herself against his hard length.

His tongue stroked hers as his hand skimmed down her hip to hike her leg over the back of his thigh. When he settled between her legs, his erection was hot and hard, making her writhe against him until she was wet with need. Regretfully, she ended the kiss, gasping for air and feeling stupidly naive.

"Nick, I'm sorry, I-I don't have any—"

He cut her off. "I do." Then he rose and retrieved his wallet from the back of his pants and pulled out several packets. He shoved two into his jeans' pocket, then sheathed himself with the remaining condom.

Her heart squeezed. *What is he doing with all those condoms in his back pocket? Please tell me he hasn't been having sex with the Napkin Girls.*

When he lowered himself on top of her again, he must

have seen the distress on her face. "Hey." He stroked her cheek. "I haven't been with anyone in months, and that was just for sex. Since I met you, I haven't wanted anyone but you."

She gave him a skeptical look. "Not even any of the Napkin Girls?"

His rumbling laughter reverberated against her chest. "Not even the Napkin Girls."

"Stop laughing at me." She punched his shoulder, turning her head away when he tried to kiss her.

He stopped laughing and clasped her chin gently, forcing her to look at him. She was too embarrassed at her confession and shut her eyes.

"Look at me." She shook her head, feeling like a jealous teenager. "Open your eyes."

Reluctantly she did, and was surprised at the seriousness on his face. "Those condoms have been collecting dust in my wallet for a long time. If it makes you feel any better, seeing that photo of you and Myer on the wall in the café every day made me want to smash it into a thousand pieces. Knowing your ex had it in his bedroom makes me crazy just thinking about it."

"You always know what to say." She lifted a finger to his stubbled jaw. "Don't you?"

"I do have my moments. So, relax." His voice had turned husky. "And let me love you."

He nudged her thighs apart and guided himself inside her. She heard the growl of desire deep in her throat as she arched against him. Her nipples grazed his chest, tingling from the abrasion. It had been a long time since she'd had sex, and she dug her nails into his back as he stretched her tight walls.

She moaned at the delicious sensations as he rocked in and out. He cupped her face, kissing her while he hiked her leg higher over his buttocks. He drove deeper, sending her closer and closer to the edge.

"Baby, you're so tight and wet. Like hot silk sliding all around me."

"Don't stop. Whatever you do, don't stop." She dug her fingers into his buttocks then dragged her nails up his back. Thick muscles rippled and bunched as he pumped faster.

Her breath came in short little gasps. Her inner muscles clenched again and again. When the orgasm hit, it was hard and fast, and she cried out. A feeling so intense and wonderful surrounded her that she wished the moment would never end.

He pushed inside her once more then groaned, letting his head fall back. She pressed her mouth to his neck, sucking at his hot skin, loving the salty taste of him. His body stilled, yet she felt the spurt of his semen against the protective condom.

Incredible. Mind-blowing. Earth-shattering. All words flitting through her head, and those she'd never used to describe making love with any other man. Not that there'd been that many, but none before Nick had ever left her body so sated. Her mind so at peace.

Her heart so frightfully open.

Another second passed, and he rolled to his side, taking her with him. They remained that way, with him still buried inside her. He kissed the top of her head, clasping her hand to his chest. Within minutes, his breathing evened out, and she realized he'd dozed off. No wonder, given that he'd been without sleep for nearly forty-eight hours.

Snuggling against him, she closed her eyes, but her mind was spinning. Moving carefully, so she didn't wake Nick, she shifted to watch him sleep. He was out cold, and yet in his arms, she felt more protected than if there'd been an army battalion parked outside. She'd also experienced more fulfillment of her body and soul's desires than at any other time in her life. The realization was overwhelming.

His words came back in a rush. *Let me love you.* She wasn't foolish enough to be misled into thinking that had been a confession of love. She'd understood it for precisely what it was—a romanticized description of sex. It had been a sweet gesture on his part to ease her concerns that he slept around a lot.

She pressed her head to his chest, inhaling the remnants of his masculine aftershave and the musky scent of their lovemaking into her lungs.

There was no denying that she could easily fall for him. But would he ever feel the same? More specifically, *could* he ever feel that way about her? No matter what had just happened between them, there was something holding him in check—a barrier still in place. Whether it was the memory of his wife, or that she was still officially a suspect, or something else, she didn't know.

Regardless, she was determined not to have any regrets. If this turned out to be a one-time thing with no strings attached, she would always remember this as a spectacularly beautiful moment during a time of chaos in her life.

Liar.

She took a deep breath, choking down the truth.

It would always be more. *Much* more.

Chapter Fourteen

Nick woke slowly, inhaling the smell of freesia. Earlier, when he'd woken to ditch the condom, Andi had been curled on her side, fast asleep.

Moonlight no longer bathed the bedroom in ethereal light, and the room was dark. He hadn't meant to fall asleep, but after being up for two days straight and then having the most amazing sex with the woman he—

The woman I what?

He wasn't sure how to answer his own question. He *did* know it hadn't been just sex.

After getting over the numbness Tanya's death had left in his heart, he'd had plenty of sex, but this was different. It went far beyond a casual hookup.

No matter how hard he'd been fighting it, he had to face facts. He might be falling for her, and it scared the hell out of him.

If the woman he loved died…if he couldn't protect her… he'd never be able to handle it again. There was still a mission to complete, and he wouldn't stop until it was done. But that didn't keep him from wanting Andi or worrying for her safety every waking moment.

She probably hadn't gotten much sleep, either, but the need to touch her again was overwhelming. Turning on his side, he reached for her. Her side of the bed was empty. And cold.

He bolted upright, searching the darkness.

"Andi?" He heard the caged panic in his voice. "*Andi.*"

He flung back the sheet and leaped from the bed. His heart pounded as he shoved his legs into his jeans and grabbed his gun and his phone, clipping the phone to his belt. If anything had happened to her because he'd let himself fall asleep…

"Fuck," he growled, then quietly padded down the stairs, gun extended. "Andi?" he called softly. No answer.

Leading with the gun, he did a quick search of the living room and the small office. Through a window, he glimpsed the patrol car outside on the street and two shadows in the front seats. Next, he cleared the kitchen. That's when he saw her through the window, standing on the porch and peering through the telescope. Saxon and Stray snuggled together in a corner by the back steps. Stray's eyes were closed while Saxon maintained a watchful eye on Andi. The only thing out of place was the air mattress he'd used for Saxon's training, which he'd propped against the side of the house. It now lay on the porch in front of the door.

He exhaled a shaky breath, then waited a moment for his heart to slow before setting his gun and cell phone on the counter and opening the screen door. It creaked, and when she turned to him, his heart began thudding again, but not from panic or fear. Something else was wreaking total havoc with that muscle in his chest. He wasn't prepared to acknowledge what it was, but his brain began flashing with images of his future. One filled with love and companionship.

The other with darkness and solitude. Which way it would go was anybody's guess.

Crickets chirped in the distance, and the air was still warm.

"Good morning," she said, smiling.

He couldn't move. Couldn't speak. Standing there in her bare feet, wearing his black T-shirt, she was the most beautiful, desirable woman he'd ever seen. And she'd scared the piss out of him.

"What are you doing out here?" His words came out unintentionally harsh.

"I didn't want to wake you." She turned back to the telescope and adjusted its position. "I'm looking for the Perseids."

"The *what?*"

"Meteor showers," she answered without turning around. "The Perseids are the most prolific meteor showers to hit the earth. The best time to view them is in mid-August, between midnight and dawn."

"Do tell." He sidestepped the air mattress and wrapped his arms around her waist, pressing his chest to her back and his lips to her ear. It took another few seconds for his racing heart to slow. "I didn't think you needed a telescope to see meteors."

"You don't. They're visible to the naked eye, but if you're lucky enough to catch one through the scope, it's even more exciting." She angled the long metal tube in a different direction. "During peak activity, sixty or more come down every hour."

He nipped at her earlobe, grazing it with his teeth. "Aren't you afraid of getting hit in the head?"

"Um, no." She lifted her head from the ocular, tilting it to give him better access to the soft curve of her neck. "Most burn up in the atmosphere..." He ran his tongue along the creases of her ear, loving how she shivered in response. "Long before they get close," she continued in a breathy voice as he trailed his tongue farther down her neck.

He slipped his hands beneath the T-shirt, hiking it higher and stroking the flat planes of her belly, confirming what he suspected. Other than the shirt, she was totally naked.

Stroking higher, he cupped her breasts, rubbing his thumbs across her nipples until they hardened to tight little peaks. "It turns me on when you go all astronomical." The erection straining at his zipper was proof of that, along with the blood racing at light speed through his veins.

"It does?" She released the telescope and leaned back against him.

He continued his ministrations, getting crazy turned on as she wriggled her buttocks against his erection.

"Yeah, it does," he whispered against her ear, then stroked down her belly, moving his hands to cup the perfect, rounded globes of her ass and squeezing them lightly. "Keep talking."

"I...can't think straight," she murmured, beginning to shiver, "when you...do that."

"That's the idea." He pressed his lips to her ear again, loving that she found his touch so distracting. "Is Andromeda really the name on your birth certificate?"

"Yeesss," she said on a breathy sigh. "I was thinking about having it tattooed on my ass."

"Don't. Your ass is perfect the way it is." He gave her buttocks another gentle squeeze. "Raise your arms." When she did as he ordered, he yanked the shirt over her head, then tossed it aside and began stroking her breasts. "Tell me more."

"Well, uh..." She gave a deep sigh of pleasure that drove him crazy with the need to get inside her again. "Did you know that Andromeda is one of the largest constellations?"

"A beautiful name for a beautiful woman." He gently pinched her nipples, and she groaned.

"You think I'm beautiful?" She covered his hands with hers, urging him on.

"I thought you were beautiful the first time I saw you. In the shower. Washing your dog and wearing about five square inches of bathing suit." He chuckled. That vision was permanently seared into his memory. "Now, I think you're the most stunning woman I've ever seen."

Before she could respond, he clasped her hands, drawing them upward to link her arms around the back of his neck while he continued stroking her quivering body, pushing his erection against her backside. "Keep talking, sweetheart." His fingers delved lower, seeking out the warm, moist folds between her thighs.

"In Greek mythology, Andromeda was the daughter of Cassiopeia." As he pushed one finger inside her, she sucked in a breath. "Andromeda was...chained to a rock to be eaten by the sea monster, Cetus, to...pacify the monster's craving for human flesh."

"Speaking of flesh..." He swirled his finger over and around her swollen folds, getting more excited by how wet she was. "So, your parents named you after a poor woman who was fed to a monster?" He pushed two fingers inside her heat and began pumping them in and out.

"It was either that, or..." She rocked against him, taking his fingers in deeper. "...be named after the eleventh brightest star in the sky."

"What's that?" Christ, she really was turning him on. He was so hard beneath his jeans he was on the verge of exploding.

"Betelgeuse."

He laughed and used his other hand to spread her slick folds apart, rubbing her swollen clit while he continued pumping his fingers in and out.

Her breath came faster, her body tightening around his fingers. "Did you know that Sirius—the brightest star in the sky—is also called, um, the 'dog star'?"

"I did." He began kissing her shoulder, loving her taste, her smell, and…everything else about her. "It's in the constellation Canis Major. That's it, come for me, baby."

Her channel squeezed his fingers. When she cried out, he turned her chin toward him, capturing her mouth with his and absorbing the rest of her cries as her body convulsed around him. The last thing they needed was for the patrolmen out front to hear her scream and come running.

And if he didn't get inside her, he really would erupt in his pants.

He yanked down his zipper, thankful he'd crammed the remaining condoms into his pocket. With fumbling fingers, he ripped open one of the packets and quickly rolled on a condom. He turned her around, then lifted her, spreading her legs as he lowered her onto his aching cock. She linked her legs around his waist and her arms around his neck.

He growled with barely controlled restraint, desperate to last longer, knowing he wouldn't. "Jesus, baby." With his hands at her waist, he raised and lowered her onto him as she arched her back. Pert nipples beckoned to him, and he caught one between his teeth, sucking it into his mouth.

Turning, he lowered her to the mattress and began thrusting more forcefully. Her legs were linked over his ass, gripping him, holding their bodies tightly together. Their breathing became labored as he held himself back, clenching his teeth, wanting to make her come again before he did.

"Can't hold out…" His body strained above hers, his muscles strung tighter than a rubber band. His entire body was primed, screaming for release.

He kissed her as she came again, absorbing her cries

while she convulsed around him, arching her breasts upward. Nick came hard and fast, pushing deeper as he exploded inside her.

Moments later, a sense of utter contentment enveloped him like a warm caress. Lowering to his elbows, he rested his forehead in the valley between her breasts. His breathing and heart rate took another full minute to slow. When he pressed a kiss to her chest, her heart thudded against his lips.

They lay that way for several more minutes, basking in the silence. Finally, he lifted his head. Her eyes were closed, her smooth skin glowing in the moonlight. As he gazed down at her, he couldn't summon any words that could come close to describing the strong emotions gushing over him. He'd never been a poet or one for flowery declarations, but making love to Andi outside under the stars had been one of the most beautiful, memorable moments of his life. And there was no way in hell she was in league with a gun dealer. He'd know it if she were.

He threaded his fingers through her hair, loving the silky softness against his calloused hand. He could get used to this. Being with her. Touching her. Making love to her. But there was still so much between them.

A warm breeze picked up, fluttering her hair against his arm. Even if she was officially crossed off the suspect list in the next five seconds, could he ever love again?

He honestly didn't know. The only thing he knew for sure was that he was standing on the edge of a steep precipice he'd only fallen from once before in his life.

• • •

Andi opened her eyes to find Nick watching her intently, his brows lowered. The look on his face was a combination of determination and something else. Did he have misgivings about what they'd just done?

A lump of anxiety the size of a softball settled in her chest. In all likelihood, their relationship had no place to go. *Too late to turn back now.* Because, without intending to, she'd already begun opening her heart to him. At this point, she had to let the chips fall wherever they were meant to be.

Remember your vow. No regrets.

Unable to meet his gaze a moment longer, she glanced at the corner of the deck, relieved to find Stray resting comfortably. Saxon lay a few feet away, snout pressed to the deck but ever alert, his golden eyes glinting in the moonlight.

She didn't know what to say or do. The last impression she wanted Nick to have of her was that of a clingy girlfriend who wasn't even officially his girlfriend. She didn't know if she was his *anything.*

"Did you know that Sirius is twenty times brighter than the sun?" she asked, hating the awkward silence.

He grinned. "Nope."

"Or that the only things in the sky brighter than Sirius are a few planets and the International Space Station?"

"Who knew?" He brushed a lock of hair from her face, tucking it behind her ear.

She shivered, wishing he could touch her that way every night for the rest of their lives. "I bet you don't know why the time period between July third and August eleventh is called the 'dog days.'"

"You'd win that bet." His grin morphed into that lopsided smile she'd begun to love.

"Ancient astronomers believed," she continued, embarrassed by the unsteadiness in her voice, "that the combination of the sun during the day and Sirius at night was responsible for extra heat in midsummer."

"You're nervous again."

"Am not." She pouted, not willing to admit that he was

making her more nervous than when she'd lost her virginity.

"Are, too."

She'd been about to deny his accusation, when he lowered his head and gave her a slow, sweet kiss, one that had her body quaking with need all over again. He lifted his head, then eased out of her and shifted so they were lying on their sides facing each other. He was watching her in a way that made her insides melt, but she wasn't a starry-eyed teenager. That look didn't mean this was anything more than sex to him. *Great* sex.

"Did you know—"

He rested his finger on her lips. "As much I enjoy hearing you quote astronomical factoids, I'd rather hear something about *you*."

"Me?" She widened her eyes. "You ran a complete background check on me. You probably know everything there is to know. My date of birth, my social security number, my employment history, where my bank accounts are located, even my associates for the last twenty years."

He laughed, swirling his fingers in slow circles on her shoulder. "Not statistical information. Why did you and Myer really split?"

"A lot of reasons." Ones she wished had been clearer at the time. "Mostly we outgrew each other. Which, I suppose, means we weren't meant to be together. At least, not meant to be anything more than friends."

"You broke up with him?"

"Yes." It had been the right thing to do, and she'd thought he'd gotten over it, until hearing his recent and unexpected declaration of love. "I sensed he was on the verge of proposing, and by that time I already knew we were done."

"Didn't you want to have children?" he asked. "I see how much you dote on every baby who rolls into the DPC."

A warm feeling bloomed inside her at the thought of

giving birth to her own child, but it was fleeting. She could still remember the doctor's words as he told her she'd never carry a child. Swallowing the rising lump of sadness in her throat, she took a deep breath. "I did want children, but I can't have any."

"I'm sorry." He tenderly skimmed his hand up and down her arm.

"Yeah, well..." She averted his gaze. "At least I don't have to worry about birth control."

He grunted, and a wistful expression came to his eyes, leaving her wondering as to its source.

"After Joe and I broke up, I tried dating again," she continued. "I even gave the online scene a whirl."

He grimaced. "How'd that go?"

"Not well." She grimaced back. "I know it works for some people, just not for me. Maybe I'm a sucker. My track record for seeing through people's crap to know who and what they really are isn't so good." She sighed. "Even Joe isn't who I thought he was. Turned out there was a side to him—the *criminal* side—that he apparently kept to himself. And what he did with my bank account... I never thought he'd use me like that. I didn't know he had that in him. Although after what happened to me in New York I—"

Woops. She bit her lower lip. *Didn't mean for that to slip out.*

His brows lowered, and he got that familiar hard-ass cop look on his face. "What happened in New York?"

"Nothing," she started to lie. Then again, it had been years, and maybe it was time to get over it. "Someone I thought cared about me—someone I trusted—lied to me. He hurt me, and he undermined my position at the company I worked for."

Nick's hand stilled on her arm. "Hurt you how?"

"It doesn't matter anymore. It's in the past." *Please don't ask me more about it.* The last thing she wanted was to ruin this moment by reliving the most hurtful, humiliating time in her life.

He stared intently at her a moment longer, then, as if sensing she didn't want to discuss the matter further, nodded. "As for Joe, don't kick yourself so hard for missing what he was capable of. In my line of work, I've seen how good people can be at hiding things. Even from the people they love," he added.

She wasn't sure if his last comment related to his job or his personal life. She was tempted to ask but didn't. "Unfortunately, I don't have access to complete personal, financial, and criminal histories the way you do." She touched her finger to his chest. "I prefer getting to know someone organically. Naturally."

He arched a brow. "You mean the way you and I met?"

She arched a brow back. "There was *nothing* natural about how you and I met."

"I suppose not." He grinned at her.

There were so many things she wanted to know about him. One thing in particular was difficult to ask, but she had to. "Do you have any children?"

A deep line creased his forehead. "No."

She waited, hoping he'd tell her more. Like how his wife had died. Whether he still grieved for her. Her insides were screaming for more information.

"I'm sorry." She instantly regretted her question. "I shouldn't have pried." She tried pulling away, but he wrapped his arm around her waist, locking her securely against him.

"*You*," he said softly, "could *never* be insensitive. I've seen you interact with your staff and customers. You don't have an insensitive bone in your body."

"Unfortunately, I have my moments. Like right now." How she wished she could take back her question.

The night air filled with more awkward silence, and she feared their line of conversation had come to an abrupt end.

"Tanya—my wife—and I tried to have kids." His eyes took on a faraway look. "She got pregnant three times but always miscarried. Twice in the first trimester. The third time early on in the second."

Her heart ached for him, his dead wife, and their unborn babies. She couldn't imagine what they both must have gone through. Losing a child would be far more painful than never being able to conceive one.

"Each miscarriage killed something inside her, and she began withdrawing from me. After the third time," he continued, "she went into a deep depression. I couldn't take what it was doing to her. I told her we should stop trying, and that we could adopt."

"Tanya wanted her own child," she murmured, inherently understanding what she must have been feeling. "She wanted a child from both of you."

"Yeah, but she could never accept that it wasn't going to happen for us." His voice had turned bitter. "I tried to get her the help she needed. Got her to see a shrink. That only seemed to make things worse. Her depression kept spiraling downward. Every day became torture. For both of us. No matter how much I tried convincing her, she could never believe that I loved her regardless of whether or not we had kids. She asked for a divorce, but I refused to give it to her. In her mind, she was trying to set me free." He shook his head. "Didn't work."

"What happened?" she whispered, starting to have a bad feeling where this was going.

He took a deep breath and raked his fingers through his hair. "It got to the point where she barely left the house anymore. I tried to get her to talk to her friends, but she refused. Then, she tried to kill herself."

Andi couldn't stop her soft intake of breath.

He paused and looked up at the early morning sky. "Her first attempt, she used pills. I found her and got her to the hospital in time to pump her stomach. A few months passed, then... I should have known something wasn't right. One night, she was almost...happy. She made me dinner, told me she would always love me, then said good night and went to bed."

Oh, no. This was going to be worse than she'd imagined.

"During work the next day it kept bugging me how she'd been acting the night before. I swung by the house to check on her." When he stopped talking, there was so much despair in his eyes, her throat constricted until she could barely breathe. "I found her in the bedroom."

She laced her fingers through his and squeezed his hand.

His jaw went harder than she'd ever seen it. "She'd shot herself in the head."

"Oh, Nick." Tears began welling in her eyes. "I'm so sorry."

"She left a note. What she wanted most in the world was to have a baby. *My* baby. She finally accepted that it wasn't going to happen but couldn't live with it. In the letter, she apologized to me for being a failure. For not being complete enough as a woman to give me a child. No matter how many times I said it, she never believed me that we could be perfectly happy just being *us*." He laughed bitterly. "To this day, I don't know where she got the gun. The serial number had been filed off. It was an illegal gun off the street."

That explains a lot.

She remembered the cold fury she'd seen in his eyes as he'd described the teenage girl who'd been struck in the head by a bullet during a drive-by shooting. It hadn't been solely the girl's death that he'd been reliving. It had been his wife's, too.

"I loved her, but it wasn't enough." He began shaking his head, clenching his jaw. "I couldn't give her what she wanted, then *I* failed to protect her when she needed it most."

"No, Nick. No." She rose on her elbow, stroking his cheek while her heart broke for him. On the outside, he was as tough as they came—a battle-scarred cop who'd seen the worst mankind had to offer. Inside, he experienced pain just like everyone else. Maybe more so, because there was a deeply ingrained protective core running through him. "There wasn't anything you could have done. You said so yourself. She planned this so there'd be no opportunity to save her."

"Christ, I do know that. Now." He inhaled deeply then let it out. "Everyone else told me the same thing. Matt, Eric, Kade… We've all seen enough suicides to know that."

"But this hit you personally, and it still hurts."

When he cupped her face, his touch was gentle, but a muscle ticking in his cheek evidenced the tension brewing inside him. "The past is just that, but I need to do everything in my power to get illegal guns off the street. *Everything.* Can you understand that?"

As she nodded, a deep, biting cold settled in her heart at the fierce conviction in his eyes. She admired it and feared it.

Rising from the mattress, he peeled off the used condom, then zipped up his jeans and went to the door. Early morning light glinted on his rippling back and shoulder muscles. The screen door closed quietly behind him, and she was left with a sick feeling in the pit of her stomach.

No matter what he'd just said, his priorities were indeed still dictated by the past, and they were focused not only on his guilt but his burning need to succeed at his job.

She squeezed her eyes shut as overwhelming sadness and futility settled in her heart. For him, getting this gun dealer really was personal. As things stood, she doubted there was room in his life for anything—or, any*one*—else.

A phone rang, and she stared at the door. It hadn't been her phone. It was Nick's.

The ringing stopped, and the rich timbre of his voice floated to her. She couldn't quite make out the words but heard the angry tone of his voice.

A moment later, the kitchen light came on, and he pushed open the door. His face was tight.

"What is it?" She bolted upright, grabbing his T-shirt and pulling it over her head. The look on his face told her something had happened. "Is it Joe?" She held her breath. Was he about to tell her the gangs had caught up to him and he was dead?

"It was." Gone was the tender look he'd given her while they'd been making love, along with every vestige of sadness and despair she'd seen only moments ago. In its place was the impenetrable man she'd first met, the one she didn't know—the cold, hard, steely-eyed cop. "He's turning himself in."

Chapter Fifteen

Nick squeezed the Explorer into a tight spot against the curb in front of the building that housed the U.S. Attorney's Office. He glanced at his watch. It was almost ten a.m.

After his pre-dawn calls to Cox and Eric, AUSA Bennett had insisted on an emergency meeting. The entire investigative team would be there, and they wouldn't leave until they cranked out a plan to get Myer into police custody. Alive.

He and Andi had swung by his place for a change of clothes and to put Saxon up in his kennel. He'd showered, shaved, then grabbed a fresh pair of dark slacks and a navy-blue polo shirt with the state police emblem embroidered on the front.

"You ready?" he said to Andi.

"Not really." She pushed open the passenger side door and stepped out of the SUV.

She hadn't wanted to be there, preferring to remain at home to make sure Stray was comfortable, but he'd insisted. There was no way he'd leave her alone again. Short of handcuffing her to him, the only way he managed to get her out of the house was to arrange for Tess to check up on the dog while they were out. But he knew Stray wasn't the only reason she didn't want to be here.

Since Myer's call earlier that morning, she'd begun distancing herself from him. Only once had he caught her eye in the last few hours, and at that moment, he'd understood. They'd made love, then he'd bolted like the chickenshit that he was.

He slammed his own door shut, and when he met her on the sidewalk, she quickly avoided his gaze. It was on the tip of his tongue to tell her how he really felt about her, but he couldn't. Hell, even he didn't exactly know. Or if part of him did, his brain still refused to acknowledge it. The sooner they could both get this investigation behind them, the better.

They walked in silence across the cobblestone courtyard to the main doors of the enormous U-shaped building, then through security and to the elevator. When the doors opened on the third floor, he touched the small of her back, intending to direct her to the reception area, but she flinched, and he dropped his hand.

I'm fucking this up. Royally.

"Andi, wait." He stopped her outside the reception door. Her eyes were filled with uncertainty, and she clasped her arms around her waist as if she were trying to shore up the steadily growing wall between them. Christ, he couldn't blame her for a second. For the last five years, he'd been doing the same goddamn thing between him and anyone who tried to get close. "After Myer turns himself in and the dust settles, we *will* talk."

Her brows furrowed. "About what?" she asked in a flat tone.

"About—"

The reception door opened.

"There you are," Cox said. "We've been waiting for you."

Nick groaned aloud. *Fuck*.

When they walked in, a dozen male eyes cast appreciative looks at Andi, particularly the FBI special agent in charge. SAC Dan Wolinski made no attempt to hide his reaction, sweeping his gaze down, then up her body.

The conservative beige linen slacks she wore couldn't hide the slim curves of her waist or the shapeliness of her legs. Her black sleeveless blouse was loose-fitting but somehow emphasized the gentle mounds of her breasts. With very little makeup and only tiny gold hoops at her ears, she was both beautiful *and* sexy in a casual, graceful way few women could achieve.

He understood the attraction other men had toward her, but as her lover, he wanted to wipe that sleazy look off the SAC's face by slamming him headfirst into the nearest wall.

The only man she smiled at was Eric, who came up to them first. "You guys both look like I feel—like crap. Get any sleep last night?"

"Some," Nick said, noting the flush on Andi's cheeks.

Their conversation hadn't gone unheard. Wolinski sent him a sly grin. Nick gritted his teeth. Stomping down the urge to kiss her then and there—branding her as his—was quickly becoming a habit. But this wasn't the place or the time to start acting on his impulses.

Focus.

"The lab guys should get started on Matteo's phone dump today," Cox said. "I've asked for geocoding on that photo. If they can give us the date, time, and location where it was taken, it may help us figure out who wound up with it after it was stolen from Myer's house. I'd like to nail down this guy's identity before we bring Myer in."

"Agreed." Nick nodded. "Once we arrest him, the gangs will want to stay as far as possible from the center of this investigation."

"Gentlemen." AUSA Bennett held open one of the inner doors. "And lady." He tipped his head to Andi. "We're in Conference Room A. Conference Room B is empty, and Ms. Hardt can wait there."

Nick escorted her to the other conference room, located in the far wing of the floor. Out of the corner of his eye, he caught SAC Wolinski and his ASAC watching them. Watching Andi, more likely.

Conference Room B was cavernous, with giant floor-to-ceiling concrete pillars in the center. Bookcases crammed with law books lined two walls, while a bank of windows overlooked the courtyard below.

"Want coffee?"

She shook her head, then turned her back to him, staring out the row of horizontal windows. "How long will you be?"

He came to stand behind her, gently rubbing her arms, but she stepped from his reach. "A couple hours." Maybe more, but he hoped not. When she groaned, he handed her a remote sitting on the long table in between two of the columns. "You can watch TV."

"Thanks," she answered, staring at the remote in her hand.

He watched her, feeling totally helpless. Not for the first time in his life, he wished he could turn back the clock for a do-over because, minute by minute, she was shutting him out and it was killing him. What he needed was more time to explain to her all the shit that was cluttering up his mind. Today, there wasn't a second to spare. Giving her space was the only thing he could do. "I'll see you later." Before she could skirt away, he dropped a quick kiss on the top of her head, then left.

Back in Conference Room A, he closed the door behind him and sat at the opposite end of the table from AUSA Bennett.

"Everyone, thank you for coming on such short notice." Bennett pushed his wire-rimmed glasses higher on his nose then pulled a legal pad from a stack of papers in front of him. "Nick will fill everyone in on what's happened."

All sets of eyes turned to him.

"Early this morning," he began, "Myer returned my call. He's ready to turn himself in."

A chorus of murmurs went around the table.

"What changed his mind?" Wolinski crossed his arms over his dark-gray suit jacket. "Last I heard, he was holed up with no indication of showing his face anytime soon."

He met the older man's eyes. "I let him know gang members tried to kidnap his ex-girlfriend, most likely at the direction of whoever he was laundering money for. I made it clear they were going to use her to get to him."

"She's a hot-looking woman." Wolinski grinned sleazily again, leaving Nick wondering if the man *had* any other facial expressions. "If anyone could draw him out of hiding, she could. With a body and a face like hers, she could make a man do just about anything." He chuckled, but no one laughed with him.

Nick clenched his jaw. Every second he spent in that arrogant little prick's presence made him want to launch across the table and strangle the man.

Eric alternated between eyeing the FBI SAC with disgust and shooting Nick warning glances not to act on what he was thinking.

"Where is he now?" Bennett asked.

"Canada," Nick replied.

"Canada?" Wolinski huffed. "How did he get across the border without us knowing? Didn't anyone notify DHS?"

"We did." With every word out of this prick's mouth, Nick was getting more and more irritated. Didn't this asshole read Cox's reports? "Somehow he got through a border crossing without getting grabbed."

"Stuff happens." Bennett made a few notes on his pad.

"We can whine about the holes in our borders all night, but it won't do us any good today. Luckily, this time it's irrelevant, since he's turning himself in."

"How'd you leave it with him?" Cox asked.

"That we'd call him today at eleven thirty with the logistics." At that statement, every man looked either at his watch or at the round white clock on the wall over Bennett's head.

"Nick? Randy?" Bennett's gray brows rose as he looked from Nick to Cox. "How do you want to play this?"

Wolinski slammed his hand down on the table. "I say we get a convoy of marked units, go grab his ass at the border, then haul him to FBI headquarters for interrogation."

Nick and Eric exchanged knowing looks. *So, the FBI can take all the credit.* Not that he gave a shit who got the credit. His only goals were to bring Myer in alive then squeeze him dry of every ounce of intel he had on the gunrunning ring and get him to vindicate Andi.

"We could take him directly to a safe house," Cox supplied.

The SAC's neck reddened as he glared across the table at Cox. Nick hoped the guy didn't get demoted for going against his SAC.

"A safe house isn't a bad idea," Nick countered. "But we don't have the luxury of time. We should bring him directly to the courthouse, so we can throw him in front of the grand jury and lock down his testimony before he changes his mind and lawyers up."

"Or somebody else gets to him," Eric added.

"I agree." Bennett nodded. "Let's not take any risks. I'll reserve a room outside the grand jury for us to debrief Myer first. I want him to give us all the account numbers and passwords for the tainted bank accounts, along with all related wire transfers, emails...whatever we can use as evidence."

Eric turned to Nick. "Did he say who he's working for?"

"Brian Argyle." He pulled out a folded piece of paper from his pants pocket—the notes he'd made earlier that morning when Myer had called. "Argyle's company is Argyle Enterprises based in Scotland. That's where Myer's been wiring some of the money."

Cox flipped open his laptop and began typing away. They all waited to see what he could pull up. The man was a whiz with the computer and had access to more government databases than Nick could remember acronyms for.

A few minutes later, he looked up from the laptop. "I can't find anything on Brian Argyle or Argyle Enterprises."

"So they're phony names," Nick said. "But someone had to open those accounts in person and provide the banks with a name and identification to do it."

Special Agent Bill Douglas of the IRS jotted something down in his portfolio. "I'll run these names through our databases. Just in case."

"I'll get started on an MLAT with Scotland." Bennett made a note on his pad. "But that will take a while to work its way through DOJ and then across the pond to our Scottish colleagues."

Too much time to bother with.

In theory, Mutual Legal Assistance Treaties were great for obtaining information in foreign government databases, but not if you wanted it ASAP. It would be months before the request worked its way through official channels.

Knowing Eric had a police contact in Scotland, he caught his friend's eye. Eric nodded subtly, acknowledging the unspoken request.

While Bennett stepped out to make arrangements for grand jury time, Nick and the others brainstormed the logistical details of getting Myer in. Before they knew it, it was eleven thirty.

Bennett had returned to the conference room, and Nick

punched in Myer's cell number. He put the call on speaker and set it on the table so everyone else could hear the conversation. The phone rang three times.

"Hello."

"Joseph Myer," he began. "This is Sgt. Houston. With me is Assistant United States Attorney Ted Bennett, agents from the FBI, IRS, and ATF. We're making arrangements to meet you at the border tomorrow and escort you to the federal courthouse in Springfield to testify before the grand jury."

At first, Myer didn't respond. He could hear him breathing, so he knew the guy hadn't hung up. "You with me?"

"I'm with you."

"Good." If Myer reneged on the deal, he was fully prepared to cross the border and drag his ass back himself. "Before we go over logistics, we have a few questions about Brian Argyle. His name doesn't show up in any database, so who is he?"

"I don't know who he is, and we've never met."

Bennett gave Nick a quizzical look.

"Then how were all the transactions handled?" Nick asked.

"By phone and by wire transfer."

"What does he sound like over the phone?" Cox asked. "Young? Old? Does he have a Scottish accent?"

"I don't know. I never spoke with Argyle."

"Then who have you been dealing with?" Nick frowned at the phone.

"His secretary, Mary. And she *does* have a Scottish accent." Myer paused, and Nick heard what sounded like boat horns in the background but couldn't place them. "I have to go. I'm not sure, but someone might be following me."

"Wait." Nick grabbed the phone. "Why did you use Andi's bank account to wire that hundred grand last month?"

A deep exhale came through the phone. "I never meant

to involve her, I swear it. My bank's system was down that day, and I was desperate. I had to send money out of the country in a hurry, so I copied down her bank information when she wasn't looking, and my friend at her bank helped me out. She has nothing to do with this. Any of it."

She's innocent. Not that Nick doubted it at this point, but hearing it from Myer's mouth made it more than just his gut impression. Now it was official.

Tomorrow, Myer would be in police custody, but Nick was reluctant to stop peppering him with questions. Something about this scenario sent up all kinds of red flags, not the least of which was that Argyle could be anyone, and they had abso-fucking-lutely nothing to go on to ID the man. But it sounded like Myer was jittery enough as it was. "Can you be at the Thousand Island Bridge border crossing in Alexandria Bay by ten o'clock tomorrow morning? We'll meet you there."

Myer hesitated a long moment before speaking. "I have my own terms."

"*What* terms?" Even though Myer couldn't see him, Nick narrowed his eyes.

"First, I'll meet you at the courthouse. I'll slip through the border the same way I got in."

"Fine," he bit out. He didn't like that idea, but it wasn't a deal breaker. They could easily remove the Red Notice and replace it with a border alert so they'd know the second Myer crossed out of Canada. "What else?"

"I'll only turn myself in if Andi is there."

"Not happening." Nick shot to his feet and smacked his hands on either side of his cell phone. "Your actions nearly got her killed once already. I won't let that happen again."

"Those are my terms. Take it or leave it."

"You're not in a position to make demands," he shouted. "I'll put her on the phone with you, but that's as close as you'll get to her." Ever again, if he had his way.

"Then the deal's off. If I don't see her in the doorway of that courthouse, I'll turn around and disappear. Forever."

"Nick." Bennett's face twisted with disapproval.

Struggling for control, Nick fisted his hands on the table. "Stand by," he said to Myer, then muted the call.

He knew damned well what had crawled up Bennett's ass. He wanted Nick to agree to Myer's terms, regardless of the risk to Andi's life. *Selfish bastard.* Like most prosecutors, Bennett only wanted the next notch on his belt of convictions, all in the pursuit of a ridiculously high-paying job offer from a prestigious private law firm one day.

"Dammit, Ted." He shook his head adamantly. "I won't let this sonofabitch dictate how this goes down, and I will *not* put Andi in harm's way again. Even if it means we have to chase Myer down some other way."

Because now that he'd found Andi, she was too important to him to risk losing.

"What's your problem, Sergeant?" Wolinski sneered at him.

"My problem"—he gritted his teeth, again struggling not to do bodily harm to Cox's boss—"is that no one but me seems to care about an innocent woman's life. They already tried grabbing her as bait once, and if they'd succeeded you know as well as I do, they'd have killed her the second Myer showed up. Now you want to put her in the line of fire again?"

"We can put more agents on the ground," Cox offered. "You'll be there. We'll all be there to protect her."

"Maybe," Eric joined in, "Matt, Kade, Markus, Jaime, or Dayne can lend a hand. Their detail at the Expo started today, but their shifts vary. Some of them may be free tomorrow morning to assist." Eric's expression was one of understanding. He was the only man in the room who knew about Nick's personal relationship with Andi. "We'll control every aspect of the meet."

Nick pressed his lips together, glaring at Eric. Not that he didn't appreciate his friend's input, but he'd seen plenty of controlled meets go bad. This one was so *out* of their control, it was a joke to call it that in the first place.

"I don't have to remind you," Bennett said in an implacable tone, "as long as you're assigned to this *federal* task force, technically you report to *me*."

"And to *me*." Wolinski shot Nick a smug, cocky look.

"Let's be clear here." He flicked a steely gaze from Wolinski to Bennett. "Officially, I don't work for *either* of you." He let out a heavy breath, knowing he was backed into a corner he didn't like. When the case was over, he was so done with this task force.

"Your concerns are duly noted." Using his pen, Bennett pointed to Nick's phone. "Get him here tomorrow."

He unmuted the call. "Myer. When can you be at the courthouse tomorrow?"

"Noon. And Andi will be there?"

He held back a snarl. "Yes." He recited the address for the Springfield federal courthouse on State Street.

"Sergeant." Myer's voice choked. "If something happens to me, tell Andi... Tell her I love her."

Swallowing the first response that sprang to his mind— *go fuck yourself*—Nick reeled in his anger. "You can tell her that yourself." *You sonofabitch.*

Even though Myer was looking at substantial jail time, there was no way on this earth Nick would allow him to start something again with Andi. No way he'd ever let Myer touch his woman.

Damn straight, she was his woman. Until that moment, he'd been too thick-headed to see it, but he fucking knew it now.

The phone beeped, and the screen went dark. Now all they had to do was throw together a foolproof ops plan involving a half dozen agencies.

From across the table, Eric caught his attention. "So we still have no idea who we're looking for."

"Then we start with the secretary," Nick said. "As soon as we get Myer's cell phone and laptop, we track her down."

"When he gets here," Bennett added, "I want to do a thorough interview before putting him in front of the grand jury."

Thirty minutes later, they'd hashed out an ops plan that would suffice, given the exigent circumstances. Through it all, Wolinski's face registered more and more indignation. The man hated not being in the driver's seat.

The door opened, and Nick recognized Brendan Sykes, another prosecutor he'd occasionally worked with. "Sorry to interrupt," Sykes said. "Nothing was on the schedule for this conference room right now. I thought it was free."

"It's an emergency meeting," Bennett replied. "We're almost done here."

"Thanks, Ted." Sykes left, closing the door behind him, but it didn't completely latch and edged open a couple of inches.

"I just heard from the lab guys." Cox held up his cell phone. "They dumped everything on Matteo's phone and are analyzing it now. I told them it's a priority, so they'll try to have something for us by the end of the day."

"I have something to add." IRS Special Agent Douglas tugged a stack of sheets from his portfolio. "I went back ten years into Ms. Hardt's financial records. She's totally clean. All her money is untainted, including funds she used to purchase and renovate the Dog Park Café. I also found this." Douglas handed the sheets to Bennett. "Two years ago, she left a prominent financial firm that was later named in a civil complaint alleging the theft of millions of dollars from their clients. Unsolicited, Ms. Hardt turned over incriminating evidence to the Attorney General's Office proving that her colleague—and boyfriend at the time—had used her to bring in clients, then scam them out of annuities by changing the terms of the contracts without Ms. Hardt's knowledge. The company got hit with heavy-duty fines, and her ex-boyfriend was arrested."

Holy shit. Nick drew his brows together. When Andi had talked about New York, she'd barely touched the surface. That asshole had raked her over the coals. While Nick had been unloading the ghosts of his past on her, she'd been keeping hers to herself.

"In addition to Myer's admission, we also have hardcore proof that Andi had no knowledge of that wire transfer." Cox handed Bennett another sheet of paper. "This is a notarized letter from her bank admitting they 'erroneously' permitted an incoming and outgoing wire transfer in the amount of a hundred grand without legitimate authorization from the account holder."

Disgusted murmurs went around the table.

"Erroneously?" Nick snorted. "Meaning Myer's friend at her bank did him a favor."

"Exactly." Cox nodded emphatically. "A team of agents interviewed the branch manager this morning, and he admitted to doing Myer that very favor."

Bennett finished perusing the bank document before placing it in a manila folder. "I'll consider filing charges against that manager. I'll also prepare the paperwork to unfreeze Ms. Hardt's bank account. It may take a week or two, but it should bring a smile to her face." He turned to Nick. "I'd say congratulations are in order."

"For what?" He narrowed his gaze on the prosecutor. Until they got an indictment, nothing was a done deal.

"For an outstanding plan and for getting Myer to turn himself in. You were being modest. You're better at undercover than you thought."

"What's this about?" Wolinski glared at Cox. "Why wasn't I told this was an undercover op?"

"It wasn't." Nick snapped, wondering who'd given Wolinski the impression it was.

"Well, not really." Cox squirmed in his seat, making it obvious he hadn't updated his SAC on the extent or method of Nick's involvement. "Nick merely suggested he could work his magic and get close to Andi Hardt. You know, spend more time with her. We figured Myer would call her eventually, and if he was stuck to her side when that happened, he could intervene and talk the guy in. Who knew he'd turn out to be a better actor than most of our trained UCs? It was an Academy Award-winning performance, and she fell for it hook, line, and sinker. Believe me, the way Nick's got her under his thumb, she'll agree to anything we need. Including being there when Myer turns himself in."

Nick shot the agent an icy glare. *What a dick Cox turned out to be.* He'd put his own spin on Nick's operation just to get his ass out of hot water with Wolinski.

Wolinski laughed, grinning at Nick. "I just figured out why you've got your state police panties in a bunch over this woman. I hadn't realized until now that you'd been spending the last two weeks *pumping* her for information." He made a gesture with his fist that no one could misinterpret.

Beneath the table, Nick clenched his hands so tightly his nails bit into his palms. If only murdering a federal agent wasn't illegal.

Wolinski's smirk deepened. "You gotta love undercover assignments with side benefits, and that Hardt woman is one fine piece of ass. No wonder you kept her all to yourself."

A startled gasp came from behind Nick.

Andi stood just inside the now-open door, one hand covering her mouth. Her cheeks were pink, her blue eyes wide.

Nick bolted to his feet. How long had she been standing there? From the horrified look on her face, she'd heard everything, including the part where Cox had made it seem like Nick had only been using her.

He rushed to the door. "Andi?" When he touched her shoulder, she swatted his hand away.

"Don't," she spat, her face an even deeper red, her entire body rigid.

Gently but firmly, he ushered her out to the hallway, then back to the empty conference room where she'd been waiting. He shut the door behind them and reached for her.

She spun on him. "Don't you dare touch me!"

If he'd had any doubts before, now it was crystal clear she'd heard every word of bullshit Cox and Wolinski had said.

• • •

Chilled to the bone, Andi wrapped her arms tightly around her shoulders. It didn't help. The temperature seemed to have dropped twenty degrees.

I can't believe I fell for it. I can't believe I fell for him.

The vicious cycle of her life was repeating itself over and over, and she was powerless to stop it. Getting used by men must be something attached to her DNA. First Steve, then Joe, and now Nick.

"Andi—"

"No!" She spun to face him, her body shaking with barely controlled rage. "Us—you and me—it was all a lie, an act on your part to get close to me and talk Joe in."

"Goddammit." He advanced on her, his hard jaw clenched. "You know it wasn't like that."

"Wasn't it?" She held up her hand, stopping him. "Are you denying what those men said?" She held her breath, hoping he would, praying he had another explanation for what she'd overheard. When he raked a hand through his hair, her hopes died.

"No. But I *didn't* use you. Not like that, and not like you think. What's happening between us is *real*."

"*Real?* You don't know the meaning of the word." Her breaths started coming quicker. She wanted to yell, to scream at the top of her lungs to keep from crying. "You said you'd acted in high school and college musicals. I was a fool not to realize you were using those talents on me. You don't care about *me*. You only wanted your 'piece of ass' on the side."

"Andi, listen to me!" Before she could stop him, he'd stepped closer, and clasped her upper arms. She tried pulling away, but he wouldn't let her. "I *do* care about you, and it *is* real, I—"

"I don't believe you." She began shaking her head, trying not to inhale his scent with every breath, but it was impossible not to. Even if she could eradicate his scent from her lungs, she'd never be able to erase the pain he'd inflicted on her heart.

Oh my God. It's happening all over again.

He stared down at her, his gray eyes radiating an intensity she'd never seen before. "Getting this gun dealer has been my sole purpose in life for the last five years. When I first met you that was *all* I thought about. I can't deny that. I would have done anything to get to this guy, including taking advantage of your relationship with Joe. At first, that's all this was. A job. Then I got to know you, and things between us changed."

"You're right, they did change. You used me, and then you slept with me to make sure you got what you wanted. That's what men do." To her, anyway. She bit her lower lip, anything to keep from crying like a baby. "Finding out about Joe was bad enough, but what you did is worse. *Far* worse. Congratulations really *are* in order, Sergeant. You went above and beyond the call of duty by leading me to believe that you actually cared, and you know what? I *did* fall for it. Hook. Line. And sinker."

As she stood there, chest heaving, the worst of it hit her. She'd been horribly hurt by Steve, and then by Joe's lies, but that pain didn't compare to what she was feeling now. Because she hadn't been in love with either of them. She was in love with Nick. Admitting it was like taking a bullet to the heart.

"Andi." He leaned in so close she could have kissed him if she'd wanted to. "Don't do this. Don't do this to *us.*"

"Us?" Uttering a soft cry, she shrugged from his grasp. "There is no *us,* and there never was. I knew something wasn't right about you." She blinked back the tears, refusing to let them fall because, once they started, they wouldn't stop. "I don't even know you."

"You *do* know me." From the rigidity of his stance, it was obvious he was resisting the urge to touch her again. "And I'm telling the truth."

"Maybe you are, maybe you aren't. Unfortunately, I can't tell what the truth is with you." Without warning, something inside her snapped, and she rushed forward, pushing at his chest. "I was nothing more than a job to you—a means to an end."

He stood there, silently taking her hits with his arms at his sides. She looked into his eyes, momentarily taken aback by the abject misery she saw reflected in his gaze.

It's not real. It's an act. Like everything else that had passed between them.

Sucking in deep breaths, she stepped back and uttered a sarcastic laugh directed at herself. While she'd been stupidly falling in love, he'd probably been logging in the names of the Napkin Girls before making a pretense of tossing them out.

She'd been taken advantage of and used so much in her life. If she hadn't caught on to Steve's scam, not only would her clients have lost their annuities, but she could have been taken down along with him. Because of Joe, she'd been on the verge of being arrested and losing her business. Now she'd lost something just as important.

Her heart. And she doubted it was possible to ever get it back.

Nick's face was an impassive mask, the same one he'd been wearing the day they'd met. *That* was his real persona.

"I'm not giving up on us." He took a step closer, shaking his head. "When this is all over, we can—"

"Go our separate ways." She backed up, putting the corner of the desk between them. Much as she tried, she couldn't keep her voice from shaking. "Maybe it's my fault— my gullibility in believing you could possibly be different."

"I'm sorry for what you overheard, but I won't apologize for something I didn't do." He held out his hand to her in a pleading gesture. "When this is over, I'll prove it to you."

"You're only saying that so I'll keep helping you. I heard Special Agent Cox. He wants me there when Joe turns himself in."

"*He* does. *I* don't. It's too dangerous." He took another deep breath as if to steady himself. "*That* part of the conversation you conveniently missed."

Unable to bear the intensity of his eyes any longer, she spun and turned her back to him. A moment later, she felt his hands on her bare shoulders. Warmth from his touch seeped into her skin, reminding her of how he'd once made her entire body come alive like never before. The urge to lean against his chest and let him enfold her in his strong arms was overwhelming.

Don't do it.

It wouldn't be real. It would be temporary, to keep her tied to him in order to get what he needed to wrap up his investigation.

She turned to look at him, gazing into his handsome face, inanely wishing he could feel even half of what she did for him. Steely gray eyes watched her from beneath lowered brows, and she suddenly understood the *only* motivating force driving him. Ironically, it was an admirable cause. "I get it. I really do. What happened to your wife was terrible."

Again, he shook his head, more adamantly this time. "That has nothing to do with—"

"Let me finish. You think that by taking down this organization you can absolve yourself of what you think is your own failure. But it wasn't your fault, and you know it."

He didn't deny it, and that was okay with her. What wasn't okay was letting him use her to find his salvation.

Steeling herself, she swallowed. "I want to go home."

"I'll take you." He went to the door and reached for the knob.

"Eric can drive me."

He turned on her. "The hell he can." His voice was low and controlled, yet his tone was hard as nails. "You may hate my guts right now, but I'll be damned if anyone else watches over you."

She shook her head. "I don't *want* you."

"Too bad." He yanked open the door. "Until this is over, you're stuck with me. That is *not* open for negotiation."

The conviction in his eyes told her there was no way to breach his stony resolution. For one supremely stupid moment, she dared to hope his adamant pledge to protect her was about his feelings for her.

It's not, she reminded herself. With that painful realization, her heartbeat slowed to a dull thud until she barely felt it beating at all.

The only truth in all of this was that if they got to her, they'd get to Joe. Then kill them both.

Chapter Sixteen

"You can drop me off at the restaurant." Andi stared out the passenger side window, her body rigid with anger to the point where it was palpable.

Those were the first—and *only*—words she'd spoken to him since leaving the U.S. Attorney's Office thirty-five minutes ago. The only time she'd shown any emotion was when they'd stopped to pick up Saxon, who'd given her a sound licking on the chin.

He ground his teeth together. Again, the silent treatment was killing him.

After parking in the DPC's empty lot, he got out and rounded the hood to open Andi's door, but she'd already whipped it open, slammed it shut, and was stomping toward the restaurant.

He clicked the button on his key fob, popping open the kennel door. Saxon leaped onto the pavement and bounded after her. When she opened the DPC's front door, Saxon poked his head through, trying to squeeze in after her. She laughed, and it was like music to Nick's ears. Sadly, her laughter wasn't for him. It was for his dog. *Fuck. Me.*

Beeping sounded, then quieted as she deactivated the alarm. She held the door partially open to prevent Saxon from entering, but she leaned down and put her arms over Saxon's neck, burying her face in his thick coat. His tail wagged back and forth, a sign of just how much Saxon loved her. Pathetically, he wondered if she'd ever throw her arms around *him* again.

Great, now I'm jealous of a dog.

As he neared the door, she gave Saxon a final scratching behind his ears.

"*Hier.*" His dog reluctantly disengaged from Andi's arms and looked up at him with a quizzical expression. Golden eyes pinned him, then swiveled from Andi, to him, then back again. Even Saxon sensed the tension between the two of them. "Let's go see Stray."

Minutes later, he'd put Saxon up in the house with Stray and come back inside the restaurant to find Andi holed up in her office, poring over a stack of bills—the ones he knew she still couldn't pay.

Crossing his arms, he leaned against the doorjamb. "We need to talk."

"There's nothing more to say." She didn't look at him. "And by the way, you're fired."

Ignoring the jibe, he sat on a corner of the desk. "Now that you're officially not a suspect anymore, your account will be released. You should be able to access your money within two weeks."

"Great, thanks. Too bad that may be too late." The tips of her fingers were white where she clutched a pen in one hand and the bills in the other. "This isn't the first time I've been late paying bills. I'll be lucky if these vendors don't tack on interest, increase their prices, or cancel my accounts altogether."

Not if I can help it. That, he could fix, but he couldn't fix things between them.

Back at the courthouse, he'd wanted to tell her what was in his heart—that he couldn't live without her. Didn't *want* to live without her. It was just as well he hadn't. She would never have believed him. Not right on the heels of what she'd overheard.

He nearly choked on the irony. She'd thrown his own words back at him. *I was nothing more than a job to you—a means to an end.* He'd said almost the exact same words to Cox the day before starting this operation. She'd been right. He *had* used her. The true depth of his deception smacked him in the face, and it was worse than he remembered. Only now did he understand that he would have kept right on using her until he got his man.

Mission almost accomplished, asshole.

Even then, he'd liked Andi as a person, but it hadn't mattered. Her cooperation had been deemed integral to the case, and he'd vowed to work her the way he'd work any cooperator. It was simply good, old-fashioned police work, a technique used for centuries by thousands of cops all over the world. The best cases were made either with snitches or cooperators. Andi had been a cooperator. Until she'd become something more.

Bottom line, *I fucked up.*

He'd had it all, and now it might be too late. He'd let his obsession over making up for the past and nailing this gun dealer destroy a relationship with the woman he'd fallen in love with. Somehow, she'd managed to get through the cracks of his thick skin and make him love again. After what he'd done, he didn't deserve her. Maybe she was better off without him.

With someone who isn't a cold-hearted sonofabitch. Someone who didn't use people for his own personal gain.

Like that piece of shit in New York who'd hurt her. Shit, hadn't he done the same thing?

No. There was no way that faceless motherfucker could possibly have cared about her the way he did. Because Nick had no intention of letting her go.

When she sniffled and turned away, he knew she was about to cry, and it ripped at his guts like nothing else could. The urge to touch her overrode all his common sense, and he rose to reach for her.

"You guys okay?"

He jerked his head around to find Tess and Eric standing in the doorway. He pressed his lips together, annoyed that he'd been so distracted he hadn't heard their approach.

"We're fine." Andi smiled, but it was obvious to him she wasn't feeling any joy.

"You don't look fine." Tess eyed him with outright suspicion, and he found himself admiring her protective nature.

Eric arched a brow but said nothing.

Nick headed for the door, about to brush past Tess and Eric when the cell phone on his belt vibrated. He grabbed the phone and looked at the screen. *Cox.*

"Houston," he answered. Much as he wanted to tell the agent exactly where to go, he held back.

"I'm sorry," Cox began. "I shouldn't have said that about you and Andi. Whatever you two have going on is none of my business. She's a great girl."

"I don't need you to tell me that." He glanced at Andi, whose eyes shimmered with hurt and humiliation. Although he fully intended to verbally rip Cox a new one, this wasn't the time or the place. "Is that the only reason you're calling?" He knew damned well it wasn't.

"No. The lab boys found something interesting on Matteo's phone." That got his attention. "They pulled geocodes from the photo used to identify Andi. Get this... the date stamp indicates the photo was taken on August thirteenth. Two days *before* the break-in at Myer's house."

Nick began processing the importance of that information, and he put the call on speaker so Eric could hear. "Go on."

"We served the warrant on Tuesday, August fifteenth," Cox continued. "Myer's house was broken into later that same day, and the photo was stolen during the break-in. That means—"

"The photo on Matteo's phone couldn't have been the same one stolen from the house on August fifteenth, because it's dated two days earlier," Nick interrupted. "Did they get a location from the geocoding?"

"Yeah, it's the Dog Park Café."

"Holy shit." Eric caught his gaze with a disgusted one of his own. "They were inside the restaurant. Right under our noses."

"You got a time stamp on the photo?" Nick asked.

"Three p.m.," Cox said.

"We can pull receipts for that afternoon, maybe get some names," Andi suggested.

Nick nodded in agreement. "It's a long shot. We can check for criminal records on anyone in the DPC that day. Maybe we'll recognize a name. But if they paid cash or didn't purchase anything at all, there'd be no paper trail."

"The lab guys also found something else in the photo," Cox added. "A reflection. It wasn't really visible to the naked eye, and given that it was a photo taken of a photo, clarity is compromised. I just texted you the partially enhanced image."

Nick's phone vibrated as a photo flashed on the screen. He tapped the image. Sure enough, a faint reflection stared back at him, one that hadn't been visible when he'd first looked at the photo on Matteo's phone. Using his thumb and forefinger, he enlarged it as much as the phone would allow. He still couldn't make an ID from the fuzzy image.

"Stand by." He handed the phone to Andi. "Do you recognize this guy?"

She accepted the phone, then peered at the screen, scrunching up her face. After a few seconds, she shook her head. "It's not clear enough." She handed it back to him. When her fingers brushed his, awareness flickered in her gaze.

She still cares. Maybe there was hope after all. Either way, he damned sure wasn't about to give up on her.

"The lab's not finished enhancing the photo," Cox continued. "They think they can do better, but it will take more time. I'll send you new images as soon as they're in."

"Later." He ended the call, then looked at Andi. "How soon can you get started on those receipts?"

"Let me do that," Tess offered. "You both look exhausted and should get out of here for a while. I'll print out all the credit card charges for whatever day you want. I'll do the same for cash sales, but like you said, we won't know who paid the bill."

"I'll help you." Eric rested his hand briefly on Tess's shoulder, and she gave him a shy smile.

Something about the gesture struck Nick as being oddly intimate. Then again, over the past two weeks he'd been observing other subtle indications that his friend had more than a passing interest in Andi's manager.

"Keep an eye out for receipts with the name 'Paul Nelson' on them," Nick said.

"Seriously?" Eric's eyes widened. "Paul Nelson, as in the chief of the Springfield Police Department?"

"Could be nothing." He thought back to the day he'd seen Nelson and his dog at the DPC. "I saw him in the parking lot the same day I began working here. Did you know Chief

Nelson lives over an hour away? That's a long way for him to come just to run his dog and grab a cup of coffee. Then again, with the brand-new Porsche he was driving, maybe it doesn't take that long after all."

Eric whistled. "Pricey ride."

Andi gave him an incredulous look. "Do you really think the police chief is the man we're looking for?"

"I hope not," Nick said. "His salary might be big enough to purchase a Porsche, or it could have been bought with dirty money. When too many things begin stacking up, we can't discount that possibility."

Eric nodded. "Okay, we'll look for receipts in his name."

"While you're at it," he added, "check for any cash sales that include a broccoli rabe and pulled pork panini with a side of mac 'n' cheese."

"Frank Feldman?" Andi stared at him. "Meera's boyfriend?"

"Frank's always been cryptic about what he does for a living, and he shows up at the DPC for a late lunch nearly every day. Right around three o'clock, the same time that photo was taken inside the restaurant."

"Here I was thinking Frank was such a sweet man." Andi rose from the desk, shaking her head. "Then again, it seems I've been wrong about most of the men in my life." Shooting him a dirty look, she slung her bag over her shoulder and began edging between him and the desk.

He wanted to grab her and shake some sense into her. Instead, he gently caught her arm. "No one is beyond suspicion at the moment, and you have to be careful of everyone."

"I'm going home." She jerked from his grasp then shot out the door past Tess and Eric.

He followed her. "I'm going with you."

"No. You're not," she threw back over her shoulder.

"Humor me."

• • •

Andi breathed hard, taking in the familiar, earthy smells of pine and moss as her feet pounded on the soft, winding, tree-lined path.

Even with the shade provided by the overhead tree canopy, her running clothes had darkened with sweat. Her muscles were screaming, and still she couldn't seem to run fast enough. Or put enough distance between her and Nick.

Unfortunately, he'd had a spare set of gym clothes in the Explorer, and over her strenuous objections he'd not only accompanied her to her house but insisted on being her running mate.

His heavier footfalls sounded behind her. He wouldn't say it, but she knew the real reason he was stuck to her like glue, and it had nothing to do with having any real feelings for her. After the botched kidnapping, he wasn't taking any chances. He needed to ensure her presence at the courthouse tomorrow when Joe turned himself in.

She wiped the sweat from her brow, sucking in breath after breath as she tried in vain to increase the gap between them. *Not likely.* They'd been running for twenty minutes, and he'd more than easily kept pace, staying a few feet behind the entire time. On the rare occasions that she'd glanced behind her, he'd looked like a thoroughbred out for a light trot. His perfect body glistened with sweat, but he was barely breathing hard compared to her. The man looked like he could go on for miles. At least he respected her need for space.

A sharp pain jabbed at her right thigh, and she pulled up, leaning against a tree while she massaged the heat cramp in her leg. The pain worsened, and she uttered a muffled cry.

"I've got this." He knelt in front of her. "Honey, let go."

The pain was steadily worsening, so intense that she

did as he commanded, barely registering the endearment. His large hands encircled her upper thigh, kneading and massaging. She'd been leaning on the tree for additional support, but when another spasm shot to her leg, her hands flew to his shoulders.

"Easy there." His voice was low and soothing, giving her something else to focus on besides the worsening cramp. "The pain should go away any second now. Hang in there, baby."

"Don't you dare," she gritted out through clenched teeth, "call me baby. Or honey. Or anything else."

Through eyes narrowed in pain, she glimpsed the look of concern on his face, and it only irritated her more. He didn't have the right to be concerned about her. Not as a person, anyway, let alone as a woman.

She wanted to hate him but couldn't. He was only doing his job. *Too well.* What she had to do was block out any feelings she may have had for him. *Still have*, she had to admit.

God help me forget him. Because she wouldn't be capable of doing it without divine intervention.

His strong fingers were magically working out the acute cramping in her thigh. Her breathing gradually returned to something resembling normal, and she closed her eyes as his hands continued massaging her muscles. They were totally alone, deep in the center of a secluded, forested area, far from any roads or houses. The only sound was the occasional whisper of leaves in the treetops.

The truth of her dilemma was horrible. Worse than horrible, it was absolutely, positively soul-destroying. After all he'd done…

…she still loved him.

His ministrations eased and turned into a gentle caress with his hands gliding up and down the front and back of her leg. Against her will, she was reminded of how deliciously talented his hands were, and how they'd once set every square inch of her naked body on fire until all she could think about was him moving inside her.

Lord, why did she have to be born with the self-destructive sucker gene?

Allowing him to touch her again was the weakest, most stupid thing she could possibly do. She regretted not having brought Stray and Saxon along, anything to provide a buffer between them. But Stray wasn't healed sufficiently for such a long run, and both dogs would have had a difficult time not overheating.

When she opened her eyes, he was watching her with an intensity that made her squirm with the need for more space. "You can stop now." Digging deep into what little remained of her emotional fortitude, she pushed at his shoulders, but he didn't budge.

He stood and dropped his hands to her waist. His chest pressed against her as heat poured off them, and her measly effort at resistance began to crumble into a pathetic heap of mush.

Don't do it. Be strong. Think about how much he hurt you.

"Let me go, you lying bastard." She pushed at him, struggling to free herself, but he pressed her gently back against the tree, pinning her against the rough bark.

"I don't want to. I can't, and I don't think you really want me to, either." His gaze flicked to her lips, and her mouth instantly went dry. When she parted her lips to lick them, he kissed her. With a half-hearted effort, she tried tearing away from him. But it was useless. The moment his lips touched hers and his tongue pushed into her mouth, her body betrayed her.

Desperate need, the likes of which she'd never known, assailed her, taking control of her body until she was clutching his shoulders. She moaned, opening her mouth to his, all the while thinking—no, *knowing*—this was a huge mistake. As much as her brain warned her to stop this madness, something else was in control. Her heart was making her do things in total opposition to every vestige of common sense she knew she ought to have. And didn't.

Of their own volition, her hands slid over the rock-solid curves of his muscled shoulders, down his arms, then to his back. His skin was hot beneath her touch, his muscles tight with restraint as he angled his mouth over hers, kissing her deeper.

She was about to hand over a piece of her soul to a man who didn't love her. A man who wasn't capable of loving her. He'd used her and was still doing it. Worse, she was *letting* him.

Weakness made her slide her hands beneath the waistband of his shorts, clutch his muscular buttocks, and pull his erection against her lower abdomen.

He groaned, throaty and deep, then skimmed his hands along the sides of her breasts before tugging her tank top up and over her head. Next came her bra, followed by her running shorts and panties, and she found herself toeing off her sneakers until she was standing against the tree totally naked beneath his roving hands and mouth.

If only it didn't feel so good, so right. But it did.

Large, warm hands cupped her breasts while he leaned over, flicking her nipples with his tongue until they jutted proudly into his mouth. He straightened and kissed her, surging his hips against hers.

"Andi," he whispered as he kissed her again and again. His warm breath and the heat from his body washed over her. "Tell me you want this. Tell me you want me inside you."

She moaned, letting her head fall back against the tree as he pressed hot kisses to her neck. *No.* "Yes," she whispered.

"Yes."

He scooped her up, carrying her to a clearing a few feet away before kneeling and gently laying her down on a bed of soft moss. All the while, his eyes never left hers.

A moment later, he kicked off his sneakers and peeled off his shorts. He was long, and hard, and thick. *And without a condom.*

He rested his forearms on the moss on either side of her head, holding his lower body inches above hers, his erection barely touching her belly. His nostrils flared. His breath came in deep, raspy inhalations, as did hers. Though he said nothing, she understood what he was asking. To make love to her. Without a condom and without commitment.

There was no chance of her getting pregnant, but in that moment, she wouldn't have cared if there was. She wanted him that badly.

Answering his silent question, she parted her legs and tugged his head down for a long, slow kiss. *One he'll never forget. Our last.*

In one smooth motion, he entered her. Her body bowed, her back arching to receive him fully as she hooked her legs over the backs of his thighs.

His motions intensified, his body pushing deeper inside her. For a fleeting instant, her heart and head began rebelling. *No, don't let them. Don't feel* anything. Except how exquisite his body felt sliding in and out of hers.

He raised his head and gazed down at her from beneath hooded lids. His nostrils flared wider, his teeth clenching as he breathed harder.

The first wave of her orgasm washed over her with the strength and speed of a late summer storm. She threw back her head, squeezing her eyes so tightly shut she saw stars.

His body convulsed as he came inside her. Wrapping her arms around his back, she held him to her while their breathing slowed. Part of her—the weak, self-destructive part—didn't want this moment to end but knew it would, and that it would be the last time they would ever hold each other this way.

He lowered his forehead to hers. "I love you," he whispered harshly, his warm breath washing over her face. "I love you."

She stiffened. *I must have misheard him.* Then her heart grew cold. She hadn't misheard him. This was merely another facet of his master plan to keep her close until he no longer had any use for her.

The need to get away from him overrode everything, and she pushed frantically at his shoulders and chest, forcing him to withdraw from where he was buried so deeply inside her. For one long heartbeat they lay on their sides, facing each other. Pain bubbled up at the pathetic realization that those three words—words that should have been beautiful and meaningful—had the power to hurt her like nothing else could.

Because they aren't true.

"I don't believe you." Ignoring the flash of misery in his eyes, she scrambled away and retrieved her clothes and sneakers from the base of the tree and quickly began dressing. Her head throbbed with anger. After everything that happened, how could he even *think* of saying that?

There'd been a time—a brief, stupid time—when she'd yearned to hear him say those words. Now they were just that. Words. Sgt. Nick Houston was good at using words to get whatever he needed.

Nick grabbed his shorts and shoved his legs into them. Next, he grabbed his sneakers and shoved his feet into them without even bothering to untie the laces.

A sickening awareness pervaded her senses, followed by numbness. That numbness would keep her going after tomorrow. After he was gone from her life, and she was left to deal with the fact that she'd allowed yet another man to use her. Knowingly, this time.

"Andi, I—" He took a step toward her, then stopped. Exhaling a ragged breath, he shoved a hand through his hair, looking as if he wanted to finish his thought but couldn't. It didn't matter. His expression said it all. Nick had just used her ass again and felt like crap about it.

She didn't. The man was out of her system. Forever.

Without looking up, she shoved her feet into her sneakers. "Don't even think of saying you're sorry about what just happened."

"I wasn't going to say that."

"Bullshit." This time she did look at him. "I can see it on your face, so don't say another word. Just let it go. *Please*." She swallowed the sob rising in her throat. If he apologized, she'd lose it, she was sure of it.

Mercifully he didn't respond, and the second she had her sneaker laces tied, she bolted to her feet and took off down the path. There was no need to check behind her. He was there. He and Saxon would watch her back until Joe was safely ensconced in police custody.

A stronger breeze had kicked up, rustling the trees overhead. She picked up her pace, running faster, her heart pounding so fiercely she thought it would explode. *Or break. Again.*

By the time they made it back to her house, she'd gotten control of her emotions. Or so she thought. Tess and Eric were waiting in her kitchen, a stack of café receipts piled high on the table.

"Andi?" Tess threw her a concerned look as she buzzed past the table. "*Andi?*" she repeated, following her upstairs into her bedroom. "What's wrong?" Her eyes dipped from the top of Andi's head to her sneakers, then back up. She reached out to pluck something from her hair. "Did you know you have moss and stuff in your hair? You were gone a long time for a run. What else did you—"

Her eyes widened, and she gasped. "You didn't. You did! You had wild, unbridled sex in the middle of the woods." She giggled. "We were about to send out a search party, but no wonder you guys took so long. That is so hot. It's *beyond* hot." Then her countenance turned serious. "What's wrong?"

"He doesn't love me. He was only using me and I—" She covered her face with her hands. "Oh God," she muttered through her fingers.

"You're in love with him." Tess pulled Andi's hands from her face. "You think that's news? Any moron can see that. And I'd bet he feels the same about you. Granted, guys like him and Eric don't exactly wear their hearts on their sleeves. It's a cop thing. I'm not a fan of cops, but even I have to admit the way he is around you, and the way he looks at you… He cares about you. A lot."

"He doesn't." She then described in painful detail what she'd heard about the award-winning role Nick played to get close to her and convince her to talk Joe in. "They were practically slapping him on the back and high-fiving him for a job well done."

Tess shook her head. "I don't believe it, and neither should you. All those long smoldering looks he throws your way are definitely not made up. So, he acted in some musicals. Doesn't mean his feelings aren't real."

"Nick didn't deny it."

"Did you ask him if it was true?"

"Yes. Later, when we were alone."

"And?"

"He admitted it was true."

"Whaat?" Tess's brow wrinkled. "This doesn't make sense. There has to be something else going on here."

"It doesn't matter whether there is or isn't. I don't want to talk about it anymore." She toed off her sneakers and began peeling off her sweat-soaked shirt. "I'm going to drown myself in the shower."

"Don't you want to know what Eric and I discovered in the receipts?"

She paused at the bathroom door. "What did you find?"

"Nick's hunch paid off. Both Frank Feldman *and* the chief of the Springfield Police Department were at the DPC between the hours of three and four on August thirteenth. The *same* day as the date stamp on that photo."

Chapter Seventeen

Nick punched the pillow on Andi's living room sofa for what must have been the hundredth time. Not that the sofa was uncomfortable, but he'd much rather have slept upstairs. In her bed.

He'd hurt her. Badly. There was no doubt he was going straight to hell for what he'd done.

Though he hadn't spoken out loud, Saxon lifted his head, skewering Nick with his golden stare. Groaning, Saxon lowered his head and went back to sleep on the floor beside the sofa. Nick dropped his hand to the dog's back and ran it along the smooth coat. He glanced at his watch. Six o'clock, two hours before they were scheduled to leave for the courthouse.

He wanted to get Andi into the building early, then patrol the perimeter, checking for signs of early surveillance by gang members or anyone else who might have been hired to take Myer out before he could set foot inside.

Nick yawned. Markus and Dayne had kept watch over Andi last night while he and Eric had gone out and interviewed Frank Feldman and Chief Nelson. Seemed as if he'd only closed his eyes ten minutes ago when, in reality, it had been around eleven when he'd returned to the house. But he hadn't gotten much sleep. Instead, he'd relived every second of making love to Andi in the woods yesterday.

I never should have touched her.

Afterward, when he'd told her he loved her, it had only screwed things up more, and she'd thought the worst—that he'd only said it because he was using her again, this time for sex. Ironically, they were the truest words he'd spoken in a very long time. Fact was, she'd been so beautiful, lying beneath him on the moss…he'd never forget her face as he watched her shatter in his arms. He'd been unable to hold back what was in his heart. But then the hurt had returned to her eyes, and he'd felt like a dick of the highest order, which was exactly what he was.

If you don't quit kicking yourself, you'll be useless.

He repositioned on the sofa and began reviewing everything they'd learned during the interviews last night. Both he and Eric believed neither Feldman nor Chief Nelson was the man they were looking for.

Turned out Feldman was a corporate salesman peddling ladies cosmetics to department stores, an occupation he was embarrassed about, so he kept it on the down-low. Said he was sick and tired of being called an Avon lady. That explained why he'd been so cryptic when Nick had tried to figure the guy out. Feldman answered all their questions and let them look through his phone log, photos, texts, and email for anything linking him to Myer or the attempted kidnapping.

They were astounded at the money Feldman was raking in. His income was off the charts, to the point where he could make his own hours and afford to swing by the DPC for grub so often and at any time of the day. Plus, he'd admitted to having a thing for Meera, and the DPC was a neutral location where he could easily bump into her.

Their next stop had been to Chief Nelson's house. To say the chief had been pissed about being interrogated was a major understatement. The guy had gone ballistic. It had taken them a good ten minutes just to get him to let them into his house, then another twenty to calm him down enough to answer questions. For a moment there, he'd half expected the chief to either lawyer up or call Nick and Eric's bosses demanding they back the fuck off. An hour later, they'd left the chief's house with the same unexpected result. The chief was innocent.

Chief Nelson not only wound up answering all Nick and Eric's questions, but explained, albeit in a voice angry enough to shrivel most men's gonads, that a rich uncle had died, leaving him enough money to fill a five-car garage with Porsches. He even showed them his uncle's will and the six-figure amount he'd inherited.

Unable to lie still a moment longer, Nick got up and poured Saxon some of the kibble he'd picked up last night at his house. At the dinging sounds of the kibble hitting the bowl, Saxon pushed to his feet, ears erect, totally awake as he trotted into the kitchen and began munching away. He freshened Saxon's water bowl, then grabbed his uniform and overnight bag before heading into the downstairs bathroom.

One look in the mirror told him he looked exactly the way he felt—like shit. Worse really. He needed another four hours of shut-eye before he'd feel or look remotely awake. His sleep cycle had been totally shot to hell by the gnawing in his gut that said something would go wrong today. Not that he could pinpoint why, but the worry was there, eating away like acid in the pit of his stomach.

He yanked open his bag and dug out his electric razor, wishing he could hit the reset button on what had happened yesterday. His timing had sucked, but he didn't regret saying those three little words. Not for a second. He really was a lucky bastard. Never in his godforsaken life had he ever expected to fall in love again. But he had, and with a depth and intensity he hadn't thought possible.

Andi was an amazing woman, and now she was in the line of fire, driving him that much harder to bring down the dealer.

I have to finish this.

Not only for Andi and Tanya, but for every innocent victim of gun crime. And who was he kidding? He wanted this over so he could have a chance with Andi. It would be one hell of a steep climb to get her to believe a word he said, but he had no intention of giving up.

The upstairs shower came on, and he glanced at the ceiling. He couldn't keep his mind from wandering, or from wishing he were in that shower with her. Sliding a bar of soap over her smooth skin. Stroking every inch of her beautiful body. He'd made love to her without a condom. *Stupid. Juvenile and stupid.*

Snatching up the razor, he turned it on and began moving it over the dark stubble on his face. Though she'd told him there wasn't any chance she'd get pregnant, he wouldn't mind if she were. If they had a child together, it would bind her to him. Unfortunately, against her will.

You're fucking pathetic.

Nick was fully dressed, sipping his first cup of coffee in the kitchen by the time Andi and Stray came downstairs.

Stray padded into the kitchen first. Saxon gave her a morning sniff in greeting, wagging his tail. The two dogs had become friends to the point where it didn't seem to bother Saxon that Stray was hovering so close to his food bowl.

Next, Stray came to Nick for attention, her body wriggling and tail wagging furiously. He leaned down to pet her soft ears, glad to see she was recovering well.

When Andi walked into the kitchen, all their heads turned. As she leaned down to give Saxon and Stray a sound ear-scratching, his throat tightened. He could easily imagine starting the day with her like this *every* morning.

She straightened and looked at him. Eyes that had once gazed up at him with passion and desire were now totally impassive. He understood precisely what she was doing, and it was more effective than if someone had slammed him in the gut with a battering ram.

She wasn't only distancing herself from him. *She's trying to cut me out entirely.*

Which only fueled his determination to win her back.

As she took in his uniform, a discernible frown came to her pink-glossed lips, as if she were only now reminded of who and what he was and didn't like it much. To him, she looked as beautiful as the day they'd met. More so, and while she fed Stray, he couldn't keep his eyes off her.

The snug sleeveless blue dress hugged her body, coming to just above her knees, and emphasizing every graceful curve of her body. A strand of tiny pearls hung around her neck, with matching studs dotting her earlobes. Her hair hung loose, and with the sun streaming into the kitchen from the window behind her, it framed her face like a golden halo.

"Any coffee left?" Without looking at him, she headed for the coffee maker on the counter behind him.

As she moved closer, he breathed in the scent of freesia, much as he had the first time he'd ever kissed her. He cleared his throat and shifted aside so that she could reach for the cup he'd already taken out for her. "There's plenty. I made extra for Matt and Kade. They'll be here any minute to follow us to the courthouse."

She poured herself a cup then went to the refrigerator for milk. "How did the interviews go last night?"

Grateful though he was for her talking to him at all, her tone was flat, emotionless, and she did her best to avoid his gaze, sending him only a quick glance before pouring milk into her cup and setting the carton on the counter. The chill between them had grown into a full-blown wall of ice, and it was driving him crazy.

Dammit.

He shook his head. "Not as we expected. Neither Feldman or Chief Nelson is the man we're looking for."

A frown flickered across her brow, and he knew that look. She was worried—for Myer, he figured, and that pissed him off as it always had, but never more so than today. If he didn't get this jealousy thing under wraps, he'd go fucking ballistic. He wished more than anything that he could go to her, take her in his arms, and tell her everything was going to work out. But he couldn't, so he settled for one out of three.

"Everything's going to work out." Even as he said the words, something about the whole setup Myer had described over the phone still bugged him.

Her frown deepened. "So, what's next? How do we find out who this person is?"

We?

Funny how she still considered herself part of the investigation. In a perfect world, he'd want her as far away from this as possible. If it weren't for AUSA Bennett's insistence, no way would he have allowed her anywhere near the federal building when Myer turned his ass in. He'd take every precaution he could drum up to protect her during this op, but he couldn't shake the feeling of foreboding pounding in his gut. "We have to rely on Joe's information to get us to the end game."

Saxon sat at Nick's side, and he dropped his hand to rest on the dog's head. "He said over the phone that he never met Brian Argyle, the man he's working for, but Brian Argyle doesn't exist." And Nick hated the not knowing.

"We're hoping Joe's laptop contains transactional records," he continued. "We'll dump everything on the hard drive and dig through it with a fine-tooth comb. Then we'll issue subpoenas for every banking institution he wired money to. Eventually, we should be able to find out who took receipt. Unfortunately, money laundering schemes usually involve deposits overseas, so tracking it and getting assistance from foreign governments and banks will take time."

"How much time?"

"Months. Maybe six by the time we get responses, analyze the results, then put an indictment package together."

More worry lines etched her forehead. "What happens to Joe in the interim, while you're waiting for all this information?"

"If he cooperates—fully—most likely the AUSA will cut him a deal."

"Will he have to go to prison?"

"Probably," he answered honestly. "It depends on the extent of his cooperation and on whether the AUSA is in a generous mood that day. Even if he is, a judge will have final say on sentencing. He won't be charged until after we ID and arrest the man at the top. If his cooperation leads us to nailing the bastard, it will go a long way toward lessening his sentence."

"Will he have to remain in custody, protective or otherwise?" she asked.

"Probably. Given that he fled to Canada, he'll be deemed a flight risk."

For seconds, they stared at each other. Silence filled the kitchen. There was nothing more to be said between them. At least, not today, and maybe not tomorrow.

Regret pummeled him from all sides. He wanted her more than he wanted anything else in his life, but he couldn't act on it. Not yet.

He had unfinished business. *She* had to believe his feelings for her were real.

Chapter Eighteen

Nick turned left toward the main road they'd follow into the heart of Springfield. Behind them, Matt and his K-9, Sheba, followed, Eric and Tiger in the next vehicle, with Kade and his K-9, Tango, taking up the rear. Cox and his team of agents would meet them at the federal building.

At the first red traffic light, he tapped his fingers on the steering wheel, recalling the team of agents that had completely bungled safeguarding Matt's wife, Trista, when she was in FBI protective custody. Those agents had made the ultimate sacrifice, but it shouldn't have gone down that way. They'd been ill-trained and undermanned for that assignment. Hence the reason he was embedding Matt, Kade, and Eric within the FBI counter surveillance teams.

Since going through extensive police K-9 training with his friends, he knew them to be tough, seasoned cops who'd back him up without question. Thanks to the national Emergency Management Assistance Compact all their agencies belonged to, Matt and Kade's assistance at the courthouse had quickly been approved by his own troop commander.

When the light turned green, he hit the accelerator. Saxon's massive head stuck out through the kennel's front access door, partially obscuring Andi sitting beside him on the passenger seat. Aside from her left hand ruffling the thick hair around Saxon's collar, she sat rigidly, staring out the windshield and saying nothing. The only sounds in the vehicle came from the occasional squawks on the police radio.

Saxon pulled his head in and settled down for the remainder of the drive. From the corner of his eye, he glimpsed Andi wedged in beside the mobile computer docking station and his MP15 patrol rifle. She eyed the rifle warily then sank farther into the seat.

"It won't bite," he said.

"It's not that." Her expression said otherwise.

He stopped at the next light. "What then?" Aside from the white elephant taking up the seat in between them.

"I'm worried about what's going to happen today."

Join the club.

He glanced in the rearview mirror to see the other SUVs following. "The plan is simple," he tried reassuring her. "The second Joe shows up, a small army will escort him into the building. He'll meet with AUSA Bennett to answer questions, then go before the grand jury to give testimony against Brian Argyle."

"You make it sound so simple." She rubbed her hands up and down her arms.

"It is." As long as everything went according to plan.

"And where will I be in all of this?"

"You'll stay safely inside the building at all times. Whatever happens, don't go outside. Once Joe is under our guard, no one can get to him."

She nodded but still didn't look at him.

He was about to turn onto the ramp for I-90 when the cell phone in his front shirt pocket vibrated. *Cox.* He pulled out the phone and slid his finger right to answer the call. "We're about fifteen out."

"I'm sending you a text," Cox said, and Nick's phone vibrated again. "The lab finished enhancing that photo. It's not totally clear, but it's the best they can do. Let me know if you recognize her."

Her?

Just before the highway onramp, he cranked the wheel hard right and parked on the side of the road. Behind him, the other SUVs did the same. He cued up the radio frequency to the private channel used for the op. "Stand by," he said into the mic.

He opened the text message and pulled up the photo. Using his thumb and forefinger, he enlarged the image. *What the—?*

His mind took off in a hundred different directions as he processed the implications of the face staring back at him.

"What?" Andi shifted in the seat to face him. "What's wrong?"

He handed her the phone.

Her mouth fell open. "It's Meera!"

He took the phone back, pressing it to his ear. "It's Meera Devine."

"Who the hell is that?" Cox asked.

"Hang tight for a minute." Setting the phone on the dashboard, he flipped up the cover of his mobile computer. A minute later he had Meera's home address, DOB, knew she had no criminal history and that she drove a maroon Lexus.

He recited the information to Cox. "See what else you can find on her. We'll hit the house on the way over. Maybe she'll talk. Either way, we're bringing her in."

"Got it," Cox replied. "I'll let Bennett know."

He grabbed the radio mic and clicked the transmit button. "Change of plans."

Ten minutes later they pulled up in front of Meera

Devine's two-story wood-shingle house. A maroon Lexus sat in the driveway.

"Stay here," he said to Andi.

"I want to go with you." Her eyes burned with anger. "If Meera really did take that photo, then I have a right to confront her. She's been in and out of my restaurant for a year, pretending to be my friend."

"Not a chance." When she opened her mouth to object, he held up his hand. "I don't want you anywhere near this woman. If I had my way, you wouldn't even be here. And there is no *if* about Meera taking that photo. That photo was found on a gang member's phone. There's no plausible explanation for that. Somehow, she's involved."

Myer had said he never dealt directly with Brian Argyle and that he'd always dealt with a woman over the phone—a woman with a heavy Scottish accent. Meera didn't have a Scottish accent, but he'd still bet his ass that woman was Meera Devine.

The rage in Andi's eyes dimmed, replaced by acceptance.

"Matt and Kade will stay here with you while Eric and I go inside. Do whatever they tell you."

After she gave a reluctant nod, he met the other men on the sidewalk. "Keep an eye on her," he said to Matt and Kade, then looked at Eric. "Let's do this."

At the front door, he pressed a small white button and heard the doorbell peal from inside the house. A dog barked—presumably Meera's Bouvier. They waited a full minute, then he knocked on the front door. Again, the dog barked, louder this time.

Nick tipped his head to Eric, indicating he should check out the back of the house. His friend hadn't gotten three steps when they heard a woman's voice on the other side of the door.

"Scottie, no bark!"

The dog quieted, and a few seconds later the door opened.

Nick immediately recognized Meera and the Bouvier he'd seen many times in the dog run at the DPC. The good-natured dog stood at her side, wagging its cropped stub of a tail.

She gave them a pleasant smile. "What can I do for—" Her eyes widened, and her gaze lowered then raised, taking in his uniform. "Nick? You're a policeman?"

"I'm with the state police." He nodded to Eric. "This is Special Agent Miller with the Bureau of Alcohol, Tobacco, and Firearms."

"I don't understand." Confusion showed in her eyes, and she shook her head as if to clear it. "I thought you were a bartender."

"May we come in?" he asked. "I'll explain why we're here."

"Of course." She stepped aside for them to enter.

When the door shut behind them, they followed her into the living room. Along the way, Nick scanned the hallway and kitchen, taking in the many photos of a rugged coastline that hung on the walls. He didn't know where the photos had been taken, but something told him they'd been snapped in another country. *Scotland.*

Scottie—and no, the symbolism of the dog's name wasn't lost on him—trotted in front of them, his long gray coat swaying with the air currents created by his movement.

Despite Meera's seeming compliance, Nick never took his eyes off the woman. Body language could provide information about what a person was thinking and feeling. He particularly watched her hands, having learned long ago not to be distracted by a person's words.

She sat on the edge of the sofa and indicated two wingback armchairs for him and Eric. Nick sat across from her, while Eric stood off to the side, so he could watch her and, at the same time, see into the kitchen and hallway. Scottie lay down at her feet.

Meera clasped her hands on her lap, then raised her

brows. "What can I do for you?"

No sense fucking around. There wasn't time.

He pulled his phone from his pocket and cued up the photo with Meera's reflection. He held it up for her to see. "Would you agree that the person in this photo is you?"

She leaned forward and peered at the screen. Her brows lowered. "Yes. But how did you get it?"

"It was found on a gang member's phone. The same gang member who tried to kidnap Andi Hardt at gunpoint. This was the photo he used to identify her as the person to be kidnapped, and that's your reflection. *You* took that photo, didn't you?"

"What?" She straightened, looking alternately from him to Eric. "Someone tried to kidnap Andi? Is she okay? Was she hurt?"

"Cut the shit, Meera." He paused to watch her as his words sank in, and he knew Eric was doing the same.

"What do you mean? I—"

"It's over," he said in a hard tone. He wasn't buying into her feigned-innocence act. "Unless you start talking and tell us who hired you, you're looking at up to twenty years for your part in a kidnapping conspiracy involving firearms."

Her eyes began darting back and forth. Her knuckles whitened as she clasped her hands tightly and rocked in place on the edge of the sofa.

Classic signs of someone stalling for time to make shit up.

Quivering lips pressed together. Her nostrils flared, and she began blinking rapidly.

"Tell us what you know," he demanded. "And don't even think of lying. You're already neck-deep in hot water as it is."

Without looking at him, she began shaking her head. "I can't tell you."

"You can. The only way to help yourself is to start talking."

"I can't!" she cried.

"Who hired you?" Based upon her body language, he was close to breaking her. "Who ordered you to take a photo of Andi and Joe Myer and send it to the gangs? Was it Brian Argyle?"

She pressed her hands over her eyes, and her body began to tremble. Tears trickled from between her fingers. "Oh my God," she whispered. "He'll kill me. Mr. Argyle will kill me."

Pay dirt.

Scottie got to his feet and rested his head in Meera's lap, looking up at her from dark eyes partially obscured by long shocks of gray hair.

Now that she'd given up Argyle's name, he lowered his voice, not wanting to frighten her more. "You were Argyle's contact with Joe Myer to launder gun money. You're Mary, aren't you?"

With her hands still covering her face, she nodded.

"You were the one Myer spoke to over the phone." Interestingly, he still hadn't detected even a nuance of a Scottish accent, which could explain why Myer wouldn't have recognized her voice even if they'd run into each other at the DPC.

She took a deep breath and let her hands fall to her lap. Scottie licked them until she rested one hand on his head. "Yes," she said on a shaky breath. "I don't know what happened. I'd been working for him for years and everything was fine. Then he told me to call Mr. Myer regarding some money transfers. I swear to you, I don't know anything about guns, and I had no idea what that photo would be used for. I would never, *ever* do anything to hurt Andi. You have to believe me."

He leaned forward, cataloging everything he'd just heard and observed. She *seemed* to be telling the truth, but something was pinging his bullshit meter. He couldn't put his finger on what.

"Are you going to arrest me?" More tears trickled down her face.

"That will be up to the federal prosecutor to decide." If it were up to him, he'd throw the book at her for putting Andi's life in jeopardy. But chances were that, if she was completely truthful, she'd most likely get a reduced sentence. By some stroke of fucked-up justice, she might even get away with probation. He doubted it, though.

He tugged a small digital recorder from his other breast pocket. "Tell me everything from the moment you started working for Argyle." He turned on the recorder and set it on the coffee table.

"You have to protect me." Her eyes went wide. "He'll kill me if he finds out I talked to you. He's a vicious man who'll murder anyone who gets in his way or disagrees with him."

Not wanting to mislead her, he told her the truth as he knew it. "What I *can* assure you of is that with your testimony we can slam Argyle with enough federal weapons and money laundering charges to keep him in prison for a very long time."

She closed her eyes and began shaking her head. "Oh, Scottie." She stroked the top of her dog's head. "What will happen to you if I go to jail?"

The dog lifted its head and stared at her as if waiting for the answer. Nick wasn't about to say so, but if Meera didn't have any family, he'd find the dog a good home.

Taking a deep, shuddering breath, Meera began her story.

When Nick and Eric walked into Conference Room B, Andi was standing by the window with her back to him. She'd been waiting there while they'd re-interviewed Meera with AUSA Bennett and Special Agent Cox.

"I brought you a sandwich and something to drink." He set the plate and a bottle of water on the table next to her purse, noting the anxious look on her face as she walked toward them.

"Thank you, but I'm not hungry." She picked up the bottled water, twisting off the cap. "Did you get anything new from Meera?"

He'd already given Andi the CliffsNotes version during the ride from Meera's house to the federal building, but now they had details. "Her story's consistent with what Joe told us. Argyle directed the whole thing. Meera provided Joe with account numbers in different countries, to which he wired proceeds from the sale of weapons. She still claims she doesn't know anything about guns."

He glanced at his watch. Eleven thirty. Myer was due to turn himself in at noon, so they'd have to get downstairs shortly. Things were happening too fast, and he didn't like it.

"What's up?" The crease between Eric's blond brows told him his friend had picked up on Nick's concerns.

The timetable he'd set for today was quickly going down the crapper. "In the rush to get Meera in for more questioning before Myer turns himself in, we didn't get the chance to ask her for Argyle's records. She's gotta have contact info for the guy, wire transfers, bank account information. We need to secure her house or office and get a search warrant."

"I can work on that after we get Myer inside," Eric offered. "You've got enough on your plate."

"Thanks." He stared at the clock, watching the second hand tick its way around the dial. Those hairs on the back of his neck—the ones that prickled when something was off—were stabbing sharply into his brain. "I can't shake the feeling that we're getting played."

"By whom?" Andi asked.

"Good question." Argyle for certain. Myer was still a question mark, and he was still suspicious of Meera Devine, too.

"Do you believe everything Meera told us?" Eric asked.

"I don't know," he admitted. Whether it was intentional or not, every defendant held something back until they'd been interviewed several times. With each successive interview, more information came out.

"You think she's holding back," Eric said rather than asked.

He nodded. "I'm sure of it. How much, I don't know."

"Where is she now?" Andi watched him from tired eyes. "And will you get Joe and her together and have them both explain the whole operation?"

"She's in another conference room down the hall." He tipped his head to the door. "A deputy U.S. marshal is with her. And no, we don't plan to have her meet Joe. They're both witnesses. We don't want them to influence each other's story, so we'll keep them separated."

She took a sip of water. "Has she been arrested?"

"Not yet." Andi looked ready to drop, so he indicated they should all sit at the table.

She pulled out a chair and sat. "Why not?"

"It's standard procedure in cases like this." Knowing she wouldn't want him to sit next to her, he chose a chair across the table from her. "Like Joe, she's complicit but also a key witness against Argyle. She won't be charged until we know the extent of her cooperation. Both of them could help us get to Argyle."

"The only things we know about him," Eric added as he sat next to Andi, "come from Meera. He's about sixty years old, six feet tall, with gray hair and brown eyes."

"Was your contact in Scotland able to dig anything up?" Nick asked.

Eric shook his head. "So far, no one by the name of Meera Devine has a criminal history in Scotland. They'll try to find something on Brian Argyle and Argyle Enterprises."

"Good." He looked back at Andi. "Bennett wants Meera

to record her next phone call with Argyle and find out when—or if—he plans to come to the U.S. If he does, Bennett will want her to wear a wire and get incriminating statements on the guy. We'll use those statements to put together a rock-solid case."

She'd been about to take another sip of water but set the bottle on the table. "That sounds like it could take a while."

While he didn't say it, the practical realities of complex investigations sucked, and no one was more disappointed than he was. As much as he wanted to be the one to put the silver bracelets on Argyle, he'd take equal pleasure in locking Meera up for her role—knowing or otherwise—in the kidnapping conspiracy.

"I'd better get downstairs on patrol with Tiger." Eric pushed from the table and headed for the door. He patted the radio clipped to his belt. "We'll keep you posted on the ground. The Feebs on top of the building will be on the same frequency."

"Thanks." When the door closed, he took in the dented water bottle clutched in Andi's hand.

"Promise me something." She released her grip on the water bottle, and the sharp crinkling sound reminded him of a gunshot.

Anything, he wanted to say. Because he'd do anything within his power that she asked of him.

"What?" he said instead, ridiculously hoping she'd walk into his arms and forgive him.

Her gaze locked with his. "As angry as I am at him for what he's done—overall, and to me specifically—I don't want to see Joe hurt. Promise me you'll protect him."

As the now-familiar spurt of jealousy hit him, he told her the words he knew she needed to hear. "With my life."

Chapter Nineteen

Through the bank of glass doors, Andi watched Nick's hard profile as he stood outside, observing everyone who entered and exited the building. Nothing escaped his scrutiny, not even a woman pushing a stroller or an elderly man with a cane slowly making his way along the sidewalk.

Saxon stood dutifully at Nick's side, his thick black coat ruffling in the strong winds that had picked up since they'd arrived. Sunlight glinted off the dog's back, and she worried about him being outside in the heat for too long, particularly with the added weight of his canine body armor.

Andi had watched in horror as Nick strapped the specially fitted vest on Saxon. The first time she'd seen Saxon, he'd been wearing his body armor, but this was different. Now she understood the danger firsthand. Someone might try to shoot Joe before he got inside the building, and Nick wanted his dog protected as much as possible. As if Saxon wasn't huge to begin with...now he looked positively enormous.

"What's keeping him?" AUSA Bennett looked at his wristwatch, then at Cox and the two other FBI agents waiting with them.

"He'll be here," she reassured him. "If he said he'll turn himself in, then he will." And as soon as they were alone, she fully intended to light into him for everything he'd done.

"He'd better," Special Agent Cox said. "He's already ten minutes late."

Nick held his cell phone to his ear, then put it back in one of the pockets on his uniform shirt. He turned and strode toward the glass door she was standing behind. He held the door open for Saxon, who was panting from the oppressive heat. A blast of hot air gushed into the building, washing over her legs.

Standing this close to him made her pulse jump, and it was all she could do not to walk into his arms and let him surround her with his strength. As if reading her thoughts, steel-gray eyes pinned her. His free hand flexed, and for a moment she thought he was about to reach for her, but he didn't, leaving her both disappointed and relieved.

Stay strong. Even though she wasn't.

If she let him touch her again, she seriously doubted the emotional walls she'd begun rebuilding around her heart wouldn't crumble into a pile of emotional rubble, and when he left her—which he would—she'd only have to rebuild. That, she couldn't take. *Never again.*

"Any sign of him?" Bennett asked.

"Negative." Nick shook his head. "I just called his cell. No answer."

A bead of sweat trickled down his temple. His face was tight. Between his uniform, body armor, and all the equipment clipped to his belt, she imagined he was suffering from the blazing sun just as Saxon had to be.

At the sight of Andi, Saxon's tail wagged, and she reached down to give him a quick pat on the head. "He'll show," she reiterated, although deep down she was beginning to wonder if he really would.

Nick arched a brow, and his lips curved into a doubtful expression. Back in the conference room, she'd sensed his irritation when she'd asked him to protect her ex. It had struck her as jealousy, and she didn't understand the source of it. Nick didn't have real feelings for her, so why should he care?

He turned to stare intently out the glass door, his eyes flicking right, then left. Despite what had gone down between them, she deeply regretted extracting that promise from him to protect Joe. When he'd said *with my life,* it had frightened her because she knew he would do exactly as he'd promised. He was that kind of man. Duty and honor were ingrained in him down to the cellular level.

Nick clicked the microphone on his lapel. "Is the roof secure?"

"Ten-four," a voice she didn't recognize said. "Window washers are standing down until we give them the all-clear."

Andi heard a faint buzzing, and Nick yanked the cell phone from his pocket. He swiped the screen to take the call. "Myer. Where are you?"

Edging closer, she hoped to hear some of the conversation but couldn't. What she did get was the scent of Nick's aftershave, bringing with it bittersweet memories of making love with him in the woods.

Taking in a shuddering breath, she realized the futility of it all. No matter how much she tried banishing them, those memories would stay with her until the day she died.

Nick's jaw went rigid. "Not a chance, Myer."

"What is it?" Bennett stepped closer.

He hesitated, clearly not wanting to repeat whatever Joe had said. "He won't show unless Andi is out there curbside when he pulls up."

"So, do it," Bennett said. "You said so yourself, there's too much riding on his testimony to risk him taking off again."

He turned on Bennett. "The hell I will. It's bad enough that she's here at all. She stays inside."

"Nick." She rested her hand on his arm, instantly regretting the contact. The mere feel of his warm skin was enough to dent her resolve. "It's okay," she said, quickly letting her hand fall to her side. "I *want* to do this. You and Saxon will be right there with me. Eric, Kade, Matt, and all those other agents will be watching. I'll be safe."

"Make it happen, Sergeant." AUSA Bennett glared at Nick.

His jaws clenched so hard his cheek muscles flexed. "Five minutes," he barked into the phone, then ended the call and stuffed the phone in his pants pocket. He clicked his mic. "Five minutes," he repeated. "All teams acknowledge."

Six men came back with "all clear," and Andi thought she recognized Eric's, Matt's, and Kade's voices among them.

Nick draped Saxon's leash over the dog's back and began unbuttoning his shirt. When he'd gotten it off, he all but threw the shirt at Bennett. "Hold this." Then he began unstrapping his Kevlar vest. The Velcro straps made hissing sounds as he yanked them open. Then he turned to her and began fitting the body armor over her torso.

"No!" Horrified, she pushed the vest away. "Then *you* won't be protected." No matter what he'd done, the thought of him injured because he'd given her his vest was unthinkable.

"No time for a spare." He winked, then grinned. "Humor me."

His body was so close to hers that she glimpsed the silvery flecks in his beautiful gray eyes. It hit her how easily he'd shed his own protective vest to safeguard her life. He didn't have to do that. But he had.

Not waiting for her assent, he resumed fitting the vest to her body. Knowing it was a compromise of sorts, she didn't say another word, but felt his touch everywhere as he tugged the two pieces of material tighter to her body then adjusted the straps.

As his fingers grazed her bare arms, goose bumps paraded along her shoulders and back, and she was overwhelmed by the heady scent of his aftershave. For as long as she lived, she'd never forget the wonderful way he smelled.

The vest was large for her slim frame, covering her entire torso. Given how bulky it was, the Kevlar wasn't as heavy as she expected, but it was warm from being wrapped around Nick's chest.

She watched him grab his shirt from Bennett then put it back on and tuck it in. "Let's go," he said to Cox and the other agents. "Make a circle around her"—he nodded to Andi— "and keep it tight." When he faced her, his tone softened. "Stay in the middle of us as we walk to the curb. Okay?"

She nodded. "Okay."

Could a sniper really be out there, lying in wait to take Joe out?

Taking a deep breath, she got behind Nick and Saxon just as he pushed open the heavy glass door. Cox fell in step behind her, and she was quickly flanked by the other two agents. Hot, blustery summer air swirled all around her, a stark contrast to the air-conditioned interior of the federal building.

An American flag whipped back and forth on a tall metal pole in the center of the courtyard, making loud snapping noises. Banging metal had her looking up and behind her to see an empty window-washer cage hanging against the side of the building, swaying back and forth in the gusty winds.

As they made their way down the short flight of stairs from the building to the curb, a blue sedan pulled up and parked. Peering around the breadth of Nick's shoulders, she glimpsed a blond-haired man get out of the driver's seat. She held her breath until she could positively identify him.

Joe.

"Andi!" He walked briskly to where she was effectively sandwiched between Nick and Agent Cox. When Saxon lowered his head and growled, Joe froze.

She squeezed between Nick and one of the agents, then threw herself into Joe's waiting arms. Only then did she realize he had a backpack slung over his shoulder. He held her tightly as she clung to him, grateful he was alive and here and safe. She held back the litany of expletives she had planned for later.

Behind her, Nick cursed, and she knew why. She'd disobeyed his order to remain within the protective circle of federal agents.

"Unknown subjects approaching," a voice said over the radio. *Matt's voice.*

"Save the teary reunion for later," Nick ordered in a harsh tone, gently pulling Andi from Joe's embrace. "Get inside. Both of you. *Now.*" He and the agents encircled them and ushered them hastily up the stairs and into the building.

As pre-planned, building guards passed Joe and his backpack through the magnetometer.

"All clear," Matt came back over the radio. "Just a couple of kids playing hooky."

Nick clicked the mic. "Copy that. I'll keep you posted."

At the elevator bank, a man in a dark suit—one she didn't recognize—held an elevator for them. Nick and Saxon stepped aside, indicating she and Joe, along with Cox and AUSA Bennett should enter first. Nick looked both ways down the hallway before he and Saxon got in. The remaining two agents guarded the elevator as the doors closed.

Cox pressed the button for the third floor, and as the elevator began a slow ascent, a wave of relief washed over her. Joe had actually turned himself in, and no one had gotten hurt in the process.

The elevator was silent, save for the sounds of breathing—panting, on Saxon's part. She hoped Nick had a water bowl for him upstairs.

Joe's hand clasped hers, although his touch didn't elicit anything close to passion. Nothing he could say or do would ever change the fact that she was in love with someone else. But Joe was her friend, and since he needed her support, she squeezed his hand.

Nick took that moment to glance over his shoulder. His gaze dropped to where her and Joe's hands were tightly clasped. His jaw tightened, and he turned back to face the elevator doors.

Not for the first time, she wondered what was with the jealous behavior. Aside from sex, he'd never wanted her. The answer was suddenly obvious. It was a turf war, and she was the turf. She'd made love with both men. Nick knew that. Joe didn't, so he'd thought nothing of holding her hand in front of everyone. She could only surmise that Nick felt some latent masculine possessiveness over her body. One he had no claim to. *Not anymore.*

Even though she was still angry with Joe, she held his hand tighter. He needed her support more than Nick needed his ego stroked.

The elevator came to a stop, and a moment later the doors opened. Nick held up his hand as he and Saxon entered the hallway. Man and dog looked both ways down the corridor before Nick indicated they should step out of the elevator.

She and Joe followed AUSA Bennett and Special Agent Cox down the long hallway. Even if she couldn't hear Saxon padding behind her, or the footfalls of Nick's boots, she would have known he was there. It wasn't quite rage or animosity radiating off him. More like annoyance, and she felt the heat of his gaze penetrating her dress, her skin, straight to her heart—a heart that betrayed her again by beating out a steady staccato at his nearness.

When they entered Conference Room A, the same one in which she'd witnessed Nick being heartily congratulated over duping her ass, he shut the door behind him then went to the sink at the far end of the room and ran a small bowl of water for Saxon.

AUSA Bennett sat at the head of the long table, with Cox to his right. Bennett indicated Joe should sit to his left, with her next to Joe. She caught Nick eyeing them as Joe sat and re-clasped her hand in his.

Saxon pranced in place, his attention fixated on the water bowl that Nick set on the floor against the wall. As Saxon drank, Nick unstrapped the dog's body armor. Saxon's coat was matted down by sweat, making her realize she still wore Nick's Kevlar vest.

"How 'bout I get that off you?"

Nick pulled her chair from the table so she could stand. He tugged open the Velcro straps, briskly and efficiently removing the vest, although one of his hands lingered at her waist—the side facing Joe, who, she noticed, flicked his gaze back and forth between her and Nick.

"Better?" Nick asked.

She nodded and sat. Yeah, except for the fact that every time he touched her, her heart broke a little more. "Thank you."

He set the vest on the floor behind their chairs, then took the seat to her left. She noticed that he rolled his chair back a few inches so that he could better observe Joe.

"Joseph A. Myer," AUSA Bennett began. "We have a warrant for your arrest."

"I know that." He hung his head.

"We'll hold off formal arrest processing until we determine the extent of your cooperation. The charges include money laundering and conspiracy to distribute illegal firearms."

He jerked his head up. "I didn't know what the money was from. I swear it."

"But you knew it was tainted money," Nick said in a blunt tone.

He nodded. "Yes."

"Are you willing to cooperate to the fullest extent possible?" Bennett asked.

He didn't hesitate. "Of course. I'll do anything you want."

"Then first," Bennett continued, "Special Agent Cox will read you your rights."

Cox pulled a card from his wallet and began reading. "You have the right to remain silent…"

Andi shifted uncomfortably in her chair. This was something out of a movie. A *bad* one.

"Do you understand these rights as I have explained them to you?" Cox set the card down a minute or so later and looked at Joe from across the table.

"Yes."

"Are you willing to waive your right to an attorney and to have an attorney present during this questioning?"

"Yes." He smacked his hands on the table. "Can we just get on with it?"

Bennett handed Joe two sheets of paper. "The first page is a waiver of rights form, essentially reiterating what Special Agent Cox read to you. The second is a cooperation agreement. Take a moment to review them both."

Joe released her hand and grabbed the documents. He quickly scanned them, then took the pen Bennett offered and signed at the bottom of both pages.

"Nick, would you sign as a witness?"

Joe reached in front of her to hand Nick the sheets of paper. Nick pulled a pen from the pocket of his uniform shirt and signed at the bottom before handing them back to Bennett.

"You have our undivided attention, Mr. Myer." AUSA Bennett leaned back in his chair. "Start from the beginning and tell us how you got into this."

He took a deep breath. "I have a gambling problem."

• • •

Nick wasn't surprised to learn about Myer's gambling problem. Most illegal money was made to either line someone's pockets out of sheer greed or to bail someone's ass out of hot water. Myer was drowning.

Cox and Bennett had each begun taking notes on a yellow legal pad, leaving him to keep an eye on Myer. Watching Myer sweat it out made him think he ought to cut the guy some slack for having a weakness. What he was having a difficult time tolerating was that after signing the cooperation agreement, he'd grabbed Andi's hand again and repositioned it firmly in his lap.

Motherfu—

He hooked his thumbs on his duty belt, when what he really wanted was to rip the guy's hand off his arm and feed it to Saxon for his dog's next meal.

Keep your head in the game. This is what you've been working for—to get Myer in front of a grand jury.

"I owed a casino in Connecticut fifty thousand dollars. I couldn't pay it off fast enough. The next thing I knew, a couple of thugs went to my office and threatened my secretary while I was out. They broke some furniture and told her I had one week to pay up in full or I'd suffer the consequences. Where was I supposed to get that kind of cash?"

"Oh, I don't know," Nick couldn't stop himself from interjecting, "sell your Mercedes, or that million-dollar house of yours and move into a condo?"

For a moment, anger and resentment blazed in Myer's eyes, but it was quickly extinguished with shame and remorse. "Yeah, I guess I could have, but certainly not within a week's time, and it would only have been a stop-gap. I have a problem, Sergeant. If I can get myself out of this mess, I definitely need help."

"That you do." In his years on the job, he'd seen every order of addiction, gambling being just one of them.

"A few days later," Myer continued, "I got a call from a woman with a Scottish accent—Mary—saying she'd pay off my debt if I did something for her."

Meera Devine.

"I didn't believe her at first. I thought it was some kind of con. She said she understood my hesitancy and offered me a show of good faith. The next thing I knew, there was a deposit for ten grand in my checking account. A down payment for wiring some funds out of the country."

"For Brian Argyle," Nick said, rather than asked.

Myer nodded. "For Brian Argyle and Argyle Enterprises. She said it was a one-time thing, but once turned into twice, and before I knew it a year had gone by and I'd wired nearly a million dollars to multiple foreign accounts. Scotland, the Caymans, Switzerland, Belize. And you're right. I guess I always knew the money was dirty, and eventually, I told her I wanted out."

"And what did she say?" Bennett asked.

"She laughed. She said no one *ever*"—he hooked his fingers into quotation marks—"gets out. Then she said that if I didn't want to help her, she could always call the boys at the casino and have them pay me a late-night visit and rough me up."

"Do you know Meera Devine?" Nick figured he might have run into her at the DPC.

"Sure, I've met her a couple of times." He narrowed his eyes. "Why?"

Nick glanced at Bennett, who nodded that he should continue with this line of questioning. "Could the woman over the phone have been Meera Devine?"

"No way." He shook his head. "Mary has a heavy Scottish accent. Meera doesn't have an accent."

Not that any of them had detected. That didn't mean she didn't have one.

"Is your laptop in there?" Nick pointed to the backpack on the table.

"Yes." He unzipped the bag and pulled a silver laptop from the center compartment. After flipping up the cover and hitting the power button, he pushed it in front of Andi so that Nick could view the screen.

Nick edged closer, gratified that this gave Myer something else to do with his hands besides holding Andi's. He couldn't type on the keypad *and* be all touchy-feely at the same time.

In an effort to give him some space—or get away from him, he didn't know which—Andi leaned back in her chair, but not enough that his shoulder didn't brush up against hers. Or the clean scent of her shampoo didn't invade his senses like a pillaging army marching him right up the fucking wall.

"Here." Myer clicked on a folder marked *Cayman accounts*.

Nick tallied the line items. "Seven wire transfers to the Caymans in the name of Argyle Enterprises over the last twelve months for a total of two hundred thousand. There are three different account numbers."

Cox continued taking notes, as did Bennett. Andi stared straight ahead at the screen, gripping the armrests of her chair so tightly her knuckles were white. Good to know his nearness was affecting her as much as hers was jumbling his brain cells.

"Keep going," he urged, and Myer opened another folder, this one marked *Credit Suisse.*

"Ten more transfers to Switzerland for one hundred thousand. Two accounts there."

Myer clicked on a third folder—*Royal Bank of Scotland.* This folder contained the most recent wire transfers, executed over the last three months. "Three more to Scotland for another two hundred. Three accounts."

"Why all the different accounts?" Andi asked. "Doesn't that make it harder to keep track of?"

"That's exactly the point." Nick turned to her, secretly admiring her astute question. "The more accounts, the less activity associated with any one of them, and the easier it is to close one if anyone gets suspicious. It also provides spare locations if money ever has to be moved in a hurry." He tapped his fingers on the table, staring at Myer. "Did *you* set these accounts up?"

"No." Myer shook his head. "I assume Argyle did. The woman gave me the account numbers over the phone."

The woman. Again, Meera.

"That's five hundred thousand dollars," Cox said.

"I'm only getting started." Myer moved the cursor to close out the Scotland folder. "Wait until I show you the Belize account."

"Hold on." Nick pulled out his cell phone and took a picture of the screen, making sure to get a clear image of the Scottish account numbers.

As Myer continued detailing the specifics of how he wired money out of the country to all of Argyle's offshore accounts, he texted the screenshot to Eric, along with a message to ask his friend in Scotland to pull some strings. It was a long shot, but if they got lucky and Eric's friend came through, it could shortcut the process, saving them a boatload of precious time.

Eric came back with a quick reply. *On it.*

Myer started to click on the folder marked Belize but stopped and looked at Andi. "I'm sorry about using your account. It was stupid, and thoughtless, and I'll never forgive myself for doing it."

Andi nodded slowly but didn't say anything. The only evidence of her internal struggle over Myer's admission was the tightening of her jaw. Nick wanted her to let loose and slug the guy, but she didn't. She was too kind a person, which was one of a hundred reasons why he loved her.

Two hours later, they finished. Nick and Saxon escorted Andi and Joe to the cafeteria for coffee and something to eat, then to Conference Room B, where Andi had been waiting earlier. She set her purse on the table next to the sandwich she hadn't eaten. Joe set his plate down, then pulled Andi into his arms.

At the abrupt movement, Saxon lowered his head, glaring up at Myer. Nick smirked. His dog didn't like the guy much, either, but probably not for the same reasons Nick didn't. Myer didn't like dogs, and Saxon knew it. Nick's reasons for disliking him went gut-deep.

Over Myer's shoulder, she met his gaze for a long moment before shutting her eyes and uttering a long sigh.

"Joe, are you really okay?" she asked.

"I'm fine, baby." Myer clasped the back of her head, stroking her hair. "I'm more worried about you."

Nick clenched his hand into a fist around Saxon's leash. Myer could be a goddamn altar boy, and he'd still hate the guy's guts—for loving Andi and for being the one she had her arms around.

It's your own damn fault. Words he found himself repeating over and over the past twenty-four hours.

Knowing the depths of Myer's feelings for her, the idea of leaving the two of them alone grated on his nerves, but he had no choice.

"I have to go verify the grand jury is ready. Don't leave this room," he ordered Myer before heading to the door, taking no small amount of gratification when Andi pulled out of the guy's embrace. "As long as you stay here, you'll be okay. Tonight, you'll go to a safe house."

Saxon shot Myer one last wary look before following Nick.

He jerked open the door, slamming it shut when he and Saxon were in the hallway. Dealing with Myer was going to be a lot harder than he'd expected. More accurately, seeing him with Andi would drive him abso-fucking-lutely nuts.

Shake it off, Houston. For now, he'd do it, but only because he had no say in the matter. Later on, he'd move heaven and earth to get back in Andi's good graces. There was no way on this earth he'd let Joe Myer or anyone else stand between him and the woman he loved.

After taking Saxon outside for a few minutes to do his business, he found Cox and Bennett back in the other conference room discussing their next move. He suspected this would be a long day, stretching well into the evening with additional interviews of both Myer and Meera. With that in mind, he'd brought Saxon inside again, not giving a crap whether Bennett objected. Not only that, when it came time to move Myer to wherever he'd be spending his first night, he wanted his partner there backing him up.

"We've been going over Myer's and Meera Devine's statements," Bennett said as he and Saxon rejoined them. "For the most part they mesh, but we'll re-interview them to button down the details before putting them in the grand jury."

Nick figured that might happen. He unhooked Saxon's leash and pointed to the wall behind him. Saxon lay down, resting his head between his paws.

Leaning against the same wall was Nick's discarded

body armor. He reached out to retrieve it when his cell phone buzzed. He looked at the screen to see an incoming text from Eric.

Call me. Interesting news from Scotland.

"Back in five." He headed for the door, preferring to have this conversation out of Bennett's earshot. The guy would throw a fit if he knew they were circumventing DOJ protocol by involving foreign officials in an investigation without filing the requisite red tape.

Red tape, my ass.

Anything that would get them to the end game faster was fine with him.

Stepping into the hallway, he pulled the door shut behind him then punched up Eric's number. "What have you got?" He leaned against the wall opposite the conference room, absently noting that the door hadn't completely shut again, and he could glimpse Saxon watching him. His snout still rested on the floor, but his ears twitched as he kept an eye on Nick.

"I sent the bank account numbers you gave me to my friend in Inverness. They checked with a security guy at the Royal Bank of Scotland, who figured out pretty quickly that the three accounts were opened at a branch in Portree."

"Where's Portree?"

The conference room door squeaked open another inch, and Cox eyed him suspiciously.

"On the north side of the country, near the Isle of Skye," Eric continued. "My friend in Inverness has a buddy in the Portree Police Department. Turns out the Portree PD is located literally thirty yards across the town square from the same branch where these accounts were opened. Apparently, Portree isn't that big, and everyone knows everyone. This cop is dating one of the tellers, and she told him who opened the accounts."

Nick straightened. *Now they were getting somewhere.*

"Portia Laird," Eric said.

Nick searched his memory. *Nada.* He'd been expecting Brian Argyle, possibly Meera Devine, or even Joe Myer, if the sonofabitch had lied to them. *So, who is Portia Laird?*

"As soon as the Portree cop heard the name," Eric continued, "he called me directly. Everyone in Portree knows the name. Ten years ago, Portia Laird was investigated for murdering her husband."

Eric paused, giving Nick a moment to absorb this information, and his heart began beating faster. "What was her husband's name?"

"Andrew Laird. Does that mean anything to you?"

"No. What were the circumstances of his death?"

"Portia and Andrew Laird were on a hunting trip on the Isle of Skye. Andrew Laird was shot in the back. Portia said she heard the shot but didn't see anyone. Problem was, there were no other documented hunters in that area, and the local police never found any evidence. Not even another weapon."

"Did they compare the weapon Portia was carrying to the one that killed her husband?"

"The bullet didn't match her gun *or* her husband's, but they were sure they had their man. Er, woman."

"Why were they so sure?"

"Several reasons. Portia had never gone on a hunting trip with her husband before, but she was the one who suggested it. Laird had been previously married, and his children hated Portia. What his children didn't know is that Laird had just changed his will. Portia stood to inherit everything, even though it wasn't an enormous estate."

"They think she killed him for the inheritance."

"You got it."

Nick's shit meter swung into the red zone. "Can they send us a photo of Portia Laird?"

"Since she was never arrested and never charged, the police don't have her photo or prints on file. They're trying to dig up her old UK driving license photo."

"Wouldn't the shooting have made the news? Is there a photo of her in one of the local papers?"

"I already checked," Eric said. "It's not only been ten years, but apparently Portia Laird did a good job of staying out of the limelight after her husband's death. Someone up there will find a photo sooner or later, and they'll send it to me when they do."

"Good work." He tried to disguise the disappointment in his voice. He really needed that picture. "What about the bank? Did they say when Portia was there last? They might have video." Then again, if Portree was that much in the Scottish sticks, he wondered if the banks even maintained cameras.

"Negative video. It's been two years since she was physically in that branch accessing her safe deposit box, and the bank video turns over every thirty days."

He wasn't surprised to hear that. Most banks didn't maintain footage forever. At least they knew she had a bank box, and they could include that in their MLAT request.

Some things about Portia Laird still bugged him, not the least of which was that she'd been investigated for murdering her husband. "Can the Portree cop or anyone in the bank give us a description of the woman?" he asked.

"The cop said she's kinda plain. Average height, brown hair, brown eyes. The bank tellers said the same thing. Aside from her being a suspected murderer, the only other thing people remember about her is her dog."

Her dog?

Nick pushed from the wall. Every one of his senses went on high alert. Through the opening into the conference room, Saxon lifted his head, watching Nick intently.

"What *about* her dog?" His voice was low and controlled, but inside he was wound tighter than a rubber band.

"Big thing, with thick wavy gray hair covering its eyes, cropped tail. Sounds a lot like a—"

"—Bouvier," they both said at the same time.

His heart began beating wildly. "Saxon! Cox!" he shouted, already taking off down the hall. "Eric," he yelled into the phone, "get in here and call for backup! Conference Room C. Third floor. It's Meera! The bitch has been playing us the whole time."

"Already on my way," Eric said. "Backup's in tow."

He jammed the phone into his pocket and tore down the hall. Behind him, Saxon's claws scrabbled on the floor as he caught up. His partner didn't need to know what was up. Saxon knew from Nick's body language that it was bad.

"Nick!" Cox yelled from behind them.

Not waiting for the agent to catch up, he and Saxon took the next corner at top speed. He shoved a few paralegals out of his way. Others jumped aside, pressing their backs to the wall as they shot past. "Get in your offices and stay there!" he shouted.

His heart raced as he pounded down the hall. Christ, he should have seen this coming. His gut told him there *was* no Brian Argyle. Worse, he suspected Meera Devine was the brains behind Argyle Enterprises.

And she'd killed before.

Chapter Twenty

"I can't believe Meera was part of this the entire time." Andi stared out the window, watching the window washers on the opposite side of the U-shaped building. "How often has she come into the DPC and talked with us as if we were friends?"

It had been her intention to yell at Joe the minute they were alone, but she was too tired and overwhelmed. The chewing-out she had planned would have to wait until later, after she'd rested up and had more time to process everything.

"I'm sorry." Before she could stop him, he cupped the side of her face. His hazel eyes were filled with concern, his expression one of utter misery. "Can you ever forgive me for involving you in this mess?"

"What's done is done." She tugged his hand from her face, and when he tried to thread his fingers with hers, she pulled away. Hearing about his gambling problem had sucked the wind from her anger, but definitely not eliminated it by any stretch. "I'm still mad as hell at you, but I understand that gambling is an addiction, and I want to help you. I'll stay with you through this. As long as it takes." And she meant it.

He reached for her again, but this time she held up her hand. "No, Joe. You misunderstand." The look of confusion on his face about killed her. This was *so* not going the way she'd expected. "I only meant I want to *help* you. I'll support you any way I can, but—"

"It's the cop, isn't it?" The elation on his face had fled. He turned and rested his forearms on the windowsill. "I picked up on it in the other room. Every time I touched you, Sgt. Houston looked like he wanted to rip my heart out. Even his dog doesn't like me."

"I'm sorry. I really am." She laid her hand on his shoulder, but he shrugged it off. "I don't know what I said or did to make you think otherwise, but you know as well as I do that our romance was over a long time ago. I thought you were okay with that. What's changed?"

His chest expanded as he took a deep breath. "Being on the run then learning you could have been killed made me rethink things. We were so good together, and I thought we could be again."

She joined him at the window, nudging his hip with hers. "We *were* good together, and I have no regrets. But we made the right decision to break up years ago. I think it's the stress of what's happening that's confusing things."

He began massaging his forehead. "Maybe," he admitted after a long moment.

"No *maybes*." Nick's handsome face shimmered before her eyes. Even though things were over with him, rekindling a romance with Joe wasn't in the cards.

"So, what's with the cop?" He faced her and rested his elbow on the sill.

Now it was her turn to stare out the window. She wasn't quite sure how to answer his question. "We were…something. Now we're not. It didn't go anywhere."

"You could have fooled me." He playfully shoulder-bumped her. "There was definitely something sizzling between you two. Pissed me off, but I want you to be happy."

"Thanks." She squeezed his hand, giving him a forced smile. "If only that were poss—"

Her cell phone rang, and she dug it out of her purse on the table.

"Hi, Tess," she said after taking the call. "What's up?"

"You won't believe this." Tess paused, and Andi tensed for more bad news. "Someone just paid all the DPC's outstanding bills."

"What do you mean someone paid our bills?" Though Tess couldn't see, she scrunched up her face. "*I* didn't. That isn't even possible. I don't have the money."

"Nick paid them." Tess laughed. "Every single one."

"What?" Her mouth fell open. "Are you sure?"

"Positive." Her bubbly giggle sang through the phone. "I called the produce market to let them know we'd be late paying our tab, and they said it was already paid. A man called in yesterday afternoon and gave them his bank card information. I asked, 'what man' and they said Nicholas Houston. Then I called every other one of our vendors, including the dairy farm, the winery, the electrical company, and the water company, to name a few. They all said the same thing—Nick paid the bill."

"Oh my God." She stared at the wall as she absorbed Tess's news.

"Andi?" Joe stood in front of her now, a concerned look on his face. "Is everything all right?"

"That's over ten thousand dollars," she whispered. "Why would he do that?"

The question was meant more for herself, but Tess answered just the same. "Because he cares about you. He *really* cares about you."

"I-I have to go. I'll talk to you later." Still in a daze, she ended the call and put her phone back in her bag.

Had he done it out of guilt? Or sympathy?

Maybe. In her heart, she dared to hope there was another reason, and at that moment his words yesterday in the woods came back to her. *I love you.* And the stark pain she'd glimpsed in his eyes. A man like him didn't throw those three words around lightly.

"Oh no." She reached out to steady herself, resting her hand on the table. Everything that had passed between them flitted before her eyes.

Nick confronting his awful past to bail her out of a major jam when her musician hadn't shown.

Nick saving her life, then guarding her with his.

Nick kissing her and making love to her as no man ever had.

Now he'd paid all her debts. That hadn't been a requirement of his job, or his duty, or something necessary to further his investigation. Not for the first time, he'd done something for her just because he loved her. *And I was too blind to see it.*

She'd judged him by all her failures with the men in her life. Not that he hadn't given her a reason to doubt the truth of his words. "I've made a terrible, terrible mistake."

"What mistake?" Joe asked.

They turned as the conference room door opened, and she hoped it was Nick.

It wasn't.

Andi gasped. "Meera."

"What are *you* doing here?" Joe shouted.

Without answering, Meera shut the door, locking it behind her.

Andi tensed. Something was very, very wrong.

Nick had assured her that Meera was being guarded by a deputy U.S. marshal, and that Meera's and Joe's paths would never cross.

What was she doing there, unguarded?

Meera dug into the purse hanging over her shoulder and pulled out a gun. "I'm here to clean up this mess," she answered in a thick Scottish brogue.

Andi jerked back, bumping into the window ledge.

"Oh, shit." Joe moved in front of her, shielding her with his body.

"Where's the laptop?" Meera glanced at Andi's small purse, then at the floor on either side of the table. "Where is it?" Her voice was low and controlled, yet there was no mistaking the deadly intent in her eyes.

Andi stared, unable to take her eyes off the barrel of the gun. Odd, but Meera was pointing a gun at them, and all she could think was that the woman really was Scottish.

"Where's the fucking laptop?" With Meera's accent, the word "fucking" sounded more like "fooking." She raised the gun, again pointing it at them.

Andi flinched. Fear shot up her spine, immobilizing her. She glanced at her purse. Her cell phone was in there, but there was no way she could get to it. Or to the second door, the one behind them. They'd never get out without being shot.

"You're too late." Joe grabbed the back of a chair. "The state police and the FBI have it, along with all your accounts and every wire transfer I ever made for you."

Meera sneered.

We're going to die.

"I'm sorry, Andi." Meera took a step closer. "I really did like you. And I'll miss your lovely café."

Did like her? As in past tense. As in, *I won't be around much longer.*

She grabbed Joe's arm, crushing his shirtsleeve in her fist. "Meera, *please*." She was surprised at how steady her voice was because inside she was shaking like a leaf.

"Don't do this." Joe pushed in front of her, holding his arms up and away from his sides as if that would actually shield her from a bullet. "She didn't do anything to you. Let her go."

When Meera lowered the gun and uttered a heavy sigh, Andi thought he'd actually gotten through to her.

Meera stepped closer, stopping when she was five feet away from them. "I told you once that you can't walk away. Ever. There's only one way out." Then she raised her arm.

• • •

Nick flung open the door to the conference room, aiming in, shouting, *"Platz."*

Saxon lowered to the safety of the floor, his head erect, his body quivering with tension.

Breathing hard, Nick scanned the room.

Empty. No Meera and no deputy marshal.

Someone groaned.

Nick bolted to the far end of the conference room. Saxon rose to his feet.

"Pass auf," he commanded over his shoulder, wanting Saxon to remain at the open door and guard it.

The deputy lay on the floor behind the table, and several rolling chairs that had been strategically placed there to conceal the injured man.

He clicked his mic. "Officer down. Conference Room C. Female suspect—Meera Devine—is loose in the building. Approach with caution." He added a quick description then holstered his Smith & Wesson and knelt by the deputy. Blood flowed from a deep gash on the man's head, but his chest rose and fell with even breaths. Nick stood and yanked a handful of folded paper towels from the sink dispenser, then pressed them to the wound to slow the bleeding. "Hang in there.

Help's on the way."

The deputy groaned again, louder this time. A good sign.

"What the hell's going on?" Cox said from the doorway, shooting Saxon a wary look.

Saxon's head was lowered, his big body blocking Cox's entry.

"*Lass es.*" Nick commanded. He didn't want his dog taking a chunk out of the agent's leg.

Saxon backed off, allowing Cox to run into the room.

"She hit me." The deputy touched his fingers to where Nick held the towels to his head. "Ah, damn, that hurts. What did she hit me with?" He tried getting up, then grimaced and thought better of it, easing onto his side.

"*Who* hit you?" Cox looked at the deputy then to Nick.

"Easy there. Stay down," Nick rested a hand on the man's shoulder. "It was Meera," he said to Cox, then nodded to the small blood-covered bust of George Washington lying on the floor beside the deputy.

The deputy moaned, and as he rolled onto his back, the hem of his jacket caught on the man's holster, and Nick froze. The holster was empty, as were the leather handcuff and spare magazine pouches.

In a nanosecond, Meera's plan crystallized. A moment of panic gripped him, and his heartbeat seemed to slow to a complete stop.

She'd go after Myer, and Andi was with him.

"Stay with him and keep pressure on the wound," he said to Cox, then ran to the door, clicking his mic along the way. "All units, she's heading for Conference Room B, and she's armed."

"*Hier!*" Saxon spun and followed Nick as he charged down the long corridor to the other conference room.

Only then did he realize how much Meera had played them. She would have had no way of knowing where Joe was, and what better way to find out than to get inside the federal building and pretend to be a co-witness against Brian Argyle. She'd orchestrated the whole thing, then played them like a bunch of chumps fresh out of the academy. With security and magnetometers at every door, she never could have gotten a firearm into the building, but she'd procured one just the same, and she knew how to use it.

Eric's voice came over the radio. "ETA five minutes."

Five minutes. Nick pounded down the hallway with Saxon keeping pace at his side. *This could all be over in two.*

Standard federal protocol didn't include security officers stationed inside the U.S. Attorneys' office space. Security's job was to guard all the first-floor entrances and courtrooms. Until backup arrived, he was on his own.

At the end of the corridor, the closed door to Conference Room B came into view. He had no idea what he'd find on the other side, but he wasn't about to wait around with his thumb up his ass.

With his pulse skyrocketing, he and Saxon charged to the door. In those last steps, he completely regretted everything he'd said and done to push Andi away. She would never forgive him, but he prayed he wasn't too late to save her.

Five feet from the door, he heard the gunshot.

And Andi's scream.

Chapter Twenty-One

She shot him. *Meera shot Joe.* It had happened in an instant, and she still couldn't believe it.

Blood seeped into his shirt, and his head lolled to the side. His eyes were closed, and she couldn't be sure he was breathing.

Andi took rapid breaths, trying not to panic. She moved toward him, intending to kneel at his side.

"Don't move," Meera ordered. Her lips curled into an evil smile as she pointed the gun at Andi's head. *Oh my God, oh my God.* She squeezed her eyes shut, waiting for the bullet to blast through her skull.

"Put these on," Meera shouted.

Something thumped on the floor at her feet. She opened her eyes to see a set of handcuffs.

Where did she get handcuffs? Probably the same place she'd gotten the gun.

"Do it!" Meera shouted. Spittle flew from her mouth, and her eyes glittered with rage. She unhooked her purse from her shoulder and heaved it to a corner of the room.

Keeping one eye on her, Andi swallowed hard, then picked up the handcuffs. Never having touched a pair of those before in her life, she didn't automatically know how to work them. Using her fingers, she pushed on one side of the metal cuffs. It opened with a loud ratcheting sound. She clamped the cuff over her wrist, shoving one end into the other until it again made that same ratcheting sound.

Meera growled her impatience. "Now your other wrist."

The door handle jiggled, then the door crashed open, slamming against the wall.

Nick and Saxon stood in the doorway. She wanted to cry with relief. Then it all happened so fast, yet she caught every movement as if she were watching a movie in slow motion.

While Nick raised his gun, Meera grabbed Andi's arm, jerking her to stand in front of her. The woman was using her for cover.

The movement of Nick's arm was subtle, but she caught it as he adjusted his aim away from her.

Two gunshots blasted. Meera cried out and winced but didn't drop her gun. Blood trickled from her arm.

"*Platz!*" Saxon hunkered down at Nick's feet.

The barrel of the gun jabbed against her skull. Meera's chest pressed against Andi's back as she wrapped her free arm around Andi's waist. As they were both approximately the same height, Meera's head was directly behind hers.

She grabbed the woman's arm, clawing at her flesh, but Meera's hold was as tight as a vise.

"Andi, don't move!" Nick shouted as he moved into the room.

"Be a good girl and do what he tells ye." Her breath was hot against Andi's ear, her brogue becoming thicker. "And don't do anything stupid." She rammed the gun harder against her head.

Nick and Saxon had taken cover behind one of the floor-to-ceiling square columns in the room. Most of Nick's body was concealed by the column, but she glimpsed his eyes. They were lit with fury.

Saxon's tail and part of the dog's body protruded from the other side of the column, his big body vibrating with energy. She understood he was only waiting for Nick's command to lunge at Meera and take her down.

But he'll be shot.

As Meera jammed the gun harder against her skull, the thumping in Andi's chest resounded like a battering ram, echoing in her ears.

"Let her go and put your gun on the floor." Nick's voice was cold and controlled. "There's no way out."

"I beg to differ." Meera dragged the barrel of her gun lower, pressing it into the soft flesh of Andi's cheek. "You'll let me go because I've got something you want."

As she breathed harder, the smell of gunpowder entered her lungs. The barrel of the gun was warm against her skin, reminding her that Nick *and* Meera had fired off a round.

Nick readjusted his position, giving Andi a brief but clear glimpse of his upper body, and her heart stilled. The center of Nick's gray-blue uniform shirt was quickly darkening.

With blood.

Nick's been shot.

But he was wearing his—

Body armor.

No, he wasn't. He'd given it to her and never put it back on. Neither Nick *nor* Saxon was wearing a Kevlar vest. He'd adjusted his aim to keep from shooting her, but in doing so, had missed a kill shot and taken a bullet to the chest.

Worry hit her with more impact than any physical pain could. Nick had been shot, and he was bleeding profusely.

He clicked his mic. "Lock down the building. Nobody gets out."

A voice came back that sounded like Eric's. "Copy that."

"Let her go, Meera." His voice was even, yet she knew him well enough to hear the pain behind his words. "We have the laptop. Shooting anyone else won't help you. The building is on lockdown, and there's no way out."

"We'll see about that." Meera backed up, edging for the door behind them.

Movement made Andi glance to where Joe lay on the floor. His shirt had dampened with more blood, but his eyelids fluttered.

He's alive.

Meera yanked the gun from her face, pointed it at Nick, and fired again.

Andi screamed, squeezing her eyes shut. The gun had been so close to her head, her ears rang from the blast. When she opened her eyes, she expected to see Nick lying on the floor, but he and Saxon were still there, taking cover behind the column. He wouldn't risk another shot at Meera, not while she still used her as a human shield.

Again, she clutched at Meera's arm, feeling something warm and sticky. Nick had shot Meera in the arm, yet she retained the strength of a gorilla.

Meera walked them backward. "Open the door," she growled.

"Andi, don't!" came Nick's harsh command.

"Do it!" She jammed the gun against Andi's temple, and this time it was hot enough to burn her skin, and she flinched. "Do it, or I'll keep shooting your boyfriend."

"No," she cried. She couldn't bear the thought of Nick being shot again. "Please don't. I'll do anything you say." Blindly, she reached behind her until her fingers contacted the doorknob. Twisting the knob, she pushed the door open.

Meera dragged her through the doorway.

"Andi, no!"

The last thing she glimpsed was the rage and pain on Nick's face.

. . .

Nick bolted to the door and peered around the doorjamb in time to see Meera back her and Andi up toward the stairwell at the end of the corridor. The absolute terror in Andi's eyes sent a shot of panic through his bones, the likes of which he'd never felt before in his life. Goddamn, he felt helpless. Helpless to save the woman he loved more than his next breath.

More than his own life.

A sudden and sharp, burning pain stabbed him in the chest, forcing him to shut his eyes momentarily. He blew out quick breaths, willing himself to remain upright. He was hit. How badly, he didn't know.

He pressed his shoulder against the doorjamb for support, watching Meera drag Andi closer to the wall, and for a moment he didn't understand what she was doing. When she reached for the small fire alarm box on the wall, he figured out her tactic in a heartbeat.

Diversion.

Meera would try to escape with the hundreds of people who—in the next few minutes—would try to evacuate the building.

With the gun still pressed to Andi's head, Meera flipped up the clear plastic cover and pulled down the lever. A piercing siren shattered the quiet. White strobes flashed on the ceiling.

Meera's arm shot back around Andi's waist. She backed them closer to the stairwell door, keeping one eye on him. People began poking their heads into the corridor, looking each way, searching for fire or smoke.

Just before disappearing through the door, Meera aimed her gun directly at Nick. And fired.

The gunshot echoed above the din of the screeching fire alarm. He ducked back into the library just in time to avoid the bullet that shattered the doorframe where only seconds earlier his head had been. He barely felt the sting of the splinters that embedded in the side of his face.

Damn, but the woman really does know how to use a firearm.

A moan had him turning to see Myer on the floor. The man's face was pale, telling him the guy had lost a significant amount of blood. Judging by the ding in the wall behind him, the wound was a through-and-through.

Breathing more heavily now, he canted his head, clicking the mic with his free hand and wincing from the movement. "All units, gunshot victim, Conference Room B. Suspect escaping via the east stairwell. I'm in pursuit. Be advised the fire alarm is bogus. Maintain lockdown." Although he couldn't be certain building security would honor his lockdown order over evacuating people from a potentially burning building.

The corridor was quickly filling up with people responding to the fire alarm and heading for the stairwell to evacuate.

"Police! Make way." He and Saxon pushed past the people heading to the stairs.

Catching sight of the gun in Nick's hand, some gasped. Others jumped out of the way as Saxon barreled through.

With every step, excruciating pain lanced through his chest. The hallway wavered, and for a moment, it looked as if there were two hallways. He clenched his jaw, staving off the pain that was so acute it was impacting his vision.

"Medics dispatched," Eric's voice came back on the radio. "Lockdown in place. We're heading up the stairwell to your location. We should intercept Meera somewhere in the middle."

"*Hier.*" Saxon followed him down the corridor, weaving in and out of the crowd as they made their way to the stairs.

Just before the door, a wave of dizziness rocked him, and he nearly blacked out. The pressure on his chest was unbearable and threatened to take him to the floor. *Got to... keep going.* Leaning one hand against the wall, he took in deep breaths, shaking his head to clear it.

"Officer, are you all right?" A woman stared at his bloody uniform shirt.

Ignoring her question, he fisted his hand on the wall.

C'mon, c'mon. Pull yourself together, Houston. If you don't, Andi will die.

Because there was no way Meera would let her live.

He pushed from the wall, shoving past more people and through the stairwell door. He and Saxon barreled down the stairs. "Police! Make way," he shouted as the number of people on the stairs increased to the point where he wasn't getting anywhere.

A few people moved aside as they took in his uniform and his unholstered gun, but most remained on the stairs, blocking his way.

"Saxon!" He glanced down at his dog who looked up at him, ears erect, waiting for his command. "*Gib laut.*"

Saxon began snarling and barking at the top of his lungs. The crowd parted like the Red Sea, clearing a path down to the next landing where, again, people were packing up, blocking the stairwell.

"What's going on?" a woman shouted.

"They won't let us leave the building," someone else cried.

"We're bogged down by the evacuation." This time it was Matt on the radio. "We're stuck in the stairwell, but still coming to you."

A woman on the landing below glanced up. *Meera.* Her eyes went wide with recognition, and she shoved Andi in front of her, pushing her toward the stairwell door. When she couldn't get through the crowd, she pointed her gun in the air and fired. The blast echoed in the close confines. People screamed and hit the floor, covering their heads with their hands.

"Move!" Meera waved her gun back and forth until her path was clear.

Nick aimed down the stairs, but people were scurrying in all directions. Getting a clean shot without risking innocent lives wasn't possible.

Meera flung open the door and pushed Andi through first.

"Make way!" he shouted, louder this time. "Saxon!" he added, urging his dog to keep barking.

As he shoved people aside, the pain intensified, but he kept pressing forward. Eventually he reached the door Meera and Andi had disappeared through. No sooner did he grab the handle and yank on it when another red-hot burning sensation speared him dead-center in his chest, and he staggered. Saxon clawed at the floor, uttering a low growl.

"*Fuss.*" He wanted Saxon to heel at his side, not launch into the hallway and get shot.

When the spasm passed to the point where he could see straight, he went through the doorway, leading with his gun. Thirty feet down the corridor Meera was shoving Andi into an open elevator.

He and Saxon charged down the hallway. Every beat of his heart made his chest throb, but he couldn't stop. *Wouldn't* stop. Not until he'd gotten Andi to safety.

Or died trying.

Just as he and Saxon got to the elevator, the doors closed. He shouted his frustration and slammed his fist on the metal door. The pain reverberating in his torso was so fierce he fell to his knees. Nausea engulfed him. His vision swam, teetering on darkness, and this time it took longer to clear. When it did, he noticed splotches of blood on the carpet in front of his knees. *Dammit.* He was losing blood quickly, and he couldn't see or hear straight. His senses were royally fucked up. Soon the energy would drain from his body like air from a popped balloon.

"Nick, where are you?" Eric's voice demanded from the radio.

Sucking in quick breaths through his nose and open mouth, Nick raised his eyes to the glowing succession of numbers over the elevator doors as it ascended. Though it killed him to wait, he did, watching the red numbers change as the car kept going up.

With the building on lockdown, he'd expected the elevator to descend, or at least stop on another floor. But it kept climbing.

Fourth floor.

What the hell was she planning?

Fifth floor.

"Nick? What's your twenty?"

"Stand by," he gasped, waiting for the elevator lights to stop changing.

The letter *R* glowed above the closed elevator doors.

"They're on the roof." Why, he didn't know. There'd be no way off.

Saxon whined and licked the side of Nick's face. His dog knew every nuance of Nick's behavior. Seeing him on the floor, unmoving and smelling of fresh blood, wasn't normal.

Keep moving. Have to get to Andi. She was everything to him, and he cursed himself for screwing up his priorities. Avenging Tanya's death for his own personal reasons seemed so pointless now.

"Help me up, buddy." He rested his hand on Saxon's back, using him for balance as he pushed to his feet. When he was vertical, his vision darkened again, and he leaned one hand on the elevator doors, waiting for the moment to pass.

Frantic, he began pounding on the up button, because there wasn't a chance in hell he'd have the strength to take the stairs three floors up to the roof. But the other elevator was on the ground floor where it would most likely remain during the evacuation. *Shit. Shit, shit, shit.*

He half walked, half ran down the corridor, all the while pressing his hand on the wall to keep from falling on his face.

After backtracking to the same stairwell he'd come in from, he pushed open the door. By this time, most people from the upper floors were jammed on the lower landing, leaving the stairs above nearly devoid of people.

Again, his vision wavered, and his knees nearly buckled. He couldn't hold himself upright, couldn't find his balance. It was as if the entire building were shifting beneath his feet, but it wasn't. It was his body trying to shut down. "No, dammit. *No!*"

He shoved his gun back into its holster and grabbed the metal railing with both hands. He let out a harsh breath, surprised that the pain in his chest had dulled to a bearable measure. *A bad sign.* When he stopped feeling any pain at all, he'd be a dead man.

I'm not going to make it.

You can, and you will. Andi's depending on you.

Beside him, Saxon walked up the steps, his nails clicking on the painted concrete.

"Almost there, boy," he said, although he was really trying to reassure himself that he was making headway.

Gripping the railing tighter, he picked up his pace, not stopping until he made it to the roof level. As he flung open the door, a strong gust nearly slammed it back in his face.

He held fast to the knob, using it for balance. Men's angry shouts came to him. Not the Feebs who'd taken point on the roof. They'd long since stood down after Myer was safely ensconced inside.

An angry female voice shrieked. *Meera.*

He eased open the door and was nearly blinded by sunlight. Squinting, he looked to the edge of the roof, and his heart nearly stopped.

Andi stood on the ledge of the building. Meera's gun was pointed directly at her head.

Chapter Twenty-Two

Blustery wind whipped Andi's hair in front of her face. She trembled, and it was all she could do not to lose her balance on the ledge.

Looking down, she swallowed the rising bile in her throat. A six-story fall would crush her bones and probably kill her instantly.

So would the gun pointed at her face.

"Get in," Meera shouted over the screaming wind, motioning with the muzzle of her gun to the empty window washer's cage dangling beside the ledge.

Even with the gun aimed at her head, Andi hesitated. The metal cage was about ten feet long and two feet wide, surrounded on all sides by metal railing but open on top. It swung violently back and forth, screeching as it scraped against the concrete wall. An even stronger gust caught the cage, twisting it and slamming it repeatedly against the building.

"Don't do it," a window washer warned. The man, along with his partner, stood with their hands in the air. "It's way too windy. You'll get thrown over the railing."

Meera whipped her gun around, aiming at the two men. "Get out of here or die." Her accent was thicker now, and Andi was amazed at how well she'd concealed it all this time.

Both men threw their hands in the air, backing away a few steps before taking off running.

Meera spun and turned the gun on her again. "I said, get in. And fer fuck's sake, be quick about it."

She swallowed, and her heart beat furiously as she took in the shaking contraption that didn't appear sturdy enough to withstand gusts of this magnitude.

Two heavy metal davit arms bolted to the roof and extending over the top of the parapet seemed strong enough, but it was the light aluminum cage that sent a shaft of terror through her. The only things that kept the cage secured were two twisted steel cables.

Taking a deep breath, she lowered unsteadily to her knees, scraping them on the ledge as she clambered backward. She grabbed one of the metal cables, clinging to it before heading backward down the short ladder.

No sooner did her feet hit the cage's platform than a blast of wind slammed the entire contraption against the side of the building. With shaking hands, she grabbed the top rail, barely able to keep her balance. The empty handcuff dangled from her wrist, clinking against the metal rail. Any second now she expected the cables to break free, sending her plunging to her death on the courtyard below. She tried unsuccessfully to swallow her fear.

Meera's crazy, and we're both going to die.

"Move to the corner." Meera stood above the ladder and flicked the barrel of the gun to the far corner of the cage.

Without letting go, Andi shuffled her hands along the rail, scooting to the end of the platform, a good six feet from the base of the ladder.

The wind suddenly quieted, as if they were in the eye of a tornado. Meera clambered awkwardly down, somehow managing to hold on to the gun and keep it aimed at her the entire time.

She held her breath. *Wait for it, wait for it.* The second the wind kicked up again, Meera would have to grab on to the ladder with both hands, or risk falling. That one moment of distraction might be her only chance of disarming the woman.

Her pulse raced as she waited for the wind to kick up again. *C'mon c'mon.*

The cage started to rock. Every muscle tightened as she readied to launch at Meera.

"Cuff yerself to the railing," Meera shouted, a sneer twisting her face into a mask of ugliness.

Damn.

"Quit fucking around and do it!"

With a trembling hand, she reached for the open cuff dangling from her wrist and snapped it closed over the top rail, clicking it tightly enough to show Meera she'd done as ordered, but leaving a small amount of space between the cuff and her wrist. Maybe enough that she could squeeze her hand out when the woman wasn't looking.

Meera moved to the platform's control panel. Another savage gust rocked the cage, swinging one end upward with such jarring force Andi was nearly knocked off her feet. Meera struggled to maintain her balance, holding the gun with one hand and the control box with the other. She pushed the green down arrow. The platform lurched and began a slow descent.

Only one thing was certain. As soon as they made it to the ground—*if* they made it—Meera would turn that gun on her for the last time and pull the trigger.

A shadow darkened the platform, and she looked up. She

pressed her lips together, stifling her cry of joy.

Nick and Saxon stood on the ledge by the primary control box, looking down. He aimed his gun at Meera when the platform dipped sharply to one side and seemed to slip out from under Andi's feet. Meera's body slammed against hers.

Abruptly, the cage jerked to a stop, forcing both of them to grab the rail. Nick hurtled onto the platform, landing with a heavy thud. The cage shuddered but maintained its position. Above them, Saxon trotted back and forth on the ledge, barking.

Before Nick could regain his balance, Meera turned to him and raised the gun. The platform rocked, sending her closer to where Andi stood.

"Nick!" Andi screamed, clutching the rail tighter. She'd expected him to shoot Meera the second his feet hit the platform, but he didn't.

He'd fallen to his knees, his head hanging low as his chest heaved. When he lifted his head, a sheen of sweat glistened on his pasty-white face. The entire lower half of his uniform shirt was soaked with blood.

Before Meera could steady herself and take the shot, Andi kicked at Meera's arm—the one with the gun—knocking it from her hand. The gun flew end over end, tumbling over the railing.

Meera clenched her hands. Venom shot from her eyes. "Fucking bitch!"

Still kneeling, Nick raised his weapon, but before he could come on target, Meera spun and kicked him square in the chest, directly on top of his wound. He let out a deep cry of pain, gritting his teeth and pressing one hand to his chest.

"No!" Andi screamed, knowing it was useless. The woman would normally be no match for Nick's size and strength, but anyone could see the damage the bullet had inflicted, and Meera meant to take full advantage of it.

Saxon let out a series of barks and snarls.

Meera lunged for Nick's gun, but he twisted away, protecting the weapon so she couldn't get to it. As they fought for control, his eyelids flickered. He was on the verge of passing out.

Something went over the side of the railing. His gun. She couldn't be sure if it had slipped from his hand, or if he'd intentionally tossed it, knowing he didn't have the strength to hang on to it.

Andi strained at the handcuff, desperately trying to extricate herself, but she'd made it tighter than she'd intended and couldn't squeeze her hand out. She stretched her body as far as it would go, trying to land a kick to Meera's head, yet unable to make contact from this far away. Again, she pulled and tugged at the handcuff, wincing as it cut into her skin and drew blood.

A soft whirring came to her ears. The steel cable on the opposite side of the cage was slipping, causing the entire contraption to list.

The cables aren't holding.

The cage twisted back and forth, slamming again and again against the side of the building, and with each impact, the other end of the platform angled more steeply.

A series of sharp barks sliced the air, and when Andi looked up, she couldn't believe what she was seeing.

Saxon was in midair.

The dog landed unsteadily, his feet clawing frantically for purchase on the metal surface, reminding her of the balance training Nick had given him on the lake.

For a moment, Saxon looked as if he'd slide to the lower edge of the platform, and Andi's heart lurched. "Saxon!" At the last second, he regained his footing and clawed his way to where Nick and Meera grappled together.

The big shepherd snarled, then clamped his powerful

jaws around Meera's leg. She screamed and beat at his head with her fists. Ignoring the blows, the dog shook his head back and forth, growling as he drew blood.

Nick grabbed something from one of the many leather pouches on his belt—a baton—and slammed it against the side of Meera's head, but she turned away in time, and it was only a glancing blow.

Meera shrieked her rage and pain, pressing a hand to her head, but only for a second before reengaging, trying to wrest the baton from Nick's grip.

His eyes were almost closed. As soon as he completely passed out, none of them would stand a chance against Meera's sick, twisted thirst to kill them all.

She really is insane. Not even Saxon's jaws clamped around her calf, or the blood dripping from between the dog's teeth was enough to cut through her escalating madness.

I have to help Nick.

She clawed at her own flesh but couldn't squeeze her hand from the cuff. Then an idea struck her with godawful clarity. There was only one way to get loose.

Taking a deep breath, she bit her lower lip. Using her free hand, she clamped down as hard as she could on her thumb joint closest to the handcuff. She screamed as bone snapped and tendons twisted. Through the haze of pain, she glimpsed Meera standing over Nick, ready to kick him full-force in the head.

Then she slipped her hand from the cuff.

In between the throbbing in her broken hand, fury—the likes of which she'd never experienced—fueled her with enough adrenaline to power a locomotive.

"Get off him, you bitch!" she screamed, hurling herself at Meera then slamming both her hands on the woman's chest. Pain radiated through her hand, and still she kept pounding on Meera.

The woman swayed but remained standing, windmilling her arms for balance. Only Saxon's grip on her calf kept her upright.

Forward momentum nearly had Andi following Meera. Her feet slipped out from under her, and she fell to the deck so hard it knocked the breath from her lungs. Gasping for air, she shot out her good hand and grabbed on to a lower rail.

"*Aus*!" Nick shouted raggedly.

Saxon released his jaws from Meera's leg just as the cable slipped again and the cage dipped a few more degrees. Meera staggered backward, flailing her arms.

An even stronger gust caught the platform, slamming it against the wall. Meera's lower back hit the end of the cage railing. The last thing Andi saw was the fear and panic in the other woman's eyes. Then she was gone—over the edge with a throaty scream.

Nick grabbed one of the lower rails. The cable slipped again, and the end of the platform dipped lower. Saxon's rear end slipped out from under him. He clawed frantically with his front paws as the end of the cage dipped lower. Another second and he'd slip off the edge.

"Nick, he's falling!" Andi screamed.

"Saxon!" Releasing the baton, he shot out his arm, grabbing one of the dog's front legs.

Stretching as far as she could, she reached out and closed her broken hand around Saxon's other leg, crying out as more pain radiated through her hand then up her entire arm. For a split second her vision flooded with white stars, but she held fast and sucked in quick, deep breaths until the stars faded.

The dog whimpered, his hind legs scrabbling uselessly as he tried to get them beneath him.

"Nick!" Andi shouted. Her heart pounded crazily. Nick was dying, and Saxon was in jeopardy of falling over the side like Meera had, and there wasn't a thing she could do. "Help!

Help us!" she screamed, looking up to the ledge, but no one was there.

Another second and Nick would black out—she could see it in his flickering eyelids. Andi didn't know if she had the strength to hold Saxon alone, and she certainly wouldn't be capable of holding on to Nick if he let go of the rail.

If Nick passed out, then he and Saxon would likely both tumble over the edge and fall six stories down. *To their deaths.*

Tears rolled down her cheeks. She couldn't believe it was going to end this way. "Nick, don't let go. *Don't let go.*" Of the railing *or* Saxon.

The dog managed to get his haunches beneath him, but the angle of the platform was still too steep for him to stand. She didn't know how, but even in his semiconscious state, Nick didn't let go of Saxon or the railing.

"Get 'em up!" a voice shouted from above. *Eric.*

"Oh, thank God." Andi no longer felt any pain. All she could think about was Nick.

He lay on his side, his large body shivering.

"Faster!" she cried.

Above her, Eric, Matt, and Kade looked over the ledge. Special Agent Cox and the two window washers stood at the roof's control box.

"Go faster. He's—he's dying." Her last words came out on a croak as she realized it was true.

"Goddammit, hurry!" another voice boomed. *Matt.*

Slowly, the platform rose until it was level with the top of the parapet.

"Swing it over," Eric shouted. "Easy does it."

When Andi's head was finally level with the roof's edge, she could not only see Nick's friends had arrived, but a large crowd of building security had gathered to assist. Matt's, Eric's, and Kade's dogs stood off to the side.

The entire cage swung up and over the ledge, lowering

slowly to the roof. A swarm of officers grabbed on to the cage, leveling it enough that Saxon could now stand.

Andi scrambled to Nick's side, clasping his face in her hands. The second her fingers touched his cheeks her heart sank, and she let out a cry. He was cold. *So cold.*

"Get the medics up here!" Matt shouted, then he and Eric swung up and over the top rail and crouched at Nick's side. He touched two fingers to Nick's carotid. His dark brows bunched, and she feared the worst. They were too late.

He's dead.

Saxon whimpered, lowering beside Nick and nuzzling his hand. That's when she noticed Nick was still holding tightly to the dog's front leg, his knuckles white.

"Is he…" She stared at Matt, unable to say the word. *Dead.*

"He's alive." But the expression on Matt's face was grim. "Somebody get a blanket!" he shouted to the security guards. "He's in shock with severe blood loss." He rested a hand on Nick's arm. "You can let him go, buddy. Saxon's okay. You can let go now."

"Nick," she whispered, leaning down to press her lips to his chilled forehead. The words came bubbling out. "I love you. I love you!" All she wanted at that moment was for him to know she loved him.

He released his death grip on Saxon's leg. Andi's breath caught in her throat as he exhaled a low yet audible sigh. His lips moved, but the wind was still blowing so hard she couldn't hear what he'd said. She leaned closer. "I'm here. It's Andi. Please, Nick." She began shaking her head back and forth. "Don't you die on me. Don't you *dare* die on me!"

When his lips moved again, she turned her head, positioning her ear nearer to his mouth. His voice was low, yet his words unmistakable.

"Love. You. Too."

"Oh, Nick." Her heart was tearing apart. He really loved her, and he was dying before her eyes.

Eric's face came into her view. "Let the medics get to work on him. You can ride with him in the ambulance. I promise. He'd want you with him."

"Okay," she heard herself say, although inside she was going completely numb.

This can't be happening.

But it was.

She let Eric help her to her feet, giving the medics more room to work. In seconds they had Nick's shirt ripped open, and she drew in a sharp breath at the sight of all the blood, some of it wet, some dried and dark.

"Get every patrol unit you've got," Matt ordered, pointing to the other officers. "The second that ambulance starts rolling, *light 'em up.*"

Chapter Twenty-Three

Andi leaned over and kissed Nick softly on the lips. "Good morning." His skin was cool, although not nearly as cold as it had been that day a month ago when Meera's bullet had pierced his chest. "And so, it begins again," she whispered.

Another day of waiting. Hoping. Praying.

He lay deathly still, his lower body covered by a sheet, his bare chest dotted with heart monitor leads. A jagged, slightly raised patch of red skin marked what was left of the bullet's entry wound. Tubes ran from his arms, attached to several IV drips on long metal poles. Monitors on the wall beeped occasionally, breaking up the silence of the hospital room.

Sighing, she let her gaze roam his body, searching for a sign that he'd moved, but there was none. Even in a coma, he was still the most handsome man she'd ever seen. And the only man she'd ever truly been in love with.

She lowered herself to a chair positioned next to the bed—the same one she'd been sitting in nearly every hour of the day and night for the last thirty days. During that time, she'd talked to him about anything and everything. She'd given him updates on Saxon, who'd been bunking with her and Stray. The poor dog was so completely lost and confused, he conducted daily searches of her house, looking for Nick and getting the most forlorn look on his face when he didn't find him. She'd even confessed to feeding him Pop-Tarts, anything to boost the dog's spirits.

Next, she'd told him how Tess had all but been running the DPC for the last month, popping into the hospital every now and then to make sure Andi ate. As it was, she'd lost ten pounds. She'd even given Nick her thoughts on Eric and Tess. Despite Tess's adamant denial, something was definitely brewing between them. When she'd run out of things to talk about, Nick's friends had stepped in, providing long-running recaps on the investigation.

Portia Laird was dead, and Andi had no sympathy for the woman who'd put so many guns on the streets and been responsible for so many deaths. Seeing Nick lying in a hospital bed—another victim of Portia's greed and viciousness—she'd come to better understand the all-consuming, driving force behind his determination to stop the flow of weapons into Springfield. He hadn't been able to prevent his wife from killing herself, but he'd dedicated himself to getting those weapons off the streets. In all, nearly three thousand guns had been discovered in a storage facility outside of Springfield.

As for her broken hand, the cast had recently been removed, although her fingers were all still quite stiff. Physical therapy would be necessary to regain full range of motion. Joe had recovered from the wound in his shoulder and signed a plea agreement with the prosecutor. While awaiting sentencing, he'd begun counseling sessions for his gambling addiction and put his fancy house and car up for sale in order to pay a large criminal fine and make restitution to an organization that assisted victims of gun violence.

The only good thing to come from Portia Laird was

Scottie, her Bouvier. Matt had graciously taken custody of the dog and was housing him at Jerry's Place, a kennel that was not only a place of healing for teens with alcohol problems, but a shelter that took in rescue dogs for the kids to work with and train. Despite his size, Scottie was a favorite at the kennel, and two families were already vying to adopt him.

She watched Nick's chest rise and fall rhythmically, wishing he would open his beautiful gray eyes and pin her with that hard-ass cop glare of his.

Please, baby. Open your eyes.

Even though she'd rejected his love, he'd shown her his in the only way possible at the time. He'd paid off all her debts, allowing her to keep the café. It was as if a bright light had been turned on, illuminating the truth. The DPC meant everything to her, and Nick knew that.

The only emotion flowing through her now was fear. She'd learned quickly over the last few weeks that if she didn't tamp down everything else, she'd go insane. At this point, she was beginning to feel numb to everything. Better that than the jagged, heart-wrenching pain she'd experienced that first week until Nick's vitals had stabilized. Now that numbness was the glue holding her together.

Needing to touch him, she trailed her fingertips along his arm. Feeling a spurt of hopefulness, she glanced up to watch the now-familiar green blips track across one of the monitors. She'd become tightly attuned to what each beep and blip represented, and there was nothing to indicate he'd felt her touch. Considering he'd coded twice during the ambulance ride to the hospital, she was grateful for the steady pattern of normal sinus rhythm.

She could vaguely recall the lights and screaming sirens from all the police cars that had given them an escort to the hospital. After that, everything was a blur. Except for the blood. It had been everywhere. On his uniform, his chest, and even on her. When the medics had used the defibrillator on him, her own heart had nearly seized, and she'd never been more frightened in her entire life as she'd been at that moment. When she'd again thought he was dead.

Miraculously, he'd made it to the hospital alive, then been transfused with so many liters of blood she'd lost count. After that, he'd been raced into surgery to repair the damage. The doctors said he'd been anoxic—not enough blood flow to the brain, and his body had shut down. The ventilator had been removed two weeks ago, and he was breathing on his own, but he still hadn't woken.

The last words he'd said to her on the roof before succumbing to unconsciousness came back to her: *Love. You. Too.*

She swallowed the rising sob in her throat and blinked back the tears. Theirs was a love that might very well never happen.

One of the nurses she'd come to know, an older woman of about forty, with the reddest hair she'd ever seen, entered the room, smiling as she began inspecting the levels of fluid in each of the IV bags. "Morning, Andi."

"Morning, Patsy." She forced a smile, one she didn't feel in the slightest. "Any change?" It was the same question she'd asked each and every day, although she knew Patsy or one of the doctors would have informed her if there'd been anything new to report.

She shook her head. "No. I'm sorry." Her expression was kind and sympathetic.

Patsy adjusted the blood pressure cuff on Nick's right arm, then turned to leave, giving her a light squeeze on the shoulder before disappearing out the door. The blood pressure machine kicked on, its motor whirring as the cuff inflated around Nick's bicep. She waited for the inevitable readout on the screen, already knowing what it would be.

One-ten over seventy. The same as it was every hour of every day. *No change.*

Her heart clenched, and she pressed a hand to her flat belly. *Keep it together.* You have to, now more than ever.

The doctors had all agreed they didn't know how Nick had the strength to survive this long, but there was still a possibility he would die before he ever woke. His injuries had been bad enough, but it was the blood loss that had taken the worst toll on his body.

Her gaze took in the windowsill crammed with flowers and cards. Since the day he'd been brought in, there'd been a constant influx of police and K-9 officers from all over the Commonwealth. Most of her memories of that night in the emergency room were fuzzy, but she had a vague recollection of the waiting area filled to capacity by uniformed officers from all over the city and surrounding areas, offering moral support and ready and willing to donate blood. Though they'd all had to wait in line behind Matt, Eric, the rest of Nick's friends, plus Agent Cox, and Nick's family.

For the last month, one or more of them had been there with her at Nick's bedside. What surprised her more than anything was that they'd gone well out of their way to provide for her every need, and they barely knew her.

Nick's parents, along with his brother and sister, had visited nearly every day. Despite the horrific circumstances, they'd been pleased that Nick had found someone after Tanya had passed. Andi's parents had been up to visit, as well, and were coming again this weekend.

Eric lived locally and had been to the hospital every day, bringing her food and coffee, along with restaurant magazines. For a man as big and strong as a Viking, he'd been gentle with her, and his sympathy knew no bounds. She'd lost track of the number of times he'd held her while she'd cried.

Kade, Jaime, Dayne, and Markus had returned to their

respective cities, but they'd rotated up on weekends. Agent Cox stopped by every other day. Matt had barely left Nick's side. He and his pregnant wife, Trista, were both on leave to be there.

As had become her habit lately, she splayed her hand over her lower abdomen, much the same way Trista did. Only Trista was a good five months further along.

"Did you tell him?" Matt's voice came from the doorway.

She'd been so absorbed that she hadn't heard him come in. "Tell him what?"

He cracked a smile. "That you're pregnant."

Her eyes widened. "How did you know? I haven't told anyone." *Not even my parents.* Subconsciously, she glanced down to reassure herself that at only one month, she still wasn't showing.

"Trista told me." He hooked a thumb in the direction of the corridor behind him. "She's in the ladies' room. Again. Says the baby is pressing against her bladder. She caught you touching your belly a lot." He dipped his head to where her hand rested on her lower abdomen. "Don't worry. Most of us—men, that is—are too dense to pick up on stuff like that."

Whether it was hormones or from outright relief that she could talk to someone about her unexpected pregnancy, the tears she'd been holding in check streamed from the corners of her eyes.

"Oh, honey." Trista waddled past Matt, grabbing a handful of tissues from a box on the windowsill, then handing them to her as she sat in a chair and wrapped an arm around Andi's shoulders. "It'll be okay. No matter what happens, we're here for you. *All* of us. You're family now."

Her body began shaking as tears rolled down her cheeks. Matt grabbed the box of tissues and brought it to her, crouching in front of her chair. He remained there, resting his hand on her knee. After a few minutes, she dabbed at her eyes and wiped the wetness from her cheeks. She gave Matt and Trista a grateful smile.

"I'm okay. Really. Sorry, I-I just lost it for a minute there." Renewed sadness overwhelmed her. Just when she thought she'd exerted control over her emotions, it had shattered in seconds, making her realize she wasn't quite as numb as she'd thought or wished she could make herself.

"Why don't you tell him?" Trista's green gaze flicked to Nick. "Tell him about the baby. He might hear you, and even if he doesn't, it will make you feel better. Besides, he deserves to know."

She shut her eyes tightly, then took a deep breath, nodding jerkily. "Okay."

"C'mon, Matt. Let's give them some privacy."

Trista started to rise, when Matt solicitously placed one hand at his wife's lower back, holding out his other for her to use for balance. There was something so loving and intimate in that simple gesture, it tugged at Andi's heartstrings. Like Nick, Matt was a giant of a man, but watching him with his petite wife gave her hope. Hope that Nick would wake any day now and they could start working on the same kind of beautiful, loving relationship his friends so obviously had.

After Matt and Trista left the room, she clasped Nick's hand in hers, threading their fingers. "I have news for you, and I hope you won't be mad. Do you remember when I said I couldn't get pregnant?" She uttered a soft laugh. "Every word of it was true, but somehow...I'm pregnant. Can you believe it? I'm going to have a baby. *We're* going to have a baby."

The blood pressure monitor took that moment to kick on, re-inflating the cuff on his arm. She watched the readout on the screen, then waited for the cuff to deflate with its usual *whooshing* sound.

"It was when we were in the woods and we didn't use a condom. I mean, who goes running with a spare condom, right?" Her tight laugh came out sounding like more of a sob. "I knew almost right away. My breasts are already tender and swollen, and my back is achy all the time. I'd really appreciate it if you'd wake up and give me a back massage with those magic hands of yours."

Clasping his hand tighter, she bent down and kissed his fingers. "I love you with all my heart. Please come back to me. *Please* wake up. I need you. *We* need you."

Overwhelmed by emotions she could no longer contain, she rested her head on the mattress while her entire body racked with uncontrollable sobs. "I love you, Nick. *I love you.*"

· · ·

I'm pregnant… We're going to have a baby… Please come back to me… I love you…

The words were fuzzy and jumbled, and Nick could swear it was Tanya's voice. But that couldn't be right. Tanya couldn't have children, and she was…dead.

Maybe I'm *dead.*

Beeping intermingled with the muted voice, along with weeping. Somebody was crying, but who?

Something soft and silky slid across his arm, bringing with it the flowery scent of freesia and reminding him of…

Andi.

With her long golden blond hair and eyes as blue as wild cornflowers. With skin so soft and smooth he could spend hours caressing her body. He wanted to get to her. *Needed* to get to her. She was in danger, about to be shot by Meera.

The beeping in the distance grew louder, faster. The weeping he thought he'd imagined stopped.

Someone gasped. "Nick?" Andi's voice, and so, so close.

He tried lifting his arm, but it weighed a ton. Worse

was how every time he took a breath, it seemed as if there was an armored SWAT tank parked on his chest. Darkness surrounded him, but he needed to escape. To save Andi. She was everything. Without her, nothing mattered.

He wanted to open his eyes, but he was so tired and weak, he couldn't find the strength to lift his eyelids, let alone his arm.

"Nick?" Andi's voice was panicked.

The enshrouding darkness clawed at him, threatening to pull him back under, but he wouldn't let it win. She needed him. He could hear her crying, screaming his name, and it was killing him not to get to her. Every sob threatened to rip his heart from his chest.

Hand over hand, he crawled up the steep incline of a deep, dark, craggy ravine, clutching at rocks and roots—anything to get closer to that pinhole of light at the top. With every inch he gained, the pain magnified, and it was all he could do not to let go and plunge back into the dark nothingness that awaited him if he did.

Finally, darkness bled to gray. Something squeezed his hand. Not some*thing*—some*one*. At first, he tried pulling away, fearing it was the blackness threatening to undo his efforts to escape the hellhole he'd been relegated to. The light overhead grew brighter, yet something kept holding him back.

Looking over his shoulder, he peered into the inky void below, straining for a glimpse of what was tying him to that place. But there was nothing.

More tugging, this time pulling him closer to the light. If only he could reach it.

"Nick? *Nick*?" Again, Andi's voice, although this time it was clearer and right there next to him. "You can do it, baby. I love you, and I'm here. Open your eyes. *Please*, open your eyes."

And he did.

"Oh, thank God." She was laughing and crying at the same time, clutching his hand, then kissing his face.

He blinked, trying to clear his blurry vision. *Bright. Too bright.* He squinted, allowing his eyes to adjust to the ambient light in the room. *A hospital room.* Like so many bad movies he'd fast-forwarded through, it all came back to him in a flash.

Meera shooting him square in the chest—no wonder his chest felt tight. Running. Andi handcuffed to the window-washer cage. Saxon leaping onto the platform, then Meera going over the side. The last thing he remembered was grabbing on to the railing with one hand, and with the other—

Saxon.

Was his dog dead?

Horror shot through him. Over Andi's left shoulder, one of the monitors began beeping crazily. When he opened his mouth to speak, his lips were dry as a bone, as was his throat. *Saxon*, he tried to say, but the name didn't come. Digging deep, he somehow found the strength to squeeze Andi's hand.

"What is it?" She leaned closer, her eyes brimming with tears. "Are you in pain? I called for a nurse."

"Saxon," he managed to whisper, although it sounded more like a croak.

"He's fine." She pressed her hand against his cheek. "You didn't let go." She sniffled and took an unsteady breath. "Do you remember?"

He closed his eyes, nodding as relief flooded his body. Saxon was alive. Andi was alive. Andi was—

He snapped open his eyes.

Pregnant? How can that be?

The first two times they'd used a condom, but the third —when they hadn't—had been only yesterday.

He was about to try speaking again when a nurse with bright red hair walked in, smiling as she immediately began checking the monitors. "I knew you'd come back to us, Sergeant. How do you feel?"

"Fine," he rasped, although he didn't. Not really. His limbs felt as if they had the strength of a baby's. Less, perhaps. And speaking of babies... His gaze met Andi's then lowered to her flat belly.

"This is Patsy." She wiped at her eyes and motioned toward the nurse. "Patsy's been with us the entire time you've been here."

He tried to say thank you but couldn't manage the words. He settled for a courteous nod.

"I'll call the doctor, then we'll see about getting you some ice for your throat. Not talking for a month will dry up anyone's vocal cords." She rested her hand briefly on his shoulder, then left the room.

He stared, shock coursing through him. *A month? A whole fucking month?* The ledge behind where Andi sat came into view, the entire length jammed with flowers and cards.

Holy sh—

"Welcome back." Andi leaned down to kiss him again, and all he wanted to do was wrap his arms around her and hold her until the end of time.

Not happening.

He wasn't close to having the strength to move his arms, so he lay there, content to have the woman he loved kissing him again and again.

"Are you all right?" he whispered against her hair, breathing her in.

"Am *I* all right?" She pulled back and laughed. "*You're* the one who was shot in the chest. You almost *died*. The bullet barely missed your heart, and you lost *so* much blood."

She pressed her lips together, and he could tell she was about to cry again.

Patsy reentered the room and placed a cup of ice on a rolling metal bed table. "The doctor is on his way. He okayed you to have some ice for your throat. Think you're ready to sit up?" When he nodded, she pressed a button on a large plastic remote and the bed gradually inclined.

After re-checking his vitals, Patsy winked at him, then grinned broadly. "I'll be back. I want to give the rest of the staff the good news that you're awake."

The second she'd left the room he clasped Andi's hand. "You're *pregnant*?" he croaked, then couldn't stop grinning.

Her eyes went wide. "You *heard* that?"

"Then it *is* true." His smile faded. *I'm going to be a father.*

"You're upset. I can see that." She pulled from his grasp, misery clouding her face.

"No, it's not that. I thought you couldn't—" He stopped when his throat dried up so much he thought it would close in on his tonsils. Andi's beautiful blue eyes glistened with more tears.

Tears you put there, dickhead.

"Oh my God!" a woman gasped.

He turned his head to the door to see Trista with her hand covering her mouth, her green eyes as big as key limes. Behind her, Matt grinned. And were his best friend's eyes wet, too?

Trista practically ran to the bed and started raining kisses all over him. "You had us *so* worried."

"Sorry, little pixie." She smiled impishly at his use of the nickname all of Matt's friends called her by. "Guess I needed to sleep for a while."

Tears streamed down her face, reminding him of a leaky faucet. She laughed. "Hormones."

Matt came forward and held out his hand, which Nick managed to clasp. Matt's face instantly sobered, telling him it had been bad. *Really bad.*

"Good to have you back, my friend." Matt cleared his throat and squeezed Nick's hand tighter. "You have no idea."

From the seriously intense look on Matt's face, he was beginning to.

"You're still as ugly as ever." Nick grinned, knowing full well how many women would kill to have been with his best friend.

"Same goes." Matt released Nick's hand.

An hour later, after Trista and Andi had hugged and cried some more, Eric and Kade blew into the room, and damned if both men didn't get all teary-eyed. Several doctors had come and gone to reexamine him and explain the extent of his injuries in excruciating detail. Bottom line was that he was looking at months of physical therapy to get back to where he'd been before the shooting.

For several minutes, he closed his eyes, content to listen to his friends talk around him. Andi never let go of his hand, and he held on to hers like it was his lifeline. As much as he loved his friends, he was tiring quickly, and all he wanted now was to be alone with her. There were so many questions, and he wanted the answers to all of them before he fell into the exhausted sleep that was coming on fast.

"Guys," he said. "I need some time alone with Andi."

His friends understood, and several minutes later he and Andi were the only ones left in the room.

"I'm sorry." She tipped her head back and stared for a moment at the ceiling. "I know I said I couldn't get pregnant, and I really thought that was true. The doctors said so as far back as when I was in grad school. I really thought it was impossible." She began twisting her hands. "My dad would have said that I hadn't been ready before, mentally or physically. He'd say that it took all these years for the stars and planets to align properly."

"You and your astronomical explanations." He did his

best to bob his brows, failing miserably. "You know how that turns me on."

"Be serious," she chided. "I don't want you to think I did this to trap you, and if you don't want to be part of my baby's life, I'll understand. I won't hold you to anything."

"*Our* baby's life." There was no way he'd let his child grow up without him. "I'm going to love our baby as much as I love his or her mother."

For several long seconds of agony, she stared at him with a blank face. Warning flags shot up in his brain. While he'd been semiconscious just before coming out of it—and in his dreams—he could have sworn she'd said she loved him. Now he wasn't so sure.

A smile lifted the corners of her mouth. "I love you, too." Her smile broadened, and she squeezed his hand, lifting it to her lips. "I'm sorry I didn't believe you. I judged you by the actions of others in my life, and I shouldn't have."

"Listen." He wanted to tug her closer but didn't have the strength. "I don't blame you. I *did* use you. I still can't deny that. I had my own personal vendetta, and I wasn't about to let anything get in my way. I would have done whatever it took to convince you to let me work at the DPC. But everything that happened between us from that point forward was real. As real as it gets."

She took a deep breath and let it out. "Okay."

"Okay." He grinned, then sobered. "And let's be clear on exactly how you got pregnant. How *I* got you pregnant. It wasn't the stars and planets aligning. It took the right man—*me*." And he was damned proud of it. "Now come here."

This time he did manage to tug on her hand, urging her to sit beside him on the bed. When she did, he rested his hand on her abdomen where their unborn baby nestled in a cocoon of warmth and love.

She covered his hand with her own. "Did I mention that I

think Stray and Saxon are in love? They run and play together all the time. They're practically inseparable."

He managed to arch a brow. "Is she spayed? Saxon isn't neutered, and I know for a fact that he doesn't carry condoms when he goes running."

She laughed, and he would have, too, if his chest weren't so tight. Tight from his injury and from his emotions spinning wildly out of control.

"Don't worry," she said, still laughing. "She was spayed as soon as I found her. There will be no more unplanned pregnancies in my house."

"Then we'll just have to plan in advance."

And he was determined to set his new plan in action without delay.

The time for putting his future aside was over, and he didn't want to waste another second of his life. Getting shot in the chest and seeing the woman he loved with a gun jammed against the side of her head will do that to a guy. Even if there were no baby, his goal would still be the same.

What he was about to do was miles away from how he would have liked to execute this operation. He had no champagne, no ring, and no romantic candlelit dinner, but the time was right, and the time was now. He knew it in his head and in his heart.

He took her hands in his and locked his gaze onto her incredibly beautiful face. "I love you more than anything in the world. I'd get down on one knee if I could, but I'm pretty sure I'd fall flat on my face, or my ass." He paused, searching her eyes, seeing all that he needed. Not only *his* future but *theirs*. "Andromeda Hardt, will you marry me?"

Epilogue

The lacy white fringe of Andi's dress fluttered in the unexpectedly warm mid-November breeze. Her pulse beat rapidly at the two little words that were about to change her life.

She looked into the eyes of the man she loved. "I do."

"Then I now pronounce you husband and wife." The state police chaplain gave Nick a brief nod. "You may now kiss your wife."

Nick slipped his arms around her, pulling her close. Looking as handsome as he did in a classic black tuxedo, he took her breath away. But it was the unabashed expression of love in his eyes that had her heart melting.

"I love you," he whispered, then kissed her. His lips were warm, lingering on hers before pulling away. "I'll finish that later."

"I'll hold you to it." Her belly tingled, though she didn't know if it was from the promise of yet another night filled with his lovemaking, or from the baby. What she did know was that her hormones were flying in every direction, and she craved making love with him now more than ever.

No sooner did they turn to face the crowd than the entire line of groomsmen—all of Nick's friends—whooped and hollered like a bunch of rowdy teenagers. The rest of the guests cramming the DPC's rear deck and grassy yard below clapped and cheered. Even Saxon and Stray, who sat obediently in a corner of the deck, began howling their congratulations.

Saxon was decked out with a big, shiny white bowtie, while Stray twisted her head first in one direction, then the next, trying to nip at the small bunch of pink flowers Tess had tied to her collar.

The reception passed in a blur, and over the next two hours, they greeted family and friends. Business had picked up over the last few months, and the guest list had included some of their regular patrons, old and new.

After waking from his coma, Nick had spent another week in the hospital, then jumped right into rehab to regain his strength. Last week, he'd returned to work on light duty only, which was driving him crazy. His house was for sale, and he'd filled his time by moving his things into her house. *Correction,* their *house.* His latest project was to turn the spare bedroom into the baby's room.

Now they sat in a corner of the deck, waiting for a second wind. Nick leaned over and rested his hand on her mounded belly, splaying his long fingers across the lacy fabric.

"Think it's a boy or a girl?" He shot her a grin that was both cute and devastatingly handsome.

"My mom says it's a girl." She nodded to another table, where Nick's parents and hers were deep in conversation. "Yours says it's a boy. Which do you want?"

Nick shook his head. "I don't care. But if it's a girl, we're never letting her bring a boy near that telescope."

She leaned over and punched his bicep. As she did, she caught sight of Nick's friends knocking back beers. Raucous laughter came to her ears. Everyone was having a good time except Eric, who stood off to the side watching Tess fill Saxon's and Stray's water bowls. The look on his face was decidedly somber.

"What's wrong with Eric?" She'd come to know him well enough over the past few months to recognize something was bothering him.

"He's transferring to New Jersey."

"New Jersey?" She couldn't contain the shock from her voice. "Intentionally? I thought he was happy here."

He shrugged. "Said it was time for a change."

"Change my ass." Narrowing her eyes first at Eric then Tess, she took a long slug of sparkling cider from her champagne flute.

"Such language," he chided. "You're going to be a mother soon."

"Congratulations."

They both turned at Joe's voice behind them. He leaned down to give her a quick hug and a chaste kiss on the cheek.

Knowing Nick still hadn't forgiven her ex for putting her in danger, she glanced at her husband to see his eyes narrowed to gray slits.

"Congratulations." Joe extended his hand to Nick.

She watched the interplay, still wondering if Nick would launch from his chair and tackle Joe to the ground the way he said he'd dreamed about every night since waking from the coma.

"Felon," he said, after making Joe sweat a few seconds longer before taking his hand.

For a convicted felon, Joe had gotten off easy. A federal judge had sentenced him to only six months home confinement and a thousand hours of community service.

The unexpectedly light sentence had been partly the result of his cooperation being taken into consideration, plus the fact that he'd been shot. A stipulation of the home confinement was that Joe's location was closely monitored, and the only things he could leave his house for were work, doctor's appointments, the wedding, and his community service.

A little bird had leaked information to the judge regarding Joe's distaste for dogs. As a result, the judge had assigned one hundred percent of his service to a local rescue shelter. Now Joe was doing something he hated: being around canines and picking up their poop.

"How's the community service coming along?" Nick grinned slyly, and she understood why.

"It sucks." Joe gave a disgusted snort.

"Good." Nick snorted back. "It's not *supposed* to be fun."

"You're never going to forgive me, are you?"

"No."

Anyone else watching Nick would think he was composed and relaxed, with a champagne flute in one hand, and the fingers of his other hand idly tapping the tabletop. Andi knew otherwise. Her husband was itching for an excuse to lay Joe out on the ground. For now, he was getting a kick out of toying with her ex.

"Thank you, Joe." She reached out to squeeze his hand. "Nick and I were just having a moment alone."

Joe took his cue and wisely left.

Nick downed the rest of his champagne. "You just saved his life."

"I realize that." She gave her husband a knowing smile.

Two hours later, Nick carried her over the threshold, somehow managing to hold her *and* activate the brand-new security system. A short time later, they were completely alone in their bedroom, and the house was blissfully quiet. Even Saxon and Stray were exhausted from all the noise and attention and promptly fell asleep in their side-by-side beds in the living room.

Wordlessly, Nick and Andi peeled off each other's clothes until they were naked and lying on top of the bedcovers. It had taken Nick nearly a full month of recuperation before he'd regained sufficient strength to make love to her, and when he had, it had been slower and sweeter than ever before. Tonight was no exception.

He pushed inside her, kissing her and cupping one of her swollen breasts. When he flicked his thumb over the rosy, distended nub, she arched off the bed. He leaned down to suck on her nipple. Given how ubersensitive they were now, she let loose with a throaty cry, holding his head to her breast with one hand and cupping his muscled backside with the other. His glute flexed and bunched as he pushed languorously in and out of her body.

Their breaths came quicker. As she neared orgasm, her heart pounded against her rib cage.

"You're so beautiful," he murmured against her ear.

She cried out, her body clenching as heavenly waves crashed over her. A moment later, Nick groaned, coming hard inside her.

He lifted his head and pushed up from the mattress so that he could look down at her. His gaze lowered, and he rested his hand on her belly, rubbing her rounded abdomen in slow circles.

"What are you doing?" she whispered.

"Feeling our baby."

As she reached up to cup his cheek, a lone tear trickled from the corner of her eye—one born of infinite joy, love, and the beautiful family that was finally theirs.

Author's Note

K-9s are a highly specialized component of law enforcement that few officers are blessed to experience, and pose challenges most of us never encounter on the job. I've done my best to accurately reflect this unique aspect of law enforcement. Any mistakes contained within this novel are entirely my own.

Acknowledgments

Once again, my thanks to Cpt. Joseph King, Lt. Patrick Silva, and Sgt. Gary Hebert of the Massachusetts State Police K-9 Unit. Your time is precious, and I thank you for allowing me an insightful glimpse into the K-9 world. My editor, Candace Havens—thanks for putting up with me! Last, but never least, special thanks to my fabulous critique team, Kayla Gray, MK Mancos, and Cheyenne McCray.

About the Author

Tee O'Fallon has been a federal agent for twenty-four years, and is currently a police investigator, giving her hands-on experience in the field of law enforcement that she combines with her love of romantic suspense. Tee's job affords her the unique opportunity to work with the heroic men and women in law enforcement on a daily basis. Tee is the author of the Federal K-9 Series: *Lock 'N' Load* and *Armed 'N' Ready*, and the NYPD Blue & Gold Series: *Burnout*, *Blood Money*, and *Disavowed*. When not writing, Tee enjoys, cooking, gardening, lychee martinis, and all creatures canine. If you'd like to contact Tee, please visit her website at teeofallon.com.

Discover more Amara titles...

TOMBOY

a *Hartigans* novel by Avery Flynn

Ice Knights defenseman Zach Blackburn has come down with the flu, and my BFF begs me to put my nursing degree to use. But paparazzi spot me sneaking out of his place, and accusations that I slept with him fly faster than a hockey puck. At first, all of Harbor City wants my blood—or to give me a girlie-girl makeover. Then the grumpy bastard goes and promises to help raise money for a free health clinic—but only if I'm rink-side at every game. Suddenly, remembering to keep my real hands off my fake date gets harder and harder to do.

HARDEST FALL

a *Dominion* novel by Juliette Cross

Even though Bone refuses to take sides in the apocalypse, there's one job she's not willing to do for a certain demon prince. If she doesn't, her head will end up on a spike. Of course, there's a good chance we're all going to die anyway, but I will do anything to protect this fierce woman—and not just because she saved my life.

HEARTBREAKER

a *Bad Angels* novel by Inara Scott

Mistakes? Tess Paplion has made a few. But now she's starting over, juggling multiple jobs while finishing her college degree. Nothing's getting in her way. Especially not the sexy angel investor with "one-night disaster" written all over him who just hired her to train his dog.

Made in the USA
Monee, IL
04 April 2022

94107544R00194